HUDSON HOUSE VICTORIAN

MYSTERIES

www.hudsonhousemysteries.com

THE MINOTAUR'S CHILDREN

ALAN McKEE

"...not even the great London Minotaur himself—that portentous incarnation of lust and wealth—fill us with such sorrow and shame as are occasioned by the attitude of some decent people who, while admitting the truth of all these horrors, would have them continue for ever rather than that their ears should be shocked by hearing of the horrors which others have to endure."

—The Maiden Tribute of Modern Babylon
by W.T. Stead in the Pall Mall Gazette
July 8, 1885

"The first principle to remember is that the human mind can do anything. The only limits are those we put on it, with our own narrow view of what is possible."

—Ralph B. Allison
Difficulties Diagnosing
the Multiple Personality Syndrome
in a Death Penalty Case

THE MINOTAUR'S CHILDREN

A Hudson House Victorian Mysteries Book

ISBN
978-0-9813524-1-1

PRELUDE: A CHILD'S NIGHTMARE

Ariana was running into the maze again, Serafina realized as she glanced up from the book she was reading. She just saw Ariana's golden curls as they disappeared behind the high yew hedge that formed the winding paths of the maze. Why the child was drawn to the one place on the grounds where she could get lost and be frightened was something the older girl could never understand. With a sigh of impatience, she put down the book, *Bulfinch's Mythology*, carefully keeping her place, and set off after the child.

"Ariana," she called. "Don't go in there. You know what happens."

As soon as the words were uttered, Serafina realized what she had done. It was the same thing she always did and it always had dreadful, inevitable consequences. As they descended, the evergreen walls of the maze gave way to blocks of stone, ancient stone, covered in places with a thick moss, like the fur of an exotic animal, but the stone was enchanted, like the stone which had held Excalibur. She heard the child's cry as she ran deeper and deeper into the maze, which formed the centre of the formal garden of their large home in Kensington. It grew darker and Serafina could hear feet running on the flags of her father's garden. How the little girl could run so quickly when she could scarcely walk always surprised Serafina. They were just inside the maze, hidden from everyone, and Ariana was lost already! The child's long wail pierced the older girl with apprehension, even though she knew there was nothing that could really hurt the child—

9

yet. The path started downward again and the darkness grew thicker. Serafina could see in the half light, but this was where the child always became afraid and moved events forward. They entered the tunnel where only a few torches lit the dark walls carved out of the earth. Ariana began to scream as she foolishly ran deeper and deeper into the dark, twisting passages. The older girl took the ball of embroidery yarn out of her apron pocket and tied its end to a sprig of the yew. She let the ball unwind as she followed Ariana. Serafina heard her little feet pattering on the stones and then, her blood seemed to drain out of her into the ground. A subtle but regular sound had been added to their footsteps.

"Oh, Heavens," Serafina said out loud.

Already, she was hearing the breath of the Minotaur as he ran behind her driving them deeper and deeper into his lair. The scream that echoed through the endless corridors was now her own. She had to catch up the child before the monster hurt her again. She ran faster and faster, ignoring her own peril of tripping on the uneven stones. Her breath came in ragged gasps and...suddenly, she felt a hand on her shoulder. It was not the huge horrible hand of the beast. It was the hand of her sister, Julia, who was trying to wake her.

"Serafina, dear Serafina, do wake up," the sweet voice was saying to her.

"Oh, Julia," Serafina burst out in a sob of relief. "You woke me again?"

"Yes, of course, I could hear you from across the hall. It was the dream?" the younger girl asked. Serafina nodded.

Julia, who was about eleven, regarded her thirteen-year-old sister with a look of mature concern.

"You haven't had one for ever so long, Serafina. What do you think it signifies?"

"It probably doesn't signify anything, little mouse," the older girl answered as she held back the bed clothes so Julia could get out of the chill air of the room. Even in fall, nights on the top floors of the old Georgian house were cold and fires were lit in the girls' bedrooms. Any cold always made Julia's twisted

foot ache. In the moonlight, Serafina thought, looking at her
sister's face above her, she was reminded of the women Rossetti
had drawn for Tennyson's King Arthur in Avalon. Her small,
perfectly formed features were marked with an expression of
compassionate anxiety, and wore the moonbeams as if they were
made for her creamy skin and auburn hair which fell below her
waist like a cloak. The young girl had taken her felt boots off
and the floor was very cold. She got under the bedclothes with a
single hop.

"Oh, your feet are like fishmonger's slabs," Serafina
squealed, as Julia put her face on her sister's bosom and they held
each other.

"Did I get here in time?" Julia asked, looking over at her
sister.

"Oh, yes," Serafina answered. He wasn't even close to
Ariana."

"I am so glad," Julia said nestling into her sister's shoulder. "Shall you sleep?"

"Oh, yes. I think so," Serafina answered.

But after a few moments, Serafina sat up and wrapped her
long arms around her knees. Julia had no choice but to sit up as
well if she wanted to remain covered and stay warm. The fire in
the grate had burned low and the orange glow cast pretty shadows from the swaying tassels of the four-poster bed. Both Serafina and Julia liked to keep the bed curtains open so they could
see the fire.

"What is it Fifi?" Julia asked, using one of her sister's secret names, names no one else knew. Sometimes her sister even
spoke with a French accent.

"I don't know. I just feel strange." Her young face was
creased into a thoughtful frown.

"You always feel strange after the dream. Shall I read the
fire for you?"

"You're not too sleepy?"

"You know I'm never too sleepy to help you," the child
said.

"Then, yes, please, it would be lovely. The fire is perfect

for it, isn't it?"

"Quite perfect," the beautiful, mature child said sitting up and adjusting the bed clothes.

The troubled child put her head in Julia's lap and gazed over at the hearth.

"Well, what do you see? Do tell me something wonderful," the older girl asked in a dreamy voice. "Tell me about fairies and kings and queens. You know what I like."

The younger child reached over to the bed table, picked up Serafina's hairbrush and began to stroke rhythmically her sister's long, golden hair. Both the lovely faces were lit with the ruddy light of the glowing coals.

"Oh, Serafina, I see a journey...and...and at the end, a handsome prince."

"What does he look like" Serafina asked.

"He's beautiful. A little like cousin Miles. Yes, the resemblance is striking."

"You're sure?"

"Yes, dear. Put your head down again," the younger child prompted.

Obediently, with the air of a cat waiting to be petted, Serafina put down her head. Julia continued stroking with the brush.

"I see that one day all your bad dreams will be gone forever and the prince will take you to his beautiful castle where you shall be his princess and be happy forever. The minotaur shall be driven out of his cave and done to death. He shall come no more."

"You're seeing that in the fire?" Serafina said.

"Yes, dear. And I shall come to visit you in your castle and we shall be ever so jolly together."

Then, she paused, looked over her sister's shoulder and saw that her eyes were staring sightlessly into the fire. She continued the rhythmical motions of the brush.

"But you have to do your part and keep out of the maze."

The slow, even strokes that the young girl administered

to her sister's hair, back and shoulders soon had their effect: the young woman's eyes were wide and staring but entirely vacant.

"Go to sleep now, Serafina," Julia said bending over her sister. "Sleep, sleep, sleep," the child chanted slowly and evenly. Finally, the staring eyes closed.

"Oh, Serafina," the child said plaintively but softly to her sleeping sister. "How can I make you happy forever and ever? So you never, never have the dream again. And I never, never have to get up to stroke your hair and make you feel better. You know you must do everything I tell you, now. You have no choice. Tell Ariana she is a wicked child to lead you into the tunnel where the monster lives. And you must stay out of the maze in the daytime. You must not allow yourself to be led in there again. If Ariana does, she will not be allowed into your dreams at all. And if you go in the maze when you're awake, I shall not brush your hair at night or read the fire anymore. Do you hear me?"

"Yes, Julia," Serafina said in what Julia called her flat voice.

The young girl watched her sister's face very intently. She watched the strong, clean planes of Serafina's face grow soft as melting wax and readjust themselves into the face of a child even younger than Julia. The transformation no longer amazed or frightened Julia. She just accepted it as a remarkable aspect of the sister she doted on and comforted.

The very young child who had taken possession of Serafina's face looked sad. Her lower lip was thrust out and she seemed on the edge of tears.

"Please, Auntie Julia, don't be cross. I hate it when you are cross with me."

"Then, you must not lead Serafina into the tunnel again, Ariana. Can you promise me you will not do it again? You must. It is very frightening for Serafina. Don't you realize that? Do you want to scare her? If you do, you are a little beast and it is very cruel of you."

"No, I don't want to," the lisping voice said. "But the butterfly goes there. I want to see the butterfly. That's all."

"Well, you must not follow it. No matter what. Otherwise, I shall put you to sleep for a long, long time and you shan't get out even in dreams."

"Auntie Julie, don't put me to sleep. Only if it hurts. Only if I am really going to be in trouble with—" The child paused in obvious terror. Her dark eyes had grown large and reflected the embers from the fire. "—you know."

"Sweetheart, you know I shall never hurt you. If I put you to sleep it is to help, not to hurt. You know that, don't you, dear," Julia said mimicking the tones and expression of her elder sister during the daytime when Serafina was the undisputed leader in all their games and studies.

"Yes, Auntie Julie. I know you never hurt me. If the monster comes, I have to go to sleep to be safe."

"That's right, sweetheart," Julia said patting the infantile face her elder sister now wore.

The first time Julia had seen this facial change, it had alarmed her. But now she just accepted it as part of Serafina. Julia lay on the older girl's shoulder for some time, and once her sister was breathing easily, Julia got up in spite of the chill and looked out the window at the garden behind the house. The yew maze was at the centre of it, a dark mass of indistinct shadows.

"If I could," Julia thought. "I should tear the maze to pieces. It's good for nothing but scaring Serafina. The moonlight, and the deep shadows it cast, emphasized the darkness and prolixity of the twisting paths between the hedges of the maze.

She looked back at her sister and, reassured by the slow even breathing, looked out at the sinister forms of the maze.

"We shall always take care of one another, always," Julia thought. "I shall never let anything bad happen to Serafina. Cross my heart and ten fingers up to God."

It was the most solemn oath the child knew.

Chapter One

KATHERINE

...a woman who has once lost chastity has lost every good quality. She has from that moment all the vices.

—The Roman Minister of Justice quoted by Josephine Butler

At five minutes to twelve on a warm summer night in 1885, as he entered Regent Street just off Piccadilly, Miles Hick-enbotham, returning to his studio after delivering a very satisfactory commission, paused to watch a strikingly handsome young woman who waited under a gaslight. The other men who walked by glanced at her with more than casual interest: Her cheek bones were high, her skin very white and translucent but blooming with a healthy rose blush in each cheek. She was small and slender but still rounded and shapely. Her fine featured face had a foreign, even an oriental quality, with dark almond shaped eyes, a long nose and a wide well defined mouth set above a deliciously small chin. Her thick dark hair fell from under her bonnet in two softly braided loops to her shoulders. She stood very close to the lamp post in what was almost a posture of defence, as though using the sculpted cast-iron pole to keep people away. Was she a domestic angel who had lost her way in the dangerous darkness of the Metropolis or a shameless creature who preyed on male weakness? In short, she was lovely and respectably dressed but, she was alone, and it was the middle of the night in the Babylon of Victoria's London. Such a woman could not fail to make herself an object of male interest and speculation, speculation because she had none of the boldness of the prostitutes who sauntered past her along Regent Street. During the day, this same thoroughfare was a focus of the new feminine past-time of window shopping, an entertainment permitted by the greater public freedom women had begun to enjoy in the eighteen-eighties. But as darkness fell, an odd inversion took place: in the evening it was men who were the shoppers and the women on the street, the merchandise. Unlike the respectable female pedestrians of the day-time who would likely turn away in angry silence if spoken to by a male "pest," the women who promenaded Regent Street at night were, generally, very ready to talk to men. But the woman who pressed herself against the lam post, Miles thought, did not look at all communicative. That she should be out at this hour, and at the same time seem so aloof made her peculiarly interesting.

If I were to approach her, he asked himself, and were to fall completely under her spell, would I find a sublime adventure, or working-class dullness with a degrading aftermath? All the energy of the night seemed to flow around the girl without touching her. She remained motionless and apart. Miles took in Piccadilly with a furtive turn of his head, a gesture which showed he was as concerned with being observed as he was with observing. Then, he brought his gaze back to the girl, who was so still she might have been made of wax, like a figure at Tussaud's.

Her worn, clean clothing was cheaply made but not tasteless, and unlike many of the women who paraded during the late evening hours, she did not wear too many petticoats, nor was she too tightly laced. Her figure did not require it. However, Miles thought, that was no indication of anything. There were countesses for sale on the streets of London, as well as young maids, certified pure by their keepers—as W.T. Stead would tell

readers of the Pall Mall Gazette starting tomorrow morning in the first article of his sensational exposé of child prostitution, *The Maiden Tribute of Modern Babylon*. Serafina Winstanley, Miles' cousin and the woman he wished to marry was an intimate of Josephine Butler and a steadfast worker in the causes of female emancipation and repeal of the Contagious Diseases Acts. Her younger sister Julia was on the staff of the Pall Mall Gazette and had actually worked on the exposé as an unnamed member of Stead's Secret Committee.

Miles paused and watched the girl, feeling the weight of his body balanced between passing and stopping. In later years, he would often think of the girl's face as he first saw it beneath the gaslight, and would compare it to one of the hieratic women in the paintings of Edvard Munch, a face strangely impassive and mysterious. He stood, suspended in mid-step for a moment, and then let his foot drop to the pavement with his full weight, no longer propelled forward by the momentum of his stride. If only Serafina would finally consent to be his wife, he would not have such conflicts, but she seemed incapable of comprehending this aspect of their relationship. For her, all was black or white. Either he behaved as "a principled man," or he did not. Either he could sustain a relationship with her based on things other than "instincts," or he could not. For her, the foundation of marriage had to be intellectual and spiritual, a mutuality of interests and beliefs, something worthier and more significant than mere attraction. And, indeed, they did share intellectual convictions and pleasures. Miles agreed that women should be enfranchised. On her side, Serafina was an excellent amateur painter and together they had enjoyed numerous day trips with their easels and brushes. They both took pride in the progress she had made since he had been teaching her. He often spoke of her talent to his professional colleagues, especially for drawing likenesses.

"I have no trouble with her views. I support them," he muttered to himself as watched the girl on the other side of the street.

Most in their circle regarded Miles and Serafina as a perfect couple, close in the special way of cousins but removed sufficiently so that there could be no scandal about their union. They were both exceptionally handsome, well-educated people and enjoyed the connections of an upper middle-class family. The only slightly odd thing was that their engagement had never been formally announced. It was more of an assumption formed over many years. Miles had avoided women at Oxford. Holidays were always spent with Serafina and her family. Miles had lost his own parents in a steam packet disaster on the Thames. His sister, too, was gone, so he was alone but for Serafina and her family. Once Serafina's father had passed away during a trip to the Continent, Miles became the man of the house whenever he resided at Twenty-one Cavendish Square, the Winstanley's townhouse.

Serafina's settlement would give them a sizeable income when added to the money Miles was beginning to earn from painting portraits for some of the better mercantile families of the west-end. Yet, at their respective ages of twenty-four and twenty-six, no formal steps had been taken toward matrimony. The settlement had not yet been drawn and Serafina refused to formalize the engagement in so many words. Her belief in female emancipation and her love of personal independence kept her from making a full commitment. Marriage, she believed, was a 'fundamentally flawed institution.' Her mother, Mrs. Winstanley, an attractive middle-aged woman seemed to be curiously disinterested in Serafina's marital plans. But Serafina knew her mother, sister and friends would be shocked if she did not marry Miles, and she certainly had not met any other man she preferred.

As with many pre-marital middle-class Victorian couples, the only kisses the cousins had exchanged were soft, childish pecks. Miles could afford a mistress, of course, but something in him resisted taking that step and so, occasionally, he went to visit one of the establishments of Mrs. Jeffries, a rich and notorious madame who ran a string of extraordinary brothels in London that catered to all tastes. Miles restricted himself to her establishment known as The Rose Cottage in Hampstead Heath where erotic whippings were administered. In fact, the birch was essential to his pleasure. Her two other establishments, one at 112 Church Street in Chelsea or the torture chamber near Gray's Inn Road held no attractions for him. If Serafina had known of his visits to the Rose Cottage, she would have been furious, not on personal grounds, but because one of the key arguments against repeal of the CD Acts was that prostitution was a social necessity for men. Men, the argument went, even men of breeding, must satisfy their sexual appetites much more frequently than any respectable woman would care to experience. This scientific fact was set out in all four editions of *The Functions and Disorders of the Reproductive Organs in Childhood, Youth, Adult Age, and Advanced Life Considered in their Physiological, Social and Moral Relations* by the physician, William Acton. Even in 1885 Acton's widely read and ridiculous pronouncements on female sexuality were still taken seriously. Historians of today regard Acton's book as the work which was primarily responsible for creating the Victorian stereotype of the sexless female. However, during Victoria's reign, nearly all scientific authorities agreed that women were without strong sexual feelings. "In men," wrote William Rathbone Greg, "the sexual desire is inherent and spontaneous. In the other sex, the desire is dormant, if not non-existent."

For years, the House of Commons based legislation on a similar view of male and female sexuality, and refused to pass laws which would make it a criminal offence to buy sex from an underage girl (the age of consent being thirteen). As one MP put it, "To pass such a bill could put our sons and even ourselves at risk of prosecution." In other words, men who used prostitutes were compelled by nature to do so and therefore could not be blamed for their actions. But women who sold themselves in order to eat, or fulfill the "needs" of men were disgusting, "fallen creatures" who lured men into immorality. Once an unmarried woman had been seduced, every door and every opportunity was closed to her. The Roman Minister of Justice and Police horrified Josephine Butler, who spearheaded the fight against legalized prostitution in Britain, by asserting that "a woman who has once lost chastity has lost every good quality. She has from that moment 'all the vices.'"

The Contagious Diseases Acts had been passed into British law to protect soldiers in garrison towns in Great Britain and in India where, by the 1880s, venereal disease reached epidemic proportions. Under the CD Acts, women could be seized and subjected to pelvic examination on the mere accusation of prostitution. If infected, they could be placed in locked wards. Men, however, even diseased army men, were subject to no such regulation! It was generally assumed that only women of the lower orders would be so degenerate as to sell themselves, so assumptions of social as well as moral superiority were intermixed in late Victorian attitudes toward sex. These assumptions strongly affected relations between women of 'higher' and 'lower' classes as well as between men and women.

Naturally, Miles' feelings about the girl he was watching were coloured by the beliefs of his time. The fact that she was alone at this time and place told against her respectability. The fact that she carried several small parcels, suggested she was not a professional prostitute. She also seemed lost, uncertain which way to turn. A few seconds more or less and Miles would not have been present for what happened next: A man in a cheap, shiny suit swaggered up to the girl while she clutched ever tighter to her packages. He placed himself indecently close to her and said something that must have been a verbal equivalent of his leering look. The burning blush which appeared on her cheek, her expression of fear and her shrinking stance irresistibly drew Miles out into the crossing. As he stepped briskly across the patches of manure on the filthy paving stones, the man continued to impose himself on the girl, trapping her with his long arm as he wrapped it around her and the post.

Miles called out, "I say, Mabel, have you been waiting long?" And waved to the girl who was facing him over the shoulder of her aggressor. She looked up at him, the man felt her attention shift and wheeled around. When he saw Miles' tall, well-dressed figure, he touched the brim of his hat and said, "Sorry, guvnor, I thought the lady was alone," and slunk off toward the thickest knots of girls who strolled back and forth across the pavement.

"Are you all right, Miss?" Miles asked as he placed the lamp post between himself and the girl.

"Yes, sir, thank you," she replied in well modulated tones. "But I don't know what should have happened had you not come." Her speech and manner were educated and lady like, Miles noted with pleasure.

"Well," Miles said, "If you really do not want to be accosted, you are standing in the wrong place."

"I was just starting to realize that when I was approached. I was looking for a hansom and couldn't see a single one. I was wondering what to do next."

"There will be one on the Strand. There's a rank there. And you certainly don't want to wait here. You can see what the other women here are up to. So come along," he said in a perfunctory manner as he offered his arm and took her parcels. There was a certainty of acceptance in his movement and voice which seemed to compel her to take his arm. They walked off together in the direction he had indicated.

"I felt quite certain the last omnibus had gone," she explained, obviously nervous and somewhat embarrassed. "But there were no hansoms either."

"Which omnibus?" he asked.

"The one east to Whitechapel."

"You live in the east end?"

"Yes, I rarely come into the City or west-end."

"Then, I had better see you home. Your name is not really 'Mabel,' is it?" he asked smiling, trying to reassure her.

"No," she said, timidly returning his smile.

"You are not afraid of me are you?"

"No. I don't believe I am."

"Then what is it?"

"What is what?"

"Your name?"

"Green, sir. Katherine Green," she said in a tone of some deference, as if in providing her name she had suddenly become aware of her shabbiness and Miles' sartorial elegance.

The night was a very fine one, the air unusually fresh and clear, so the street lamps actually lit the broad thoroughfare. The parade of women and their customers thinned out and up ahead, Katherine could see four or five cabs lined up near the curb.

"There are the cabs," Miles said. He could feel that her arm was stiff in his. "You must allow me to see you home."

"Oh, I should be glad after what just happened, but it is such a very long ride sir."

"Hickenbotham, Miles Hickenbotham," he said.

"Mr. Hickenbotham, it is really quite a long ride."

"Please, I should worry if I did not see you to your door at this hour. Especially in Whitechapel—if it's even half as rough as west end papers say."

"It isn't really that rough, but I thank you for your kind intentions, Mr. Hickenbotham."

"How did you happen to be out so late, Miss Green?" Miles asked.

"I went to the White Horse Cellars Inn to fetch some parcels that were coming from Plymouth. The coach was terribly late in arriving. They kept saying the coach would arrive and I knew my acquaintance needed the packages. So I waited way past any decent hour. If the parcels had been mine, I should have left them until tomorrow."

The pair drew abreast of the cabs. Miles handed the girl into the hansom and said, "Where, then, are we going?"

"You really need not trouble yourself, Mr. Hickinbotham."

"It is no trouble. It is a fine night. A ride through the City should be pleasant."

"Dorset Street and Commercial Street, then" she answered.

Miles repeated the address to the driver. "Yes, yes, I'll be coming west again with you," he told the driver as he settled into his seat.

"Now, what do you do when you are not waiting for parcels, Miss Green?"

"Oh, I work in Bow on Fairfield Road. I make matches at

Bryant and May."

"If I may say so, Miss Green, you are very well spoken for a factory girl." Neither one of them thought his condescending remark inappropriate.

"My father was an army man in India, sir, but my education was not altogether neglected. Right now, I am studying photography at the studio of a practitioner on Fleet Street. I am anxious to leave the match factory."

"Really? I am a photographer. An amateur, of course. I am an artist by profession."

"How wonderful to be so talented, sir," she said in a dull, disinterested tone and she turned away from him to look out at the passing streets.

There was something so distant about the girl, Miles felt, even her responses seemed remote. It was the quality he had first noticed about her when she was standing alone on the street. She had a curious aloofness that drew him to her. It was more than the common social distance which separated their sexes and classes. Her apartness was of an altogether different order than ordinary propriety demanded. It was considered, as if she harboured some conviction about herself and the world, a conviction that placed her in an altogether different sphere than those around her. He found her strangely inert and impenetrable, which made her mysterious and desirable.

Most women responded to Miles immediately, and he could feel their interest in him. Accordingly, most women seemed transparent to Miles and gave him the illusion of insight, but this girl was hidden in an obscurity which admitted of no connection or contact with anything outside herself, as if she were a visitor from a distant star. Her essential self was suspended in a vast interior space, of which he had been somehow aware when he first saw her. Now, he felt impelled to cross the distance of her inner solitude and touch the woman at its centre. It was an attraction by the law of contraries: the strength of her self-possession and containment inflamed his desire for some strong response. Some of his reaction was vanity. It was a little provoking that this working girl should remain at an

Olympian distance from him. He felt she would ride all the way to Whitechapel in silence if he did not prompt her. She was not lumpish or awkward. In fact, she was unusually poised, extraordinarily so. Few women of his own caste bore silence so well.

The dark hair which grew low over her forehead was like the edge of a luxuriant cloud floating out from beneath her cheap bonnet. On a sudden impulse, Miles reached over and pulled the velveteen ribbon which held the bonnet in place, and in one sweeping motion he removed her hat. It was a gesture he never would have made with Serafina or with any woman of his own class, and he was aware that it implied a degree of familiarity incongruous with their short acquaintance. It was a crude way to get a response and seemed utterly inadequate to accomplish the connection he sought.

A rich shiny cascade of auburn highlights fell to her shoulders and was visible even in the half light of the moving cab.

"Oh, what are you doing?" Her tone was an odd mixture of surprise and boredom. Once again, he felt, he had failed to rouse her.

"I just had a feeling that you had a mass of beautiful hair beneath that bonnet. I wanted to see it. I suppose I should apologize for being so familiar."

"What sort of photographs do you make?" she asked, giving her disordered hair a shake and ignoring his apology. There was a certain self-consciousness in her gesture which afforded a glimpse of her spirit and pride. She refused to respond to his gesture in any direct, personal way.

"Mostly portraits."

"And what processes do you use?"

"In the studio, wet collodion. Do you know what that is?" he asked.

"And, you generally print on albumen paper?" she replied, without acknowledging his question.

"You really do know something about photography."

"I told you I want to change my employment. I am learning as much as I can. It is too costly to be merely a past-time. For pleasure, I must limit myself to charcoal."

"Then you sketch, as well?"

"A little," she answered. "But even a pad of newsprint is expensive to me."

"We share several enthusiasms, then, Miss Green."

"It would seem so," she said, in a neutral voice and turned to look out the window.

What is it about her, he wondered, that makes me want to break through her opaque surface? He resolved to change his subject and tactic.

"You know, you must be more careful, Miss Green. There are unprincipled men and women in London who would abduct a handsome girl like you—especially at this hour. I—I had a little sister who was taken years ago . And was never again found."

He was surprised at the feeling he could hear in his own voice. Self-revelation was not what he had intended. Yet, for the first time, she turned toward him with real interest.

"How long ago was it that you lost her, Mr. Hickenbottham?" she asked.

"At least ten years. She would be almost eighteen, now. She was a late child, eight years younger than I am. I was only twelve when she was taken. I was supposed to be watching her at the time. Foolish of me still to feel responsible after all these years."

"No, Mr. Hickenbottham. Not at all," she said looking directly into his eyes for the first time. "It shows your fine feeling. It is a very terrible way to lose a loved one."

Her extremely dark eyes reflected the passing lamps and seemed to draw him in without revealing anything. A few moments later he was embarrassed to find himself still staring into the opaque depths.

He looked away and spoke, using an authoritative didactic tone which he felt would help him regain control of the situation.

"It seems you've taken my remarks very much to heart, Miss Green. I did not mean to impose my feelings on you, but rather to warn you of very real dangers."

Then, to withdraw even further from his embarrassment, he added, "In fact, those dangers will be detailed tomorrow morning in the *Pall Mall Gazette*. My cousin has helped do the research for the articles. I assure you, the facts are shocking. A handsome young woman like yourself is in real danger alone on the London streets after dark."

"I'm sure that is true, Mr. Hickenbotham. But as I told you, my being out this late is entirely accidental."

"Do please be more careful in future, Miss Green. Piccadilly is a notorious place for prostitutes—and their keepers. A young girl of your appearance seen in such a place at such a late hour is particularly at risk. A carriage stops in front of you, you go to speak to a genteel looking woman who leans out the window and in moments, you are seized and whisked away to one of the great clearing houses where English girls are shipped to brothels here or on the Continent, never to be seen again by family or friends—and to suffer a fate worse than death."

"After what happened to your sister, Mr. Hickenbottham, I can understand your vehemence, but once more I assure you..."

"How do you know you are safe with me?" he suddenly said. "You took my arm, got into this hansom and seem completely unconcerned."

To his surprise, she smiled very broadly. It was a revelation to see her blank look become so suddenly alive.

"Would you like me to be frightened of you then, Mr. Hickenbotham? My judgement of people is excellent. I am certain I have not mistaken the goodness of your intentions."

"No," he said after along pause. "You have not. But you shouldn't trust so completely to your own feelings. That trust could exact a terrible price from you."

"I thank you for your concern, sir, but you see I am something of a gypsy and have had to trust my own intimations about people and situations for many years."

"You mean you are alone in the world?"

"For many years. I was orphaned when I was ten."

"Good heavens, you are certainly a fine grown girl for

such a history. I was orphaned, too, but have had a good home with dear cousins."

"I should have done much more with myself if I had had the advantages of a family and trustworthy friends."

"But—excuse me for asking— who reared you, then?"

"There were some people who took me from where I had been living after my parents died. They sheltered and schooled me, yet cared little enough about me, and used me for their own ends." She turned away from him again and they both lapsed into a long silence.

Finally, Miles reached into his jacket pocket and took out his card case. He drew out one of his cards and gave it to the girl.

"Perhaps it is providential that we have met, Miss Green. Your story resembles in some ways what my lost sister's may have been, though I doubt I shall ever really know. I have a photographic studio which I would be happy to place at your disposal along with chemicals, papers, plates and all the costly apparatus of the art. Allow me to aid you in this small way."

"Oh, that is very good, sir," the girl said with a slight thrill in the first syllable of her reply. Then she looked away and was quiet. Finally, she spoke again in her usual flat tone, "but I should feel too indebted to you. I am very unused to relying on anyone other than myself." She handed his card back to him.

"Please, keep my card," he replied. "If you change your mind, you can find me at that address most mornings. I have my portrait studio there as well. I paint best in the morning light, so I have no use for the camera or the glass room before noon."

The hansom was slowing to a stop and the girl gathered up her parcels and made ready to disembark.

"No. Wait," Miles said. "I shall hand you out and help you with those to your door."

The girl sat passively with her arms around her parcels until Miles came to her side and opened the door, relieved her of the parcels and took her gloved hand.

"That is my doorway," she said pointing to the entrance of an ugly narrow lodging house. "My room is just inside," and she took back her parcels. "Goodbye and thank you, Miles Hickenbotham. I shall not forget your kindness."

Before Miles could reply she had disappeared into the dark, foul smelling hall. He stood for a moment looking into the impenetrable darkness and then climbed into the cab.

All the way back to his studio near Soho Square, whilst the hooves of the quick stepping horse beat out a brisk rhythm on the paving stones of the empty streets, thoughts of the girl preoccupied Miles. After trying to examine his own feelings and being confounded by them he spoke out loud.

"I was not merely attracted by her appearance. It was something more than that. Her self-sufficiency—not at all like Serafina's—was passive and patient and had what one might even call a spiritual quality about it. A kind of knowing, a certainty. I wonder if we shall meet again. She certainly lives in very straitened circumstances."

His thoughts about the girl went on and on, but began and ended nowhere, and by the time he got home he was wide awake. He smoked three cigars in his studio and pointlessly examined his latest work in the flaring gaslight. The gray dawn was filtering into his bedroom before he finally slept.

Chapter 2

SERAFINA

"Mr. ———, (is) another wealthy man, whose whole life is dedicated to the gratification of lust. During my investigations in the subterranean realm I was constantly coming across his name. This procuress was getting girls for ———, that woman was beating up maids for ———, this girl was waiting for ———, that house was a noted place of ———'s. I ran across his traces so constantly that I began to make inquiries in the upper world of this redoubtable personage. I soon obtained confirmation of the evidence I had gathered at first hand below as to the reality of the existence of this modern Minotaur, this English Tiberius, whose Caprece is in London."

—*The Maiden Tribute of Modern Babylon*
by W.T. Stead in the *Pall Mall Gazette*
July 8, 1885

Given the late hour at which he had retired on the previous night, Miles was late for his breakfast with Serafina and Julia. It was well after nine in the morning on a perfect summer day when he vaulted up the well-known steps at number twenty-one Cavendish Square in London's fashionable west end. The house stood in a neighbourhood where the streets were lined with trees, gardens and iron fences. Most of the buildings were imposing, three-storey, single-family homes, constructed of stone or brick. Ornamental shrubs abounded, and even someone as disinterested in gardening as Miles could not help but appreciate the wonderful scent of lilacs which permeated the porch of the Winstanley's large handsome home. Slender boughs heavy with blossoms drooped over the white wooden railings, as if tempting him to pluck their bounty. He capitulated to the temptation almost immediately and broke off a small cluster of the deep purple blooms to take inside, as a peace offering and tangible evidence that he was sensible of the offence of his tardiness. Then he rang the bell and waited for Rossiter's creaking step. Anyone seeing Miles in the full sunlight would have thought him an exceptionally handsome young man, just the sort of young man who would be calling at such an elegant house.

He heard the brass bolts snap back and before Rossiter could get the door fully open, Virgil, the spoiled bloodhound, stuck his large, melancholy face out at him. Miles felt for the sugar cube he had secreted in his waistcoat pocket and used it to pay the agreed upon price of admission.

"The ladies are in the south drawing room, sir," Rossiter said in his slow, sepulchral voice, which would have been the envy of a bishop.

"Thank you, Rossiter. I thought I should miss breakfast. Which ladies?"

"Miss Julia, Miss Serafina and Mrs. Winstanley, sir."

"I see," he said, squaring his shoulders.

He had expected to find Julia with her sister, but not their mother, Mrs. Winstanley, who was rarely seen before noon. She generally showed little interest in her daughters' suffragist work, or the articles of the notorious crusading journalist, W.T. Stead. She was even less interested in such things than in her daughters' suitors.

Julia and Serafina were planning to read the first of Mr. Stead's articles exposing child prostitution in London. Julia would be the one most excited about the reading since she had been swimming in the mud of London's underworld for months doing much of the background research for Stead. She would certainly be proud that publication of the exposé had finally begun. He glanced down at his little cluster of blooms. A poor olive branch, he thought ruefully, if he had kept three ladies waiting for over an hour and missed breakfast into the bargain.

He passed through the familiar rooms quickly, getting impressionistic glimpses of dark stained oak and lighter polished fruit woods, soft carpeting and fine paper on the walls, which boasted patterns recently designed by the prominent socialist and king of Victorian design, William Morris. The furniture was an unconventional mixture of some elegant old Chippendale pieces with claw feet and rounded curves set artfully against the straight lines and square shapes of some newer tables and chairs produced by Morris, Marshall and Faulkner in the '60s. Most of these newer pieces had been selected by Serafina. With an image of her in his thoughts, Miles soon regarded the original in the brilliant sunlight which flooded the south parlour. "What an exquisite picture," he thought as he looked inside.

Serafina knelt on the thick carpet, chin resting on her palms, her long slim torso curved above an open newspaper which lay on the floor. As usual, rebelling against the current fashion, she wore a walking dress of yellow silk with no trimming or bustle behind. A tiny, tightly confined waist with exaggerated hindquarters was the keynote of 1880s fashion. Her naturally elongated waist and elastic hips recalled to Miles the branch from which he had plucked the blooms he held in his hand. Her unusually long arms and legs, which gave her such an advantage at tennis, a game she played very aggressively, seemed to surround the newspaper. Her sister, Julia, not at all unattractive in a layered green plaid 'handkerchief' dress, peered over her left shoulder. Both women refused to be hobbled by their clothing and so wore their dresses short, even for walking costumes. Both wore their hair loosely gathered at the backs of their heads. Neither were tightly laced and neither wore crinolines or other awkward foundation garments. Both were picturesquely displayed on the carpeted floor. Serafina's golden hair seemed to catch every ray of light in the bright room and magnify it, while Julia's rich brunette colouring contrasted with her elder sister's and gave them each extra charm. Like the face of the goddess in Botticelli's *Birth of Venus*, Serafina's features were irregular and imperfect but somehow combined to create a face of striking beauty. Julia's much more regular features were handsome but lacked the glamour of her older sister.

Mrs. Winstanley, a high-nosed, proud looking woman of handsome middle-age sat demurely back in an armchair on Serafina's right side.

"Horrible man," Serafina said glancing up at Miles and taking the proffered blooms without even glancing at them. "And men say it is women who are never on time."

"Mea culpa, Serafina," the contrite looking young man said, looking, if possible, even more handsome in his contrition. "Mea maxima culpa. I offer no excuse."

"Well, we have serious business this morning, so I won't bother to castigate you. Isn't that a new waistcoat? You are such a dandy, Miles." she said as her face broke into a smile that managed to intensify the already bright sunlight in the room. "Now, sit down next to me and turn the pages. Julia and I have been agreeing on a digest of the article."

"Digest? Mrs. Winstanley and I are not judged competent to hear the whole?" Miles asked.

"As usual," Julia spoke up, "Mr. Stead has employed many lumbering pieces of rhetoric which overbear the content. We thought we would select the important points for you. It is the content of the series that will stand the nation on its head— not the bombast."

"That is unfair, Julia," Serafina put in. "Mr. Stead is an excellent gutter journalist who well knows precisely how to stir the reading public, especially those among them with prurient tastes. The thing I object to, though, is what you told me about the 'Minotaur, the incarnation of lust and wealth."

"What about him?" Miles asked.

"He is no longer in London. And Mr. Stead was very evasive about him when I asked who it was. It makes me wonder if he exists."

"But it is really the facts, not personalities which are most striking and important," Julia insisted.

"I agree with you, Julia," Mrs. Winstanley interjected. "Even though we experienced the horror and pain of little Amelia's abduction, other people cannot fail to be moved by the simple fact that such monstrous things are a common occurrence in London. It is entirely unnecessary to embroider them. I can hardly speak about it without feeling rage. None of you, who were children at the time, can possibly feel the horror of it as I did—and still do. Your parents were devastated, Miles." The odd thing was, however, Mrs. Winstanley's manner and expression were at odds with her words: she looked appraisingly at her elder daughter but seemed entirely untouched emotionally.

Miles sighed quietly, hoping that Mrs. Winstanley would give them the abridged version of his sister's abduction. It was true that none of his generation could feel it as Mrs. Winstanley did, however, sometimes the emotions she claimed to feel seemed out of proportion with a tragedy that was nearly ten years old. Life must go on and for all the younger Winstanley's it had done so easily enough. If Miles' own parents had lived, Mrs. Winstanley would have had contemporaries who might have shared her revisitations of the past, but then she would not have been able to be so uniquely aggrieved. Neither Miles nor his fair cousins could feel much sympathy for what they viewed as the emotional indulgence of Serafina's mother. Miles, in particular, did not like having his own sore point touched. Mrs. Winstanley's pronouncements about grief didn't let him forget that he had been left by nurse for only a few moments to watch his little sister, Amelia. He had turned his back on her and walked only a few paces away from her to look at a particularly colourful bird, which later proved to be a South American parrot escaped from a neighbour's aviary. He had turned back to see a man running away and his sister's perambulator empty. He had not been able to tell the police inspector anything about the abductor. As a rational adult, he knew that he had not been to blame, but throughout his childhood in the Winstanley's house, he felt a nagging guilt and sometimes wondered if he had allowed the abduction to happen in order to get rid of Amelia, his family's beautiful late arrival, whose blonde curls and precociously well-formed face had charmed everyone. The deaths of his own parents six months previous to the abduction, reinforced this feeling of guilt and rejection. After his own family was gone, Dr. Winstanley, his cousins' father, became the guardian of Miles and Amelia. Nurse, of course, was dismissed and Miles had immediately begun his career as a student of the rather harsh, Dr. Winstanley. The unfortunate convergence of the two heavy losses, and Dr. Winstanley's distant nature might have made his life with his cousins's family bleak. But actually, Dr. Winstanely was a good teacher and with the help of several private tutors prepared him well for Oxford. He also had the Sunday afternoon company of his two charming cousins. It was the only time the male and female cousins were allowed to be together unattended by Mrs. Winstanley. Otherwise, boy and girls were kept separate with Miles leading a disciplined life under the direction of the doctor.

After Miles had lived five years in the Winstanley house, tragedy struck again. Dr. Winstanley was drowned during a very rough channel crossing. The night before he sailed, there had been a break-in in the house which ended by rousing the whole family. As a consequence of the crime, Dr. Winstanely had departed suddenly for the continent. During the rough winter crossing, the boat had been hit by a larger vessel and Dr. Winstanely, who had been promenading on the upper deck, was lost overboard. Serafina was twelve, Julia ten and Miles fourteen when the head of the house was lost. Mrs. Winstanley, who had always been distant with the children became even colder. Miles was sent away to school and finally on to Oxford. He was not permitted to return to Cavendish Square until the end of Michaelmas term in his first year of university. When Miles once again saw his cousins, they were two very pretty young girls of twelve and fourteen, respectively. The seventeen year old boy in his school blazer and long pants immediately became their hero and romantic idol. Miles and Serafina remembered little

of their tragic earlier years and met as strangers. Unfortunately
for Julia, she was just a little too young to compete for the young
man's attention, so the lovely Serafina became the first object of
his affection. It was Julia, however, who remained unswervingly
loyal to her first love through all the years of her adolescence,
and remained quite ready to be an adoring, unmarried sister-
in-law for the rest of her life. Serafina, on the other hand, had
many suitors before she returned to a serious consideration of
Miles. For the young man, the mere fact of being considered
by Serafina had erased every other woman of his acquaintance.
Julia, who had grown into a very clever young woman, saw that
the game was finally up and began to concentrate on writing and
other intellectual pursuits. No man other than Miles would do
for her.

Just short of Julia's eighteenth birthday, she and Serafina
became active members of the National Vigilance Association
founded by Josephine Butler, the charismatic woman who led
the fight for repeal of the CD Acts and broke the taboo on female discussion of sexual issues. Though Serafina became close
to Mrs. Butler, Julia surpassed her sister intellectually by winning
a position on the Pall Mall Gazette. W.T. Stead, editor and chief
of the journal and the most sensational journalist of his time,
himself, hired her based on several sketches of London life she
had written. The family was amazed when she came home and
announced that she had become a salaried employee, an ambitious young journalist, the very pattern for the New Women of
the 1880s. Mrs. Winstanley was disapproving, saying that young
men of good families would take no interest in an office girl. The
glamorous Serafina was proud of her sister, but a little jealous.
Only Miles offered her unalloyed approval, which was everything and more than Julia could have desired.

Sometimes, when Miles thought of the past, he believed
that it was the abduction of his sister that was the secret main-
spring of Julia's muck raking career and her quiet, concentrated
attention and capacity for intellectual work. The abduction had
certainly affected them all. He did not realize that his choice of
Serafina was the real motive power behind Julia's attainments.

On that morning, when the first of the *Maiden Tribute* articles was published, and he turned away from looking at Julia to watch Serafina in the golden light of the Winstanley's south parlour, he was more conscious than ever that Serafina's character defied his analysis. She was a wonderful golden bird whose beauty and self-centered confidence had pierced him before he'd been old enough to realize what was happening to him. His dim recollections of those first Sundays when they were allowed to spend long afternoons together gave him no clue to his deep bond with her. The inner life of this golden bird was hidden from him, by his own lengthy infatuation and desire for her. For years, he'd watched other young men enter and leave her circle of friends, always fearing that the latest one might win her. Even now, he was still not entirely sure of her. He had never acknowledged to himself that whenever he wanted good judgment, strong affection and sound advice, Julia was the one he sought. But Serafina was the prize he wanted to win, and always would be. On the way over to Cavendish Square, he had decided that his attraction to the match girl of the night before was some kind of strange anomaly. No woman of that class could ever be a serious rival to Serafina.

While Julia was speaking, Miles regarded Serafina with the eye of an artist, which of course, he had done many times, having painted at least four oil portraits of her during the six years he had been painting seriously. Their relationship had now advanced to that degree of intimacy where a woman has a right to give orders to a man. However, familiarity had bestowed no concomitant rights on Miles, only the obligation to respond to Serafina's commands. Even now, he was allowed no liberties with her person. She would tolerate only the slightest physical contact even when they were alone. Occasionally, she let him take her gloved hand.

While Julia was very pretty, she could not compare to the tall, beautiful Serafina in Miles' eyes. This was an unfortunate fact for the younger sister, however the young artists did enjoy the admiration written in two matching but contrasting volumes. Julia's admiration often gave him a pleasure which he knew he should resist. Yet, he could not help but enjoy feeling the cynosure when the three of them were together. Julia sometimes left the couple feeling annoyed with herself for her susceptibility to Miles. Serafina never even noticed her sister's feelings, taking her own superior power of attraction entirely for granted. In spite of this uncomfortable triangle, Julia would not have given up her place in it for any degree of repose. She thought Serafina had more dash and spirit than any girl of her acquaintance, and Miles was the most attractive man she had ever met. She often missed seeing her own gifts, which were great, so bright, in her eyes, was the brilliance of her elder sister—magnified by having won Miles.

Serafina deferred only to Josephine Butler, one of the most beautiful and magnetic public women of her time. But in the family circle and among the Winstanley's intimate friends, Serafina was always perceived as the most glamourous women in the room, while Julia merely had penetration, steadiness and was "somewhat pretty". Both were in love with their cousin, each according to her nature. Serafina had enslaved the handsome artist from an early age and often treated him with a presumption of her power—a presumption that could seem almost cruel at times. Julia sometimes wondered if it wasn't that power which Serafina loved better than Miles himself. It was strange because at times, Julia thought that Miles actually liked being ill-used by Serafina. The younger sister was mostly content to be the close spectator of romance, assured of her place near to the object of her affections. Only occasionally did any dissatisfaction manifest in a sharp or judgemental remark, pinpricks which were always administered to Miles, never to her sister. By the time Julia was a young adult, her twisted leg which had singled her out as a "defective child" had been entirely corrected.

"This morning," Serafina announced in her most ringing public voice, "you are going to hear excerpts from a series of articles that will shake Parliament to its foundations. It is called, *The Maiden Tribute of Modern Babylon*, by W.T. Stead, and while I do agree that some of his devices are ponderous, they are perfectly suited to stir people's passions. I hope you are ready, sir," she said, flashing her dimples at Miles, to be extremely shocked."

"Please," Miles said blandly. "Astonish me."

"Very well," and she began to read.

July 6, 1888…crime of the most ruthless and abominable description is constantly and systematically practised in London without let or hindrance, I am in a position to prove from my own personal knowledge—a knowledge purchased at a cost of which I prefer not to speak. Those crimes may be roughly classified as follows :—I. The sale and purchase and violation of children. II. The procuration of virgins. III. The entrapping and ruin of women. IV. The international slave trade in girls. V. Atrocities, brutalities, and unnatural crimes.

That is what I call sexual criminality, as opposed to sexual immorality. It flourishes in all its branches on every side to an extent of which even those specially engaged in rescue work have but little idea. Those who are constantly engaged in its practice naturally deny its existence. But I speak of that which I do know, not from hearsay or rumour, but of my own personal knowledge.

Serafina and Julia both looked over at Miles to see his reaction.

"Yes, well, you have certainly caught my interest," Miles acknowledged.

"It really is dreadful to hear such things in a respectable west end paper," Mrs. Winstanley said. "If Julia had not laboured so hard, I shouldn't listen at all. I know Serafina takes a positive delight in shocking me."

"I shall go on," Serafina said sententiously and continued.

For days and nights it is as if I had suffered the penalties inflicted upon the lost souls in the Moslem hell, for I seemed to have to drink of the purulent matter that flows from the bodies of the damned. But the sojourn in this hell has not been fruitless. The facts which I and my coadjutors have verified I now place on record at once as a revelation and a warning—a revelation of the system, and a warning to those who may be its victims. In the statement which follows I give no names and I omit addresses. My purpose was not to secure the punishment of criminals but to lay bare the working of a great organization of crime.

"A great organization?" Miles said. "Now my credulity is being meddled with. I have a hard time believing that the girls I see around Piccadilly late in the evening have anything organized other than getting their doss money for the night as quickly as possible."

"It is not the prostitutes who are organized, poor creatures," Serafina said in a lofty tone, "It is the men they serve."

"You shall hear his proofs, Miles, if you will just listen," Julia said, a little more sharply than was necessary.

Miles turned to her to make some charming reply when he caught sight of Mrs. Winstanley. He was shocked by the sudden change in her. Her full cheeks, which were ordinarily rosy and well-shaped, had fallen in. In moments, she looked years older than her normally youthful appearance. Her light colouring and sharply defined features had aged well, but now she looked far older than her forty-odd years.

"Mrs. Winstanley," he exclaimed. "Are you all right?"

Serafina turned around and looked up at her mother.

"Gracious, mother. What's the matter?"

"No, no, read on. I want to hear it all. I am quite all right, really."

"But you look..."

"I tell you, I am well."

But it was clear to Miles that she was anything but well. Her cheeks were now bright with colour where a moment before they had seemed white as chalk.

"I really think..." Miles began.

"Thank you for your concern, Mr. Hickenbotham. I insist, Serafina, that you carry on. This is still my house and you are still my daughter, no matter how advanced you are."

The total silence absorbed the shock of all the younger people. None of them had ever heard Mrs. Winstanley speak so vehemently to her daughter. It was often remarked by

Serafina's friends that it was the daughter who ran the house, not her mother. Ordinarily, Mrs. Winstanley's manners were perfect, if somewhat reserved. Serafina's large blue eyes dilated with surprise and concern. Then she turned back to the paper in front of her and re-commenced her reading.

Before beginning this inquiry I had a confidential interview with one of the most experienced officers who for many years was in a position to possess an intimate acquaintance with all phases of London crime. I asked him, "Is it or is it not a fact that, at this moment, if I were to go to the proper houses, well introduced, the keeper would, in return for money down, supply me in due time with a maid—a genuine article, I mean, not a mere prostitute tricked out as a virgin, but a girl who had never been seduced?" "Certainly," he replied without a moment's hesitation. "At what price?" I continued. "That is a difficult question," he said. "I remember one case which came under my official cognizance in Scotland-yard in which the price agreed upon was stated to be £20. Some parties in Lambeth undertook to deliver a maid for that sum ----to a house of ill fame, and I have no doubt it is frequently done all over London." "But, "I continued, "are these maids willing or unwilling parties to the transaction—that is, are they really maiden, not merely in being each a virgo intacta in the physical sense, but as being chaste girls who are not consenting parties to their seduction? " He looked surprised at my question, and then replied emphatically: "Of course they are rarely willing, and as a rule they do not know what they are coming for." "But," I said in amazement, "then do you mean to tell me that in very truth actual rapes, in the legal sense of the word, are constantly being perpetrated in London on unwilling virgins, purveyed and procured to rich men at so much a head by keepers of brothels?" "Certainly," said he, "there is not a doubt of it.

"Now that really is astonishing," Miles ejaculated. "I don't suppose he could just make all of this up?"

"Miles!" Both young women admonished in chorus.

"Pardon, me."

"You know that Mrs. Butler has been working with Mr.

Stead for some time. You have met her. She's an angel, you must admit. Nearly a female Christ. Can you honestly think that she would be connected with a fraud?"

"No, Serafina. Of course not, but, it is just, so, so shocking. These claims."

"And entirely true," Julia said. "I have seen the signed affidavits upon which these articles are based."

Serafina began reading again:

So startling a declaration by so eminent an authority led me to turn my investigations in this direction. On discussing the matter with a well-known member of Parliament, he laughed and said : "I doubt the unwillingness of these virgins. That you can contract for maids at so much a head is true enough. I myself am quite ready to supply you with 100 maids at £25 each, but they will all know very well what they are about. There are plenty of people among us entirely devoid of moral scruples on the score of chastity, whose daughters are kept straight until they are sixteen or seventeen, not because they love virtue, but solely because their virginity is a realizable asset, with which they are taught they should never part except for value received. These are the girls who can be had at so much a head ; but it is nonsense to say it is rape ; it is merely the delivery as per contract of the asset virginity in return for cash down.

"That fellow is a Member of Parliament?" Miles cried. "Why he speaks as though he is actually in the trade himself... good heavens, Mrs. Winstanley," Miles suddenly cried. "She's fainted. Get her smelling salts."

But the middle-aged woman came around on her own. As her head cleared she turned to Julia and said, "Really, my dear, I cannot congratulate you on working for a man who writes such things, true or not."

"Mother," Serafina said, "I think we should call Dr. Jarvis. You still do not look yourself."

"I realize you have acquired the permanent habit of command, Serafina," Mrs. Winstanley said as she rose to her feet. "But as long as I am in my own house, my daughter shall not issue commands to me. I am not one of your marching women."

Serafina and the other young people were shocked into silence. Never had anyone heard Mrs. Winstanley speak so sharply to anyone, let alone her imperious daughter.

"Yes, mama," the shocked and chagrined young woman said.

The silence lasted for some time after Mrs. Winstanley left the room. Finally, to distract everyone, Julia spoke,

"Miles, don't you think the articles will create enough pressure to get the Criminal Amendment Act through the Commons this time?"

"Well," he said, looking toward the door, "it certainly affected Mrs. Winstanley."

"But really, Miles," Julia went on, doing her best to change the subject, "Don't you think it will affect the politics of the case?"

Serafina remained in shocked silence as she looked through the door where her mother had passed from the room.

Finally, taking his cue from Julia, Miles answered, "I can't see why anyone would not want to raise the age of consent. The way the law is now, a woman of twenty-one at least owns her own property. But I don't see that a girl of thirteen should have the legal right to sell her body to the highest bidder. Mr. Stead's talent for, ah, publicity will undoubtedly put pressure on Mr. Cross and the government."

"You know what they said during the earlier readings of the bill," Serafina snapped, now fully engaged in the subject. "They were afraid that raising the age of consent and making it a criminal offence to lie with an under-age prostitute, might leave some MPs and their sons open to prosecution."

"But this article is also talking about abduction and entrapment," Miles said as he looked over the paper. "I should think any MP would be afraid to oppose the bill, now. How could they defend their opposition—even if prostitution is a social necessity—prostitution with abducted children surely isn't."

"Prostitution is not a social necessity in any form," Serafina said in her softest, angriest voice. "That is a disgusting, male prevarication and has no place in a Christian society. I cannot bear to hear such words in your mouth, Miles Hickinbotham."

Under the strange law of contraries by which our inmost thoughts are often governed, the face of the girl from Piccadilly rose into Miles' mind, until he could see her gas lit face as clearly as Serafina's in the bright light of day.

"Yes, of course, you are right, Serafina," he answered. "But I know it is one of the key arguments that Mrs. Butler faces in trying to achieve her goals."

But Serafina was now in full sail. She stood up and rushed on, basing her oration on the platform style of Mrs. Butler, striking the palm of her left hand with her other fist to emphasize each statement.

"Just think, under the *Contagious Diseases Acts* any woman in a garrison town can be accused of prostitution and forced to submit to a most degrading medical examination. And all that's required is an accusation. A few words brand her for-ever as a prostitute. And none of the army men are ever required to be examined at all. Perhaps worst of all is that sick women are placed in Lock Hospitals and treated like criminals. But sick men are never treated so. How these laws were ever passed in the first place is beyond my comprehension."

"Well," Julia said, "It is obviously a prelude to a con-tinental system of legalized brothels. Mr. Stead's articles will expose the whole shocking system, the ways in which young English girls are stolen from their homes and sold into the Con-tinental brothels. Sold like cattle."

'No unprotected woman is safe from these monsters, until the Criminal Act is passed." Serafina said, her eyes bright with asperity.

"But even if it is passed," Julia added, "We must get the CD Acts themselves repealed."

"Absolutely," Serafina said. "And we shall. Mrs. Butler will not be beaten."

Miles, who had settled on the carpet near Serafina, found himself glared at by both women.

"There can be no other stand possible for an ethical man," he said in answer to the silent prompting of the two young women. He was not insincere, only lukewarm in his concern about the issue.

"This article is only the beginning of the series," Julia said. "There will be three more days of the exposé."

"Yes," Serafina said. "So, Miles, I should like you here early tomorrow and since you live near a stand where the papers are first delivered, please bring a copy with you. Seven sharp, if you please, sir."

"But I thought we were going out," Miles protested. "It's a beautiful day and…"

"I can't leave Mama alone," Serafina said, dropping her voice. "You saw how she looked. I must be here if the doctor is needed."

"Yes," he said. "I had forgotten."

"Well, then, get along with you. Don't you have some work to do, you idle bohemian," Serafina said with only the hint of a smile.

"I just delivered a commission late last night. That is why I was tardy."

Julia watched and felt some envy as Serafina exercised her power over Miles .

"Well, don't be late tomorrow. We shall need the paper."

"Don't you have to be at work, Julia?" Miles asked.

"I worked additional hours to help get the articles ready, so Mr. Stead gave me the week off."

Rossiter lurched through the door and announced, "Mrs. Winstanley would like to see Miss Serafina in her chamber."

Miles stood and lifted Serafina to her feet.

"Goodbye, Miles," she said airily as she slipped from the room. "Seven sharp."

"Goodbye, Serafina," he replied, trying not to show his irritation at the way she dismissed him. He glanced over at Julia, who remained sitting on the carpet.

"Goodbye, Julia," he said. "You must think me a terribly tame fellow."

Julia put her hands out and shrugged. "She tames everyone, does she not?"

Miles gave a curt nod and walked out.

The following morning, Miles was astonished to see his favourite news vendor mobbed by wildly gesticulating people.

"What's all this?" he said as he pushed his way toward the publications.

The news vendor, who was a prosperous member of his tribe, having obtained a stand right off Piccadilly said, "It's the PMG, sir. The exposé they are running has driven the city clean off its head. I'm sold out. No sir, none left. But you never take the PMG. Sorry, sir. Nothing I can do. Probably will go a h'extra h'edition. If they're as sharp as I think they are."

"Who else gets early delivery?" Miles asked. He dared not show up without a copy for Serafina.

"If I was you, sir, I'd go right to their offices. Yes, sir, Northumberland Street, sir. Number 2. Very near the Strand, it is."

It was a fresh, clear morning and the newspaper offices were not far from the news vendor, so Miles decided to walk. When he arrived in front of the three attached houses which the newspaper occupied, there were men and carriages clogging the street. The congestion, the excited voices of the crowd and the carnival atmosphere were unlike anything he had ever seen.

"Good heavens," he said out loud. "This will be everything and more than they were hoping for."

After fighting his way through the crowd and slipping a few extra shillings into a boy's hand, Miles came away with a tattered but complete copy of the latest PMG. He jumped into a cab and dashed off to Serafina's.

To his surprise, Julia opened the door.

"Rossiter's waiting on Mrs. Winstanley, Miles. I'm afraid she really is unwell. Dr. Jarvis has been. There's no immediate danger but he seemed rather puzzled."

"I am truly sorry to hear of this," Miles said, as Serafina

joined them.

"Well, did you get it?" she asked.

"Of course, Serafina. I am sorry to hear about Mrs. Winstanley."

"Well, there is nothing certain, yet. Mother has always been healthy. Let's see what Mr. Stead is up to today."

"Apparently," Miles told them, "the series has already created a huge stir. They were sold out at the news vendor's and I had to go directly to the PMG offices. The street was packed with people. I literally risked life and limb pushing my way through the mob until I could find a boy who worked in the offices and bribe him to steal the last copy for me."

"Marvelous," Serafina said as she led her guests into the room they'd occupied the day before. "We are going to win this time. The Commons won't dare adjourn until the bill is passed."

"I do believe you are right," Miles said. "I have the bruises to prove how effective just one article has been."

"I do hope mother will soon be better," Serafina said as they entered the bright parlour. "It seems very strange to think of her lying in bed while we gloat over our triumph."

"What exactly is her complaint?" Miles asked.

"The doctor is not sure. He's to come later with a specialist. It seems to be some sort of numbness or paralysis in her legs. He didn't want to tell me, but I made him. Poor mama," she added as she sat down on the carpet again and spread out the tattered paper.

"This does show signs of having been fought over," Serafina remarked. "Well done, Miles."

"Yes," Julia added. "Well done."

While all of London boiled with the scandal caused by the exposé, the house at 21 Cavendish Square became strangely quiet after the morning of July 7, 1885. The following morning, when Miles called with the third day's installment of the exposé, he found the house silent. The knocker was muffled. He was not admitted and at first, only glimpsed Serafina at the front door.

She told him that Mrs. Winstanley was mysteriously paralyzed and bed ridden and the best medical attendants of Harley Street were baffled by the causes. Absolute quiet and rest had been ordered, so for an indefinite time the only callers would be professional men.

Then, to the young man's delight Serafina opened the door wider, stepped outside and added, "If you come each morning and see me, Miles, I should be very glad. I shall tell you how Mama is doing and we can sit on the porch. It will give me a welcome respite from the grayness of the sick room. Oh, Miles, Mama has stopped speaking altogether." And to his inexpressible amazement, Serafina began to cry.

"My dear girl," he said huskily as his shoulder received her tearful face and he put his arm around her. "I am sure it will all come right. You said yourself that your mother has always been healthy."

"But the doctors are not even sure that it is her body that is ill. They think it may be her mind."

"Good heavens, have you noticed any signs of her intellect failing? I certainly have not."

"No, Miles. I have not."

"Well, what is to be done, then?" Though delighted with her outbreak of feminine helplessness, he was also rather shocked by it. It was so unlike the Serafina he knew.

Chapter 3

THE ANTEROOMS OF HELL

If Hell has anterooms, one of them is surely to be found in the rookeries on the north side of Dorset Street, hard by Christ Church, Spitalfields, in London's East End. By the late 1880s the infamous 'Old Nichol' area in Shoreditch was gone. The only comparable place in the Empire might have been the worst of the back streets of Calcutta. But the poor natives of the subcontinent are on the other side of the globe and have lived primitive lives for centuries. They have never seen London. They know nothing of the tree-lined, golden streets of the west end: Portland Place, The Mall, Cumberland Terrace, Cavendish Square and many others where enormous wealth is the rule. But in the Metropolis, itself, the two extremes of human life eye each other across a distance of only a few miles, in some cases a few streets. If someone unfamiliar with London consults Charles Booth's map of poverty and wealth, he will see, with some surprise, that the very poor live, in many cases, across the street from the very rich. With a little mobility the contrasts can be even greater: a maimed freak from a penny gaff along the Whitechapel Road can, if he desires, stand and look through the gates of Buckingham Palace. Starving children from Frying Pan Alley can press their hungry faces against the plate glass windows of Regent Street bakeshops where cream-filled pastries are displayed, or a thirteen-year-old Dorset Street prostitute can eye west end bloods who are slumming in the pubs along Commercial Road, and hope for a good night's price for her degradation. Lisson Grove in St. Marylebone is not far away, the ugly, narrow, street where filthy children play in the gutter, the place where a procuress acting for W.T. Stead, Julia's employer, found the girl Eliza Armstrong, whom he used as the centre-piece of his exposé, for whose maidenhead he paid £5—a small price for equality and social justice. Yet, no journalistic crusade did any good for the women who lived in the narrow lanes and cramped filthy rooms along the north side of Dorset Street, or the rookeries of nearby Flower and Dean Street. It would require a far stronger purgative to cleanse the insanitary lodging houses of these courts and alleys. Yet, even in these sinister and dangerous streets, among the stench of rotting garbage and open sewers one might also find souls who had some apparent refinement. Katherine, the girl Miles had watched at Piccadilly was such a one. Unlike many other girls of the east end, her face was not "wise with wickedness". She had managed to preserve the appearance of gentility. After a very strange and difficult life, transplanted from a different continent and culture, she got on quite serenely, even in the narrow ugly lanes. At nineteen she was quite handsome in a shabby way, even in the torn and faded fustian dress and jacket she usually wore. As Miles had observed, her small figure was rounded and nicely formed. Her face and small chin were finely modeled. Her skin and colouring was dark, too dark to be European. She was sexy, to use today's term, rather than handsome— in the Victorian sense of the word.

Poverty reformers who believe that moral sloth is "bred into" east end people, or even worse, the dregs of army families from the subcontinent, would have been baffled by Katherine's apparent health, direct speech and penetrating glance. In the alleys where she lived, cruelty and insensitivity often did seep into the young like dirt from the gutters. Many of the children were hideously cruel, having not yet had time to reflect on their own suffering. The adult Katherine once stopped a group of youngsters who were amusing themselves by the sight of the dying fits of a cat whose eyes they had gouged out, and whom they had hanged by the tail. When the bleeding, tortured animal jerked with his feet to get away, they struck at it. Katherine brought the mangled beast to her room, where it died within the hour. Her presence brought a subdued additional light into the narrow lanes where the sky was barely visible. She lived close by Dorset Street at number 18 Thrawl Street, a common lodging house where she had an eight foot by eight foot room that she shared with another girl, Frances Coles. Frances lost her job soon after moving in and took up prostitution. Katherine finally asked her to leave because her earnings were sporadic and she began to drink more and more. Before getting this wretched room, Katherine had had a very bad time of living on the street. But she also had an epiphany. Through some work she did for an older man who had a photographic establishment on Fleet Street, she found what she believed would be her life's work— in the new science of photography. She was so excited by the magical new art form, she worked without pay in order to learn photographic skills. The first time she had seen an image emerge out of nothingness, floating onto the paper treated with albumen and silver nitrate, she could scarcely believe her eyes. The magic of watching images rise out of the darkness stunned and thrilled her. Capturing and printing images fascinated her and shaped much of her waking thoughts. Her fascination motivated her to find a second job for a time so she could buy her own paper and chemicals. The photographer for whom she worked allowed her to use an old camera and his printing equipment.

Soon she was dividing her time between the studio on Fleet Street and the Bryant & May match factory in Bow. She worked at the Fairfield Road factory where she earned 5s for an eighty hour week. She tried not to think about the possibility of getting 'phossy jaw'—necrosis of the bone through inhaling yellow phosphrous fumes—a condition that could result in disfigurement and death. Not everyone in the factory was afflicted with the disease, and Katherine did not plan to work there long. She was ambitious. Photographic technology was in its infancy but had already taken England by storm, with many new picture-taking establishments springing up all over the metropolis. Katherine's encounter with photography had given her a clear goal which shaped her life. Instead of dropping into her bed at the end of a long day, or gossiping with other girls in the street, she went to the library and struggled to read and grasp all she could about photographic chemicals, papers and processes. She regularly looked in the windows of the several photographic shops on the Whitechapel Road whenever she could. Her ambition was to have such a shop one day, herself. Adversity had made her disciplined and also made her realize the value of autonomy. The young men who presented themselves to her were ignored. She preferred the company of the middle-aged photographer for whom she worked because he could teach her something she wanted to learn. Her co-workers at the match factory noted that Katherine was different from them. She had an education superior to theirs—she knew how to heal certain kinds of ailments by applying unusual skills she had brought from India. But it was her driving interest in photography that gave her emotional self-sufficiency. That self-sufficiency was part of what drew people to her. The other factory girls did not resent these attainments, but began to seek her advice on many subjects, everything from love to health. Katherine carried with her an aura of inner quiet, which Miles had noticed when he first met her. In spite of being cold in winter and never having enough food, Katherine rarely felt unhappy. Her life in India had often been far harder than in London. She thought only of what she wanted to do in the future and tried hard not to think about her past.

One July day in the summer of 1885, shortly after meeting Miles, Katherine saw Susan, a very young, very pretty prostitute come stumbling into Thrawl Street. It was a dark morning in the east end, the air thick with smoke reputed to be from a large fire somewhere near Shoreditch. The smells of burning wood and fabric overpowered the normal stink of unwashed flesh which usually reached into the street from the doss house doorways. Susan, like many people of the east end, laboured just to earn the right to sleep indoors for a night. She had no room of her own—even among the narrow, crooked brick lodging houses where seven or eight women often slept in a single room hanging from straps. The best she usually did was to doss among the warrens of falling down shacks which choked every court and alley in Whitechapel, pathetic habitations which, because they were never empty, were some of the most valuable real estate investments in London.

In spite of Susan's miserable, peripatetic lifestyle, Katherine had noticed that the young girl had always managed to retain possession of her hat, a rather shapeless wide-brimmed felt with a jaunty green feather in it, of which the young girl was very vain. Now, she was bareheaded. There was some mud in her dark hair and her young white breasts, whose buds were displayed by her torn bodice almost down to their nipples, had large purple bruises on them. One eye was puffy and nearly closed. In spite of Susan's extreme youth and attractions, her present state made it doubtful that she would find customers necessary to raise even her doss money—the four *ds* that most lodging houses charged for a night's shelter. Susan's uneven swaying movements led Katherine to think that the girl was probably drunk, as well as bruised. Katherine had noted the girl wandering the ugly Whitechapel lanes and taken an interest in her because of her extreme youth. She identified with the girl's struggle and there was a certain refinement in Susan's bearing—even when bruised, dirty and drunk. Her glazed eyes failed to register Katherine's presence, so the older girl called out to her, "Susan."

Susan stopped, did a shaky turn and blinked owlishly at Katherine.

"Kat, what are you doing here?"

"I live here, you goose. What happened to you? Who hit you?"

"That bleeding ponce, Bob. He's no right, either. He don't look after me." She swayed from side to side.

"Why don't you come to my room and sleep it off, Susan?" Katherine said. "I am just going to work. You can have all day to sleep it off."

"God, Kat. You save me life. Really need to doss."

"I'll be back tonight. You can stay. But, no men in my room. Yes? Promise?"

"Bloody hell, Kat. I look more like cat's meat than man's meat right now. At least, that's how I feel."

"Come on, then," Katherine said, taking her arm and leading her back to the room she had herself just left.

Katherine returned that night to find Susan seated on the front steps of the Thrawl Street lodging house with an older girl who was brushing her own thick brown hair. Katherine had never seen this other girl before, but she looked sober and was clean and quite pretty. Katherine had no need of companions but neither did she turn her back on other girls. When Susan saw Katherine she hailed her.

"Hello, Kat. This is Mary. We stayed down here cause I know'd you don't want strangers in your lodgings."

"Hello, Mary," Katherine said.

"Hello, Kat." There was an odd lilt in the girl's voice which Katherine noticed.

"Not from London?" Katherine asked.

"Oh, I've been many places. Lived in France for a while but I was born in Wales."

"Susan, you're going all purple and yellow now," Katherine said as she leaned forward and took the young girl's face in her hand and turned it from side to side.

"That's the worst part of a beating. It makes you too ugly to work," Mary commented.

"You sound like you've traveled more than most," Katherine said, looking over at Mary as she released Susan's chin and leaned back against the wall.

"Well, I don't know as I'd make it sound that grand, but I've seen a few things," Mary replied as she twisted her long, thick tresses into a tight bun.

"Do you live near here?" Katherine asked.

"Breezer's Hill, Pennington Street."

"I have no idea where that is." Katherine remarked.

"Aye, well I was working down here last night. Came

down by cab and dossed here, but early this morning I saw this child getting a terrible beating right out in the street. I saw her stumble off this way and when I finished my business, I looked for her. And here she was, just sitting in the doorway, comfortable as anything. Here I'd been afraid I might find her dead."

"Take more than that ponce to kill me," Susan said with a hoarse swagger in her voice.

"Not much more, from the looks of you," Katherine remarked. "You should go to Miss Steers' under the bridge, or the Salvationists on Hanbury Street. I had a few good meals there before I got work."

"You mean you won't let me stay till I'm well? I been thinking all day that I could end up in the bastille." Susan said, suddenly sounding young and frightened.

"You'd get better food at the Salvationists or Miss Steers," Katherine said.

"I have a few pence for my dinner, Kat. Can't I stay, please? Just tonight? I made the bed. I didn't touch nothing. Truly."

"I would take her myself," Mary suddenly put in, "but my landlady would see those bruises and throw us both out. Won't have any rowing. She runs a very quiet, respectable house."

"That's very good of you," Katherine said. "I appreciate your interest in the girl."

"Well," Mary said, "we girls have to look after each other. No one else will. But none of us wants to see any girl go to the bastille."

At the mention of the "bastille," the Whitechapel Work House, Susan quailed. The harsh discipline imposed by the so-called Guardians who ran the place was designed to make the poor see any labour as preferable to the work house routine: oakum picking, rock breaking and other useless boring jobs. The thin gruel and boiled tea that was served in the bastille could barely sustain the lives of inmates who did hard labour each day.

"Please, Kat, can't I stay tonight?"

"All right, Susan," Katherine replied patting the girl's head.

"I told you, Mary, Kat's not a whore," Susan said with sudden fierce pride. "She's a factory girl. Works regular."

"Then, she's a deal kinder than most," Mary said looking up at Katherine.

"We've all been hard up," Katherine said.

"Well, I'm not," Mary said. "At least, not right now. So why don't I buy you girls some dinner?"

"You must have had a good night," Susan said, envy in her voice. "Say, how come you're down here. A woman like you could work some place nice, like Piccadilly."

"I have done," Mary said. "Told you I come down here in a cab. With a slummer from Piccadilly, as a matter of record. Just before that I made five pounds for fifteen minutes work."

"Lor," Susan said, her eyes growing large as saucers in spite of her injuries. "What did you have to do for that?"

"Just listen to a gentleman talk."

"Really, I never had one of them. That's nice work. Mostly old blokes, I guess. The ones who come down here to spend money expect more."

"Yes, it's light duty when you can get it. Then, I met the chap who brought me down here—all the way from Piccadilly in a hansom."

Susan looked over at Katherine, "Our talk too low for you, Kat?"

" I'm not a magistrate, nor a clergyman."

"Are you one of General Booth's lasses out of uniform?" Mary asked. "They're the only good girls I know who don't mind listening to whores talk trade."

"No. Besides, the only difference between a whore and the rest of us is the degree of hunger. That's not wickedness."

"But many surely do think us wicked, " Mary said.

"It's the swells who think we're bad," Susan said. "They like us to be low. They like the wickedness, as long as its us that's wicked, not them."

"It's not really wicked, anyway," Katherine said.

"What do you mean, Kat?" Susan asked.

"The only person we can ever really hurt is ourselves. If

you hurt someone else, in the end, they'll be all right. It is you who will suffer. That's the true meaning of the Golden Rule.

"Oh, my," Mary said with a chuckle. "That's over my head. You may not be a Salvation Lassie, but you certainly are a deep one Katherine...ah..what's your family name?"

"Green."

"You are a deep one, Katherine Green."

Susan reached up and took Katherine's hand. "She's more than deep. She's the best one on these mean streets," she said leaning her head against Katherine's thigh. "I'd be in the Spike now if Kat hadn't come along. And if the Guardians found out I wasn't thirteen, yet, I might not have got me freedom again for ever so long."

After pleading to be allowed to stay at Katherine's for another night, Susan set about to make her stay as permanent as possible. It was not only that she wanted physical shelter, there was a warmth that Katherine gave her, an acceptance she only knew as the dimmest of memories. The older girl let Susan be herself, for good or for ill—as long as she did not bring men or drink into their room. Kat had made those rules clear from the first night. Other than that, Katherine seemed to require nothing from her. For Katherine, the child-woman was not an impediment and she respected the girl's combative spirit. Susan responded by trying to help Katherine in any simple way she could. She offered to pay rent for her part of the room, but knew if she did not have 4d she would still have a place to sleep along-side Kat on the bedstead, which was their only piece of furniture. She cleaned the room when Kat was at work and tried to make it look pleasant. It was the first time in her life, the twelve year old child had ever had a home. It was also the first time anyone had touched her physically to express affection. She felt that Katherine cared for her and she reciprocated. Sometimes the pair would wake at night and find themselves wrapped in a strange, heated embrace. Neither said a word about such encounters in the morning. Susan didn't understand it, but as long as she could stay with Kat, she didn't care. Instinctively, Katherine knew that a clear set of rules and a complete absence of moral judgment was the only way to make Susan feel cared for. She was surprised by the strength of her own attachment to the young girl. She had thought herself entirely self-sufficient.

One night Katherine saw Susan through the glass front of the *Three Bells*, a pub in nearby Flower and Dean Street. The young girl was drunk and her expression, which mingled contempt with meanness and hatred, still did not obscure her finely formed features and intelligent eyes. This, in spite of the fact that her right cheek was scratched and her hair fell over the left side of her face in wild disorder. Susan's teeth were faultless. Her petite curvaceous body was advantageously displayed by her disorderly dress, a dirty linen *saque*, which was torn open, as if with brazen intention, and revealed to view her childlike white breasts, whose bruises had long since healed. Standing across from her was a young West-End blood of about twenty, with dark curling hair and dark gray eyes. His linen was spotless. From where she stood on the street, Katherine could feel Susan's lust, both for the young man himself and for his money. As Katherine watched, the young girl came up to the young man and placed herself breast to breast against him. She looked at him with her large blue eyes sparkling with morbid desire. But she did not speak. The young man looked down at her for a moment, was obviously struck by her, but then turned away and walked to the door.

"You are a fool!" Susan shrieked drunkenly, a sudden indescribable rage twisting her features. Then she saw Katherine watching her through the window, and she hid her face with her hands, pushed through the crowd and ran out the back door of the pub.

Susan did not come home that night and Katherine lay awake until she finally had to leave for the match factory, well before sunrise. Bryant & May girls were fined for lateness, using the toilet too frequently and a long list of other offences. The next day, on coming home from the factory, the older girl almost burst into tears of relief when she saw the little woman sitting in the doorway of her lodging house, waiting for her. Katherine, who had been self-sufficient for years, hadn't realized until that moment the depths of her feeling for Susan.

Susan ran toward her and actually did burst into tears as she threw her arms around Katherine.

"Oh, Kat, I am so sorry." The child's sobs racked her body.

"It's all right, Susan. It's just that I was worried about you last night. If you are not going to come home, perhaps you could put a note under the door."

Nodding agreement and sobbing as she walked arm and arm with Katherine up the narrow staircase to their room, Susan began to know what it was to want someone's good opinion.

When they entered their room, Susan said, "Kat, I don't want to go on the street no more."

"I see," Katherine said in a neutral voice.

"I've got some pence saved for me rent..."

"Don't worry about that Susan. I can pay for this room myself. I'd rather you used that money for yourself. You'll need it to find steady employment."

"I know Kat. I was thinking...could I do outside work for the match factory? I'm quite clever with me hands...really, I am. I thought perhaps I could make match boxes here at home. I know the piece work don't pay much, not 'til I could get really fast. But I could clean the room and have it nice for you and you could take some of me earnings before I could spend it on drink or a pipe."

"If I withheld some of your wages, Susan, you'd end up raging at me when you wanted drink or to go to the chinaman's."

"No, no, you'd be like me strongbox. I'd know you was keeping it for me and it was safe with you."

"You're welcome to stay and I can talk to Mrs. Willis, who's in charge of outside work. But if I talk to her, you can't change your mind when you get bored with the work. If I vouch for you and you don't do the work, it will be a black mark against me."

"Oh, Kat, then, I don't know. I don't know as I'm trustworthy enough..." the girl looked down at her hands. "I'm ascared of doing anything to hurt you." After a few moments of silence the girl finally said, "You're right, Kat. I can't be trusted."

"Now, I didn't say that," Katherine replied. " You did. I want to trust you, but for both our sakes I can't risk my job, especially with winter coming." Katherine also thought of the cost of photographic materials and wondered how she could ever replace the elderly photographer who had been her patron. Bringing a third girl into her tiny room seemed out of the question.

"Cors not," Susan said.

Katherine understood that Susan was really divided in herself. She wanted to be trustworthy and improve herself, but she knew something of her own highs and lows. Right now, the young girl was impatient to make a change after being humiliated in front of Katherine, but she liked opium and alcohol too much. She probably also wanted to find out if Katherine would take a real chance on her and risk something as valuable as her job. Katherine had acquired her penetration by using it as a survival tool from an early age.

"I'll tell you what I'll do, Susan," Katherine said.

"Yes, Kat?" the young girl's bright blue eyes looked up hopefully.

"You know I want to help you, Susan. But I've got to protect us both. So here's my offer. We'll take some of your money and buy some materials for making match boxes. You practice for a month here at home. No going on the street. No drinking or smoking. Well, maybe once in a while...If you persist, I shall talk to Mrs. Willis. You will be a lot faster than most beginning girls and you'll earn more money. What do you say?"

"A whole month of working for nothing?"

"All day, every day. You go to work each morning when I leave and quit when I get home. I have to be sure you'll stay with it. It can't just be feeling badly about last night— because I saw how much you wanted that young man. And I saw him turn away from you."

Susan was quiet. Her eyes showed she was thinking about Katherine's offer. She gave her friend a sidelong glance. "You're terrible clever, Katherine. I'll try. But can I have a drink or a pipe in the evening, after you're done work?"

"Not here. And I won't give you money for that."

"You're terrible hard on me," Susan whined. "I don't know if I can go a day without a pipe at the chinaman's."

"Where is the chinaman's parlour?"

"Down Shadwell near Tiger Bay."

"How do I get there?"

"What do you want to get there for?"

"Never mind, yet. Just tell me."

The child shrugged and said, "Make for Cable Street, and keep along east till you spy a lane. Turn south toward Shadwell High Street until you spy the Hoop and Grapes; next to it is another tavern, the Gunboat, and opposite is another, the Golden Eagle; within spitting are three other taverns, the Home of Friendship, the Lord Lovat, and the Baltic - the Baltic is at the corner of the very street. From the end of this street you turn and make out another dirty little public house, called the Coal Whipper's Arms. The chinaman's house is just handy - up a court. Everyone knows where. What you want to know all that for, anyway?"

"If you agree— if I think you've gone to the china-man's— I'll come and fetch you home. Otherwise, we'll forget about the work."

"You'd go all the way down there to find me? It's danger-ous down near the water, Kat. Specially for a nice-looking girl like you."

"I know. That's why you shouldn't go there. But, yes. I'd go there to find you."

"Very well, Kat. I'll follow your rules."

"Wait," the older girl said. "I know you could cheat and get men to take you up a dark lane and get money that way..."

"No, Kat. I won't do that. I promise."

"I was just going to say that if you do, I'd rather you tell me than lie about it. Yes?"

The young girl put her arms around her friend and let her head fall to her shoulder. "I know you're trying to make a good girl of me, Kat. I want to be. But it's hard. I couldn't do it without you."

"I know, my darling," Katherine said, kissing the dirty tear-stained face as she rocked Susan in her arms. In those few moments Katherine felt the pain of her own lonely years before meeting her first mentor. She held the younger girl and kissed her full lips.

"Oh, Kat, you are so good to me," Susan purred.

Next day, when Katherine brought home the lavender paper, glue and wood for making Bryant & May matchboxes, Susan could scarcely sit still for her excitement. She was like a child at Christmas opening presents.

"Oh, thank you Kat, thank you. How much do I owe you?"

"You don't owe me anything. I told Mrs. Willis about you and said you were trying to get off the street and she gave me these things out of leavings at the factory."

"That's grand, Kat," the young girl said throwing herself onto the bedstead in her delight. "I'll start right away."

"No," Katherine said. "Wait until tomorrow. We'll get up early and I'll help you get started when the light is better. You have to learn how to make a good matchbox. It won't just come on by itself."

"Oh, Kat. What do you know about piecework? You're a factory girl."

"I started doing piecework. Just like you. Right here on this floor."

"Really? The same as me?"

"The same as you."

Dawn found the two girls setting up Susan's workplace: a heavy board from a broken holding which Katherine had found and carried home long ago.

"This will be your work table, Susan. We'll set out all your materials on it. When you're through for the day, you'll clear it off and throw away all the scraps. Be sure to keep the glue covered when you're working. It dries very fast. Now, watch my fingers," Katherine said. "It's very important to do things in the right order."

When Katherine got home that evening, she wasn't surprised to find Susan gone. There were signs of the girl having worked during the day. There were scraps but no finished boxes. She had expected that Susan would want to see if she were really ready to help her, even if rules were broken. Still, Katherine was tired. It was a long walk to Shadwell, and it was dangerous for a woman down near the river. She was torn between leaving right away and waiting to see if Susan came home. Finally, she decided to go to *The Three Bells*, which is where Susan would probably go if she had stayed in the area. She pulled on her boots, tied on her bonnet and shawl and went down to the street. Just as she turned into Flower and Dean Street where the pub was, she saw Susan. She wasn't drunk and she smiled and waved when she saw Katherine.

"Hello, Kat."

"Hello, Susan. I'm glad to see you."

"Have you been home? Did you see my work?"

"No."

"Come," Susan said taking her hand and playfully tugging her back the way she had just come.

They entered the room and Katherine said, "Where are the finished boxes, Susan? I don't see them anywhere."

"I was going to surprise you. They're in the tin box what keeps the rats off the bread. Here."

To Katherine's surprise and delight there were over two dozen neatly turned out boxes, which Susan took out of the tin.

"Susan," Katherine exclaimed. "These are wonderful."

"I ran out of wood," the girl said blushing with pleasure

at the effect of her work on Katherine. "So I thought I'd go to the Bells and just have one beer before you got home."

"These are excellent, Susan," Katherine said as she slid the little drawer of each box back and forth.

"I think I'm good at them," Susan said. "I just want to get faster."

And in the weeks that followed, Susan did get faster. She was a very neat-handed worker. Katherine was overjoyed to see her working so well each day. There hadn't been a single incident of back-sliding for nearly three weeks.

"I showed Mrs. Willis your work," Katherine said at the beginning of the fourth week. "She's ready to hire you as an outside worker, tomorrow."

"It ain't four weeks, yet, Kat."

"I know, Susan. But you've done so well."

Chapter 4

MISSING

When Katherine came home after telling Susan that she would soon have regular employment and found the room empty, she knew she had made a mistake. She felt certain that Susan, drawing close to her goal, had gone to the chinaman's in Shadwell. Katherine had been after her time for leaving the factory and it was now quite dark outside. Wind whipped through the streets and lanes and turned the rain into stinging strands sharp as a cat o'nine tails. Katherine had been lashed all the way from Bow and was soaking wet. The gale shrieked through the cracks and holes in the walls of her room and sobbed like a child in the chimney. The 'billy sweet', a sticky sort of mortar that never dried, had long ago dropped away from the cheap exterior brick walls of the building. The foul weather would make the streets on the way to the chinaman's very empty and consequently more dangerous. Near the waterfront, the out of work casuals who laboured on the docks often preyed on ones weaker than themselves. There was little work just now and it was a hard time for everyone, but especially for the dockers. Soon the fogs and cold of autumn would make it that much easier to be injured or even drown alongside the quays.

Knowing conditions at the waterfront, Katherine decided she would ask Dave Cullen to come with her, a neighbour who had worked the docks for years and had gradually saved enough to start a brisk coffee business of his own near the waterfront. He was a huge, shuffling giant of a man—as kind and gentle as a Newfoundland dog. He had never forgotten the plight of casual dockers who waited for hours in all weather at the Cage on Nightingale Lane in the hopes of work, and he often brought free coffee to them. He had helped Katherine find lodgings when she first left the bed of the elderly photographer with whom she lived for a short time after leaving her first home in London. Dave generally just sat at home on bad nights, reading the bible or Pilgrim's Progress, waiting for the following day when he could wheel out his barrow with his pride and joy on it: the polished copper kettles which were tricked out with elaborate brass billy cocks in the shapes of mythological beasts. They represented his life savings.

Dave lived just around the corner from Katherine on Fashion Street. In less than five minutes, she was tapping on his window. The wind had picked up and screamed like a hungry wife down the narrow street as she waited for Dave. The rain had let up only slightly since she had come down from Bow.

Dave loomed out of his doorway. He was head and shoulders taller than Katherine. She barely came up to his chest.

"Katherine, dear, what are you doing out on such a night as this?"

"Oh, Dave, I am sorry to trouble you, but I am afraid I have to walk to Shadwell and find Susan."

"The wee thing is out on a night like this?"

"I fear she may be at an opium den off of the Shadwell High Street. I am afraid to go on such a dark night by myself."

"Don't think of it, dearie. Now I know what you're about, I wouldn't let you go alone. You know that."

"Thank you, Dave."

"Step in while I get me coat and pipe. Get into the snug before we start out."

In moments, they were on their way. Though she was

cold and wet, Katherine was glad to be doing something active to find Susan. It helped give her hope.

"Off the Shadwell High Street, you said?" Dave asked.

"Yes. That's what I was told," and Katherine managed to repeat the litany of pub names from Susan's directions.

"I think I know this place. I've pulled some mates out of there in times past. Now the Bowen Refuge is down there."

"Bowen Refuge?" Katherine repeated into the wind as she clutched her shawl around her.

"Like Dr. Barnardo's, only smaller. Good place for children, I suppose. Better than the street. Specially on a night like this."

"Susan would never go to such a place. She is frightened by anything that reminds her of the Bastille."

"Aye, well, we all feel that way. And who can blame a poor mite of a thing like her? You think she went down there to smoke?"

"I fear it may be so."

"Well, I believe that chinaman remembers me. I smashed his place pretty good one night when I thought he was helping a bad German shanghai some of me mates. Yes, that was a night. You wouldn't think it of me now, would you, lass?"

"No, Dave. You always seem to me the most gentle of men."

"I am. 'Cept when I'm roused. Then, I get up on me big elephant legs and stump around. I bet I could still scare that chinaman. If he's done anything to your wee friend, he shall pay for it."

"Oh, don't even mention such a thing, Dave. I couldn't bear to have anything happen to Susan. She is doing so well. She's off the street, you know."

"Well, that's good. She won't last long in that life. And in the end, she'd come to the Bastille, a worn out woman. Especially such a tiny one as she is."

The pair tramped through the empty, wet streets as the rain gave the bricks and paving stones a lustre they never otherwise attained. Here and there lean faces loomed out of the darkness into the flare of the occasional gaslight. When the predators caught sight of Dave's bulk they disappeared back into whatever hole from which they had emerged. The closer the pair got to the water, the louder the wind howled and the closer Katherine walked to Dave. The sound of breaking glass and drunken laughter came to their ears The suddeness of the noise startled Katherine.

When Katherine cringed against Dave, the big man patted her shoulder. "Don't be scared, Lass. You're safe with me. I just hope your wee friend isn't on her own down here."

More breaking glass, mixed with angry voices and a woman's cry of pain. The sounds seemed all around them now. A man leapt out of the darkness suddenly with something bright in his hand. Dave pushed him away as if swatting a fly. The man slammed into a wall of dirty brick and without looking back, the pair continued onward. How long they passed through the wet, ugly streets, Katherine couldn't tell. She had no idea how far they had walked.

Finally, Dave said, "This is the Lane, lass. If I'm not mistaken."

Katherine glanced around and in the midst of the howling wind and darkness, five bright, odd-shaped windows shone out from all points of the compass, each one a public house where poor seamen and dockers threw their money away. Dave led her past them up to a dark open doorway, whose gloom was impenetrable.

"Here we are, Lass. I'll go first. You hold onto my jacket tails so you don't get lost or fall on something. If you trip, just grab onto me." With these words, Dave stumped up the groaning stairs which seemed barely adequate to hold his weight.

The gloom and stink of the ancient hallways was unlike anything Katherine had ever known except in the markets of India. The building seemed abandoned. Rats scuffled across their path, but finally, little thin lines of bluish light shone ahead of them. There was a sudden crash and she saw that Dave had kicked open a door.

A yellow skinned man was bent over a frying pan where

he was cooking a brownish mass in water over a charcoal brazier. A few candles lit the room and the smoke from the brazier added to the gloom. A white woman was holding a long needle and twirling the sticky stuff onto it. It seemed as if every crease in the yellow man's face and clothing was outlined in dirt. A large bedstead had three smokers lying side by side, staring glassily at the ceiling.

"You!" the chinaman exclaimed when he saw Dave, nearly dropping his pan of water and goo.

"You remember me, matey? That's good. Tonight, I'm looking for a wee lass. A tiny person. Very pretty with dark hair. Have you seen her?"

"She didn't come here. No one like that here. See?" And he held up a lamp over the three stuporous men on the bedstead.

"Not here now," Dave growled. "But what about earlier?"

"I did see someone like that. Not here. Not here. She talk at door of Bowen's Refuge down street. She didn't come here. Not here at all."

"You wouldn't lie to me now, would you, matey?" Dave said advancing on the man.

"No. No. I no lie to you, sir. No, sir.

"Bowen's Refuge, huh? We'll go there. But we may be back."

All through this dialogue, Katherine's teeth had been chattering from cold and fear. It was only when she heard that Susan might be at the refuge that she began to feel better.

Dave and Katherine made their way back through the Stygian darkness of the hall and stairs. After traversing these Tartarian realms the street looked bright and well lit by comparison.

"Down this way, lass."

"I can't understand why Susan would go to the refuge instead of coming home," Katherine said as they tramped through the slush which had reached an accumulation of three or four inches.

"Oh, it is so wet," Katherine said.

"Here, lassie," Dave said as he took off his coat. "An old

bear like me doesn't feel it much, long as I'm walking."

"Oh, are you sure?"

She felt the weight of the heavy coat fall on her shoulders. The old melton cloth felt thicker and more impenetrable than the walls of her room.

"Here we are," Dave called out to her as he banged on the door loudly enough to wake the dead.

"We don't open at this hour," a voice called out when Dave began shaking the door in its jamb.

"You'll have it open or I'll have it down. We're looking for a wee lassie." Dave bellowed, and he shook the door so it seemed he might pull the old wood from its hinges.

A band of light appeared.

Katherine stepped forward so she could be seen.

"I am looking for my little sister. Someone told us she came to your door earlier this evening. She's about this tall, dark hair, very pretty. No! You haven't seen her. Oh, she came and went away. Did she say where? No? Thank you."

And the band of light disappeared.

"Oh, dear God, poor little Susan, lost near the waterfront on a night like this," Katherine said into the howling wind.

"We can go back to the chinaman," Dave offered.

"No. He told us the truth. She was here. But now she is," and she paused for a moment, "gone."

"Perhaps she's gone home by now," Dave suggested.

"Perhaps. I suppose going back is all I can do. It's not fair to keep you out anymore."

"Think nothing of that, dearie. If I knew where to look, I'd look all night."

"I know, Dave, thank you," and she turned away from the wind, away from the river and back the way they had come.

After work the following day, Katherine came home to

an empty room. There was no sign that Susan had returned during the day, so Katherine resolved, in spite of the long walk she had just taken from the factory at Bow, to go again to the chinaman's in Shadwell. Perhaps he would speak more freely to her if she were alone. He had been afraid of Dave.

In the fading daylight, Leman Street was much less threatening than she had found it the night before. Along the broad thoroughfare, which the heavy traffic to and from the docks had churned into a sea of mud, she could see a handful of carters finishing the day; their tired horses nodding into canvas feedbags, the men resting against wagons whose rough wood was transmuted into gold by the sunset. But it would be dark by the time she got to Shadwell, Katherine thought, and she didn't know what she might find at the chinaman's parlour when she got there. It was reputed to be a place where high and low rubbed shoulders on his mouldy mattress—dockers and dukes craved his skillfully prepared poison. The night before, the darkness in the tumbledown building had been like the smoke of the drug itself, murky, thick, almost viscous. It had tugged at objects— making ordinary shapes unrecognizable and phantasmagoric. No matter, Katherine had resolved to find Susan no matter what the obstacles. The strength of her feeling for Susan had been unknown to Katherine, until the young girl was lost. Now, nothing else existed for her but to find the child—even her photographic ambitions had been temporarily displaced.

As she walked, the sky's heavy brown curtain merged with the muddy ground into a single field of murkiness. In minutes, everything lost its form and colour and became nearly indistinguishable. The long rows of buildings lining the street, seemingly made from the same material and built to the same height, melted into the watery brown exhalations of the city which hovered over the streets near the river. Katherine could feel her legs moving but they moved in relation to nothing. She could almost have lost the sensation in her feet, so disconnected from the earth did the fog and half-light make her feel. She turned east into Cable Street and walked on until she reached a nameless, tiny, dismal lane which runs down toward High Street,

Shadwell—a lane where many policemen would dare not venture, the access to the chinaman's court. As Katherine walked through the passage, she could have stretched out her arms and touched the slimy bricks on either side of her. It was not until she saw the windows of the five public houses as they stared across the irregular intersection of lanes that she ceased to move blindly. She could believe for a moment that she was back on dry land in a borough of London. Then, once more, she pressed on, walking away from the comparatively bright corners and up into a dark slit between buildings where the single window of The Coal Whipper's Arms seemed to glow particularly red and menacing then, up into an even darker court where the parlour of the chinaman lay in abysmal gloom. She paused at the doorway—there was no door— only because the black emptiness of the opening seemed impenetrably solid. Then she stepped inside. In a few moments, the hall seemed brighter, but not because there was more light. There were more sounds, and the echoes of her footsteps and the scratching of nearby rats gave her a better sense of direction in the darkness. The cracked banister was sticky with something that she didn't want to touch, but she was afraid of losing her footing, so she held tightly to the slimy wood. The revolting stench of the rats, dry rot, charcoal smoke and endless pipes of opium clutched at her throat. It seemed worse than the fumes of the match factory.

As she got near the top of the stairs, she had expected some light from the chinaman's door, but there was none. The door was slightly ajar and offered nothing more than a gray gash in the gloom. Katherine waited for what seemed a long time. All she could hear were the rats. Not the faintest light shone forth from the opium parlour. Pushing the door open with sudden resolve, she stepped into the chamber and almost immediately something fastened onto her ankle. Through the confusion of her terror, she became dimly aware of another sound, a kind of gurgling which rose and fell while the strong grip held her. She could go neither forward or back, so she knelt down to be closer to the sound, which she began to discern was a voice, a voice somehow dreadfully impaired.

"Bonekil," the voice gurgled three times in succession.

Katherine realized someone was struggling to talk to her. She bent close

"Bonekil talkkkkgorl," the hand clutched her ankle convulsively "Bonekil tak gorl," the voice gurgled, and gasped once more, and Katherine, who had seen death often, knew someone had just died next to her. She felt the hand drop from her and she reached out, running her hand over the floor. There was something cold and heavy near by. The frying pan! She remembered that was how the opium was being cooked when she came last night. There had to be matches somewhere close at hand, and almost the next moment she felt the familiar shape of a matchbox. She opened it and struck the tip against the box. Though her eyes were overwhelmed by the sudden flare she could see that the chinaman lay dead on the floor. His face had been gnawed by rats and his throat had been torn open by something sharp. That was why the voice had been gurgling in its own blood. She heard something else now and didn't know what it was. It was some moments before she realized that someone was coming up the stairs. Frantically, she looked around and found that the only refuge was a small cupboard at the back of the room where she stood. She crouched low and desperately thrust herself into the cramped space as the heavy footfalls progressed up the stairs. Just before the heavy feet came into the room, she closed the cupboard door. A small gap between the door and the frame allowed her to see a narrow slit of the room. A man in a dark suit of poor quality and moderately clean linen quickly crossed her narrow field of vision. Then he came back the other way, this time pausing so she could just see his face. He wore large mustachios, and had the strong features of a rapacious wolf, a long straight nose and cruel, thin lips. She felt that his dark eyes were burning through the walls of her hiding place, exposing her to view. The thought of being found by this man was more frightening than the clutch of the dying chinaman. Fortunately, she was so frightened that she could not move even if she had wanted to. She could see by the speed of his movements that the man was in a hurry. He stamped around the room for a few seconds, peered into some buckets that were sitting close at hand, muttered a couple of oaths and left, his heavy footfalls crashing on the stairs as he descended.

As soon as she was sure of his departure from the building, Katherine struggled out of the tiny compartment, and in gaining her freedom also banged against some pails that had been left at the back of the cupboard where she had been hiding. When she got out of her confinement she pulled one of the buckets out after her. She struck another match. What she saw was a bloody stew of mostly unrecognizable shapes, but floating in the confusion of fluids and raw meat was a tiny human hand, a child's hand. A moment later, some other pieces took on identifiable shapes. An eye seemed to wink at her. The next thing she knew, she heard a sound she did not recognize: it was her own voice shrieking with horror. She threw away the box of matches she was holding and lunged for the door. Somehow, she stumbled down the stairs without falling. But all the while she was in motion, the dying man's voice was in her ears: "Bonekil tak gorl." The senseless syllables kept ringing in her mind as she burst out into the alley and rushed out of the rookery onto Cable Street. She ran up the street narrowly avoiding collision with some costers and a few small knots of pedestrians, not thinking of anything except the horror of what she had just seen, the chewed face, lying in its own blood. But what really blinded her to the street and the people around her were visions of the dreadful, grisly bucket. She kept seeing the floating eye and little, helpless hand. Her ears rang with the chinaman's absurd syllables all the way home. She was out of breath by the time she reached the Whitechapel Road and, from the burning in her chest, realized she had been running for a long time. Then she thought of Dave and began to run again, this time to Fashion Street.

By the time Katherine threw herself against Dave's door, her chest was on fire.

"Oh, heavens, Dave, please answer," and she began crying. But the big man was not at home. With a heavy tread, she returned to her lodgings and stretched out on her bed. Some time later, in the small hours of morning, Katherine woke from deep sleep, sat bolt upright in her bed and muttered, "Bowen, kill, take girl."

"How horrible," she said out loud. "Could he have been talking about Susan?"

Chapter 5

VICTORIA PARK

My window shows the travelling clouds,
Leaves spent, new seasons, alter'd sky,
the making and the melting crowds:
The whole world passes, I stand by.

—Gerard Manley Hopkins
The Alchemist in the City

During the latter part of the nineteenth century, the large central lawn of Victoria Park was a favourite place for London people interested in political and social questions of the day. Here, one could listen to speeches and debates on a huge range of subjects. On this lawn, the listener could hear discussions of Malthusianism, atheism, agnosticism, Calvinism, socialism, anarchism, Salvationism, Darwinism, and even Swedenborgianism and Mormonism. In the few decades since the publication of *The Origin of the Species*, rigid adherence to religious ritual had, in many persons lives, been replaced by a spirit of inquiry and practical social application of Christian ideals. Service had become the core of religious ideology at Oxford. Service to God, to Man and to the Empire. Orthodoxy, by itself, was no longer enough to make a good Christian. The men and women who worked for the improvement of 'darkest London' in the 1880s were not content merely to improve attendance at east end churches. They were interested in better education, sanitation, housing—any of the things that touched on the daily living conditions of the underclass. It was a 'muscular' Christianity rather than orthodoxy which characterized the beliefs of educated middle-class sons and, increasingly, daughters. They recognized, for example, that sexual morality had a practical importance which went beyond adherence to scripture. A poor man and woman who thoughtlessly had children were wastrels. They wasted their resources instead of adding to their small store with industry and labour. They diminished their own lives and in the process diminished the life of the community. A few decades earlier, morality had been largely a matter of blind obedience to a sectarian creed. In the 1880s it was a social as well as a religious value, more a manifestation of Christianity in broad terms. This broader, less sectarian Christianity didn't mean that Salvation Army members were not attacked in the streets, or that Methodism was not still associated with a certain class, or that there wasn't social discrimination against anyone who was not an Anglican. But these differences began to fade, overtaken by the Victorian ethos of social improvement which grew in intensity until at least the end of the century. Serafina and her sister emphasized in their own minds the practical value of Christian ideals. Miles was more a pagan worshiper of beauty and less a Victorian Christian than his cousins. He was more at home with the spirit of Byron and Shelley than that of Robert Bridges' and his as yet unknown *protégé*, Gerard Manley Hopkins.

When the weather was fine, Serafina often led family and friends into the greenery of Victoria Park for an afternoon of instructive oration. So it was that some two weeks after publication of the final Maiden Tribute article, Miles found himself carrying a hamper of sandwiches while he and his cousins sought a place on the grass where they could sit close to the speakers. The air was fresh and the park offered a fine prospect, painted in the golden tones of late summer sunlight, muted to a glow by the

pendulous branches of the trees. The sky was a delicious ceru-
lean blue and could not have been more brilliant. The clouds
were huge and fluffy, tinged with a poignant burnished bronze.
The young ladies had provided themselves with two thick alpaca
rugs, and Miles carried the basket with tea and cucumber sandwiches. In many ways, it was a celebration. Miles had finished
several large commissions which promised to bring him others. Serafina was in high spirits and Julia was more carefree and
less watchful and solicitous of her sister. It was the first pleasure
outing any of them had enjoyed together since Mrs. Winstanley
fell ill. She seemed now to be on the mend, though none of the
medical men had said or done anything more than mumble the
word "hysteria."

Because of the Park's proximity to the east end, the
crowds were mixed groups of working people and middle-class
intellectuals. Often one saw a good number of foreigners, especially Germans. When Serafina and her friends arrived, a red
haired German orator was speaking. He was fulminating against
the collectivists.

"You want to reduce man to a state of slavery worse than
that of the those nations who live under the yoke of a tyrant.
..you want to destroy liberty and individuality."

His adversary soon cut in to claim his right to reply.

"Our friend here accuses us of wishing to convert men
into slaves and machines; our friend accuses us of wanting to
stop the development of brains. Our friend is mistaken...We ask
our friend where he sees the liberty of a workman who works ten
hours a day for a morsel of bread. We ask him what sort of liberty
is it that if the man out of work has to go and knock at the door
of the workhouse? We are curious to know what he thinks of
the poor girls who are reduced to sell themselves in our streets.
Does not our friend know that labour is the source of all riches?
Doesn't he know that a big capital cannot be created without
one man oppressing another?"

Back and forth, as the two foreign Socialists sparred in
the heavy-handed manner of their nation, Miles, Julia and Serafina settled onto the lawn for an afternoon's entertainment and

enlightenment.

"What is the latest news about the Criminal Amendment Act, Julia?" Miles asked as they sat down. "It seems clear that your paper has put Mr. Cross under intense pressure to pass the bill immediately. Every journal I pick up is filled with indignant letters from readers, demanding that something be done to stop the trade in young girls."

"Mr. Stead believes the bill will be passed before the month is out," Julia replied.

"Then we have won," he said.

"Yes, it would appear that justice has triumphed in a grand manner, for once."

"And my little sister has been at the very centre of the triumph," Serafina added.

"Well," Julia responded, "let us wait for the vote in the House. Political factions and opinions can be the most treacherous things. I sometimes think that the most damning thing about the radical cause in England is that even the Socialists often can't agree with each other. I think if women led the Socialist party, as we led the agitation for the Criminal Amendment Act, the wrongs of society could be redressed much more quickly."

Miles leaned back on his elbows and looked over at Julia, "Well, there are women socialists like Eleanor Marx and Mrs. Besant. And are you trying to tell me there are no disputes among the suffragists on points of political dogma?"

"Not on the essential points," Serafina replied.

"I have to agree," Julia said. "Men are much more likely to argue about ideas just because they each wish personal ascendency in the group. Women are freer of such intellectual posing. We just want to get the work done and help those in need. It is women who do the hard work in the slums. Look at the Hallelujah Lasses who go into thieves' kitchens and many terrible places where even policemen won't go."

"And consider the work Octavia Hill is doing," Serafina added. "How many homeless people has she helped? And there is the invaluable business training she gives the women who look after her buildings. I agree, Julia. If we are ever to have justice, it shall be women who bring it into being. The sooner we have the vote, the sooner there shall be social justice in England."

"And, who created the Hallelujah lasses, I should like to know?" Miles asked and then answered himself. "General Booth."

"And his wife," Julia said quickly.

"But without him there would be no Salvation Army," Miles said. "And if not for John Ruskin's help, where would Octavia Hill be now?"

"But it is the women who do the really hard work," Serafina said. "I have seen Mrs. Butler stand on a stage when people were throwing brickbats at her. Eventually, she tamed even those roughs with her divine patience and the warmth of her sentiments. That kind of selfless devotion is what has carried us this far in the fight against the CD Acts."

"And what about Stead?" Miles said.

"You know perfectly well the point we are making, Miles," Serafina said.

"I know it, but I don't agree with it. If men and women are to be equal partners, woman cannot be better than men any more than men can be better than women."

"Well," Julia said, "let us say that the differences between men and women can be advantageous or disadvantageous under different circumstances. I believe that in the political arena, the feminine ability to speak directly without striking poses is a great advantage."

"Oh, wait, look, he's about to speak," Serafina said as an imposing figure stepped up to the podium. This was the address for which they had all been waiting. William Morris, the most famous socialist of his time, fixed his thoughtful gaze on the audience and waited for the crowd to subside. No other artist of the century was as protean and cast such a large, benignant shadow across late Victorian England. Morris worked in such widely differing art forms as architecture and literature, furniture and graphic design. His tall figure and white beard gave him a physical presence which added to the power of his words. He had been at the forefront of eminent people who had struggled to make the wave of Jewish immigrants settling in the east end accepted and welcome. He stood in the bright summer sunlight and spoke passionately about the rights of the Jews to come to England. He attacked several anti-semitic polemicists and insisted that sweatshops had not been caused by the Jews. There was no rebuttal to his remarks.

And so the afternoon went. After debating and listening to debaters, Serafina and her friends became captivated by the beauty of the afternoon, especially as the day began to fade and people started to leave. The roof of the rose granite monument seemed to blend into the sky, and the water of the little pond where a weeping ash bathed its drooping branches fell into shadow. The swans appeared motionless against the dark water. Gradually, as the shadows lengthened, silence obtruded itself across the vast lawn of the park. The constellations emerged above the clouds, and the sparrows sang vigorously as they flew upward to the branches which would give them shelter for the night. Miles and his cousins took in the melancholy beauty of the fading day and sat quietly.

"Oh, look," Serafina said suddenly as she shaded her eyes. "Do you see that girl with a camera, Miles? On the other side of the field. If she can capture this subtle light in a photograph, she must be quite an artist."

Miles stood up and looked across the lawn. He could not be sure at such a great distance but the figure with the wooden box and tripod could be the girl he'd met at Piccadilly.

He looked across the field for some moments and suddenly said, "I think I shall go and speak with her," Miles said.

"She will think you're a pest who is trying to flirt with her," Julia said.

"Then why don't we all go?" Serafina said.

"She won't think me a pest if I talk to her intelligently about what she is doing," Miles answered.

He looked off into the distance. He could not analyze all of his thoughts and feelings at that moment but was only conscious of the need to keep Serafina and Julia from accompanying him.

"No," he finally said. "You and Julia stay here. We would have to bring all our things with us. And I don't want to approach her with a caravan. It would be deuced awkward. Besides, we would only have to carry everything back this way in any case." He lit a cigar.

"I suppose if you meet as two enthusiastic amateurs," Julia said, "it will not seem impertinent."

"Of course not. I've never had any woman call me a pest." Miles said as he strode off.

Even as he walked away from Serafina and Julia, he wondered, "Why am I doing this? If it is the girl from Piccadilly, what does it matter? If not, she may well regard me as an intruder with some kind of design, even if I can speak intelligently about photography. In addition, I shall have to give Serafina and Julia a reasonable précis of my conversation."

He would have turned around immediately had he been able to think of what to say about why he had changed his mind. Did he want to turn around? He wasn't sure, apart from his desire not to involve Serafina and Julia in his meeting at Piccadilly. He was conscious that his every movement was being watched across the open expanse of the field, and so, he pressed on. As he got closer to the figure in white muslin, sharply outlined against the shadowed green of the lawn, it began to look more and more like Katherine, and the discovery affected him more than he would have thought likely just moments before. Having labeled and dismissed her as nothing more than a handsome working class girl, albeit with a little extra refinement, he had deliberately dulled the memory of her attraction for him. Even as he drew closer and felt that attraction once more, he remonstrated with himself, "Why should any of this matter? I have nothing to hide. I gave a ride to a girl at a late hour. That is all." The more honest aspect of himself immediately replied, "And now you've prevaricated again by not telling Serafina that you probably knew this girl photographer."

By the time he was certain of the girl's identity, he could hear the scratching movements of her cheap muslin skirt as she

81

walked around the camera. On the ground next to her was an open suitcase containing glass plates coated with collodian and silver halide, each fitted into a holder which kept the light from converting the salts into silver.

"Good day, Miss Green," he said as he tipped his hat to her.

She looked up blankly from her work. It seemed to take some seconds before she knew him.

"Typical of her," he thought to himself. "I come all the way over here and risk upsetting Serafina for the blandest of greetings."

But a moment later, his vanity was gratified by Katherine's smile. He could almost feel her thoughts collecting themselves, returning from the peculiarly timeless place where an artist's vision must go to see what is most essential.

"She was very far away in her thoughts," he said to himself. "Profoundly focused on her art."

Actually, Katherine had been thinking about Susan, and the ghastly opium den where she had searched for her. For weeks, the dreadful bucket Katherine had seen slipped, unbidden, in and out of her mind. She had told Dave but he advised her not to go to the police, who were regarded by most eastenders as enemies. All she had been able to learn that might touch on Susan were some snippets of information from the Salvationists on Hanbury Street.

Katherine had found the Salvationists' building just a few blocks to the north of where she lived. A woman had been sweeping the sidewalk when Katherine approached. She wore a red guernsey and an armband with a cross on it. When Katherine drew close to her she could see the armband clearly. It bore the words 'Salvation Army, Blood and Fire'. In spite of the heat, the woman wore a coal scuttle bonnet. She looked very maternal and friendly. The hair that escaped her bonnet was greying and her cheeks rounded and blushing with health. Her eyes sparkled. As Katherine approached her, she smiled.

"Are you Mrs. Cottrill?" Katherine asked, repeating the name she had been given by some of the neighbourhood girls.

"Yes, I am. May I help you?"

"I am looking for a friend. I thought she might have come here. She used to go on the streets before she came to live with me. But now, she's disappeared. I was hoping that perhaps she had come here."

"What is her name?"

"She answers to Susan. She's very young. Not yet thirteen. And very pretty. With dark hair," Katherine said.

"I'm sorry, my dear. I have no one like that right now. Would you like to come in and fill out one of our Lost Persons Forms?"

"Lost Persons Forms?" Katherine repeated.

"Yes. So many people go missing off the streets, now. And many do come to us. So the General decided to start an enquiry department to help people find their lost loved ones. If you fill out a form, it will be copied and circulated by our new department to every Salvation Army Mission in England. The police don't have enough men to search for all who need looking for. If the person wants to be found, we shall notify you. Would you like to fill out a Form?"

"Oh, yes. If you please."

"Where was she last seen?"

"At the Bowen Refuge."

"Oh, dear," Mrs. Cottrill said, frowning.

"Is there something wrong?" Katherine asked.

"There have been rumors about that place—that it might be involved—involved with sending children to Europe. To— to the bad houses there. They are just rumors, of course. The Bowens have powerful friends in Parliament. The General has said they are well protected. So we can say nothing about it until there is evidence. And we have none. I am sorry to trouble you, my dear. But the General says that truth is always best for those who are searching for loved ones."

"Yes, thank you."

And that is where Katherine had let the matter rest—at first. There was no way she could confront the Bowens and find out if they had seen Susan. They probably didn't even live at the

Refuge themselves. The only one who might have seen someone from Bowens was the chinaman and he had had his throat
slit. She thought of the terrible looking, dangerous man she had
seen at the chinaman's and wondered if he were connected with
the Bowens. That was the question she put to herself just before
Miles greeted her.

In the sharp contrasts of late afternoon sun and shadow,
Miles was more aware than ever of Katherine's attractiveness
and her poverty. The waistband of her skirt was separating from
the rest of the garment and had been pinned to hold it in place.
Her cheap cotten gloves were frayed and darned in many places.
The straw hat which lay beside the camera on the ground was
bent and battered. In spite of all this and in spite of seeing her
poverty so clearly defined by the sunshine, her face still had that
strange magnetism, that strange opacity of character which had
drawn him to her at Piccadilly. He tried to analyze the quality
and could not. Her profile was finely and definitively cut and her
dark eyes, which were nearly black, gave her a dramatic appearance. Seen from the front, her nose was rather broad and flat.
Her complexion was very dark, perhaps exhibiting an Asian
heritage, but her black eyes looked inward to something apart
from the ordinary world.

"Oh, excuse me, Mr. Hickenbotham. When I am composing, I often become so concentrated on what I am doing it is
difficult to reconnect my thoughts to the present moment."

"What exactly are you photographing, Miss Green? May
I remove the plate you just exposed and have a look through the
camera?"

She did not politely acquiesce as most women would
have done but instead answered, "I shall remove it. I was just
about to do so."

She expertly detached the wooden plate holder and then
lifted it from the camera. Then she removed the lens cap.

"You may look now. The light changes so quickly at this
time of day, I am not certain you shall see what I did."

Miles bent over the back of the camera, slipped the cloth

over his head and looked at the dark, fuzzy upside down image on the ground glass.

"Unlike you," he heard her say through the muffling cloth, "I mostly take landscapes. I thought the shadows and light particularly beautiful when I was here yesterday, so I came today with the camera to be ready if the poignancy of the scene repeated itself."

He pulled himself out from the cloth and smoothed his ruffled hair, which grew in handsome dark ringlets.

"A difficult picture to print," he said. "It has many subtle tones. Poignant was exactly the right word."

"That is what made it beautiful," she said in a tone of positive authority.

"At least you are certain of your own esthetic judgments," he said.

"We must feel certainty before we expose the plate. The images are so evanescent. In the dark room, they can so easily become a poor faded thing that does not capture at all what we believed we had seen on the glass. We must at least start with certainty in our thoughts and intentions. Otherwise, what can be the result ?"

The vehemence of her response surprised him. There was a long silence as he considered her words.

Finally, he said, "I think what you mean is that our conception of a work must be clear. We must see it before it is actually there."

Her face became blank as she thought about his words. He noticed that one of her hands played with her hair the way a child would. He found the gesture very innocent and charming. After a few moments she answered, "You have said it much better than I. The conception is everything. All the rest is just technique."

"But technique is important, too," he said, trying to match her vigour of expression. "In painting and photography."

"Yes," she admitted reluctantly. "But it must never become an end in itself."

"Of course, you are right. What a cunning little camera

this is," he said abruptly as he moved the bellows on their wire frame tracks. "You can easily correct verticals or horizontals and yet it packs down to nothing. Canvas bellows are lightweight. Dubroni. Of course, it had to be French. I've not seen its like before. Where did you get it?"

"It isn't mine. It belongs to the man with whom I—I've studied. He has an establishment on Fleet Street. He is very kind to let me use it occasionally. Actually, this will probably be the last time."

"Why is that?"

" He is—ah, he is closing his establishment."

"Then he has a complete studio with a glass room?" he asked as he looked at the camera. "You would use dry plates with this?"

"Yes. But I don't believe he will keep his studio for long. He is trying to sell. He— He is quite elderly."

"What will you do then?" Miles asked.

"I don't know. I suppose I shall have to give it up. I shall never save enough to buy my own equipment."

"But what about your wish to become a photographer? Shall you give up on that and keep toiling as a maker of matches?"

"I honestly don't know. I don't know what I can do. I have so little money, and photographic studios are so expensive to arrange." She shrugged, "However, if it is my karma..."

He did not notice the strange word because he was absorbed in his own words. He rushed into what he wanted to say:

"Indeed. My glass room was horrifyingly expensive to build. It seems a great waste that it is idle at least half of every day. Why not accept the offer I made the night we met? Use my studio in the mornings. My glass room has north light, too. You could start doing some portrait work. I have a few different backdrops. And I have a multitude of drying frames."

Once again, he saw her gaze turn more deeply inward as she thought about what he had said. Katherine was thinking of her empty room and the missing child. It would be good to fill up some of that emptiness with more photographic work. She could

no longer allow herself to use her teacher's studio. She thought
of her past in India and wondered how much she dared reveal
to the beautiful young man who was offering her so much. She
let her hair slip between her fingers and began twisting it into a
tight rope. There was no childishness in her action, this time,
Miles thought. It was more expressive of the nervousness of an
adult.

"Perhaps you were right, Mr. Hickenbotham," she said in
a halting, strangely reluctant way. "Perhaps it is providential that
we met. Since that night I have thought of a way I might aid
you, as well. But you must promise to take me at my word and
not cross question me if I tell you what it is."

"But of course, Miss Green, I would take seriously anything you told me."

Her next words were spoken more to herself than to
Miles, "Others have said that before, yet it has always ended
badly."

"I give you my word, I shall listen passively, without
judgement, to anything you wish to say," Miles said.

She looked within again, but this time her brow was
furrowed in an expression of outright concern. Her conflict between speaking and remaining silent was palpable.

"I shall trust that you really are as good as you seem, Mr.
Hickenbotham," she said without meeting his eyes. "I may be
able to help you find your lost sister."

Miles was so surprised by the object of her discourse that
for some moments, he said nothing. The thought occurred to
him that perhaps the girl might be a little mad. Perhaps that was
the meaning of her odd distance, her separateness. Who could
know what had befallen her if she had been orphaned at ten?
The seconds passed as they stood together silently among the
shades of the trees spreading out over the great lawn, and the
longer the silence lasted the more plausible did madness seem
to him. Yet, another part of him felt the depth of the moment,
a strange pause in which some kind of secret pulse of the world,
of which he had never before been aware, had ceased to beat for
a time. He was conscious of taking a deeper than normal breath

and suddenly the spell was broken. Everything began moving again, the eternal stillness was gone, and all things were once again caught up in the motion of each moment following the next. It was like something he could not quite recall. He wanted to speak but remembered his promise not to do so.

Instead, she spoke directly of his inmost thoughts, "I cannot explain it. Something shifts and I can see things, as if through a rip in a veil."

Surprised at having his mind read so exactly, he played with the camera for some moments before saying, "Seeing things such as where my sister might be?" he asked, feeling her statement had given him permission to reply.

"Yes," she said.

"Even if she is dead?"

"Yes."

"You are a spiritualist medium, then?"

"No. Not in the generally accepted sense. I see things. I don't know how else to say it. I have done so most of my life. Unfortunately, I can't do it for people who are dear to me. Only for strangers."

"You are a seer, a clairvoyant?"

"Of a kind. Yes. I have been called that."

"Miss Green, I can see that for some reason you are suffering under some great inner pressure of emotion. What is it? Can I do anything to relieve you?"

"No. It is only that you are only the second person in this country I have told."

"Then you are from some foreign place?"

She nodded affirmatively.

"May I ask where?"

"India," she said.

"And that is where you were orphaned?"

She nodded again.

"Heavens. What a place for a child to find its way."

"I told you, Mr. Hickenbotham, that I was something of a gypsy. I am also of mixed blood. My father was a native sergeant in the Ninth Bengal Lancers."

"I wondered."

"Why I was so dark? Now you know." There was something almost haughty about the way she spoke of her heritage, as if in defiance of a disapproval she anticipated.

"But there is no shame in that— if your father was loyal."

"He was true to his salt and fought for the Queen during the Mutiny, but his loyalty did nothing to help me and my mother, later. And after she died..."

"There is no need to tell me all this, Miss Green. Not if it gives you pain."

"Yes. I must finish. If I am going to accept your help and to work in your studio, you should know these things about me. I would not want one of the slurs society casts on me to affect you in any way. That would be poor repayment for your kindness." She paused for a moment but clearly had not finished her statement.

"Take your time, Miss Green."

"Thank you, once again, Mr. Hickenbotham. You are very kind. I have had another loss in the last few months and it has affected me."

"There is no need to say more."

"Yes, I must go on. I must finish my statement by saying that while still a child, I was exhibited publicly and made to give demonstrations of my clairvoyance and mesmeric abilities at various army stations around Calcutta and upcountry. I am sure that to many who saw me, had I not been a child, I would have been thought a fraud, no better than a common mountebank."

He gave her a few moments to regain possession of herself and then spoke, "I understand that there might be some who would find fault with the respectability of your background, but I, personally, can find none. I think you have been most unfortunate, especially so since your own innate sense of refinement is so strong and causes you such pain about things you could not help."

"That is very generous, sir."

Miles poked at the ground with his stick for a moment and then said, "The material point is whether or not you are going to pursue your photographic aspirations. The past is of no consequence. One can do nothing about it. Why fret over it? Especially a past over which you had so little control. The future is what you must think about and act upon. Shall you use my studio and equipment or not?"

"Yes, if it is still offered. With deep gratitude, Mr. Hick-enbotham."

"And do you still have my card? Ah, I thought not. You've thrown it away, you headstrong girl. Then, here's another. Any morning before noon, Miss Green, the studio is yours."

He tipped his hat once more and wished her a good day before she could find another reason not to come.

What a history, he thought as he walked away from her. No wonder she seemed out of the common run. That sense of timelessness she was able to conjure was quite eerie. Her remarks about finding Amelia—well, it was better to keep her mind on photography and not wander off into the swamp of occultism. How many people had lost their footing in that black mud? Even a scientific observer like William Crookes had reportedly lost his grip on reality under the spell of the charming medium, Florence Cook. Miles might have been a pagan or a poor Christian but he was clear-headed and wanted nothing to do with the murky waters of spiritualism. For more than thirty years those waters had washed over England. Everywhere there were groups of people engaged with table tappings, ouija boards, flying trumpets and glowing hands. Even the nobility had been drawn in, fasci-nated by the Scottish-American, D.D. Homes, the most famous and sensational medium of the age, the intimate friend of kings and emperors. Among all the fraudulent mediums who had been reported during the nineteenth century, Homes had never been caught out, yet his feats of levitation and immunity to fire were by far the most astounding ever seen.

Miles had tried to find his sister through occult means, but one experience of fraud and the intense disappointment he had felt was enough to convince him that spiritualism was the hope of fools. Not only did he want to protect himself from the delusional experiences of the spirit cabinet, but more especially

his aunt and cousins. He had banished all the half truths of psychic phenomena forever. It was better for the family never to let
that sort of thing into their home again. This was reason enough
not to tell Serafina or Julia about all that had just transpired.
Especially so since the girl had spoken to him in confidence
about her history. Nor was there any need to mention she would
be working in his studio. She might never appear. He felt the air
growing cooler as he walked back toward his cousins, who, he
was certain, had observed him intently, albeit from a distance,
while he was speaking with Katherine.

Chapter 6

THE GLASS ROOM

List of a Photographic Outfit

1. Glass-house, or room in the garret furnished with a sky-light.
2. Dark room, for sensitizing plates or papers.
3. Operating room, for collodionizing plates, mounting prints, etc.
4. Screens (white, gray, blue, and artistic) for the glass house.
5. Lenses, (1/4, 1/3, 4/4, etc., stereoscopic and orthoscopic.)
6. Cameras, (for portraits, views, stereographs and (for copying.)
7. Ornamental carpets, chairs, stands, curtains, pillars, balustrades, etc.
8. Head-rests, etc., camera-stands, mirrors, brushes, combs, pins, needle, and thread.
9. Washhand-stand. pitcher and basin, soap and towels, clothes-brush and nail-brush.
10. Stove, tongs, shovel, poker, coal or wood-box.
11. Antechamber, suitably furnished with lounges, etc.
12. Show-cases for artistic productions, and cases for chemicals, etc.
13. Collodion, (negative and positive,) acetic acid, nitric acid, citric acid, tartaric acid, etc.

—JohnTowler ,*The Silver Sunbeam* 1864

The weeks following the outing to the Park were gray and overcast, leaving the light in Miles' studio diffuse but gray and uninspiring. Of course, there were many days like this in London, especially at a time before efforts had been made to clean up the air of the metropolis, and Miles knew that his lack of industry was not the result of the weather. He needed another commission on which to focus his energies for, he did not have a genuine artistic calling, though he would not have described the emptiness he felt in those terms. But the fact was he did not have the essential motive power of creative work: the ability to set himself problems which required new and unique solutions. A capacity for hard work, an exactness in perceiving spatial relationships, a good colour sense and the willingness to spend long hours mastering technique were his gifts. His paintings were workmanlike, sometimes even brilliantly so, but originality eluded him. In one sense, he could not be blamed for his lack. His circumstances were such that he needed to make money from painting. This meant his artistic choices always had to be certain and conventional, sure to be accepted by the people who paid him. He never gave himself the luxury, nor derived inspiration from asking, "what if?" So he could repeat past successes but rarely had new ones and this often left him feeling bored with his own work. There was no mystery for him when he stood before a canvas, the uncertainty which every genuine artist accepts as his true mistress, a mistress who demands that her aspirants always risk failure to gain the greatest reward. The uncertainty demanded by his art was directly opposed to the demand he felt from Serafina. To win her, he must succeed in making money. His father's legacy had provided a good education and a respectable place in society, and Serafina's settlement, along with eventual ownership of the house at 21 Cavendish Square, a comfortable life. But Serafina would never want to live only on her settlement. She would demand that her husband excel in some way, some way that earned a good income. For the last several years, Miles had been making his own way, but he had arrived at the critical point in his career. He must now direct his energies to building a durable reputation among the new money of the west end. His thoughts were focused on this, not on being more original. He had sought and generally found clients who wanted well-executed second class work. No mysteries or magical manipulations of light and colour for these wealthy men. Reality was just what it seemed and had no mysterious inner dimensions. For this class of patron, artistic experiments were to be left on the Continent. In England, with the exception of Turner and a few other bold souls, a painting was a straightforward representation of its subject and as predictable as a bank balance. A portrait might flatter the original, as long as the resemblance was obvious to the dullest of the client's friends and family. Bankers from Portland Place, Railway barons, Quakers who had made fortunes in the grocery business, this was the class from which Miles drew his clientele. Ambitious men of this sort were the most reliable source of patronage for the arts during the later years of Victoria's reign.

It was tantalizing for Miles to be engaged in a field where he could see the spirits of great explorers unfold before his eyes. He did make the occasional trip to Paris to see what was being done in the garrets of the left bank. His French was fairly good so he was not limited to the *ateliers* of ex-patriot Englishmen who flocked to Paris, supposedly for the chance to study but more often for the easy women of the *demimonde*. He could believe at times that he shared something with the boldest explorers, but the need for safety had early dulled his appetite for experimentation. The impact, what would soon be called the trauma, of losing Amelia and the changes it had brought in his life, had taught him the importance of safety, in a very visceral way. If one abandons duty and what is certain, dangerous elements could enter one's life. The truth was, had Amelia not been lost he might have had the courage to live a life which compromised less between the bohemian and conventional. However, had the forces which resulted in the girl's disappearance not existed, Miles life would have been altogether different. As Miles stood in the faint, watery light of his studio and experienced the *ennui*, the inner pressure, of choosing convention over excitement, he still did not comprehend that mystery, danger and passion were the things for which he thirsted most. His outward conventionality had shaped his life, but also suffocated him, emotionally and professionally. Certainty is an impossible condition to impose on art, whose primary purpose is to continually reinterpret what we see in new ways.

He already lived a life judged too unconventional for many of the wealthiest west end families who aspired to see their sons and daughters presented at Court. His occasional trips to Paris acted as something of a relief from the pressure of conformity. There, he could drink absinthe, forget his social position, unleash his demons and indulge in unusual games with French tarts.

The astonishing revolution that would be fomented by Matisse and Picasso was still some twenty years in the future. Its spirit, which flared again briefly during the nineteen fifties, is now nothing but a heap of sacred ashes kept in the sepulchre of museums. In our own day, the spiritual and personal nature of art flickers even more dimly than it did in Miles' time. After the Second World War, the Americans showed us that art was a commodity just like any other and could be bought, sold, and invested in for economic gain. Uniqueness has since been cloned and is now a mass produced item marketed for money. We buy goods with designer labels, the facsimile of a facsimile, without examining them too closely if they make us believe we possess something unique. We even tell ourselves that owning something is equivalent to creating it. That lie is one of the cornerstones of what is now known as "codependency". We have exchanged our unique, genuine experience of creation for someone else's, to which we attach a monetary value and proudly hang on our walls or wear on our backs. We wait for journalists to tell us what is "good" and what is not. Most have even lost the desire to have strong aesthetic opinions.

Miles, at least, had the passion to learn the disciplines which art requires from any serious votary. In our own time, few get that far, and even fewer can discern the difference between technique and art. The fact that Miles was a fine technician was one of the reasons he liked photography. It is an art form where technical excellence is often the primary goal of the photographer, and that was even more true in his time than in ours.

The *atelier* where Miles pursued his vocation and avocation was located on the entire top floor of a large gray stone Georgian building, probably originally built as a printing plant. It was tucked between Reid's Brewery and Leather Lane in the only row of decent buildings on that block. It was not an elegant address, but it was centrally located for sittings and was convenient to the train. Miles had broken the space into four main divisions: the north facing glass room where photographs were taken, the dark room where he printed and dried photographs and, which for chemical reasons was completely separate from his painting studio, and a large open living space. A quiet, middle aged manservant who did not live in looked after essential needs, and during the day kept his own quarters on the ground floor of the building in an arrangement not unlike that of a French concierge.

It was from his glass room that Miles looked down over Portpool Lane, on the gray day already described. He watched as the unusually sharp wind battered a plane tree which grew in the narrow court three storeys below. The many panes of glass in the large cast-iron framed window rattled ominously against the pressure of the wind and mixed with the noise of the Soho Bazaar just a few streets away. Occasionally, the railway which ran along Gray's Inn Road also added its thunder to the street noise. The massive three sided glass and iron bay window recalled the architecture of the Crystal Palace, and made the room seem even larger than it was. Some people experienced a sense of vertigo when they entered the room through its south wall and looked across the room at the enormous, unobstructed view of the rooftops and streets through the huge, north-facing window. To the left, at one end of the forty foot room was a large fireplace, facing it was a storage area from which spilled period pieces of furniture, a well-grown auracaria, a rubber tree and other house plants, parts of costumes, interesting sheets of fabric —in short—props of all kinds. Facing the three-sided bay of the window was the sitting area where, presently, Miles had a empire chaise positioned. Even in the diffuse light of the overcast day, a subject would not have to be still for an uncomfortably long time in the light which washed the glass part of the room.

He turned away from the window and wandered aimlessly around the big room and then passed through the door and black silk velvet drapes into the smaller dark room where drying racks of different sizes hung from the walls. He had not used the room for some time so the unpleasant chemical odours from the processing of the plates were not evident except as a faint presence. He passed through the darkroom and operating room quickly and entered his painting studio, another large room with a sloping skylight, which bathed easel and canvas in diffuse north light. Here, the odours of mineral spirits, damar varnish and linseed oil permeated the space and made Miles feel more peaceful than he had felt in the glass room. There was something unsettling about the openness of the glass room. He had spent a small fortune to have the window built and to outfit the photographic studio and he had hardly used it since he moved from his old lodgings. He sat down on the piano stool he liked to use when he painted, then immediately got up, found one of the small, cheap Italian cigars he favoured and lit it. He looked critically at the half-finished hunting scene on the easel. It was not a commission but something he thought might be saleable to a Mr. Grant, a rich Manchester industrialist who was mad for anything connected with fox hunting, which the merchant regarded as the most ennobling activity any true Englishman could undertake. The figures looked wooden and lifeless to Miles. He resolved to wipe down the canvas and start over. Three days of work would be lost, but he didn't want anything with his name on it to look as badly drawn as the fox and its pursuers.

He wondered at his own restlessness. Perhaps he should pay calls today and see if he could stir someone into commissioning a new work. He hated what he called 'making the rounds.' It made him feel like a tradesman, but there was no denying that paying calls brought in commissions. He could visit Hewitt at his bank. The last thing he had done for him should be back from the framer's by now. He might be able to convince the banker to cover more of the bilious green paint in his office with another soothing scene of country life. If he went out, he could end up at Cavendish Square and see Serafina and Julia before dinner.

As he watched a smoke ring drift away from him, the image of little Amelia came to him. In the muted light of the gray day he could see her so clearly it was as if she were present, dressed in the same clothes which she had worn on the day she disappeared, a dark blue dress which was reminiscent of a pinafore. He quickly walked to the easel, pulled the hunting scene from it and put up a canvas he had stretched and sized with rabbit skin glue the day before.

He roughed in Amelia's dark curls, tied up with her favourite coloured ribbon, a blue he would mix with Prussian and ultramarine blue and white. There were no extant likenesses of the lost child but for some reason, in the soft light of the overcast morning a clear image of her seemed etched into his otherwise idle thoughts. Fleetingly, it occurred to him he might be able to sell the painting to Serafina's mother. But, no, he would have to give it to her as a gift. He couldn't take money from his Aunt, especially for a portrait of Amelia.

As he worked and smoked, Miles became griped by his subject. There was something very special about bringing an image of his lost sister into the physical world, where none had existed before. The thought energized him. In one corner of his mind he wondered why he had never painted his missing sister, but he was too busy seeing all the details of his interior image of her to speculate at length. He kept seeing her as Ophelia, lying prone, though he wanted to paint her standing. He had to re-arrange his vision of her. Thoughts related to Amelia which were barely at the threshold of his awareness kept begging for his attention but he was too occupied to register any of them. They flitted past like memories of half-forgotten dreams. He felt himself in a strange, trance-like state. The cigar went out in the ash tray and the work connected him with a curiously timeless realm, as if in trying to reduce the three-dimensional world to two dimensions, the dimension of time was utterly erased. Nothing existed but a vague awareness of passing thoughts and what was before his inner eye. He was suspended and in motion at the same time. He ceased to exist apart from his subject, often feeling in a tactile way the shape or texture of what he painted. If his concentration faltered and he became aware of himself for a moment, there was a strange confusion of touch, vision and other senses. As he drew the child's ringlets the odour of candied violets came to him, her favourite treat, another thing he had forgotten which would now be permanently remembered in the painting, interpreted by the shape or colour of the candied flowers.

He didn't stop until he was forced to let the underpainting dry. He re-lit the cigar and looked at the canvas. He had accomplished a great deal. The underpainting for the flesh tones, the hair and the white muslin dress would be ready for top coats once it dried. The shape and stance of the roughed out figure stood forth convincingly from the canvas. Though only an outline, Amelia already had the vividness and presence which had been lacking in the hunting scene. It was as if he were bringing her back from wherever she had been. It was a kind of *renaissance* for Amelia and for him. He hoped that when he began working tomorrow, he would still see her as clearly as he had during the morning just passed. He would not mention the painting to anyone at Cavendish Square, but would present it as a surprise when finished.

Only when he put down his brushes and pushed back his piano stool did he consult his watch, which he pulled out from under the smock he habitually wore in the studio. It was three-thirty in the afternoon. Too late to pay any professional calls, he was relieved to discover. He picked up an open copy of the second edition of Baudelaire's *Les Fleur des Mal* and began reading at the second stanza of the open page, *L'invitation au voyage*. These words evoked for him the life he would have liked to lead—a Parisian esthete's life, a voluptuary of the mid-century, with a mistress who was present and at the same time was simply another beautiful thing in a wonderful chamber, a place worlds apart from everyone, a place where he could do whatever he liked with his playthings:

Des meubles luisants,
Polis par les ans,
Décoreraient notre chambre;
Les plus rares fleurs
Mêlant leurs odeurs
Aux vagues senteurs de l'ambre,
Les riches plafonds,
Les miroirs profonds,
La splendeur orientale,
Tout y parlerait
A l'âme en secret
Sa douce langue natale.

He tried to imagine Serafina in such a room, speaking such a language and could not. Miles was a romantic who had been born too late. He could not trust his own tastes and indulge them for they ran contrary to the extraverted Victorian currents of upward mobility and outward expansion. Art itself was suspect. It wasn't practical. It was too self-absorbed. Art with a sensuous or interior bias was worse. It resulted in nothing but vague dreams and questionable morality, and Miles did not want to be an outsider, for to be isolated was dangerous. The emotional disaster of Amelia's abduction barred him from abandoning the safety of Victorian ideals, and as a man or artist it was a little too early to be encouraged by *les grands sauvages*, Paul Gaugin and Vincent Van Gogh, who were just beginning to paint their masterpieces—if anyone could be encouraged by their sufferings, even for the sake of such luminous images. Like most of us today, who partake in the second-hand life which flickers across the television screen, Miles wanted mystery and desire to be safe and predictable. However, he could not control his dreams. So, in spite of wishing to remain protected by the rigid proscriptions of Victorian ideals, it was not Serafina's face he saw in *les miroirs profonds* of his mind's eye. He could not impose conventional mores on his hypnogogic state, not even for the sake of the

obvious and, the as yet, secret ties which bound him to Serafina. The face he saw was one of *splendeur orientale*. The dark but beautiful skin, the black irises and black ringlets, floated on the ripples of a liquid mirror, which was somehow bound in a dense frame of flowers, thorns, and thistles, wound together even more intricately than a moulding carved by Grinling Gibbons. It was an exotic face that vaguely reminded him of Katherine. Some of the thorns were pricking the forehead and there were one or two tiny threads of blood where the skin had been broken. As he looked into it the girl's face he thought, "It has an opacity that shuts me out and reflects myself."

When Miles woke, the light in the room had dimmed considerably; he was very hungry and had no memory of the dream of the magic mirror, a mirror which could have revealed much to him. He made his toilet, changed his linen and dressed for dinner at the Winstanley's. where he was charmingly accommodated by Gertrude, Mrs. Winstanley's cook, who always set an extra plate for him. Only Julia complained if he did not come and did not write to say so. Serafina and her mother took his bohemian dining habits quite in stride. This violation of protocol was part of the convenience of being all but engaged to a family member who was virtually the head of the household. In most middle-class homes, dining was by no means casual, though by the latter part of Victoria's reign, the formal fifteen course dinners of earlier years had been reduced to five or ten courses, probably by the exigencies of stomach disorders and other diseases due to overeating. In any case, the tragedies of Arthur Winstanley's premature death, Miles' loss of his parents and the abduction of Amelia had knit the remaining Winstanley's into a fabric which could not be strained by violating the lesser rituals of polite behaviour.

As he walked southwest along Clerkenwell, in what seemed the day's constant twilight, Miles looked forward to presenting the picture of Amelia to Mrs. Winstanley. The older woman suddenly rose out of his memory like a column of fire. She was suddenly vividly present. No doubt when he presented the painting there would be a quarter hour of tears, but after that the older woman would be positively alight with happiness. The painting of Amelia was a whim, something he was really doing for himself. It had no special purpose, he believed as he walked toward Cavendish Square. He had yet to discover how complex motivation could be, even his own. Like many of us, he would comprehend the complexity of his life at about the same time he realized there was nothing he could do to simplify it.

There was a minor *contretemps* when he arrived at the Winstanley's. He had forgotten Virgil's sugar cube so that the beast followed him into the dining room, eliciting protests from the ladies. Miles had to go downstairs to the kitchen and petition cook for the needed article before the bloodhound resumed his post in the front hall. Then, each of the three women held out their cheeks for a kiss from Miles, which he dutifully delivered. There was no difference between the light pecks he distributed to Serafina, her sister or mother. Reflecting on that fact made him feel a little petulant as the footman seated him. He was still breathing the exotic perfumes of *les plus rares fleurs* and was struck by how commonplace everything seemed at the Winstanley's.

Finally, Julia elevated the conversation from utter insipidity by talking with real concern about the plight of the dock workers. Little had changed for the dockers since the middle of the century when Henry Mayhew wrote of them saying, "a single day of east wind, which prevented ships from reaching dock, could put 8,000 men out of work, with no income when they were not working." In the 1880s, the narrowness of the old docks meant that many of the newer, larger ships could no longer be unloaded at the London or Ste. Katharine docks. So the dockers' work was more scarce than ever.

Julia summarized the case by saying, "All of us in the west-end are still living on the labour of nearly starving men. One day soon, they shall make us pay for our complacency. They are the ones who will offer a real chance for Socialism to take hold in Britain. The Fabians and other intellectuals will never do anything except talk. They are too comfortable. Too safe, ensconced in front of warm fires. It is the dockers and their hungry wives and children who will bring social enlightenment to our country."

A vague memory flickered feebly in Mile's thoughts for a moment but was extinguished by Serafina before he could see it clearly.

"I am sure you are right, Julia," Serafina said as a servant scooped a large portion of fresh vegetables onto her plate. "I only wish those men were not so dirty. I sometimes think every n'er do well in London ends up on the waterfront."

"What other sort of men could you find to risk their lives for a few pence?" Julia asked. "During the winter fogs it is quite common to have at least one drowning a day. I am trying to get Mr. Stead to let me do a series on the dockers."

"Speaking of him," Miles said, "What is happening with him now? Is he going to trial?."

"Oh, yes. He has already appeared at Bow street," Julia said.

"And what of his old scourge, Mrs. Jeffries, queen of brothel owners?" Serafina asked, "Is it true that she actually came to the court and passed out rotten eggs to throw?"

"Yes, disgustingly true," Julia answered.

"It astonishes me that the woman is still free to attack respectable people with impunity," Mrs. Winstanely said. Her face wore a curious expression as she spoke.

"The Criminal Law Amendment Act certainly didn't affect her at all, did it?"
Miles said.

"No," Julia replied. "She grows richer every day and actually sends circulars to MPs in the House itself, telling members about the new women and children she has imported for their low tastes. Cavendish Bentick acts as her ponce and passes the circulars to his degraded band of well-placed cronies. It is incredible that Bramwell Booth and Mr. Stead are to be tried as criminals while an acknowledged procuress mocks them in the street with a band of hired ruffians— and in the House itself with an even more shocking coterie of degenerate MPs. She has sent her thugs to our offices as well," Julia added. "You must have heard of the riots there."

"And no one arrests them?" Miles asked.

"Mrs. Jeffries has too many powerful clients," Serafina said.

Miles listened to Serafina's bitter reproach and thought, "What would she say if she had seen me exchanging pleasantries with Mrs. Jeffries the last time I visited her cottage in Hampstead?" Of course, he knew it was a question that would never be asked let alone answered.

Eventually, dinner ended and Miles had a chance for a *tête a tête* with Serafina. She had a small room at the front of the house which was filled with her books and two of Miles' most flattering portraits of her. It was just off of the front hall, and by keeping the door open the proprieties were preserved by the thinnest of margins. They were actually quite alone when they sat in Serafina's room. The pair slipped away from table without being followed or questioned as most couples would have been in similar circumstances, and after passing Rossiter dozing in the front hall, they entered their sanctuary.

Miles reclined on the settee but Serafina sat down at her desk and trimmed an old quill with her penknife, disdaining to use the newer steel nibs, which had practically replaced the softer, more graceful pens of the past.

"Are you writing a letter, now, Serafina?"

"As you see, sir."

"I hoped you would come and sit by me. 'Which you well know,' he thought to himself. You can write letters when you are alone," he added out loud.

"You are such a boy sometimes, Miles. I just have to dash off a short note to Mrs. Butler to enquire after her health. The trial has been most taxing for her. She nearly stood in the dock herself."

Her back was to him and his eyes touched the curve of her neck as if he were drawing it. The charm of the subject proved too great for him and he stood and moved to a position directly behind her chair. The scratching of the quill was the only sound in the room as he looked down at the deliciously feminine neck, completely exposed by tortoise combs that swept up her thick blonde hair. He ran his index finger very lightly down the centre of her neck where the muscles formed an indentation that was normally hidden, a secret part of her person. It made him think of other such places. The thought surprised him and he was shocked at himself for thinking of Serafina in terms more appropriate to a prostitute or the mistress of a French poet. Then Serafina, herself, interrupted his fantasy.

"Miles, don't do that." Serafina said. "I am composing."

The lewdness of his thought rather than the slight transgression of his finger made his hand jump away from her as though galvanized.

But moments later, his desire to be her lord and master, led him on to mutiny and he bent and kissed the delicate curve he had admired from the settee.

"Miles, please don't make me stop to remonstrate with you. I have but one little task to do. Then I am yours," perhaps choosing her words to be deliberately bold.

Miles took the bait without hesitation.

"Mine?" he said huskily. "Are you? Really?" And he traced the delicate spiral of her ear with his finger.

"Sir, you must sit down immediately and let me finish. I am having enough trouble with my old pen."

"Why not discard it as you are discarding me at this moment?"

"Because I am fond of you both. You have your own characteristic ways of sputtering and making a mess. You see how I cannot make a clean 'e', no matter what? And in your presence I cannot finish a letter."

"And if I persist in persecuting you? How shall you punish me?" His voice was harder and clearer, a change she chose to ignore.

"I should have to ask you to leave," she said, enjoying the game she had always won in previous innings.

But she had not reckoned on the way in which Miles' latent desire for her had been stirred into a sensual response by the *splendeur orientale* of a dark-eyed face which had rippled in a magic mirror. Her self-absorption and lack of experience permitted no idea of the frustrations which Miles felt. She was astonished a few moments later when she turned around to find that he had silently left the room, his footsteps muffled by the Turkey carpet. Then she heard Rossiter bidding him goodnight, and the sounds of the front door being opened and closed.

Miles stood on the front steps and lit a cigar. "What a ridiculous tyranny," he murmured to himself. "Is she such a child that she doesn't know it? Or that she expects me to tolerate it, indefinitely?"

By the standards of her time, Serafina was playing a dangerous game. Men were in short supply in the 1880s. A respectable, good-looking bachelor was hard to find. Such a young man had thousands of young women to choose from, all sexually available in a variety of situations from a maid who warmed her master's bed to keep her job, to a kept mistress, to the denizens of houses of ill fame, not to mention the tens of thousands of prostitutes on the London streets. Women, on the other hand, hardly existed socially unless they were married, and after marriage they literally did not exist as far as the law was concerned. Before 1882 a married woman's identity was completely absorbed by that of her husband. It was legally assumed that anything a married woman did, she did at her husband's direction. Hence, Mr. Bumble's famous remark in *Oliver Twist* about the law being an ass. Only the poorest work was open to most women, which often provided incentive for a career change to prostitution. For all of these reasons, marriage was considered the most desirable condition for a young woman, and a condition which should be adopted at the earliest opportunity, since a second opportunity might never present itself. Serafina's reluctance to be married was rare, even among the "new women" of the 1880s. Unlike Serafina, many "new women" who eschewed marriage had few personal charms and used the suffragist cause to make a virtue of necessity. But rich or poor, young or old, educated or illiterate, pretty or ugly, there was no situation in which an unmarried woman could have a man in her bed without being reviled by "respectable society," an epithet which included the middle-class, as well as the more prosperous people of the working class. To be known to have slept with a man outside marriage made any woman a prostitute and an utter outcast for the rest of her life. Premarital sex for a respectable woman was considered, "the fate worse than death." During the Indian Mutiny of 1857, men involved in the great sieges at Lucknow and Cawnpore, openly discussed with their wives whether or not they should be shot if the enemy prevailed. Henry Mayhew, who was otherwise quite liberal in his views said, "Literally every woman who yields to her passions is a prostitute." However, Mayhew was writing in the middle of the nineteenth century. By the 1880s changes in sexual mores were being felt and seen. Annie Besant was even able to publish her scandalous book on birth control. In our own day, Serafina's consistent attitude about not being touched by an accepted lover would seem incredible. But in 1885, Mr. Acton's notion's about female sexuality still held sway, as did a slightly less absolute version of Henry Mayhew's dictum. So the type of sexual control Serafina demanded from Miles was common and accepted, though, it often concealed many different kinds of sexual secrets, ranging from frigidity to homosexuality. Miles' right to rebel against his cousin's tyranny rested on the fact that Serafina refused to make a definite engagement to marry him. Once married, Serafina knew that her wifely duty would oblige her to let Miles "have his way with her."

Chapter 7

A NEW FORM OF MAGIC

...the chemist has only to persevere in a systematic exploration among the infinite number of chemical substances, in order finally to meet with success; but Daguerre could not à priori be furnished with such positive knowledge; hence our admiration at his success...

—John Towler
The Silver Sunbeam, 1864

Serafina was surprised but not upset when no letter of apology came from Miles the following day. She was deeply gratified by receiving a reply to the letter she had sent to Mrs. Butler, and wrote to her idol again. Julia said nothing, but felt deeply pained by any misunderstanding which might alienate their cousin from the family. Julia knew that she could not write to him unless Serafina gave her leave to do so. No one was surprised that Miles did not come for dinner that night, but the three women were very dull at table with each other. Julia, who was ordinarily far less moody than Serafina, looked positively morose, and provided none of the usual news of the activities at her office. Mrs. Winstanley had nothing to say, except that she was feeling better and was nearly recovered from the mysterious attack she had suffered during the reading of the *Maiden Tribute* newspaper article. Even Serafina was muted. When two more days passed in a similar manner, Julia took it upon herself to speak to her sister. She approached Serafina in the same room where the lovers' quarrel had occurred.

Julia could hear the scratching of Serafina's pen from the hall.

"Serafina, may I interrupt you for a moment?"

"As soon as I finish this paragraph." More scratching. "What is it, Julia? You look in low spirits."

"I am in low spirits, Serafina. Miles has not been to see us for four days. Your quarrel must have been a serious one."

"Oh, not really. I just think he is being stubborn. He's probably waiting for me to write, which I shan't do."

"But Serafina, one of you has to make it up."

"He will have to do it, then."

"Don't you care for him at all?"

"Of course I do, my little mouse, but he must know that he can't take liberties with me."

"But how shall you feel if he does not write? What then?"

"Oh, Julia, don't take it all so much to heart. He left the house without speaking to me or saying goodbye. I shall not reward such behaviour by writing first. He is probably thinking of me day and night. He will fly back here at the first plausible excuse."

But Miles was not thinking of his cousin at all. An altogether different subject was occupying him.

The morning after his quarrel with Serafina, Egbert, Miles' servant, had just delivered a steaming cup of *café au lait* and a brioche when the two men heard the bell ringing in Egbert's snuggery on the ground floor.

"Are you at home, sir?" Egbert asked, glancing at Miles' dressing gown and slippers. He was a lean, silent, colourless man with an air of suppression about him, as if he were continually in danger of not acting like a servant. Yet, he had never been anything other than punctilious regarding his duties, and had been with Miles since his college days.

"It is hard to imagine..." Miles said reaching over to consult his watch which lay on the table in front of his chaise. The bell rang again.

"They are persistent and the tone of the ring has an imperative sound. My curiosity overwhelms my usual lassitude and bids me to be at home. It might even be a client, though they usually write first."

"Very good, sir. Even if it is a lady?" he asked, casting a final disapproving glance at the dressing gown and slippers.

"Especially, if it is a lady," he replied, thinking particularly of Serafina and his exit from her home. He still believed that she had been very provoking in ignoring him and persisting with her letter, but he also felt that his behaviour had also been bad. If he didn't want Serafina to behave like a spoiled child, he must set her an example. Though she pretended to have the mind of a man she was, after all, a woman, a young and spoiled woman. He should have sat very coolly as she wrote then, when she was finished, chided her with a pointed remark on her manners and taken his leave in a quiet polished fashion. He listened to the two sets of footsteps on the stairs as they drew closer to the landing, and prepared himself to say what should have been said the night before. Then the door opened and Egbert said, "Miss Katherine Green, sir."

The surprise was an agreeable one. Except as a fleeting image in a dream, he had not thought of the girl at all since the meeting in Victoria Park. Instead of having to excuse himself and remonstrate with Serafina, he could now have the pleasure of showing Katherine the photographic equipment and instructing her in its use.

He rose as Katherine was shown into his apartment and held out his hand to her, greeting her as a complete equal, remembering that Katherine had shaken hands with him at their last meeting. In the tempest that the suffragists and other new women had stirred out of their teacups, it was not always clear how they expected men to greet them, especially if there was an inequality of rank.

"I fear I have surprised you, sir," Katherine said looking at Miles undressed hair, dressing gown and slippers.

"Hardly that, Miss Green. The peal of the bell could not escape notice. I am delighted that you have taken me at my word and decided to use my studio."

"Tea, sir?" Egbert asked as he was closing the door.

"Yes, thank you. And an extra cup."

"Do please sit down, Miss Green."

There was something about seeing her indoors which made the girl seem even smaller and more delicate than he remembered. She removed her hat and held it on her lap. She reminded him of a well-made doll with a fine china head. Though her skin was darker than some girls', the darkness of her eyes and tightly braided black hair made it seem very white. There was a perfect rose coloured circle on each cheek which he felt certain was not paint, and he remarked how slender were her wrists as she sat down and crossed them on her knees. The way she balanced herself on the very edge of the chair made him think of something very delicate, placed carefully on a shelf. He had the fleeting fancy of picking her up and putting her in his pocket.

"Should you like to see the glass room and the dark room? Or shall we have our tea?" he asked.

"I should like to see the photographic rooms if it is convenient. But it was not my only purpose in coming here."

"It wasn't?"

"Mr. Hickinbotham, I was very touched by your kindness to me the night we met and the friendly way you greeted me at the park. I believe I mentioned your sister."

"You did, but I did not tell you that I have tried your method of trying to find her. The result was an encounter with an entirely fraudulent medium."

"Oh," her mouth in uttering the syllable formed itself into another perfect circle, making her seem more doll-like than ever. Her expression combined surprise and sorrow. There was a delicacy in her face and body which would appeal strongly to any man. Her small, well-formed chin and large black eyes were particularly fetching. Her voice was high pitched and soft, a voice that could almost be a child's voice yet, was not. She seemed so young and vulnerable, especially compared to Serafina's definitive deportment. He could not seriously take her to task for bringing up a painful subject.

"I am so sorry, sir. I had no idea."

"Of course not. But we shall speak of it no more. Would you like to see the glass room?"

"Yes," she said almost reluctantly. "But first I must tell you, Mr. Hickinbotham—she paused and almost seemed to be holding her breath before blurting out— your sister wants you to know that she will make a determined effort to speak with you. I—I thought she might have even appeared to you yesterday."

Miles flushed and was about to speak angrily when Katherine cut him off.

"I am compelled to tell you this sir, because—because she wished it. Did you not have some sign of her yesterday?"

Miles felt a strange tickling sensation around his neck just before he thought of the painting he had just started.

"If I get messages for someone," she said. " I must communicate them. I must do it even at the risk of provoking anger."

"It's all right," he said recalling the strong sense of presence he had had when he started the painting. He dropped into a brown study and the girl looked away without speaking. For the second time, he felt the strange sense of time slowing down, until it stopped. It was akin to the feeling he got when he was painting, but it was different. He was not focused on one thing, as when working. It was more like being keenly aware of all things, as if his mind were hovering on the brink of a kind of omniscience.

"You feel it again, don't you?" Her voice moved in a liquid medium, drifting toward him in a single long strand of motion which he saw rather than heard.

He nodded, and everything began to speed up, growing faster and faster, until he felt himself again.

"How do you do that?" he asked.

"I don't know. It is the way my visions usually begin."

"You did not hypnotize me?"

"Not deliberately. But maybe we are already in some kind of hypnotic rapport."

"You grow too mysterious for me, Miss Green. Are you a hypnotist or not?"

"I know something of it," she said.

"But you didn't hypnotize me?"

"No sir, I would never do that unbidden."

"I am glad to know it. But there was a kind of appearance here, yesterday. In a much more mundane fashion. Come, and I'll show you." He stood up and led the way into his painting studio.

"Oh, what wonderful scents," Katherine said as they crossed into the painting studio.

"You like them? I didn't think anyone but a painter could like the smell of mineral spirits and paint. Certainly not a young women. My cousins can't abide the odours in my studio. They rarely come here because of the smell."

"It is not the scent itself that I like, but my inner vision is sometimes affected by scents or colours. My physical senses can at times help me to see clairvoyantly. I see the energy and vitality that the paint draws out of you."

"You are too mystical by half, Miss Green," Miles murmured as he led the girl through the painting studio and the dark room and operating room, finally entering the glass room. The north light was very bright but diffuse. The sky outside was clear. Everything in the room was brilliantly and evenly lit.

"Oh, the light here is wonderful," the girl exclaimed. "I have had little opportunity to work in a glass room since—since I stopped studying. The friend who was teaching me keeps his own glass room constantly in use."

"Well, as you see, this room is not in use. Please come and use it in the mornings, when I shall be engaged in painting in the outer studio."

"I should be able to take formal portraits, here," she said, casting glances around the room. "So much equipment and so many backgrounds. And how cunningly the shutters are hinged to offer a multitude of lighting possibilities. It is much finer than what I am used to. How good you are to allow me to work here, sir."

"I should be glad to feel that the room is being used," Miles replied.

He walked across the room, picked up the canvas of Amelia and placed it on a hook fastened in the south wall. He always kept works in progress in the glass room and hung them in the full north light to view them. The girl looked at the painting very quietly and, once again, Miles felt that strange impression that time was slowing down.

"It gives me a very strong feeling of her," Katherine said, "though I can see it is only just begun."

"Yes," Miles said, "I have high hopes for it. But that is enough about me and my work. Let me acquaint you with my equipment, though from what I saw at the park, you seem quite accomplished."

"Your camera is beautiful."

"It is made in America by Gannet. The lens design is especially good for portraits as you shall see. It has a very nice fall off at the edges, and you can take multiple portraits on a single five by seven inch plate."

"Would you sit for me if I prepare a plate?" she asked. "Do you have some extra glass?"

"Oh, yes. I've got four or five pieces cut. I should like to see you prepare your plate. That way, I can show you the other rooms."

The two enthusiasts adjourned to the operating room where, under Miles' critical eye, Katherine prepared the collodion plate she would use. By today's standards, making such a plate was a messy and tiresome operation. Collodion is a solution of a substance very much resembling gun-cotton dissolved in ether and alcohol. The photographer began with a clean piece of glass of the appropriate size for the camera, and then used the collodion solution to bond powdered nitrate of silver to the glass. When exposed to light in the camera, the silver nitrate crystals became silver on the glass and formed a negative of the image. Like modern photography, the excess crystals had to be washed away and the silver chemically fixed on the plate. If the plate were used while still wet, it was more sensitive but very difficult to handle. This now commonplace chemistry was a new kind of magic in the late Victorian age, even to photographic practitioners themselves.

Katherine had already mentioned that she preferred the wet collodion process when in the studio, though in the park she had been using a dry plate. Miles watched the girl expertly mix and handle the materials, evenly coating the glass. She was neat-handed and obviously competent. He would have no concern about having her work with his equipment. The room was well ventilated so there was little danger from the ether fumes, which could be very explosive when concentrated in an enclosed space. Ordinarily, a photographer would prepare a number of plates but Katherine only made one.

"Do you not want to make several?" Miles asked, as he slipped the glass plate, into the plate holder which would be placed in the camera.

"No. I shall just take one picture of you. I had not actually expected to be able to work today. It is very kind of you to take your valuable time to help me."

"I don't think you need my help, Miss Green. But I had to make certain before I gave you command of my studio and equipment."

"Of course. Are we ready?"

"Yes. Mind your eyes when we come out. I forgot to pull the shutters over the window. After this darkened room, it will be blinding."

Miles sat on the chaise. He was still wearing his dressing gown, which the girl commented on as soon as she looked through the camera.

"If it is not too much of a liberty to ask, would you mind, sir, putting on your jacket and tie?"

"Not at all," but he thought her request another indication of her forwardness in matters relating to photography. "I should have thought of it. I shall return shortly."

Katherine looked around the magnificent glass room

and hugged herself with sheer delight. "How fortunate I am. If I could find Susan, I should have everything I want." Then she thought of Miles' beautiful face and added softly, "Almost everything." she whispered to herself. She pulled the dark cloth at the back of the camera over her head and looked through the ground glass. She experimented some with moving the gate in the interior of the camera. It controlled the placement and number of images that could be made on the plate. The she carried the camera closer to where Miles would sit. She wanted to photograph his full seated figure and exclude anything else. The blank wall behind the chair would do nicely as a background for dark trousers and jacket.

"Ah, you are ready," Miles said when he returned, now fully dressed.

"Yes, sir. I think I understand the mechanical devices. But please sit down so I can frame you. I don't think you'll need the head stand with the light in here. And I think I shall adjust these shutters." She stepped to the large shutters on the window and used them to redirect the light. When she looked through the camera, Miles right side had been darkened.

"Better to use it anyway," he said. "I wouldn't want to be responsible for ruining your photograph. I hope the plate is not too dry."

He got up and pulled over an odd looking device mounted on a tripod stand. A thumb screw on the iron base allowed adjustment of a vertical shaft at whose end was a padded metal support to go at the back of a subject's head. In poor light requiring long poses, such a device was essential, in the glass room on that morning, it probably was not needed.

"A little more to the left, if you please, sir," Katherine said from beneath the cloth. "Yes. That's perfect. It is very bright in here."

"And you'll find the lens quite fast," he said. "How curious to be on this side of the camera."

The two enthusiasts were enjoying themselves.

"I hope I don't ruin it. Conditions are usually so much darker than this. And the lens I've been using is very slow."

"You'll be all right, I am certain. F16, I should think."

"Yes, be still. Hold the pose, please."

She lifted the dark slide and then removed the lens cover for a moment. Then she slid the dark slide down, removed the covered plate holder from the camera and began walking toward the dark room.

As she worked in the dark room with Miles at her side, Katherine did not really expect a good result. "His face is so lovely, she thought, it would be a shame to spoil it by some photographic error."

"I'm sure it won't come out properly," she said. Everything she was using was unfamiliar. She didn't know the lens, or how old the chemicals were. Actually, Miles had just mixed them that morning.

"And I'm sure you are quite wrong. I couldn't have done better myself."

Both heads were close together over the tray which held the plate's final bath.

"Good heavens," Miles exclaimed as he saw what remained on the plate. Out of the darkened, swirling liquid of the bath something totally unexpected began to emerge: a large luminous patch just off to one side of Miles.

"I was afraid it would come wrong. It's because..." Katherine said.

"But look at this light area," Miles interrupted her. "It isn't a mistake or an accident, Miss Green. Don't you see how much it resembles my own painting of Amelia? You have taken a spirit photograph! Something which I believed couldn't exist—and you've done it in my own studio. It is extraordinary. Do you not see the small figure to my left? That is my missing sister, Amelia, standing next to me. It is the only photograph ever taken of her! And it has been taken when she is not physically present. Astonishing. Incredible. If I had not been here I should not have believed it."

"Oh, no. It cannot be. It is just a fault in the plate. I am sure."

Miles took the plate from her. "We'll print a positive of

this on some albumen paper and then look at it in the full light. That will settle the question. But I know it is a perfect likeness of Amelia." He walked to a cabinet against one wall. "Now, I shall sensitize it, so stand still since you don't know the room, Miss Green."

After what seemed a long period of total darkness Miles spoke again, "All right, Miss Green, I've got the plate and paper in the holder. I'm going to open the shutter. Prepare yourself for intense light."

With the clank of an iron lever, the shutters covering the skylight in the dark room were thrown open. After a few moments all was once again dark as Miles moved the paper from one bath to the next. Finally, he opened a small shutter which covered a window with amber glass in it. Then he removed the paper from the holder.

"I told you," he said. "It's a remarkable spirit photograph of my sister, Miss Green."

She bent over the print and drew back like one stung. "Please don't call it a spirit photograph. Photographers have been attacked and criticized for such claims. In America, people called Mr. Mumler a fraud."

"But this is obviously no fraud. Please don't alarm yourself, Miss Green. If it unsettles you so, of course I shall say nothing publicly."

"To anyone, sir. Any statement regarding the spirit world spreads quickly. Promise me you'll say nothing."

Soon, the photographers were examining a clear print in the full light of day.

"Extraordinary," Mile said. "I can see her face here as clearly as I did in my own mind's eye yesterday when I was painting. It really is a remarkable achievement, Miss Green. I must confess, I have been a sceptic about spiritualism and about such photographs. But you are extraordinary..."

"I did nothing, sir. It is your little sister who wanted to make herself known to you."

"But you are the medium, Miss Green. The one who has made her visible. And it's as clear as day. Much clearer than the prints William Crookes took of Miss Cook's manifestations."

"But you will not speak about it to anyone?"

"I shall only tell my two cousins. My immediate family. They must see this photograph."

"But please ask them to be discreet."

"Of course, Miss Green. We shall all respect your feelings in this matter. I promise. I wish to buy this print from you and the plate as well. We have no pictures of Amelia. This is the only one. I know my Aunt and cousins will each want prints."

"I could not take money from you, Mr. Hickinbotham. I used your equipment and facilities to make the picture. It is yours by right."

"Absolutely not. I insist that you be paid."

"But..."

"I will brook no denial. You must be paid." He reached into his pocket and pulled out two ten pound notes and put them in her hand.

"I have never had such payment, Mr. Hickenbotham. It is many month's wages for me, far too much."

"Not a penny less," he said. "And I should like to have more sittings with you, Miss Green."

"I should prefer not to, sir. If I may say so without seeming ungrateful. I have delivered the spirit's message. If she wishes to speak to you, she will. I do not wish to be a medium under any conditions."

"I am sorry you feel that way, Miss Green. My sister's loss affected the entire family and this is the first sign we have ever had from her. I wish you would pursue this with me when it has started so well."

"I really cannot, sir. If you wish me not to come here any more, I understand. I..."

"No. No. Of course you may use the studio. I am not such an ogre as that. Though you do suprise and disappoint me."

"For that I do apologize, but I cannot be other than I am."

Miles watched as she picked up her battered hat and mended gloves and tied on her old floridly patterned shawl. All her things seemed too large on her. She looked like a child wearing an older sister's clothing. There was something very winsome and appealing about her, but she certainly needed new clothes, he thought. She was tiny but she had a fetching little figure. Her shoes were cracked and missing buttons. She was almost ragged enough to be one of the flower girls from Covent Garden, who were so poor that when they could not sell enough violets, they would sell themselves.

The pair passed through the apartment to the door and out to the stairs.

"May I please come next week?" she asked, thrusting out her little chin like a defiant child who feared a negative answer.

"I told you, Miss Green. You are welcome any morning. I think you are a most able photographer and I am glad to help you pursue your art."

"You are very generous, sir," she said giving her broken hat one final adjustment before starting down the stairs.

"What a curious little slip of a girl," Miles thought as he watched her descend, "She looks as if a strong wind would knock her down, is as poor as a church mouse, yet has a good opinion of herself— and lets one know that she dances to her own drummer and none other. She won't be brow beaten into doing something she doesn't like. Not by me, even in my own studio. But she is a remarkable medium and I have a photograph to prove it. Her competence in the dark room was impressive. She would always play down her abilities. She would always say less rather than more about herself."

There was something oddly attractive about her, though she no longer looked the same to Miles as she had when they met. Now, he was more aware of that spacious quiet which seemed to emanate from her at times. It was this quality which had made him first notice her on the street. In spite of her elfin appearance, he told himself, she could be tough as saddle leather, and probably would have been more than a match for the fellow who had approached her at Piccadilly. The thought of her strength made his pulse race.

He re-entered the apartment and picked up the print. He

felt obliged to bring it to Cavendish Square at once, yet, he was
not certain he wanted to tell his cousins or Aunt about Katherine's visit. It would invariably lead to the discovery of his meeting with her, prior to Victoria Park. At the very least, his cousins
would certainly find fault with him for his lie of omission. He
also felt that Katherine was not a woman who would quietly tolerate rivals, even a rival who was her social better. If he spoke of
Katherine to his cousins, there was a chance they would meet. If
the women met, the option of having some other kind of relationship with Katherine would be ended. After her visit, he was
reluctant to give up such a possibility, though he was hardly clear
about his motives when he wrote to Serafina saying, "Have been
working hard. Will bring family surprise next week. Miles."

Chapter 8

A DANGEROUS EXPLOIT

"Picture to yourselves, fathers and mothers, what that state of degradation must be to which the men of a country have sunk who can require and take a vile advantage of the forcible subjection by money-grasping traders of terrified little girls to the service of the brutal lusts of male animals, men sunk in vice, diseased, cynical, worn out, old enough often to be these children's fathers or grandfathers."

—Alfred Dyer
The European Slave Trade in English Girls

In spite of her discipline and habits of self-abnegation, or perhaps because of them, Miles' praise went straight to Katherine's head. To be lauded by such a beautiful, elegant young man gave her hope and energy that lifted her out of the narrow lanes of Whitechapel. He admired her in a very genteel way, she knew and it quite turned her head. If one such as he could believe in her, anything might be possible, even finding Susan. The one carking thought that followed her home from Miles' studio was his mention of spirit photography. It resonated with the painful events of her past and recalled to mind incidents she wanted to forget.

"I shall keep my attention focused on my happiness," she

told herself. "I shall turn my back on the past and I shall find Susan."

She said this to herself in a special decided manner that today would be called a "post-hypnotic suggestion." This form of inner speech was one of the mental disciplines she had learned in India and with it she could pacify even physical pain. Under the influence of her own fixed purpose, she turned her steps toward the river and the ugly neighbourhood of the Bowen Refuge. In spite of the proximity of the chinaman's den and the grisly things she had seen there, she felt no fear, now. She had blocked it out, shut it off as one would snuff a flame. She walked up and down the street, looking carefully at the old warehouse building. After nearly half an hour she could see that there was only one point of entry she might try, a tiny window at the bottom of the building. Looking over her shoulder, she tried to lift the sash, but found it latched inside. Dave could break it for her, if he would. The big man felt badly about the loss of Susan, for he knew how much she meant to Katherine. He and Katherine had formed a very special bond: she had used her mesmeric skills to re-enliven his memories of his dead wife, making her seem, at times, actually present, once again. He was fully aware that his wife was no longer alive but when Katherine magnetized him, the past became the present and his memories were, as it seemed to him, magically brought into his mind with a vividness that made them seem real.

The eighteen eighties was a time of intense experimentation with mesmerism, which in 1843 James Braid re-named, "hypnosis." All the extraordinary phenomena it could produce was avidly studied: clairvoyance, telepathy, anesthesia— a host of extraordinary powers. Learning about hypnosis, from the great jailer and photographer of madwomen, Charcot, Freud and Breuer used hypnosis to treat their own madwomen, the famous Anna O, among others. From their questionable but well-publicized experiments with hysteria, Freud and Breuer formed the basis of much of twentieth century psychology. But while the muddy depths of this "main stream" were growing deeper and murkier, there were other less known but more wholesome uses of hypnosis taking place in the 1880s. While Freud was analyzing and hypothesizing, Pierre Janet was curing afflicted people with post-hypnotic suggestions. Hypnosis was also popular in theatrical performances with stage hypnotists like Dr. Flint and his daughter, Marina, who became international celebrities. Mesmerism and hypnosis was "in the air" during the 1880s.

But Katherine had learned her arts in a unique school. Her knowledge came to her by way of a native step father who had worked in the Indian hospital run by James Esdaile, a scottish doctor who performed thousands of painless surgical operations using hypnosis in the time just before chloroform and ether. She had practiced what she learned while making money for her family as she performed in the cantonments of northern India. She had become what was called a "somnambulist" and "magnetic healer." She would enter trance states and give clairvoyant readings on health, the future and most often, on what was happening, "at home," the only word anglo-indians ever used when they referred to England. With our present biases of the physical sciences we might interpret Katherine's activities as that of a "quack" but nothing could be farther from the truth. These same modern biases have led to nearly universal ignorance of the work of the most respected psychologist of the early twentieth century, F.W.H. Myers, because he believed, on well-reasoned, experimental grounds, that human personality survived death. His notions of the "subliminal" self prefigured many theorists of Duke University's famous ESP laboratory. Katherine had few theoretical ideas about what she did, but she could treat many kinds of ills very effectively with her skills.

As she walked home from the Bowens' she thought, "I must get into that building and see if there is any sign of Susan. I cannot let her be taken and do nothing if there is the least chance of helping her."

So instead of returning to her own room, she went directly to Dave's tiny chambers on Flower and Dean Street and told him what she wanted him to do.

"I don't know, lassie. It could be dangerous for you, going into such a place. If they are bad people, you might be at risk. I would go in for you but it doesn't sound like I could fit."

"You're right, Dave. But please, just get me into the building. I can't do it without you. The window must be jemmied and I don't have the strength and skill to do it. And this may be my only chance to find Susan. If she is at the Bowens' and leaves, I may never find her. That's what the salvationists told me."

"I understand your fears and it's not for myself that I worry. It's you, lassie. You're a handsome girl and if these people are supplying the bad houses across the water, they might take you as well as your friend. I don't know if I could live with myself if that happened."

"And I can't live with myself without trying to help Susan—if there is even the remotest chance. If you won't help me, I shall just knock on the door and ask to be sent to France with her."

"Oh, no, lass. You don't know what you're saying. Those poor girls live terrible lives over there, locked up in bad houses that are like prisons—with locks on the door and bars on the window."

"I know. I've heard these things, too. That's why I have to try to help Susan."

"You're too innocent to know what you're risking."

"Dave, please. I must try. I love Susan. My arms ache to hold her."

The big man got up and poked at the fire. He was clearly upset. "It's hard for me to refuse you anything, lassie. But I think you're wrong to go."

He poked at the fire ruminatively, the coals illuminating his fleshy face. Katherine could read his moods very well and knew that she must wait until he had absorbed the idea. After what seemed like an eternity to Katherine, he spoke, " We'll have to try late at night. We'll go after midnight. But I'm going to wait outside for you. If you don't come out in half an hour I'll break down the door. Better to be taken by the police than by people like these."

"I'm sure you are right about that," she answered thinking of the dreadful buckets at the chinaman's. She had not told Dave about returning to the chinaman's and what she had seen there. "I'll go home and eat" she said, "and come back on the stroke of twelve."

She went back to Thrawl Street, put on the oldest of the two fustian dresses she had. She made some tea and ate a stale crust of bread. By the time she returned to Dave's the weather seemed to be cooperating with their plans: a heavy fog filled the lanes and alleys, and it would be even thicker near the water. It was one of those London nights of late summer that prefigures the wet and cold of fall.

"I am sorry to take you out on a night like this, Dave," she said when he came to the door.

"I'll be all right, lass. It's you I'm worried about."

"Do you have a jemmy?" she asked as they turned away from his door and started down Flower and Dean Street.

For an answer, the big man patted the breast pocket of his coat.

"I'm very grateful, Dave. I couldn't do this without you."

"As long as we come home together safe and sound, I don't mind."

"Yes, with Susan."

"I hope so."

By the time they reached Cable Street, neither could see two feet ahead; the few street lamps were muffled by the fog and gave off as much light as a flickering candle. The pair crept around the old warehouse building as silently as they could, each creaking board magnified in their minds to the sound of crashing dust bins.

"It's over here," Katherine said, kneeling down on the ground. In the utter darkness, she put her knee in a mud puddle. The only sounds were lapping of the nearby river and the creaking of the old quays.

Dave ran his hands around the window, for in the total darkness it was invisible. After a few moments he reached into his coat and pulled out the jemmy. He slipped it between the sash and frame and there was a cracking sound which seemed to

Katherine as loud as cannon fire. They were both quiet and still, waiting to see if anyone had heard. Then she heard the window being raised as Dave lifted it for her.

"I'll wait here and if you don't come out soon, I'll go around to the front door and wake the dead."

"I understand," the girl whispered, as she put one leg through the window, trying to spread her heavy skirt between the rough wood and her skin. The sound of crunching glass was heard as she put her foot down on the cellar floor of the building.

Curiously, it was lighter when she pulled her head through the opening. Somewhere in the murky distance of a seemingly endless passage was a light. She was grateful for it but also realized that it meant there were people about even down in the cellar. No one would leave a lit lantern burning by itself. She could hear distant noises, and thought perhaps they were footsteps but couldn't be certain. Smells of damp rotting wood mixed with creosote and another chemical smell that was unfamiliar to her. The light seemed to grow brighter as she advanced but it was still so dim that she could hardly tell if she imagined the increasing luminance. She began to see that there was an end to the passage up ahead. She approached what looked like some kind of junction of passages and some large shadows. She tried to be absolutely quiet. Dirty as it was, she got down on her hands and knees to creep forward toward the junction. Suddenly, a powerful arm snaked around her waist and seized her in an unbreakable grip. The hood of a dark lantern was pulled back and she was nearly blinded with the light. Then a huge, hard hand was clapped over her mouth and she got a much strong sense of the chemical odour as a rag doused in chloroform was held across her face. After a brief, futile struggle Katherine went limp.

When she returned to self-awareness, she was lying on cold stone. She was in a strange, tangled heap of little girls lying all around in a strange unnatural sleep. Their eyes were closed but there were unnaturally still and sleeping like tangled puppies. Something was wrong with them.

"Drugged" Katherine thought as she crawled over to the

children. There were seven or eight of them with arms and legs akimbo. All beautiful and utterly unconscious. Their little chests rose and fell, so she knew they were still alive. How could she save them all? And what had happened to the poor creature whose hand she had seen at the chinaman's. Were these lovely children doomed, too? As she looked over at the children, she also realized that she no longer had her clothes on but was wearing some kind of loose shift, like a kind of nightgown. She was cold and there was a weak tallow candle which had nearly burnt out and was guttering. She had a terrible headache. Then, she heard footsteps approaching. There was no time to reflect. All she could do was run out the door and into the passage. She ran in the direction away from the approaching footsteps and found herself at the bottom of an ancient set of stairs. All she could do was to start climbing. She had no idea where they led, she only knew she had to get away from the footsteps which she heard somewhere behind her. She did not feel the splinters in her bare feet from the old wood, nor was she even aware of her own terror as she raced upwards for what seemed like many flights. Finally, there was a faint yellow light in the shaft which contained the stairs. The sounds of other feet on the old wood were gaining on her. She thought her heart would burst as she grabbed the sash of the window and threw it upward. Far below her, she saw the oily water of the river. Heavy footfalls were right on her heels. There was no choice but to jump. She pushed herself away from the building to try to make certain she landed in the water. An eternity of falling followed and she felt the rushing air against her naked skin as the shift she wore billowed up around her head and blocked her view. This was followed by a shock of cold as the river closed over her and she found herself clawing her way to the surface for air. She could not remember exactly what happened next but then she saw that Dave had wrapped her in his coat and was carrying her in his arms as he ran down the street. She fainted again and woke up sometime later in her own bed. Dave was sitting on a crate near her.

"Thank God you're awake, lass. I was beginning to be afraid that your adventure had been too much even for your brave little heart."

As soon as she heard the words, she immediately fell asleep again. When next she woke, there was a bowl of steaming chowder next to her bed. Dave sat on the floor, his back to the wall, watching her.

She sat up suddenly. "Oh, Dave, the children. There was a pile of drugged children in that building. They were younger than Susan. Seven, eight and nine. It was horrible. Oh, what can we do?"

"I doubt we can do anything, lass. Those children are bought and paid for by rich degenerate men over the sea. The Bowens are protected by the law, which is same as saying, by wealth. Their 'refuge' is the perfect place to trap such innocents. You would only be a housebreaker and you can be sure the children you saw are already gone from the place."

"It was horrible, Dave. Like a litter of puppies piled on top of each other on the cold, hard floor. I think they had been given something. They gave me some, too, but I woke up. It had a terrible smell."

"Thank the Almighty you got out alive, lassie. More than one young girl has met her end in that foul place."

"I'm sure you are right," Katherine said. "But to be so young and doomed. I know there are worlds other than this one. There have to be...Oh, that smells good, Dave," she said leaning over the chowder. She started to sit up before she realized she was naked. Oh! Dave, get my dressing gown from the cupboard, please."

After she was dressed and had eaten Dave looked at her sternly and said, "You'll go there no more, lassie. Promise me. You'll have to find Susan some other way. Any way, if they collect children so young perhaps they wouldn't want her in any case."

"A terrible consolation, Dave," she answered thinking of the dreadful bucket and the unknown, once living child who had made up the stew. For some reason, that child had not been wanted. "I promise I won't go there again," and she shivered as she drank her hot soup.

Chapter 9

AMELIA

Miles spent the following week making an intensive study of the photograph Katherine had taken. It showed him sitting on the chaise, looking stiff and uncomfortable while the child stood off to one side, her face and body transparent, fainter than the rest of the picture. She was wearing a blouse which he actually remembered from the nursery. A rose outlined in small beads was stitched on the front of the yoke. In spite of the transparency, all the child's features were well-defined and visible. He made many drawings of Amelia's face from the photograph and used what he learned to add detail to his painted portrait of her. Looking at the photograph also began to enliven his memories of childhood, the time before he started boarding away from home. The shy smile on the child's oval face, which had been captured in the photograph, was an expression he well remembered. She had often looked at him that way when she asked him to tie her hair ribbons or button her shoes. Father was often from home on business and Miles quickly became for the little girl, the male presence in their house. As he looked at the photograph, he recalled more details about his sister, quotidian things: how she had liked him to put brown sugar on her oatmeal, how she liked the winter season, the icicles hanging off the steeply sloping roof, the smell of the Christmas tree and the baking gingerbread men, and how they had lain down in the snow and made angels in the park when nurse wasn't watching. For the first time in years, he remembered the many long hours they had spent together, alone in the nursery. Their nurse, a dried up, middle aged scottish woman named Ross, had no real interest in either child and left them alone except at meal times. Fortunately, Miles loved to read and draw and developed some of those same tastes in Amelia. The little girl had adored him for the pains he had taken to read and explain Walter Scott's romances, and she, he now realized, had developed his taste for feminine company. Occasionally, they went to their cousins' house to visit, but there was something about these visits which, remembered even now, however dimly, inexplicably made Miles feel anxious and unhappy. It wasn't long after he had gotten a tutor and began to study seriously that Amelia was abducted.

A short time after Amelia's disappearance, Miles found himself at St. Swithins, the well known preparatory school not far from the western edge of the great gloomy heath of Exmoor where, as Miles remembered, the sky was usually gray and weeping, the wind keening through the low hills, calling to mind a female mourner behind her veil. From that time to the day Katherine took the photograph, memories of Amelia had been embedded in vague shadowy, recollections of his home. All the colourful details had been lost. There was only a sense of unease and feelings of loneliness in the large, high-ceilinged and drafty rooms of his home. He could not attribute these emotions to any particular thing. All things from this early time seemed swathed in an indefinite sense of dread. Then came Amelia's disappearance and the later accident which claimed the rest of his family. The pall of these dark times had buried the happiness of the earliest years with his little sister and playmate. He had entirely forgotten reading *Ivanhoe* to Amelia as they sat before the nursery fire, explaining who the Saxons were, while he toasted bread for her on sticks. Katherine's photograph had won all this back for him. He felt he had recovered a part of himself. He had always scoffed at the idea of spirit photography, even when he had been willing to investigate other kinds of mediumship. Now, he had no doubt about the reality of such images, and he felt indebted to Katherine. He was eager to see her and express his gratitude.

It was over a week before she came back to the studio. In the interim, he did not go to Cavendish Square. He wanted to finish the painting, remain isolated and under the spell of the photograph. He also got a terse, irritating note from Serafina which read, "People are beginning to notice your absence. It is quite absurd to pout this way, especially for a grown man. I trust we shall see you shortly."

The note affected Miles like a bucket of cold water thrown in his face. For the first time in memory, he could think of Serafina with a degree of detachment. It cemented his intention not to visit before the painting was finished. He thought her just as lovely and desirable as ever, but he also felt unwilling to let her continue as a spoiled child who had no awareness of her own selfishness. He felt determined that their relationship had to resume on a new footing where she paid some greater deference to his needs and desires. He could support himself without her settlement, not as sumptuously as he would like, perhaps, but his pride would not allow him to bend to purely pecuniary considerations. Serafina must realize that she had been in the wrong. She would no longer be allowed to proceed in her usual high-handed fashion with him. She must realize that after marriage, she would have to yield to him in the most elemental way. If she could not make some small concessions in that direction now, what sort of marriage would they have? He was not at all clear about what those concessions should be, but she must at least begin to treat him with the respect and interest which a young woman owed her future husband. Julia understood these things instinctively, and even a woman as disadvantaged as Katherine behaved with a delicate kind of submission when they were together. It was a matter of taste and feminine decorum, not politics. A woman could vote and read and think, but in the end, she must submit to her husband's rule. Julia was as independent as any woman could be yet, she had a kind of tender deference toward him even when they disagreed. Miles' unwillingness to continue to be Serafina's "tame fellow," as he had once described it to Julia, might have told him something about himself, had he been paying attention. But there were many things on his mind. It never occurred to him that he had received many similar notes from Serafina that had not produced this effect. He never even considered that his changed attitude to her could have anything to do with Katherine.

He was still mulling over the note and the reflections it had engendered when he heard the distant bell in Egbert's chambers blow. A short time later he heard footsteps and Egbert ushered Katherine into the apartment. Her expression was sad and troubled.

"Miss Green," Miles said getting to his feet. "I've been looking forward to your visit. I wanted to tell you how helpful your photograph has been to me."

She was much better dressed than the last time he had seen her. She wore a new hat trimmed with green ribbons and a simple green dress with flounced shoulders and long sleeves. The costume followed William Morris' fashion dictum that, "The period most worthy of reproduction is the ninth to the fourteenth century costume, perhaps those of 1250 being the most simple and elegant." The lines were easy and natural, not stiff or padded and showed her tiny rounded form to great advantage. It was a style that had been known a few years previously as an "aesthetic dress." Miles thought her very pretty. There was a compactness, a lithe animal muscularity in her small figure that suggested to him a potential for unusual passion. This time, however, he recognized the danger of such a thought as clearly as a flash of summer lightning. It came to him in the words of one of his favourite poets, Sir James Wyatt, who had put a memorable phrase in the mouth of his cousin, Anne Boleyn, with whom he had had a potentially deadly affair, "...and wild for to hold though I seem tame." Katherine seemed tame, but he felt she would be wild to hold, emotionally and physically, and those qualities fired him.

"I am glad that it is useful, Mr. Hickenbotham," she was saying. "But your sister is the one who made it possible."

"Please allow me to say how very handsome you look in that costume, Miss Green. Is it new?"

She blushed very prettily, showing rosy colour under her dusky skin.

"I bought it with some of the money you paid me for the photograph, sir." She did not tell him that her old skirt lay somewhere in the cellars of the Bowen Refuge.

"Excellent. Very tasteful, Miss Green. You have the perceptions of an artist."

She said nothing but the soft, dark glances of her long oval eyes told him that she was pleased with his compliment. He saw again that there was a mystery in her which had a great power of attraction for him. The fact that she was poor and humble prevented him from being really frightened by the fascination she exerted, as he would have been had they been of the same class. The fact that she was abashed by his attention and showed him her feeling was the perfect antidote to Serafina's acerbic note.

"Come into the glass room and let me show you the use I made of your photograph. Tea, Egbert," he added over his shoulder.

"Wait, sir," the girl said placing her hand lightly on the crook of his arm. "There is something I must say, first," her expression darkened once more.

"Yes?"

"I, I realize I should have thought of this sooner, Mr. Hickenbotham, but it has occurred to me that if any of your family should find out that I am coming here on a regular basis, it would almost certainly create the wrong impression."

"It had not occurred to me, Miss Green. I have only my aunt and cousins. They, need not know you come here. They almost never come."

She thought for a moment and then said, "That is almost worse." She looked very ill at ease. Her long, deliciously slender neck bowed submissively. "I don't wish to feel that we are doing something illicit, something that has to be hidden from your family."

Miles was eager to show her his painting and tell her about the memories the photograph had elicited from him. He began to feel impatient with the girl's working class deliberations, but he realized he must treat her qualms seriously or she would be insulted and might leave.

"There really is no one to know or care if you come here, Miss Green. Except myself," he added without thinking.

She looked up at him with eyes so full of surprise and pleasure, he felt her glance like a shot. Part of him knew that his response was another warning, a warning which he again chose to ignore.

"Come into the glass room and see what I have done with your photograph." He took her hand, turned and started to lead her deeper into the apartment toward the glass room. This time, she offered no resistance.

Miles was an intelligent man, but he was not reflective. He did not analyze and look ahead, his temperament was more modeled on Byronic lines. He loved the mythic, the sensuous, the larger than life qualities of the character's of Scott's romances and poets like Baudelaire, Verlaine and Rimbaud. Though somewhat disciplined, feeling and sensation ruled his thinking. Where Serafina could control him with her greater coolness of temper, Katherine had a temperament which, he sensed, was capable of fiery rapture and self-forgetfulness. He told himself he could share that rapture with her in many innocent ways, such as their interest in photography and her untrained but sympathetic interest in art. Yet, he did not let himself look far enough ahead to see that setting alight such sentiments in her would ultimately be ruinous to the girl. Part of him knew that there could be nothing between himself and the poor little match girl. He truly wanted to help her, but he also wanted something detrimental to her. He used the one intention to hide the other from himself so that he would not have to give her up. In other words, he paved the road to that well-known place with the very best and smoothest stones, and there was no one he knew who would have pointed out the downward nature of the road he was taking, except for his very practical cousins, who were the last people in the world he would consult about Katherine.

"It has a wonderful presence," Katherine said when she stood in front of the painting. "I get a very definite feeling about her character."

Inwardly, Miles commented on how well she was able to describe the painting's strongest quality. Her instinct justified spending time with her to try to enhance her understanding.

"And of course," he replied, "that is the essence of good portraiture. It should be more than an external semblance—but thanks to you, it has that as well."

"Then, I think you must have succeeded, though I have never met her."

"I would go even farther and say that when a portrait is really good, it can even have its own soul, apart from the subject. When it feels alive in that way, resemblance is the least important aspect of it."

She said nothing, but he felt that in some way she resisted the thought he had expressed.

He walked to where her own photograph of himself and Amelia hung on the wall. It had been neatly matted and framed in silver.

"I could not have done it without your photograph," he said. "I thought I could paint her from memory, but when I actually began to work, I realized my recollection of her was too vague. Looking at your picture actually brought back memories that had disappeared long ago. In fact, I am quite amazed at how much I had forgotten. The really happy times we had together as children. Thank you."

"It is very kind of you to say that Mr. Hickenbotham. You can't know the value I place on your good opinion of me."

"You and your work deserve that good opinion, Miss Green. It is you, not I, who has brought Amelia back to me. My painting draws most of its vividness from your photograph."

She looked down and there was something about the heaviness of her eyes that almost made him think that streams of hot tears were about to scald her cheeks. Part of him feared such a display, part of him desired it. But the next moment, she looked up and he realized that it was a trick of her physiognomy. It was the shape of her eyes that gave the impression of weight in the eyelids and impending tears when she cast her gaze downward. She was actually smiling when she looked into his face.

"I am so glad," she said, and he could see that her pleasure was also a kind of relief for her, as if she might have expected ill treatment for taking the picture.

"You are gifted," he said.

"I have had many people question my abilities—in the past."

"You make it sound as if you are an elderly woman when you speak of the past."

"It sometimes feels that way. It seems very long ago—in a very distant place."

"You are not speaking now about photography," he said.

"No," she said in a rasping syllable voiced with indrawn breath. It was bitten off so sharply that the word was almost a cry. Her upper teeth did actually bite down on her lower lip.

"Well, if the past is distressing," he said, finally, "why not live in the present?

He felt a little overwhelmed by the sudden force of her pain, a palpable darkness whose tide had swept close enough to touch him. He immediately saw that it was rooted in a feeling of profound separation from others, a feeling he well understood, though, he believed that he had experienced it in an entirely different way than the friendless girl. It made him want to comfort and help her, believing himself the stronger of the two.

"We are alike in our constitutions, he thought. We are both over refined. We both suffer from being too highly strung.

"Would you make another photograph of me?" he asked.

"Does your family think the likeness of your sister is true to the original?"

There was no malign intent in her question, it was not a strategem, yet it suddenly and unexpectedly exposed him. He had not foreseen it, though it was a perfectly natural enquiry. If he said his family had not yet seen the photograph, she would want to know why or, worse, would know that he was hiding his relationship with her. After just experiencing the profound nature of her isolation—rejection as a psychological term belongs to the twentieth century—he could not bring himself to make her feel he was concealing her from his family. He felt too much sympathy for her particular kind of pain, so much like his own. But he certainly could not allow either of them to know that the real reason for his secretiveness was his sexual desire for her, an attraction which was enriched by her woundedness, her ineffable silences and feelings from his own past. If he did acknowledge it, he would have no excuse for allowing it to continue. Like most of us who become fascinated with an inappropriate stranger, Miles was only dimly aware of all the volatile elements in his response to Katherine, and he knew nothing of the lies and secrets of his own family which were acting on him.

"I have not shown it to them yet. I wanted to get it matted and framed and have my own painting ready as well. I wanted you to see them both, first. The finished painting. Obviously you've seen the photograph."

"You are so kind to me, Mr. Hickenbotham. But wouldn't your family be eager to see a likeness, even a poor one, of your sister?"

"I just finished framing the photograph and have yet to frame the painting."

"I could help you do the framing."

"I wouldn't think of it. You came here to do your own work. Use the camera and the dark room. But, if you wouldn't mind using me as a subject again, you could take another photograph of me? Perhaps a profile."

She looked down at her hands and then up into his face.

"I hope, sir, you are not seeking another spirit photograph. The one you have is the only one I have ever taken."

"No. You need a subject and, I am volunteering to sit for you."

"Then I should be very glad to photograph you again. But I would rather try a close up of your face, looking directly into the camera. Most faces are not symmetrical enough to admit of such treatment, but your face is," she paused for a moment, "is very handsome and quite perfectly proportioned."

Though she spoke in a very even tone without a hint of emotion, she could not prevent herself from turning red.

"Take a comfortable position," she said, turning her back, "and I shall move the camera into an appropriate place." There was a pause while she moved the camera and tripod. Then she said, almost speaking to herself, "I don't know why I like photography so much. It is such a sad art."

"Sad?" Miles asked.

"Yes. One photographs a moment, then it is gone forever. Everything in the picture is dead and can never come again. It is like trying to stop the pain of time's passage with a spoon, or some other hopelessly inadequate tool."

"But in photographing me with Amelia, you brought her back. You snatched her from the past and brought back my memories. That is good, not sad."

"She is still gone, yet there is the photograph."

"Which is better than nothing at all."

The girl shurgged as she adjusted the tripod again.

"Perhaps you like feeling melancholy," he said.

"Anyone who loves deeply is bound to feel melancholy."

"And why is that, Miss Green."

"Because we can never hold onto what we love, or even to love itself. It will turn to other passions—even hatred. But there is something even worse about photography. We see each image of ourselves, each separate image, and we immediately realize that our idea of being a permanent soul with a single identity is an illusion. We are really composites of unique beings which time blurs into one entity. It is something I heard often from my *ayah* when I was a child. Of course, she explained it differently. But I have come to it again through photography."

"*Ayah?*"

"My hindu nurse. The woman who took care of me when I was very little."

"Then by your own philosophy, we must be content with our moments and selves frozen in photographs. Those we shall always have. Perhaps that is why you like photography. You have been looking only at the melancholy side, but the camera does allow you to capture something and keep it forever. I have been feeling an intense appreciation of that fact all week as I studied your photograph."

She was quiet for some moments, her eyes gazing downward once more, then suddenly she threw off her mood and gave Miles a quick smile.

"Then I am very glad I took the image. Now, I need to make some more plates.

This time I should like to make several images. So I shall prepare three plates, if that is not too many, Mr. Hickenbotham?"

"Please, feel free to use everything as if it were you're own, Miss Green."

"You are very, very good, sir."

"Let me help you."

"No. I should like to do it all alone, to test myself in the dark room. To see that I can do it on my own."

"Very well," Miles said, watching her leave the room. "What a strange and remarkable girl," he thought. "She is someone who sees the world inside out, as if it were an allegory. She sees what is inside, first, and only if that is interesting does she look at anything else. How very different from Serafina—almost the diametrical opposite."

This new aspect of her character made her seem more ephemeral and more desirable at the same time. He wondered if in possessing her he might also grasp the mystery of those fathomless moments which seemed to emanate from her and take possession of some of the mystery missing from his own paintings. He tried to feel his way around this new complexity of her character, circumambulating the deep silence at her centre for a long time. The next thing he knew, he heard her voice.

"You seem very far away, Mr. Hickenbotham. Are you ready to sit, now?"

"Yes, of course."

"Then place your head back into the headrest," Katherine said as she walked behind the camera, slid in the plate holder and pulled the cloth over her head. She looked at the ground glass for a few moments, pulled the cloth back and walked over to the shutters, adjusting them slightly. She got under the cloth once more and then once more returned to the shutters and adjusted them. She also pulled out a mirror which was attached to a folding rod and threw more light off to one side of Miles face. Finally, she seemed satisfied with what she saw on the ground glass.

"All right, Mr. Hickinbotham," she said coming out from under the cloth. "Please hold your pose. I am about to remove the lens cover."

Another second and the moment had been magically trapped in the darkness of the camera's wooden box.

"Please don't move," she said. "I shall change my position for the next photograph," and she dragged the camera backward. She adjusted the shutters and mirrors and went through a version of the same processes twice, moving the camera each time before removing the lens cover. After the third and final exposure, Miles sprang off the chaise.

"Let us see what we have," he said eagerly.

"Yes," she agreed, her brow furrowed with intense thought.

"So you don't mind if I come into the dark room with you this time?" he asked.

"No," she said, her eyes not seeing him but something which seemed to lie at a great distance.

The first plate, the close up, came out of its final bath and was strangely blotched, a complete failure.

"I can't understand what I did wrong," she said sounding distressed.

"It looks to me as if the silver nitrate was not well-distributed. I have had plates that looked like that."

"I never have before. It is very disappointing."

"You must not stress each failure. We are bound to fail at times. Every photographer does."

"I suppose you are right. I have been fortunate in earlier attempts."

"That's right. Let's see the next one."

The second plate was strangely wrong. It was almost as if a very blurry second picture overlay the image of Miles. It was a man's face but it was impossible to see it clearly. The third plate was the greatest surprise and greatest success of what was now the late afternoon. Miles was scarcely visible. He appeared surrounded with a cloudy darkness, but off to one side of his murky image was a brilliantly clear picture of Amelia. She was not at all transparent against the dark background and her hand was pointing upward to a partial outdoor scene of a street. She looked backward over her shoulder at the camera, as if making certain that her meaning might be understood.

"Astonishing," Miles said. "We must print it."

"No. Wait. Let us see if she will come for another image. I feel it is the time to press on with this. She wants you to know something about her. I feel certain."

"Then, yes. Let's press on. I shall help you make the plates. Do you think four will be enough? That's all the glass I have."

"Then we shall do four. I don't want to waste time getting more glass now," Katherine replied, obviously also feeling the grip of excitement.

They continued working until the light failed, forcing them to quit. They were disappointed to discover on developing all the plates that they had nothing as interesting as the two earlier plates of Amelia.

"Still," Miles said, looking at the two sets of prints they made, "It is a remarkable achievement. Quite extraordinary. I am sorry you are so insistent on secrecy regarding these photographs. They prove quite conclusively the validity of spirit photography. If you exhibited them, it would make the point."

"Perhaps. But I have seen what people do when they are faced with things which cannot be explained. They become frightened and jealous. I do not want to become the target of such emotions."

"I take it you have been such a target, before. In India."

She did not reply , but kept on working until the light

failed.

It was about nine-thirty at night and the last of the summer sun was fading out of the sky, when Miles moved to light the gas in the glass room.

"Oh, no. Leave it. It is beautiful to see the sky fade through this enormous window."

"Very well. Shall you tell me of your experiences in India, then?"

"Should you mind very much if I did not tell you just now? Let me wait a while longer. It is time for me to go home. You must realize that I do still have employment tomorrow. I was late the morning after the last time I worked here with you, and was fined. I really should leave now."

"If you must," he said. "Let me see you home. You leave me memories of an extraordinary day, Miss Green."

She put on her new shawl, hat and gloves. "Thank you, but I know my way and it is early, yet. Thank you so much for sharing your...everything with me," she said giving him her hand on the threshold. Her long, dark eyes were sad, he felt, as they swept over him before she turned away.

Miles stood at the top of the stairs and listened to her retreating footsteps until he heard the outer door open and close. She was gone and he felt an unexpected emptiness. As he stood contemplating the feeling, it grew stronger until he decided that the only sensible thing to do was to turn his back on the mood, which he did.

He entered his studio and walked through to the glass room where the prints had been hung. "What a remarkable girl," he said out loud. He felt very lonely and suddenly resolved to take all the pictures to Cavendish Square and tell the girls all about Katherine. He wanted to have someone to talk to about her and, after all, nothing improper had happened.

He dressed, collected the pictures and rousted Egbert.

"Go out and find a cab for me and bring it back here. Tell the driver to wait at the curb until I come down."

Chapter 10

AMELIA POINTS THE WAY

'The qualifications of an artist are very distinct from those of a mere operator; the former, by reason of his qualifications, can associate with gentlemen and the intelligent; the latter can aspire to no higher companionship than with the ignorant and vulgar"

—John Towler
The Silver Sunbeam, 1864

As Miles had anticipated, a great fuss was made over him and his pictures. He did feel pangs of conscience when he saw Julia's large, dark, hollow looking eyes. The poor girl had obviously been very distraught by his absence.

"She is too attached to me," Miles thought. "We must find her a husband, soon. Preferably before Serafina and I marry."

Serafina, of course, looked much like herself. She greeted him with a kiss on the cheek as if he had dined the night before. The quarrel seemed entirely forgotten, or she feigned complete indifference to it. She looked ravishing in an opulent green and purple silk gown, whose skirt was overlaid with a long drapery of fabric in front. She also wore a tight-fitting jacket with points in the back. Only her tall slender figure could have carried the

144

weight of the draperies and layers of her costume without looking misshapen. Julia was simply dressed in a costume not unlike
the one which Katherine had worn, recalling the simple lines of
a medieval gown, though Julia's costume was made of silk and
Katherine's had been only merino and had not quite fitted her.
Mrs. Winstanley was wreathed in smiles, and said only, "I am so
glad we are all together again, dear Miles."

"What are those packages, Miles?" Julia asked as eagerly
as a child. "They look like pictures."

"They are pictures. Quite remarkable pictures, actually."

"Well, if you say they are remarkable then they must be,"
Julia said.

"Let's see them," Serafina said, throwing herself on the
brown paper wrappings.

"Wait," Miles said. "I must say something first." He did
not want the images to take Mrs. Winstanley unawares. "These
are pictures of my lost sister, Amelia. I felt inspired to paint her
portrait and then something truly astonishing happened. Three
photographs were taken of Amelia, as well."

"How could she have been found?" Mrs. Winstanley
asked looking strangely terrified, "After all these years?"

"No. But I met someone who was able to take spirit photographs of her. According to my memory, they are quite perfect
likenesses of Amelia as a child, around the time of her disappearance."

"And who took these remarkable photographs?" Julia
asked.

"The very girl photographer we saw taking pictures that
day at Victoria Park. Do you remember?"

"Really?" Serafina said. "And how did you find her
again."

"She found me. I had given her my card that day at the
park and told her that since she had no equipment of her own,
she was free to come and use my studio and dark room."

"You said nothing of this, Miles," Serafina said.

"There was nothing to say. I had no idea whether or not
she would even come."

"But she did come," Julia said. "And took these remarkable pictures."

"Yes. That's right."

"Well, let us see them, then," Serafina said.

"I just wanted to warn Aunt May, first," Miles explained.

"Thank you, Miles," the older woman said. "You are a dear boy to think of my feelings, first."

"Well, I am all atwitter with impatience," Julia said. "Since I am now closest to them, I shall open them," and she began tearing off the brown paper wrappings.

"The large one is the portrait I painted," Miles explained, "The others are Miss Green's photographs."

"What a beautiful frame," Julia remarked as the ornate gilt edge appeared through the paper. Without realizing it, Miles had chosen something that was not unlike the frame in the dream he had had about Katherine.

"Oh, yes," Serafina added. "The frame itself is quite beautiful."

"They are old Italian mouldings that I found and had cut down for the canvas."

Julia pulled the painting from the last shreds of paper and held it up for everyone to see.

"Oh," Mrs. Winstanley exclaimed with a catch in her throat. Her face took on a deadly pallor, seeming harder and more frozen than he had ever seen her. But there were certainly no tears. "It's a remarkable likeness, Miles. I don't know how you could remember her so clearly after all this time. Do you have many clear memories from your childhood?"

Julia put the painting down on one of the largest chairs.

"I didn't remember her that clearly," Miles said. "I thought I would, but when I started to paint her, I realized my memory was faulty. I could not have finished it without Katherine, without Miss Green's help. Look at her astonishing photographs." He took hold of the two smaller parcels, removed the wrapping and placed both pictures on the mantle. For some long moments the only sound in the room was that of the paper which Miles had removed and crushed into a ball. The crackling sound of its expansion seemed peculiarly loud to Miles as he waited for his family's reaction.

"They're certainly clear," Julia commented.

"Oh, they are too clear by half," Serafina said. "They must be frauds, Miles. This girl has taken you in."

"She could not have done," Miles said, his face growing red and angry. "They were made with my own equipment, in my own studio. I was present in the dark room when she prepared the plates."

"But..." Serafina began.

"Serafina," Julia broke in, "Mr. Stead has shown me Mr. Boursnell's spirit photographs. Mr. Stead has absolute confidence in the veracity of his pictures. They are perfectly clear. They look like these."

"Perhaps he's a fraud, too," Serafina said shrugging.

"No," Julia said, looking at her sister with some asperity. "Mr. Stead has sent absolute strangers to Mr. Boursnell and the spirit images are always of people whom the sitter knows or has known."

"So are you saying that these pictures prove that Amelia is dead?" Mrs. Winstanley asked her younger daughter.

"No, mama, not necessarily. Sometimes pictures are taken like this of people at a great distance. In America, for instance."

"What is the explanation for this, then, Miles?" Serafina asked.

"I do not have an explanation," Miles said. "All I know is that the girl has been clairvoyant all her life."

"Who are her people?" Julia asked.

"Her father was a native sergeant who acquitted himself with honours at the time of the Mutiny. Of her mother, I know nothing except that she was English. The girl is very poor and works in a match factory."

"So there is no one to vouch for her?" Serafina said.

"Not in the sense you mean, Serafina."

"Well, then, before we accept these as genuine," Serafina said standing before the mantle where the pictures rested. "I think we should give her a test. What did she charge you for taking these pictures?"

"Nothing."

"Nothing?" Serafina said, unable to hide her surprise.

"I paid for the glass, the paper and the chemicals. She used my camera."

"You needn't sound so smug, Miles. I am just trying to get to the truth about your new pet."

"She is not my pet."

"Oh, but I think she is," Serafina replied, smiling just a tiny bit. "And it sounds as if your pet is something of a mongrel. Does she look it? Is her skin dark? I couldn't see all the way across the park."

"That is beside the point, Serafina," Julia said. "I am shocked at your saying such a thing. Her heritage is immaterial. The material point is what test would convince you of her genuineness as a medium?" Her face was flushed, showing her irritation.

"Let her take a picture of me. I am intimate with no one except our father who is dead or distant. We have no pictures of him, either. Let me see who appears in my photograph."

"I can only ask her to take a portrait of you. This sort of thing is not exact. We tried four other plates which didn't come out at all." Miles said.

"Hah," Serafina cried. "You are already making excuses for her."

"Serafina," Julia interjected, "I have spoken with Mr. Stead at some length about spirit photographs. Even Mr. Boursnell often comes up with nothing unusual on the plate. It is no proof of fraud."

"But Mr. Stead is a dyed in the wool spiritualist, is he not? He would be forgiving of any lapses on the part of a spirit photographer."

"No. I don't think that is true," Julia said. "He has exposed a number of fraudulent mediums. He has great respect for Mr. Boursnell."

"If Miss Green does agree to your test, Serafina, you must

promise not to be rude or a doubting Thomas when you meet her in the studio."

"Let her produce the results and I shall not doubt."

But we shall have to pay her as we would any professional photographer. You would have to come to my studio."

"Tell me when," Serafina said. "I shall bear the ghastly stink of your chambers."

"I should like my portrait to be taken, as well," said Julia. "I shall pay the going rate—I shall pay the same as what Mr. Boursnell charges. I shall get his charge from Mr. Stead."

"I shall ask her," Miles said, "when she comes to the studio again."

"And when will that be?" Serafina asked, visibly annoyed by Miles' praise for the match girl.

"I don't know."

"You have no appointment with her? No *rendez-vous?*" Serafina pressed in a mocking tone.

"No. I have only said that I paint in the mornings so that she may use the photographic studio any day before noon."

"Ah, she has the run of your studio. A *carte blanche,*" Serafina said archly.

"And why not, Serafina?" Miles said. She can only come on weekends. The rest of the time she is sweated in a match factory in Bow. Surely, you are not jealous?"

A very quick flush appeared and faded on her cheeks. "Of a mongrel match girl? Of course not."

"But there is still one picture we have not opened," Julia pointed out. "I want to see that one, as well."

"Yes," Miles said glaring at Serafina, "In some ways it is the most remarkable of all. It may even obviate the need for a test."

Miles angrily tore the paper from the last picture and put it on the mantle next to the others. All three women collected around it.

"Do you see that street which Amelia is pointing at?" Miles asked. "Do you see the street number, the number twenty-seven?"

149

"Yes, well," Serafina said, "What is remarkable about that?"

"That is a partial image of Church Street in Chelsea. You can see that the house number is twenty-seven. That is where..."

"...is where Mrs. Jeffries sells women and children to rich gentlemen," Julia finished for him. " I have actually visited the building, from the outside only, of course, when I worked on *The Maiden Tribute* articles. It is by far the most elegant brothel in the city. The stained glass in the entrance way cost upwards of ten-thousand pounds. But Mrs. Jeffries has two other establishments which are even more remarkable. One in Hampstead where corporal punishment is used to spice up the activities of depleted men and one off of King's Road where, I was told, one can pay to take the life of a woman or child. The windows are padded so screams cannot be heard outside."

The next moment, several things happened at once: Mrs. Winstanley turned the colour of chalk and began to faint; Serafina exclaimed, "Julia, how can you relate something like that in front of mother?" Miles reached over to catch the older woman around the waist and gently lowered her into a chair, as Serafina said, "Oh dear, mother. I hope she is not having a relapse. I shall never forgive you, Julia, if she is ill again." Miles rang for Charles, the footman, and sent him upstairs for smelling salts.

After it was established to Julia's satisfaction that her mother was not having a relapse but was merely fatigued, Mrs. Winstanley was taken upstairs by her eldest daughter, leaving Miles and Julia alone in the parlour.

"What do you think, Julia?" Miles asked. "Is she all right?"

"I think so, but I shall write for Dr. Jarvis. I should like him to see her."

"It seems that anything touching on those articles or their subject affects Aunt May very strongly."

"Yes, it is odd," Julia agreed. "But she has always had a curious constitution. She runs the gamut from cloying sentimentality to icy rage and cruelty."

"Rage? Cruelty?" Miles said. "I have never seen her even angry. *Sang froid* is the expression that comes to mind. Always the perfect hostess, mother and wife—even her piano playing sounds like a machine."

There was a long hiatus in the conversation while the pair looked at the photographs on the mantle. Then Julia broke the silence.

"I have particularly wanted to say, sir, that you have been both rude and cruel to your family during the last week. Really, Miles, not one letter. And you and Serafina are almost engaged."

"Almost is the operative word in that statement," Miles answered. "I don't mind telling you that we had a quarrel the last time I was here because she preferred to spend time writing to Mrs. Butler rather than speak with me."

"She told me about your row, but I understood it was not conversation which you desired from her, sir," Julia said raising her eyebrows in a pert manner.

"And what of it? Physical desire is hardly to be considered abnormal, especially when Serafina keeps me in suspense for so many years."

"So you have found this girl to amuse you," Julia said in a bantering tone.

"No. That is not true. You see her work. Is she not talented and worth aiding?"

"Is she handsome or is she not? That, as you like to say, is the material point. You can charm us all, dear Miles, but I shall not let you off without an answer."

Miles did not exactly blush but he was a little more pink as he moved toward the fire and the mantle where the photographs were displayed.

"She is interesting looking," he said without facing Julia.

"Well, to a gentleman the term 'interesting looking' certainly means she is not ugly," Julia goaded. The sharp, questioning expression on her face gave her fine features a provoking pixieish quality.

"No. She is not unattractive. But, as I said, she works as a match girl and wears fustian, or did until I paid her a few pounds for her pictures. Surely you don't accuse me of throwing over Serafina for a match girl?"

"If you did, I don't know what punishment I might inflict on you."

"I may grow old waiting for Serafina, but I certainly wouldn't marry someone like Miss Green."

Anyone seeing the interlocutors would have found their poses singular: Miles appeared to be studying the photographs with his back to Julia while she looked past him out the french doors.

"You had better not," the girl said in a changed tone. "You know perfectly well there is another 'office girl' who has a prior claim on you if you do not marry Serafina."

"Julia..."

"Do not try to charm me, sir," she said as she turned to face him and held up a slender index finger in a gesture of warning. "I know you cannot resist a woman who says she cannot resist you. I expect you to bring Serafina to the altar, soon."

"Tell me how to do it and I shall."

"Not by inviting factory girls to your studio. Serafina has far too much pride to react well to that kind of strategem."

"It is not a strategem. Look at these photographs. Tell me they are not extraordinary. The girl is an artist. That alone gives her a claim on my time and exertions."

"They are remarkable," Julia said turning to the photographs.

"What is remarkable?" Serafina asked as she re-entered the room.

"These photographs," her sister answered.

"They must be frauds," Serafina said, in a decided tone.

"How can they be?" Miles replied. "I was with her every minute she worked on these. And how did she just happen to get the right building in this last picture? I believe it was seeing Amelia again, captured so clearly in these photographs that just now overwhelmed your mother. You know how she used to carry on about the abduction."

"How is mama, Serafina?" Julia asked.

"Oh, she is fine. Miles may be correct about the cause of her faintness. I feel certain she will be fully recovered by morning."

Julia looked at her beautiful sister for a moment with an intent but blank expression that was hard to read. Then she turned back to the photographs.

"You are wrong about these, Serafina," she said. "I feel sure they are genuine. Though I was young, I believe I remember Amelia very well. How could this photographer know what she looked like? There were no plates or pictures ever made of her, except when she was a baby. How could she have done these, except by some combination of clairvoyance and photography?"

Miles looked at her in surprise, but neither adverted to their previous conversation.

"How can you possibly know, Julia? All spiritualist phenomena is questionable, I believe."

"What about the test, then?" Miles asked.

"Yes," Serafina said, "Let us conduct a test. We shall hold our own investigation. And she will have to satisfy, me."

"All right, the next time she comes," Miles said, "I shall write immediately. You can either send back a convenient time, which I shall submit to her, or come to my studio. Remember, she works from eight to seven. She only has light for photographs on week ends."

"I work during office hours as well, Miles," Julia said. "And Serafina has mama and the house to look after."

"Yes, Miles," Serafina observed dryly, "Let us not confound poverty with virtue."

As he walked home that night, Miles knew that Katherine would not like the circumstances in which he had placed her. Everything related to a display of psychic ability was abhorrent to her, and now he had created a situation where she was to be tested by women above her own station. It was not at all what he had intended. He had merely wanted to show his cousins why he had been absent and to make gifts of the photographs and paintings to Aunt May. Even the gifts had not produced a good effect, quite the opposite. He felt certain Katherine would hold herself aloof from the test proposed with the other women. Then, he would have to put up with his cousins' barbed remarks about the girl. Better that than have Katherine, herself, subjected to ridicule, he thought. The strength of his desire to protect her surprised him and he lit a cigar as he walked along and thought of her. There was already a slight chill in the air, Miles noted as he hurried toward his quarters. It had been months since the night he'd first met Katherine at Piccadilly. As he walked, he realized that the talented, orphaned girl had already become a part of his life. She was often in his thoughts, though he'd only seen her four times. He had never worked closely with anyone, except for team sports at college, nor had he been a mentor for anyone before, and the role was one he enjoyed. Except for his cousins and a handful of artists, he had few friends, a fact which he had always put down to the large empty house in which he and his sister had lived as children. As far as he could remember, poetry and art had filled most of his hours before he had returned from college and had interested himself in his cousins. Almost immediately after coming down from Oxford, he had fallen in love with Serafina. From then to the present, her interests and family had occupied him outside the studio.

"I should never have shown them the photographs," he thought to himself, exhaling plumes of smoke into the fog of the damp night as he walked along. "I could have given the painting to Aunt May without showing Katherine's work. I wanted them to see and admire what she had done as well as myself. It didn't seem fair, somehow, to take all of the credit. She is too talented to be ignored. It's not just that she is clairvoyant, she really does understand light, the sine qua non of photographic art. And apparently she has learned most of what she knows without instruction, which makes her accomplishments even more remarkable. My clever cousins must not throw cold water on her achievements. I shall make certain that they don't."

Then he began thinking about the photographs, the last in particular, in which the girl was pointing to the street address. Had Amelia really been taken by some minion to Mrs. Jeffries?

Then, for the first time a chilling thought occurred to him. He felt it go down his spine: Had he, himself, perhaps seen her in the brothel and not even known his own sister—and committed unspeakable crimes with her? As he walked through the dark night a creeping horror and loathing of Mrs. Jeffries glittering establishment overtook him. Of course, anyone who read the papers knew about Mrs. Jeffries activities, and *The Maiden Tribute* articles, though not mentioning her by name, described the trade in which she was a leader. For the first time, Miles really felt the weight of such a possibility. He resolved to visit the Rose Cottage no more unless, and the thought shook him, unless he went to try to identify Amelia and bring her home. He wondered if Katherine had any idea of the significance of the address in the picture? She had said nothing of it and he had not told her. It was absurd on Serafina's part to think the photographs fraudulent. There was no possible way they could be. He had been with Katherine in the darkroom every minute. Nor could Katherine know anything more about Amelia than what he had told her. It was unlikely that she knew the significance of the address. But now, he had his own reasons for wanting to see Katherine tested—though he already felt certain of her authenticity. Of course, he could say nothing to Serafina and Julia about the possibility which now haunted him. If Amelia had ended up on Church Street, Miles might have unknowingly birched his own sister and committed incest.

He arrived at home depressed and out of spirits. There was no point in going to bed. He felt certain he would have trouble sleeping and threw himself down on the chaise in his sitting area. But the strong cup of *café noir* which he had foolishly taken at dinner did not prevent him from falling asleep almost immediately, it simply gave him dreadful dreams which made him finally wake feeling disheveled and exhausted as the morning light filtered into the apartment.

He woke thinking that it was Monday morning and that he would have to wait a whole week before seeing Katherine again. It seemed an interminable length of time to bear the irresolution he now felt. He had to find out if Amelia was at Mrs. Jeffries' establishment.

Chapter 11

CONFESSIONS OF A SYBIL

"I was sitting on December 16, 1868, Lord Adare's rooms in As-
leym Place, London, S.W., with Mr. Home and Lord Adare and
cousin of his. During the sitting, Mr. Home went into a trance, and
in that state was carried out of the window in the room next to where
we were, and was brought in at our window. The distance between
the windows was about seven feet six inches, and there was not the
slightest foothold between them, nor was there more than a twelve
inch projection to each window, which served as a ledge to put flowers
on…The window is about seventy feet from the ground."

—Lord Lindsay

As he bathed and dressed, the one thought that kept running
through Miles' head was the impossibility of not seeing Katherine for a whole week. He felt he must speak with her and
arrange a demonstration for his cousins or, as was likely, have
her refuse to cooperate with Serafina's investigation. Of course,
he would like her to cooperate, but he could not blame her if she
refused. His cousins would certainly disbelieve in her powers if
she did not allow the investigation. But Miles was now more in-

terested in the possibility of discovering Amelia's whereabouts—
knowing with certainty whether or not she was to be found at
Mrs. Jeffries' establishment in Chelsea. The remote possibility
that he might have committed a horrific crime with an unknown
woman who was actually his own lost sister was almost unbear-
able. He lay in bed the night before trying to recall the faces of
the prostitutes he'd seen at Mrs. Jeffries. The dreadful possibility
made him melancholy and he dared not speak of it to anyone.
What was worse, he felt there was an even larger lacuna in his
memory than he'd previously thought; something connected
with Amelia that he needed to remember. As he grappled to
recover this memory, he set out for Katherine's place of employment in Bow.

Miles didn't really care for the noise of the train, but
it was the only practical way to get to Fairfield Road in Bow.
Otherwise he would have to drive all through Whitechapel,
Mile End and only then get out to Bow. A cab for that distance
would not only be expensive, it would be slow and in his current state, he craved speed. Eventually, with the help of the
Metropolitan train, just before noon, he found his way to the
huge match factory way out in the suburbs. The sulphurous smell
of the place hung over the entire district, but once he made his
way inside to where the matches were actually being made, the
fumes burned his nostrils and chest. Before he could reach Katherine at her post near the machines, he was stopped by a dried
up looking man in a baggy uniform who carried a billy club. He
looked like an absurd parody of a policeman, but it was only after
assuring the man that he was there on important personal business was he allowed to enter. The noise and smell was a strange
contrast to his earlier experiences of Katherine.

She started when she looked up and saw Miles smiling
down at her.

"Gracious, sir. What are you doing here? I cannot talk
with you now, sir. No. Not at all. No. Not even for five minutes.
I could lose my employment, sir. Yes, I can come tonight if there
is a special reason, but you must leave now. Please."

She carried on this short conversation without taking

her hands from their tasks, and she was once more in her fustian rags. He felt sorry for her anxiety about losing her place and so left as soon as he arranged a meeting for that evening. Her role at the factory seemed an odd contrast to the way he usually thought of her. Her artistic sensibility seemed at antipodes to the dull repetitive job of running match making machinery day after day.

Knowing that he had many hours before she came, he walked the long distance back to his apartment, arriving late in the afternoon. Even then, he had many idle hours before she came. It was too late to start working. It had started to rain and the light was gone. His mind wasn't quiet enough to paint, in any case. It was a very long day for Miles, roaming back and forth in his rooms, looking out of the glass room. Then, as the shadows of the early fall day were starting to grow long, he decided to send Egbert for more glass which would eventually be needed for plates, even if Katherine did not agree to take more pictures.

"Sooner or later," he thought to himself, "I shall want to take more photographs."

Once the servant was gone, Miles was reduced to reading to keep himself occupied. Suddenly he jumped up to write to his bookseller and ask for copies of D.D. Homes' book about his extraordinary life. Finally, he just wandered through his rooms, noting the changes in the light as the day waned. It was after seven when he, at last, heard the bell.

"Egbert, go out and get Miss Green some sandwiches," he ordered, as he brought the long awaited guest into the apartment.

"Thank you, sir. I am fatigued after standing at the factory all day. Also my late evenings have been occupied as well."

"With what?"

"Trying to find a young friend who has gone missing under very suspicious circumstances."

"Tell me about it."

The girl hung her head for a moment. "I must tell you, sir, before you listen to this sad history that my friend, young as she is, has been for some years a degraded prostitute."

Miles stood up.

Katherine looked up at him, obviously expecting to be dismissed. "Do you want me to go?"

"Of course not. I want to hear whatever you are willing to tell me. Don't forget that I have lost a young sister." This gave him a perfectly natural opening to ask her opinion about Amelia's whereabouts.

"Yes, I remember."

"And do you have any idea about the significance of the address she was pointing at in your picture?"

"No."

"One of Mrs. Jeffries establishments is at that address."

"Oh, dear. So you are very concerned? Do your cousins know?"

"No. I did not tell them. I thought it best."

"Of course. I understand."

Uncertain of how to proceed now Miles suddenly said, "You must find that factory work very dull, Miss Green."

"If one is really concentrating, it is not so bad. The day rushes by. But your visit and my curiosity about it did make it harder to work."

"I am sorry, Miss Green. I had planned to talk to you on the spot."

"They are very strict at Bryant and May. They can have their pick of girls."

"I feel sure that you could do better than a match factory, Miss Green."

"Not as a photographer, sir. I do not have a large enough portfolio of work and I do not have my own studio..."

"Yes, yes, I know all that," he said interrupting her. But if you took more pictures like the ones of Amelia, you could name your price and quickly become known."

"I have a very strong aversion to making money from the practice of anything which could be regarded as mediumship," she said, thrusting out her chin defiantly.

"I gathered that, Miss Green but, why? Your pictures

159

have excited great interest in my family. And you may have even provided an important clue to my sister's whereabouts. Do you have any idea what establishment graces the street that appears in your last photograph of Amelia? One of the most notorious brothels in London. I have been wondering how we could have it searched for, for Amelia. Unfortunately, I'm certain the police would never give us a warrant based on your photograph. Your gift could do a vast deal of good for others and could free you from the drudgery of the match factory. Why do you object so strenuously to mediumship?"

A strange, veiled look came over the girl's eyes. She was seeing something from the past, Miles knew, but what it was, sad or happy, good or ill, he could not tell. After what seemed a long interval of silence, she finally spoke.

"You have been very kind to me, Mr. Hickenbotham. Perhaps you are entitled to know more of my history."

She looked down and once more, Miles had the impression of impending tears. When she looked up, her dark fathomless eyes held him with a mute appeal of some kind. As she held his eyes with her own, he knew that he wanted above all else to spare and protect her.

"No, no," he said breaking the silence. "If it is painful to speak of for you. You must remain quiet. I ardently desire that you should be happy, Miss Green. Discomfiting you is the last thing in the world which I wish to do."

She looked down again and then, to his astonishment she took his hand in hers, which were as hot and dry as those of a fever victim. She lifted his hand to her lips and placed a kiss on the back of his hand.

"I shall trust you entirely, sir. You have opened your door to me and encouraged my meagre talent. I owe you nothing less than complete candour," and again her pained look was so intense, he felt the prick of incipient tears in his own eyes.

"The girl's intensity of emotion is sublime," he thought to himself. "I have never seen its like in anyone. But she seems to regard herself as a criminal of some sort. She cannot be wicked or bad," he thought. "I know the pictures she took here were authentic." Miles watched as her beautiful eyes overflowed with silent tears.

"My dear Miss Green..."

"No, please. Wait. I shall do better. There. There. That is enough." And she looked at him and smiled radiantly with tears still clinging to her long, dark lashes.

Miles was aware of her with a keenness of perception he had never before known. It suddenly seemed that every person he had ever met had appeared in dull neutral colours. Only Katherine was vividly alive. He felt they were connected at the most profound level of his experience. "It is as if I could hear her heart beating. " he thought. Between them he felt a kind of force, an energy that defied analysis. It was beyond mystery. It was like the infinitesimal silent centre of a seed which contained every possibility of his future life. He thought, "Even the stray lock that has fallen onto her shoulder is like a hieroglyph signifying something eternal." And he reached out and twined the lock around her ear, not reflecting that he had just brought eternity to an end.

The next moment, her face blushed with shame.

"Oh, what have I done. I wanted you to think well of me and now you cannot help but think me an immoral woman. No, please do not touch me again. I must collect myself to tell you my story." Her slender throat fought its own contraction and she swallowed with great difficulty.

"Drink some tea," he said.

"Yes, thank you," and she reached over and drank from the now cold cup before her.

Everything about her had suddenly taken on great significance; the slightest change in expression was a portent great as any recorded by Nostradamus. He had no idea what she was about to disclose, only that it would be enormously important to him.

"You have never been to the subcontinent?" she asked.

"No."

"Then I must tell you something about it to make my history intelligible. Its society away from Calcutta and Delhi is narrow and hypocritical to a degree not even imagined here. In upcountry stations, each little clique jealously guards its prerogatives. Even if it is only a matter among the native servants of who gets to eat the master's leftovers. Boredom is the prevailing emotion. The main occupations are writing endless letters home, and endless spiteful gossip. People in trade are beyond the Pale. Soldiers' wives are not permitted to consort with anyone who works for the commercial or civilian side of the government. The civil servants are all keenly away of their rank and its privileges—even if the privilege is as petty as the lining up of servants when they go to fetch household ice from the store. There is little for European women to do except measure themselves against those of their own sharply demarcated rank. The children of European soldiers rarely live to maturity. I don't say these things to excuse myself, but only to give you a context for understanding what happened to me. Half breeds like me..."

"Miss Green," Miles said sharply.

"Very well," she replied. If you prefer another term, the offspring of Anglo Indian marriages are called Eurasians and socially, are the lowest of the low. I was fortunate because I had light skin and people often thought I was European."

"I understand," he said. "You need not make any excuses."

"Wait and see," she replied. "At any rate, the degrees of preferment among civil servants, the elite of India are split into the smallest possible degrees of preference, and rarely does anyone rise except upon the rungs everyone else must climb. Everything is ruled by protocol. Everyone is jealous of everyone else's possessions, wealth, spouses and even prostitutes. But all are exiles and live in constant fear of premature death from disease, snakes, natives and the horrible climate which exudes a devil's spawn of biting, stinging insects. Life expectancy is half of what it is here. Every girl is judged on her looks and compared with every other girl in any given station. Really pretty girls who come out, almost invariably wind up as well situated wives of civil servants. The most fortunate of these will have summer residences in one of the hill stations. The most fortunate among this select group go each year to a residence in Simla, jewel of the hill stations and summer home of the Governor General of India. Simla is where I lived for much of my time in India. It is certainly the place where I became notorious."

"Notorious?"

"Yes. There is no other word."

"Your history amazes me, Miss Green."

"In Simla, pleasure was pursued with great energy when the GG was in residence. There were constant balls, fêtes for the Queen's Birthday and other holidays. As a child I saw all this pleasure around me, but none of it was open to me. I got no bubbling wines or smoked salmon from Scotland. No invitations. I was hardly even noticed. Everyone in Simla knew I was a Eurasian, even if my parents were not present. I should have known my place, but I am a curious little beast..."

"Do not speak of yourself, so, Miss Green. You pain me."

"I am a curious little beast and I determined that I should have my share of the pleasure enjoyed by my betters, whom I saw as vicious and small minded bigots, living off the natives while abusing them. I lived at the back of my mother's little stationary store on the main street of the town, which I now know had been built to look like a poor imitation of an English village. My father died in the Mutiny. My real mother was dead as well. The woman I lived with had been her friend, but she was not mine. She used me mostly as a servant. She used me hard, too, until it began to seem that I might be rather handsome when I was grown. Then she gave me better food and a little more freedom to roam about the village. She was probably planning to sell me to a native brothel when I was old enough. I am told that light-skinned girls bring a premium in those establishments. Anyway, one day she came home with a distinguished looking native man. He had the long drooping mustachios of a cavalry trooper and his hair was worn short. His name was Krishna. He ruled my home and my adopted mother without opposition, and he drew me to him. Perhaps we were drawn to each other because we were both knaves, at heart. But he had been educated in Calcutta and knew our ways. He had read widely from English classics.

He said he'd lived in the GG's house as Khitmutgar, a kind of head butler in an Anglo Indian household. But he had also been a yogi and had known a great Swami, when he was a boy. He could do amazing conjuring tricks. He was a skilled mesmerist and, I believe, a genuine clairvoyant. He was a remarkable man. Old Krishna could do things which would make the greatest mediums of Britain seem like children playing with toys. He could mesmerize anyone in seconds and make them see things which were impossible. He called his art 'the science of miracles.' He showed me a little of what he could do, and I immediately asked him to work some magic so I could have the balls and food and status that I wanted. He laughed.

'To make that spell, little daughter, would require that you work harder than you have ever imagined. Years of toil, day after day.'

'Would the result be sure?' I asked.

'Yes, after a long time, you would be able to have the things you want. Only, you would no longer want them.'

Well, I assumed he was old and mistaken. I burned to have the things I saw around me and I was sick of my step-mother, nor did I want to go to end in a brothel. 'I will do anything to get those things. I shall wait on you, wash your feet, anything,' I told him. I guess he thought I would be a good investment. Old Krishna never did anything that did not benefit himself, or so it seemed to me. At any rate, he began to take pains with me. He made me read any books he could procure, including his own copy of Shakespeare's plays. He drilled me until I could write a good lady's hand. He taught me to meditate and taught me the power of a silent mind. Then, he began to teach me prestidigitation. Once he began teaching me to conjure, I improved by leaps and bounds and in less than a year, I was a skilled little magician. Then, he mesmerized me and taught me about the multiple nature of our souls."

"Good lord, what a tale, Miss Green."

"But it is not a tale. I have never told it to anyone before. But you have been so kind, and I believe you won't hold it against me. Let me hurry to an ending. Within two years, Krishna got me invitations to perform at various *conversaziones*. The mania for supernatural demonstrations was, if anything, even stronger in India than here. I did conjuring and table rapping and the usual tricks and, once in a while, gave a genuine clairvoyant demonstration. My clairvoyant abilities grew and soon I was able to do some quite remarkable things. Like the French, somnambulist, Didier, who came to England in the forties, I was good at remote seeing. Krishna magnetized me and I was often asked to see things back in England for people, and a number of my visions were confirmed by letters from home. After a few years of performing, I began to have what I wanted: Money, servants of my own and even a kind of status in the community. But I wanted more. The bargain I had made with Krishna was that I would pay him almost half my earnings for ten years or until he died, whichever came first. This rankled in me until it grew into a real hatred for the man. In those days, I had a real demon of anger in me. And I fed that demon with greater and greater desires. I grew so angry at Krishna, that I began to think about how to kill him without getting caught."

"Miss Green!" Miles expostulated.

"I know. And it sounds even worse here in London. In the mountains of India and with the intemperance of my heart, the death of an old Hindu did not seem such a great thing. But I shall keep nothing back from you. My thoughts terrified me for one reason. I did and do believe in Karma, the universal law of cause and effect that all in this world live under. I knew that the price for such a crime would be many lifetimes in the lowest hell.

"You are not a Christian, Miss Green?"

"No. That, too, I confess to you. The religions of India agree more closely with my own observations. I cannot reconcile my own meditations with the story of Christ. At any rate, I ran away, so as not to kill the old man who taught me. I began to perform in very remote villages. For my first performance I got a handful of uncooked rice. Eventually, I worked my way down toward Calcutta, whose broad lanes and white palaces drew me like a magnet. I built up a very striking demonstration of hypnotism, fortune telling and messages from the dead..."

165

"Were these genuine phenomena?" Miles asked.

"I shall come to that," she said. "I was talented as a mesmerist and a medium. I became known in Calcutta, and the best homes on the Chowringchee opened their doors to me. No one in Calcutta knew I was a Eurasian and I certainly didn't tell them. I lived, not in the very best society, after all, I was a performer, but close to it—close enough for someone like me who had washed dishes, emptied bed pans and been kicked like a dog for years. But just about the time I had everything I wanted, Krishna's prophecy came true: material things lost all value for me. I knew their hollowness, and the gay broad avenues of Calcutta seemed like false, painted faces. Eventually, I decided to return to Simla. I don't know why I wanted to go back there. I told myself it was because that apart from Delhi, Madras and Calcutta, Simla had audiences who could appreciate my abilities. I knew from experience how bored they were and hungry for novelty. But I think I was motivated by a kind of revenge. Though I no longer cared for wealth and material things, I wanted to succeed and be known in the place where I had grubbed in the dirt as a servant."

"I can certainly understand that, Miss Green. A perfectly natural impulse."

"You just asked me if all the demonstrations I gave were genuine," she went on. "The simple answer is that some were and some were not. That is, when my abilities failed me, which they can for any medium or mesmerist, I resorted to trickery. Krishna taught me how to do conjuring, sleight of hand, the sort of thing that is done by a good stage magician. I became adept at blending tricks and real phenomena. I wanted to see my mother grubbing in the dirt while I plucked pound notes from rich audiences. By this time, I had fine clothes, a few bearers and a beautifully carved Lucknow palanquin in which to ride. I was all of fourteen years old and thought I knew all the secrets of the universe."

"Good lord," you must have been an unnatural child."

"I believe I was. I shall hurry to the end, now. The one thing I feared about returning to Simla was Krishna. He was a real magician. He was a powerful clairvoyant who could often look into the past or future. He never used his clairvoyance for money. Instead, he made little woven purses out of pebbles and grasses and sold them for next to nothing. Of course, he didn't mind living well from what I gave him. He claimed to know about previous incarnations and told me that I had actually been his chela or disciple in an earlier life. I have seen him do remarkable things, and as long as I took his advice, I prospered. If it had not been for my anger and desire for revenge, I would probably have become a wandering ascetic in the hills of northern India. But I looked forward to mesmerizing ladies and gentlemen and making them act like the beasts of the forest. I knew my desires were chains but I could not cast them off. It was my karma. When we first met, Krishna had told me that if he trained me, I would no longer desire money and the power it bestows, and it was true. I was not greedy for money. But the demon of anger and revenge had a firm hold of me and this aspect of my character, he had not foreseen. He could see very far, though. I sometimes wonder if he was human or a spirit who had put on a physical body to instruct me..."

"Do you really believe such things? That spirits can create physical bodies for themselves?"

"Krishna said so. Such things are far beyond me. It would take many lifetimes of devout study to accomplish such a thing."

"What a strange idea" Miles said.

"The outer form of religion doesn't matter to me. All that matters is the quality of the devotee. A good and really devout Buddhist beggar is worth a palace full of Christian Bishops. Does that not make sense to you?"

"In principle, but..." She could feel his disapproval hang in the air.

"Let me get to the end. I performed in Simla and, for a while, prospered. I saw my mother and had the satisfaction of making her beg money from me. Then, one night, I was confronted on stage by a senior civil servant. He was a stupid, fat, middle-aged man but somehow, he saw my sleight of hand tricks and grabbed my wrist at an important point in my demonstration. I dropped the coins I had palmed and was exposed as a fake. After that, everything went wrong. I treated a young woman for hysterical paralysis with mesmerism. She seemed much better, but then she suddenly died and some of her jewelry was missed. Even though I had never been in her room and could not have taken her things, my unsavoury history caught up with me. I was tried and convicted by the Resident in Simla. I was sentenced to work in a kitchen on the Anadaman Islands for five years, a term that certainly would have killed me with the heat and humidity of that dreaded penal colony. Instead, the wife of an Evangelist, a Methodist, interceded for me and sent me back to England. It is only in the last few years that I have ceased being a resident in her house for reclaimed Asian women. Now, you know all my shame," she ended in a voice that was nearly a whisper.

"But it is not all shameful," Miles said. "You are also very wise, I feel. You have great skills and powers. You did what you could in very difficult circumstances."

"Any wisdom I have was taught to me by Krishna or learned by my own suffering. But yes, I have learned some important things."

"What are those important things, Miss Green? I should be very interested to know what you regard as important."

"They will sound very strange to you."

"I am prepared for that. Please speak freely."

"Then, probably the most important principle I've learned is that no human is a single being. A handful of western medical men are just beginning to learn this through the use of hypnosis. There are some French doctors who are leading the way in this work, now. "

"I am familiar with Janet's book, "Double Consciousness," Miles said.

"Yes, he has made a good start, but we have only begun to understand these great issues," she said. "Some day, our idea of humankind and even the world we live in will change utterly."

"How?"

"I cannot pretend to know more than I do but," she continued, "but one of the chief things is already starting—with all this table rapping and so on. We have begun to look inside ourselves for answers. Yet, all this so-called psychical research is absurd. It has missed the most important point."

"And what is that?" he asked.

"A thing can be true and not true at the same time. We think of truth as either-or, Krishna thought of both-and. In the east, a thing can be true and not true at the same time."

"Well, obviously things are different at different times."

"I don't mean that. I have never tried to explain this. But in the Highest Reality, there is no time," the girl said in a quiet, reflective tone. "We all live in a single moment, like tiny creatures in a drop of water. There is only now. When you feel that stillness in me you have described, I believe that is what you are feeling."

"That I cannot understand," Miles said.

"Old Krishna would call it the eternal present."

They both lapsed into silence. Finally, Miles spoke, "I thank you for your candour, Miss Green. It explains many things about you, and it also leads to something I wanted to ask. After your narrative I am reluctant but, I shall ask anyway."

"Wait, first, sir, I must ask something."

"Yes?"

"Shall you permit me to continue working here? Even though I have been judged a thief by the English Resident of Simla?"

"Yes, of course. You were fighting for your life in those days and were a mere child. But, I wish to repay your candour with my own confession." He reached over and took her ungloved hand, which was feverish to his touch. "My feelings for you are not as disinterested as they should be, Miss Green. I do admire you very much..I..think of you often even though I am practically engaged to one of my cousins."

She removed her hand from his and clasped her hands together in her lap. There was a sudden flash of colour in her face and she was obviously deeply embarrassed.

"I..I have known that, sir, for some time. Yet, I thought you good enough to trust myself with you here in your apartment. I truly believe that you would do nothing to dishonour me or our friendship—or endanger your relationship with your cousin."

There was a long pause. Miles tried to reclaim her hand, but she would not allow it. He stood up. "I have not always been so certain of my goodness—with you," he answered, also flushing red.

"But your desire is to be good, sir. And I believe we can both trust to that."

Miles walked away from her to his silver humidor on a small occasional table, took out a cigar and lit it.

"I hope you are right. It is my fixed purpose to be of use to you. I want only to help you, not to hurt."

"I have felt you resist your temptations," she answered. "And I believe your desire to help me. I know you are a good man."

"With all these things having been said, Miss Green, it is easier for me to advert to something I wanted to ask. My family, my cousins and my aunt, have been thrilled and amazed by your photographs. They would all like you to take photographs of them."

"To test me," she said. It was not a question.

"I could lie to you and say it is not a test, but yes, that was the spirit of the thing. I am ashamed to admit it after what you have told me."

"If you can promise me that no one outside your family circle will ever know of it, I shall do it. I shall do it," she continued after a pause, "so that your betrothed can see for herself that there is nothing between us which is dishonourable. For I believe that is what she really wants to know."

"Thank you, Miss Green. Whatever you may believe about yourself, I know you have a kind and loving heart. When shall we have the sittings?"

"The only time I have during daylight hours is Sunday," she said. "Otherwise, I must be at work. You know, too, that I may produce nothing?"

"Yes, of course. Would this Sunday be convenient?"

"I should be happy to spend the day here, making photographs. I shall come early and stay late. I look forward to meeting your cousins—as long as they do not look down on me too much."

"No. They are good women, and—I would not allow them to patronize you."

She put on her hat and walked to the door. Miles opened it for her and watched her start to descend.

"Until Sunday, Miss Green," he called.

She turned to look at him once more and then continued going down.

After the sound of her steps had ended in the opening and closing of the front door, Miles turned back to his apartment. Though he had accomplished his object, he felt dispirited. His mood was melancholy. After the confidences that had been exchanged and the projected sittings with his family, it was impossible that he and Katherine could only be friends. Now more than ever, he felt intimately bound to her. He had never spoken so openly with a woman, not even with Julia. He felt a great sense of loss, and he had still not retrieved any more of his past. Perhaps Katherine could help him with that, as well. And he still had to find some way to find out about the possibility of Amelia's presence at Mrs. Jeffries establishment.

Chapter 12

WHAT A CAMERA COULD SEE DURING THE 19TH CENTURY

"That picture contains in itself a volume of proof of the reality and reliability of spiritual manifestations. I have indubitable evidence that in this instance it is true; and if this is true, may not other similar pictures be bona fide? It also proves the truth of all that Mabel has told me in her communications, as she has sealed the document with her honest and truthful face.

It also proves the immortality of the soul of man, and that that immortality is a blissful one. It also negatives the idea of there being any misery for the soul after it has left this body of clay, in which alone are garnered all the seeds of temptation and sin. Freed from that body, it is a spirit-form, and is free to act itself; and that it will advance in brightness and glory during the endless ages of eternity."

—Moses A. Dow, as quoted in
The Personal Experiences of William H. Mumler in
Spirit-Photography. Written by Himself. (Boston: Colby
and Rich, 1875)

The balance of the week was for Miles a strange fever of impatience and anxiety. The night after he met with Katherine, he went to Cavendish Square for dinner to retail some of what he had learned about her and to tell his Aunt and cousins of their sittings. He might as well have gone the very next morning for, he accomplished little in the studio. He spent his day pacing back and forth through his apartment.

Egbert, like most servants, could read the slightest nuances of his master's behaviour, and concluded that something momentous had happened with the young lady, if lady she could be called. He had glimpsed her making mesmeric passes in the air over the supine body of his master. But, it was not for him to examine his betters too closely. But he, like others of his class, made it a practice to know what forces were acting on his master and to comprehend clearly how those forces might affect his own situation. Not even the editors of Debrett's are more keenly aware of fine distinctions in rank than a house servant. The time had long since passed when a domestic situation offered tenure for life. In the 80s, when so much of society was in flux, Egbert knew, a good situation had to be assiduously studied and guarded. He listened carefully to the cadences of his master's footfalls throughout the day, with the close attention of a physician reading a pulse. He shaved his master with special care that evening and could see it was hard for Miles to sit still. Though Egbert knew he had brushed his master's frock coat scrupulously, Miles found fault with it. After Miles' departure and before settling down to drink some of the best brandy in the house and enjoy a really outstanding cheroot from Burma, Egbert reflected that his master was clearly nervous about seeing the young ladies that evening. Since no author in his or her right mind would contest the personal evaluation of a man by his servant, we will try to describe what was disturbing Miles when he set out for Cavendish Square on foot.

The primary concern which occupied him as he walked through the damp fog, was that he had feelings for Katherine that were clearly inappropriate and potentially scandalous. He worried that they might be observed by his cousins, particularly Julia, whose feelings for him made her very sensitive to his moods and thoughts. Because of the social distance between herself and Katherine, Serafina would hardly take seriously any such attachment and would only react badly if a *liason* became publicly known. Then, and only then, would it reflect adversely on her own position as undisputed mistress of her cousin's heart. In short, Katherine's social position, or lack of position, placed her beneath Serafina's notice. Katherine's personal attractions might provoke some feelings of competition and hostility on Serafina's part when the two women met. But Serafina's appearance was much more statuesque, and she had the blonde and cream colouring for which English girls are still famous everywhere. Katherine's dusky skin would make her much less a rival in Serafina's mind. As he walked to Cavendish Square, Miles examined these emotional nuances of his amours as closely as Egbert had listened to his master's footsteps.

The next matter upon which he ruminated was more creditable to him: he was concerned that Serafina would make some hostile and ignorant remarks about Katherine's photographs. He had no idea how Katherine would react to such illtreatment. That she was sensitive about such things, there could be no doubt. Serafina had a gift for sarcasm when she chose to exercise it, and Miles had a horror of seeing Katherine cut up by the other woman. Julia would side with Katherine, at least as far as authenticity went, but that might make Serafina even more antagonistic. Aunt May, he knew would say little.

What Miles did not allow himself to realize was that his greatest anxiety lay in seeing the three young women together, comparing one to the others and finding Katherine the most desirable. What would he do if he found himself seriously in love with Katherine instead of Serafina? He could not marry her. No. That, thank heavens was impossible. Still, he knew he was now in a somewhat false position with both women, even though he had told Katherine most of the truth about his feelings for her. He could never make such a revelation to Serafina. Her pride would end their relationship the instant he confessed, and Serafina was too much a part of his life to lose. The history of their relationship was unique and not replaceable by any other. The bonds of quotidian things are the strongest. This remains true to some extent in our own time, but in the 1880s the difficulty and stigma of divorce, and the legal and financial aspects of relations between men and women added tremendous strength to the links of habit and familiarity that are forged in even the dullest marriage. Miles and Serafina were far from such interpersonal staleness.

When Serafina removed her chemise at night and admired her statuesque, athletic body in the glass, she often imagined how Miles would react once he was admitted to her most personal mysteries. She would be granting him something very special, for which he would be grateful. This was her notion of marital sex. Giving birth was an unthinkable eventuality. She would resort to a good midwife to find out how to prevent it. She did not imagine her own feelings in the throes of physical passion, because for her, pleasure lay in her partner's admiration, not in her own responses to him. If Serafina were alive today, she might well have her bedroom lined with mirrors. As it was, she made do with a single large cheval glass which pivoted in its frame to show nearly all her figure. What she liked best about her own beauty was the power it bestowed, a power not to be found even among those of high rank. Wealth and personal beauty created today's aristocrats, she often told herself before the glass, though she was secretly jealous of aristocratic women who were both handsome and rich. Fortunately for Serafina's self-regard there were few woman who rode on Rotten Row who could turn as many heads as she did. One of her chief reasons for finally choosing Miles as a companion was that, like herself, he was strikingly good looking. Miles had good manners, sound ideas and ability. Most important, she was completely certain of his affections. They were both clever and educated, and Miles had the mysterious gift of creating beauty, a gift that was increasingly patronized by those who wanted emblems of their own quality. Her own interest in art was merely for the sake of being accomplished. It wouldn't do for her to devote herself to it in a serious way. Not when there was so much more that needed to be done for the social good of women, especially working women. Serafina kept conflicting ideas and principles in strictly separate mental compartments. She was a snob and a Socialist, a profligate spender on her own clothing and yet a critic of the foolishness of Fashion. She would give large sums to a pictur-esque beggar and keep her servants poor, and the next moment complain about the way working women were sweated by east end clothing makers. Yet, she was neither frivolous nor stu-pid. She would face mounted police and water cannons for her causes. Her character was simply a good example of the divisibil-ity of human self awareness, or in common parlance, 'one hand not knowing what the other was doing.'

Miles was eager to speak about Katherine and the sittings she had offered the Winstanleys. He liked thinking about the girl, and wanted to do all he could to gain acceptance for her by his family members, but he had to do it without appearing at-tached to her.

"Why shouldn't we all be friends?" he muttered to him-self as he waited for Rossiter to answer his knock. Under the circumstances, it was a question that could only have been posed by a man under thirty who wanted to hide his feelings from him-self.

He had given considerable thought to the problem of how to present Katherine's history to his relatives, and he really did his best. But he was not a quarter of the way through her story before Aunt May said, "Miles, are you certain this girl is quite safe, I mean, respectable? She sounds as if she has lived the life of an itinerant circus performer."

"Yes, I know her history is quite strange," Miles agreed, "But she has lovely manners and there is nothing uncouth about her, I assure you, Aunt May."

"But can she be relied upon, Miles?" Serafina asked. "More than ever I think her pictures likely to be frauds. The more I hear of her, the more likely she seems to be a skilled fraud."

"I thought that is why you were testing her, Serafina. See what comes up in your own photographs. Have you had any further reasons to find fault with these pictures since I saw you last?"

"I have not, Miles," Mrs. Winstanley said. "And I feel certain that I have the clearest memory of Amelia."

"And you are quite satisfied with the resemblance in these photographs?" he asked.

"Oh, yes. Certainly."

Miles looked over his aunt's head to Serafina with an expression that said, "There, what more do you want?"

"But they are rather odd looking, Miles," Serafina said. "I mean, the little girl looks as if she might have been added to the picture of you."

"I tell you, that is absolutely impossible. I was there every moment, at every stage of the processing and printing. There is no way in which the girl could have defrauded me."

"I think, Serafina," Julia said, "That you object to the idea of spirit photographs as a species, not to the girl. And I tell you that I have seen many such photographs. There is even talk of having a public exhibition of Mr. Boursnell's work."

"But he is known. He deals with respectable people and has a studio on Fleet Street. It is the girl I object to. Why do we not go to Mr. Boursnell? This girl's antecedents are shrouded in mystery and crime. An Asian half-breed who lives in a lodging house and who, by her own admission, was found guilty of theft."

"But the whole idea was to prove her ability or catch her out," Miles said a little too warmly. "And she is not asking for any money."

"To my mind," Serafina replied, "that is also very odd."

"Not at all. I told her how you had received her work— that you were doubtful —and she suggested the test without compensation, so she would have nothing to gain by it. I think it shows that she is honest and wants us to see that these pic- tures of Amelia are real. She has nothing to gain from publicity through us or our friends. She has asked me repeatedly to show the photographs to no one," Miles added.

"You would give any of Mrs. Butler's fallen women the benefit of the doubt," Julia said to her sister. "This unfortunate girl deserves at least that much. As far as we know, she is no prostitute and our sittings are only day after tomorrow."

"Not only is she not a prostitute," Miles said, "she is almost a prude. She was concerned what you would think if she came to my studio to work unchaperoned."

"Well at least she knows what appearances are supposed to be, even if she does not observe them," Serafina quipped.

"Serafina, please don't be witty at this girl's expense," Julia remonstrated. "She sounds as if she has had a hard life. I am interested in trying to find out objectively if Mrs. Jeffries did have anything to do with Amelia's disappearance," Julia said. "That would give this entire episode a real value. We might even trace her."

"That seems unlikely after all these years," Serafina said.

"I admit, it is unlikely" Julia answered.

"Then let us allow the photographs to speak for themselves," Miles suggested. "I only ask that no one attack the girl without good cause."

"Of course, she may not get any results," Julia said. "Mr. Boursnell often gets no unusual phenomena except bright spots of light on his plates which otherwise only show the physical subject. I think we should let it rest until after we have seen the plates on Sunday. If we are going to go through with this, let us give this poor girl the benefit of believing she is honest."

And that is how the matter was left until they all met at Miles' studio on Sunday, after the sisters had accompanied Mrs. Winstanley to matins.

Miles was glad that Katherine arrived very early. It gave her time to do a review of the mechanism of the camera back, set up materials in the dark room to her own liking and, most important of all, arrange the shutters, backdrop and seating in the glass room. The sunlight that morning was intense, a brilliant yellow fall light. It had been slightly more than a year since they had met at Piccadilly and it was early in the fall of 1886. There had been a storm the night before and most of London's bad air had been blown out to sea, for a little while at

least. Miles brought in a maid of all work to help Egbert clean
the apartment, for the manservant could become petulant if his
master asked him to dust and sweep too much. Miles wanted his
servant to wait on his guests with all the poise and aplomb of
which he was capable. He even arranged with Fortnum&Masons
to send over a huge basket of delicious prepared foods and
champagne, so that all would be perfect. By twelve-thirty, Miles'
shabby bachelor quarters had been transformed into a dining
hall with a buffet of delicacies fit for royalty, a fact attested to by
the Royal Warrants granted to the Piccadilly caterer.

When Katherine emerged from the dark room into the
living quarters, she was overwhelmed by his preparations.

"Mr. Hickenbotham, you are making too much out of
this meeting. It frightens me. The food will be superior to the
photographs."

"You must learn, Miss Green, when one meets with
paying customers, one must impress them with quality and
professionalism in all things. Sometimes the quality of the
refreshments will be more important than the quality of the
photographs."

"If this is what is required, I shall never have sufficient
capital."

"It isn't required," he said standing close to her as he admired her artistic gown, But I wanted everything to be as perfect
as you are," and he chucked her under the chin as one might a
child. It was a gesture that was inappropriate but not indecent
between two people of such differing social stations. But Katherine blushed deeply.

"If you touch me in such a familiar way in front of your
family, sir, they will think I am your harlot. And though we are
alone now and I know it is a jest, if the habit is formed..."

"I might do it in front of them. Yes, of course. You are
right. I apologize."

He was standing very close to her as he spoke. He added
in a softer tone, "I shall confess to you, and only you, though,
that it is deucedly hard not to touch you," and he punctuated his
statement by running his index finger down her cheek.

She looked up at him and this time there really were unshed tears clinging to her eyelashes.

"Sir, you have done, are doing, so much for me. But surely you realize I must never come here again if you speak to me in that way. I have lived a rough life for a woman, I know, but I have not done anything to deserve other than respectful treatment from a man. If you are to be my friend..."

"...I must, of course, give you that respect. Yes, yes," he said, turning away from her abruptly. "How could it be otherwise?" he said in an aside to himself. His brow was contracted and his lips wore a pout. He looked like a hurt little boy.

She took two quick steps toward him, one hand extended as if to comfort him, and was frozen by the ringing of the bell. He looked at her, catching her in the frozen attitude of tender remonstrance.

"Then, you do care for me?" he asked.

"Sir, do not make me answer that question with your family on the threshold. Else, how should I face them?"

"Yes, yes. But you will stay—afterward. You won't leave with them?"

"If you wish it," she said, looking down from his face. "Now, please, go and answer the door."

Footsteps could now be heard on the last flight of stairs. Their proximity put an end to further conversation and Miles moved toward the door.

A moment later the *frou frou* of silk skirts and crinolines swept into the apartment along with the scent of rosewater, partially overpowered by other, stronger perfumes. His cousins and aunt had arrived.

As Egbert took the wraps and carried them away, Miles reflected that even in the height of their elegance, his cousins did not entirely eclipse Katherine's fine-boned, exotic beauty.

"Oh, Miles," Aunt May said, "how can you live in such a place with so many stairs."

"I must, Aunt May. For the light."

"Oh, yes. How tiresome to have an occupation which forces you to live in a garret."

"I should hardly call it a garret, Aunt May, but allow me to introduce you to Miss Katherine Green. Mrs. May Winstanley, my aunt, Miss Katherine Green.

Katherine dropped a very pretty curtsey that was not too deep or obsequious.

"And this is Miss Serafina Winstanley and her sister Miss Julia Winstanley."

"How do you do?" Katherine asked extending her hand to each of the other young ladies in turn.

"Tolerably well," Serafina replied, somewhat distantly.

"Your photographs are superb, Miss Green. I couldn't be in a higher state of anticipation," Julia said giving the other girl's hand a firm and decidedly masculine shake. Miles was struck by the fact that there was some resemblance, at least as to type, between the two dark-haired finely-made women.

"I hope I can live up to your expectations Miss Winstanley."

"Of course you shall," Julia said, smiling.

Miles noted Julia's encouragement of the other girl, and was very glad of it.

"Miles," Julia said, turning to look around the sitting room. "I am going to have one of your poisonous little Italian cigars. I can't smoke them at home but here..."

"I wish you wouldn't, Julia," her mother remonstrated. "It is not a ladylike habit."

"Mother, you know perfectly well that neither of your daughters are ladylike women, in your terms. Though, Serafina, at least, does do a tolerable impersonation of a lady," was Julia's pert retort as she walked to the table with the humidor, picked up a cigar and expertly judged its freshness by rolling it between thumb and forefinger. As she lit it, her mother said, "Julia that is a shocking gesture."

"It may be shocking, mother but not all men are as fastidious about fresh tobacco as Miles, and I hate a stale cigar. Oh," she exclaimed as she caught sight of the buffet, "look at the food!" and puffed out a huge cloud of blue smoke. "Perhaps we shall just eat. Reverend Hardcastle bored me into a state of utter starvation. Look, Serafina, Fortnum & Masons. Your favourite Scottish salmon. And French champers, too! How delightful you are as a host, Miles. If I had known, I should have come sooner."

"Julia eats like an infantry regiment," Serafina said to Katherine, in an easy, confiding manner "but she never gets any larger than she is now. It is most unfair, isn't it mama?"

"It is because I work hard. I don't just move across the drawing room from one ravishing pose to another. I run all over London each day of the week," Julia retorted.

Rather than listen to the reply, Miles noted that Serafina's light tone with Katherine boded well for the social success of the afternoon.

"Don't start eating, yet, Julia," Miles called to his cousin as she scooped up some black caviar and dropped it onto a little piece of cold toast.

"But it's all fresh, now," the girl said.

"It's on ice, you glutton," Serafina said. "It will be just as fresh after we have our sittings. And mama will not be dozing."

"I am not an old lady, Serafina," Mrs. Winstanley protested. " I don't doze over my lunch."

"Perhaps, though, it would be better to walk through to the glass room. Through here, please," Miles called out waiting for the women at the entrance to the passage. Katherine was the last to pass him.

"They are delightful, sir. Such lovely manners. So elegant, but so unspoiled and natural."

"Everyone is behaving splendidly. I agree," he said, surreptitiously taking the girl's hand and giving it a squeeze.

"Everyone but you, sir," she said, removing her hand from his. "I want them to think well of me, also," and she walked by him into the passage.

"Who is going to sit, first?" Katherine asked the ladies as she stepped into the glass room.

"Mother?" Serafina asked.

"No, you go, first."

"Very well. I'm glad to see, Miles that you've replaced your cheval glass with something better. Did you see the old one?" Serafina abruptly asked Katherine.

"No, Miss Winstanley, I never had occasion to look in it."

"I have not had that old thing for ages, Serafina," Miles said, reflecting that her question could have been a way of finding out how long Katherine had been coming to the studio. "In any case, I should have replaced it before today. I know your standards, my dear."

Along one end of the room, Miles and Egbert had placed an old settee where one could sit while waiting to be photographed. Katherine had taken command of the glass room and indicated the seat.

"Please do sit down, ladies," she said. " I'm afraid I am inexperienced enough to require quiet while I work. Miss Winstanley, this is where I should like you to sit."

Miles watched Katherine with interest. He was impressed with her manner of handling the other women. She was polite but firm. Even Serafina met her instructions with full compliance. The sittings went off without any difficulty. When all three of the Winstanleys had been photographed several times, Katherine gathered up the plates and excused herself from the others.

"We said nothing to her about spirits," Mrs. Winstanley said.

"I believe they shall appear or not depending on their own desires. Miss Green's comments would have little effect."

"Miles," Serafina said, "you must have albums, something to look at for clients, do you not? I should prefer to follow Miss Green into the dark room, but since I know I would be in the way, and my petticoats could do real damage in there, at least get me something to read."

"Excuse me, all of you," Miles said. "Shall we have tea in the other room?"

"Oh, yes," Julia said, immediately. "Let us have some of that jolly food you have out there."

Everyone got up and filed out of the glass room.

As Miles had hoped, the dainties in the basket from Fortnum's occupied everyone so that it was some time before Julia enquired how much longer it would take before the first print came out of the dark room.

"It should be very soon," Miles said.

"Is she a quick study, then, Miles?" Serafina asked.

"Oh, yes. She has used my dark room before."

"Many times?"

"Only once."

"I am surprised that you let her work by herself."

"She is very neat handed," Miles answered.

"Then you are quite sure she will not make an explosion with the ether?" Serafina asked.

"Do you think I would expose you all to danger?"

"I hope your assessment is an accurate one, sir," Serafina said and turned to pick up the latest number of Punch. For some time, the only sounds in the apartment were of eating and pages turning.

Finally, Katherine reappeared.

"Are you done?" Julia asked.

"The prints must dry, but the plates look all right except for one."

"Whose?" Serafina asked.

"I'm afraid it is yours, Miss Winstanley. There is a large black spot on the plate which shouldn't be there. I do apologize."

Serafina was too well bred to flaunt her triumph, but she couldn't help allowing some expression of pleasure on her face.

"I suppose that the art takes a very long time to master," she said to Katherine, somewhat less condescendingly than she might have done.

"I am going to see if the print might be dry enough to bring it out in its drying frame," Katherine said in a very even, business-like tone.

Miles was impressed with the girl's *sang froid*.

Once Katherine was gone, Serafina turned to Miles, "She is quite new to the art, is she not, Miles?"

"Not so new, Serafina. Let us see the print before we pass judgment."

They had not long to wait. Katherine came out with a

wooden frame which held the print.

"It is not as bad as I thought," she said coming to Serafina's side and holding out the frame.

Everyone crowded around the print.

"There's the spot, down near her feet," Mrs. Winstanley said.

"It is not a spot all, mother," Julia said. "It is a large black dog. Can't you see?"

"I do believe you are right, Julia," Serafina said. "Good heavens, it is old Jewel. Remember, Julia, our favourite friend from the nursery? Oh, gracious. It really is Jewel. His face is quite unmistakable."

"Black animals are extremely difficult to photograph," Miles said. "But there seems to be a strange kind of fluorescence around him, a glow."

"It is very ghostly," Julia said.

"But actually to see old Jewel again after all these years," Serafina said with a catch in her throat. "I said I didn't know anyone other than father who had passed on, but I had utterly forgotten about Jewel."

"It does really look like him," Julia said. "Remember how you used to call him, 'Fat Nose' when you were angry with him, Serafina? Look at how fat his nose is here," she said pointing to the print."

"You're right, Julia. I was a perfect beast to him at times."

"So then, Serafina," Miles said, "You pronounce this photograph a success?"

"I have to. The camera has seen something that I myself had forgotten. You have an astonishing, an extraordinary gift, Miss Green."

"You are very kind, Miss Winstanley."

"Look, Julia," Serafina went on, pointing to the print. "It is as though he was lying right at my feet, just as he used to do."

"I remember, Serafina," Julia replied, watching her sister's preternaturally shining eyes.

"I'm afraid there is nothing on the other plates. They are just pictures of the sitters." Katherine said.

"One such photograph in a session is a great deal," Julia said. "Mr. Stead has told me that Mr. Boursnell sometimes goes for days without capturing any unusual phenomenon."

"I am certain that is true," Serafina said, unable to take her eyes off the picture of her old playmate. "I cannot get over Jewel's appearance. It is just as though he were lying there waiting for me to take him out into the garden as I used to do. And to think I had been so unkind as to forget him, altogether. Do you believe he was actually present at the moment you took this photograph, Miss Green."

For the first time that day, Katherine looked suddenly nonplussed. All her poise deserted her in an instant. She blushed and said softly, "I—I was able to see him at your feet, Miss Winstanley. I thought perhaps you saw him, too."

"You really are genuine," Serafina said, a tone of awe in her voice. "I have always doubted the spiritualists. But after this...I cannot." She propped the print up on the table where she could look at it.

"You always were the skeptic, Serafina," Julia said.

"Yes, I know. How extraordinary. It does alter everything, somehow."

"Saul on the road to Damascus," Mrs. Winstanley murmured.

"You are right, Mother," Serafina said. "I am a convert. You have made a convert of me, Miss Green," and she took both of Katherine's hands in her own. "You make me astonished at myself."

Serafina looked back at the print, regarded it closely and turned back to Katherine.

"Miss Green, will you please hold a seance for us? Just for us, please?" she tugged on both of Katherine's hands like an imploring child. "Miles has told us of your distaste for public display. Will you do it for us—no— for me?"

The girl glanced uneasily at Miles, but Serafina saw the appeal for his counsel.

"No, Miss Green, I do not care what Miles thinks, nor should you. I am asking you for myself, and I shall pay you well."

"No, no," Katherine suddenly cried shrinking away from Serafina. "No money, I beg. You will think I am false if I take money from you. If you could condescend to think of me as a friend, I should be happy to do it for you out of friendship, Miss Winstanley."

"When?" Serafina asked.

"Next Sunday. Every other day I am at the factory."

"Excellent," Serafina said. "And Miles, I shall pay for the hamper next week."

"Oh, yes," Julia said. "Let us eat well, while we are seeking spiritual improvement."

"Whom do you wish to contact, Serafina?" Julia asked.

"I shall tell you when we reconvene here next Sunday," she replied.

Later that afternoon, as everyone was tying on bonnets, buttoning wraps and getting ready to depart, Serafina offered Katherine a ride to her lodging house.

"Oh, thank you, but I must clean the dark room."

"Miles' servant can do that, Serafina replied.

"No," Katherine said. "One must know the chemicals one is handling. Some of them are dangerous. I don't believe the servant knows anything about the dark room, does he, Mr. Hickenbotham?"

"No. I should prefer that you did the washing up."

"Very well. May I presume, sir, we shall have your company later this evening?"

"Certainly, Serafina," Miles answered, as everyone but Katherine walked out into the hall.

Once they heard the downstairs door open and close Miles turned to Katherine, "You had an extraordinary success, today, my dear," and he slipped his arms around her waist and gave her a light kiss on the cheek.

"Oh, please, sir," Katherine said, twisting away from him, while he retained a light hold of her wrist. "Don't spoil it all. If you make love to me, I shall lose the respect of my new friends. I should not be able to come here any more. Then, all the dear hopes you have given me would burst like a soap bubble."

She stopped pulling away and looked up at him. There were streaks of tears on her cheeks, making her eyes appear deeper and darker than ever. Her face was softened by her tears and he could see the native blood in her features more clearly than ever—see it in the high rounded cheekbones, the faint, dusky underpainting of her skin and her full lips. He felt he could fall forever into the mystery of those dark eyes, drawn as irresistibly, as helplessly, as a bird before a snake. For some moments he felt himself balanced on the brink of the chasm, slowly slipping downward before the final plunge. All he had to do was pull her to him. She would not fight him, he felt sure, but would twine around him, passionately. He was certain that he could divine the heat of her appetite just beneath the stiffness of her waist, the rigid set of her shoulders and her fearful demeanor. But, afterward, then what? What would be left of his fondness for her and faith in her talent? Wouldn't he feel repelled by her immorality—and the violence of the passions which she compelled from him? She might not do what he asked of her in any case. She might consider it "unnatural." Wouldn't he thrust her away afterward? Or worse, use her a few more times and then cast her off? If he let himself succumb, what would happen to her talent? How would she develop it? On the edge of the abyss, his flash of self-examination showed him that he would not like himself if he let this happen. He released her wrist and told himself he had triumphed against the worst natures in both of them.

She turned quickly away from him and walked rapidly into the apartment toward the dark room. A few moments later, Miles heard the water running. He would not pursue her. Far better for them all, himself, Katherine, and Serafina, that nothing had happened. It only would have been cruel, otherwise. He would have had to lie to Serafina, all the while knowing he would never marry Katherine. If he cared for either of them, he must leave Katherine to herself.

"*Noli me tangere*," he murmured, quoting the inscription which Sir Thomas Wyatt had imagined encircling the fair neck of the doomed Anne Boylen. At that moment, Miles sincerely wished Katherine a much happier life than the one lived by the poet's infamous cousin.

Chapter 13

A DIFFERENT SORT OF 'CONVINCING EXPERIMENT'

O, Brothers Grimm; O, Madam D'Anois, O, SultanaShe-
herazade and Princess Codadad, why did you die? O, Merlin, Al-
bertus Magnus, Friar Bacon, Nostradamus, Doctor Dee, why did I
implicitly believe in your magic; and then have my confidence utterly
abused by Davy, Brewster, Liebig, Faraday, Lord Brougham and Dr.
Bachhoffner of the Polytechnic Institution? What have I done that all
the gold and jewels and flowers of Fairyland should have been ground
in a base mechanical mill and kneaded by you — ruthless unimagina-
tive philosophers — into Household Bread of Useful Knowledge ad-
ministered to me in tough slices at lectures and forced down my throat
by convincing experiments?

—Charles Dickens' *"Fairyland in 'Fifty-four,"*
Household Words 193 (3 December 1853) 313-17

In the week after the photographic sittings, Serafina amazed her family with a whirl of frenetic activity. She attended three lectures on spiritualism, visited the Museum reading room twice and had the photograph of herself and Jewel framed and hung in the drawing room. And this was in addition to overseeing all the servants in the house, fulfilling her commitments for slum visits as well as attending a meeting of the Social Democratic Federation, where she delivered a brief address on the current state of sweating in the east end clothing trade, an address which even Julia said was very well written.

"You do leave me quite breathless with the intensity and range of your activities, Serafina," Mrs. Winstantley commented coldly at breakfast one morning. "I wish you showed as much interest in being presented at Court, the season's balls or other genteel obligations."

"Pooh," Serafina said between mouthfuls of Scottish oatmeal which she was wolfing down.

"Pooh? What sort of an dreadful word is that?" her mother asked.

"I think it is a word that indicates a recent association at the Museum reading room. It sounds like an Eleanor Marx word," Julia said.

"No matter whose word it is, it is decidedly uncouth," Mrs. Winstanely remonstrated. "I don't want you to use it anymore. In my day even young ladies of your age could be birched for indecent language."

"Very well, mama," Serafina said, smiling into her oatmeal. She turned to her sister. "Aren't you excited about our coming foray into the supernatural?" she asked.

"I have been a believer for a long time," Julia answered. "It is difficult to work for Mr. Stead and not be one," Julia replied. "But you are acting like a true new convert."

"But this girl Miles found is an astonishing medium. Don't you think so?"

"I understand how you feel. I would be even more impressed if I had not been allowed to observe a demonstration given by Mr. Home."

"I did not know you had seen Mr. Home," Miles said.

" Mr. Stead was away and got permission for me to attend in his place. There is no medium anywhere who produces such remarkable but perfectly genuine phenomena. I saw him levitate up to the ceiling and mark it with a pencil. I climbed a ladder before and after the demonstration and examined the mark myself—from only inches away."

"Well, Mr. Home only performs before very select audiences," Serafina said, "to which I do not have access. "But I believe this girl will produce some remarkable phenomena for us."

"So it doesn't bother you," Julia asked, "that we are encouraging familiarity between dear Miles and this girl. She is quite pretty, I thought. And while certainly not refined, her manners are not bad."

"I suppose she's pretty," Serafina acknowledged. "In a dark, foreign sort of way. Of course her artistic costume is at least three years out of date. I'm sure you can't mean that Miles would..."

"You are very severe with him, Serafina," Mrs. Winstanely chimed in. "I've heard you say so yourself on many occasions."

"But surely don't think that Miles would take advantage of her?" Serafina said. "Even if it were not for me, I am certain he wouldn't dream of marrying anyone of her station. Or of abusing her confidence."

"I agree with that," Julia said. "But the poor fellow is only human, Serafina. When are you going to get married?"

"I really don't know. I don't even know if I ever shall."

"Then what about Miles?" Julia said, looking at her sister sharply.

"Oh, that will work itself out," Serafina said, blandly.

"Serafina," Mrs. Winstanley exclaimed, "sometimes I think you lie awake at night thinking of shocking things to say in front of me. We all expect you to marry Miles, and so does he."

"I shall not be bullied mother. I have told Miles and said often at this table that marriage should not be based on anything but the most spiritual ties; certainly not on physical instinct. I feel that way more than ever after seeing Katherine's pictures. Marrying for mere physical attraction reduces human society to sex, the most commonplace place thing in the world, according to the doctrines of Mr. Darwin."

"But marriage is the foundation of society," Mrs. Winstanley said.

"Precisely why it must not be debased," Serafina answered.

"But sex does have first place," Julia said. "The first priority of any species is to reproduce itself," Julia said.

"Oh, please, girls. I don't want this kind of talk at table," Mrs. Winstanley said. "Next, you'll be comparing Miles to a monkey."

Julia tucked her tongue into her cheek. "I think he has some beast in him, though where he keeps it is more than I can guess" she said saucily. "What do you think, Serafina? You can be sure it will come out, especially if you ignore it, indefinitely."

"I am going to my room," Mrs. Winstanley said, her face expressing distaste. "Owens has made some suggestions for the garden next year and I want to consider them."

The two sisters interrupted their duel of words long enough for Mrs. Winstanley to leave the room, then Serafina turned to Julia and said, "I confess that right now, I am more fascinated by the powers of this girl, than I am by Miles."

"That's a dreadful thing to say," Julia said. "You do not value him enough."

Serafina shrugged. "You have seen Mr. Home. I have not. You must admit that her pictures are remarkable."

"I do. I am only surprised that she has stirred your interest to this degree. You were bland even when I reported Mr. Home's feats."

"It is different to see something for oneself," Serafina said. "And there is something about that girl, some energy or power. Don't you think?"

"She seems intelligent, and tolerably pretty, but beyond that, she is nothing special. Were it not for her mediumship I should put her on the same intellectual level as perhaps Janis Morrison. And I do not believe she has had as good an education as Janis."

"Oh, no. She is a much brighter blade than Janis."

"Well, be that as it may, Serafina, I must go to the office."

"And I shall go to the Museum," the elder sister replied.

Given Serafina's enthusiasm for Katherine's powers and Julia's long-standing interest in spiritualism, eventually, Mrs. Winstanley became interested in the 'experiments' which her eldest daughter proposed to conduct with the medium. The three women sat through matins the following Sunday with less than devout feelings. It was difficult for them to pay close attention to the old dusty formulae while anticipating the spiritual wonders of the afternoon.

Mrs. Winstanley said she was hoping for a message from Amelia. Then she began to wonder if this would mean the child was dead. As they rode to Miles' she asked Julia, the family expert on spiritualism, to clarify this point for her.

"No, mother," Julia answered. "I have read of many verified instances of clairvoyance where lost people made themselves known to mediums. On the continent, mediums are even used to help solve crimes. If Amelia does come to our seance, I don't believe you have to worry that she has necessarily passed on."

"Thank you, dear. This is all quite new for me. I am really not certain what I think about it all. Miss Green has nice manners for someone of her station, but I am not at all sure she is really respectable. I worry about Miles being alone with her so much. Who knows what she might do to — to involve him."

"Seduce him, you mean. My concern as well, mother," Julia said.

"Oh, Miles is quite capable of taking care of himself," Serafina added. "I don't know why you both make so much of this. You act as if the girl were some kind of sorceress, capable of taking control of Miles. I grant you she has a nice figure, but her skin is dusky and opaque. Perhaps it is just dirt. Who knows? In my opinion, it is more likely that he might take advantage of her."

"Serafina!"

"I only said it was more likely. I did not say he would. Indeed, I believe it is all nonsense. You are forgetting his attachment to me. Do you think I am so easy to set aside? Let us just wait and see what occurs today."

Miles' manservant opened the door for them and was about to lead them up the stairs until Julia dismissed him.

"There is something uncomfortable about that man," Julia remarked. "He is so suppressed. The discomfort of the constraints he places on himself make me uneasy."

"Would you rather have him speak in tongues or burst out the way some of the evangelicals do?" Serafina asked.

"No. But I can't help but feel he is about to burst out somehow."

"You pay too much attention to servants, Julia," her mother said. "They are bound to be different from us."

Katherine was standing at the door as they came up the last flight of stairs. Her long dark hair was unbound and fell across her back and shoulders in a thick uneven mane. Critical as all the women were of Katherine's unkempt appearance, Serafina had to admit to herself that it made the girl more striking.

"Perhaps," she thought, "she is trying to affect the appearance of a gypsy fortune teller. This girl has seen much of life. We must make certain she doesn't hoodwink us."

Miles stepped out onto the landing next to Katherine.

"Forgive me for not meeting you," he said, "I have a new commission and I started to work on it before you came."

"Oh, that is excellent Miles," Serafina said as he handed her in through the door.

"It could be important for me. It is a portrait of a very valuable horse. A derby winner, in fact."

"Well, anyone who owns such a horse should be able to pay well," Julia remarked.

Serafina had taken Katherine's arm and the pair were leading the way into the apartment toward the glass room. Serafina was leaning toward the girl saying something to her.

"No, Miss Winstanley," Katherine said. "I have no objection to having my hands tied. But we shall be sitting in the strongest daylight, not in a dim cabinet. You should certainly see me if I tried any trickery."

"It is very good of you to humour me, Katherine, ah, Miss

Green."

"Oh, please, Miss Winstanley, I am flattered that you do not stand on ceremony with me."

"Thank you, Katherine. And I appreciate your willingness very much."

A few moments later they found themselves in the glass room, but now all photographic equipment had been pushed out of the way and a large mahogany table and five chairs were set up in the centre of the room. As Katherine had said, there was no cabinet and the room was in bright daylight with all the shutters opened wide. When all were seated, Katherine spoke.

"Please understand, I have no idea what is or is not about to happen. I shall go into a mesmeric trance and seem unconscious, and I shall be unconscious of anything that transpires. Then, I shall open my eyes. Once my eyes are open, you may ask what you like. You may or may not get answers. There may or may not be phenomena. It is some time since I held a sitting. I was much younger. We needn't join hands unless you want to. Miss Winstanley, if you like, you may bind my wrists or arms to the chair."

"No. I think you were right, Katherine. It seems hardly likely that any trickery is possible under these conditions."

"Very well, then. Shall I proceed?"

"Please," Serafina said.

The girl closed her eyes and drew several long breaths. Then she began to shake slightly as if she were shivering with cold. Then she became still and her eyes opened. They seemed utterly devoid of sight.

"What a strange, glassy stare," Serafina murmured. "Miles, get your flash device and fire it close by. I want to see what happens."

"That seems unkind," Miles said. "You might injure her."

"I must see if the girl is aware of her surroundings or not."

Miles got up from the table, got the flash holder and poured some magnesium powder into it. He then moved to a position about four feet from the glassily staring girl. He took a pair of dark blue glasses from his pocket and put them on.

"Everyone close your eyes," he said. "I shall watch through these dark glasses."

"No," Serafina said. "Give me the glasses. I shall watch."

Miles obediently removed the glasses and handed them to Serafina.

"All right?" he asked.

"Yes, yes, yes, yes," the participants acknowledged in turn.

Miles fired the flash.

"Not a quiver," Serafina called out. "She passes the first test. She is really unaware of her surroundings. I accept her state as a genuine trance. Now I have another test before I ask questions" Serafina reached up into her hair and drew out a long hat pin.

"Oh, Serafina," her mother gasped. "You aren't going to..."

"Yes, I am. If she is really in a deep trance, she will feel nothing. I have read that this is commonly done at hypnotic demonstrations."

"But really, Serafina," Miles said, "It does seem rather cruel."

"I am merely approaching this in a scientific fashion. I have done some study and know what we should be able to expect."

"But it is hardly an exact science," Julia said. "You might hurt her."

"It will not hurt her nearly as badly as it would us if she hoaxed us," Serafina replied, as she thrust the long needle into the girl's forearm. There was no blood and the girl did not flinch or cry out. The needle passed right through the thick part of the muscle.

"Very satisfactory," Serafina pronounced.

"Please remove it, Serafina," Julia said. "It makes my flesh creep."

"But it does demonstrate that she is unquestionably in a deep hypnotic trance. Her awareness has been shut off and is no longer connected to her senses." And she drew the long needle out of Katherine's arm with a single quick pull.

"What shall we ask?" Miles said.

"I have given a good deal of thought to our researches," Serafina said. "I think we should pursue something we want to know —but something that is verifiable. I think we should try to find Amelia. Let's see if the girl's clairvoyance can help find her. That would provide incontrovertible proof of her talent and clear up the family mystery, as well. What do you think, mother?"

But Mrs. Winstanley was slumped in her chair, quite unconscious. She looked as if she were having a peaceful sleep.

"She must have fainted when you pushed the needle into the girl's arm." Miles remarked.

"She looks quite peaceful," Julia said. "I think we should let her sleep until she wakes."

"Then, can the rest of us agree on that investigation?" Serafina pressed.

"I think it is an excellent idea," Julia said.

"Miles?"

"Yes, why not. If there really is any way to verify any of what she says."

"Either we find Amelia, or we do not," Serafina answered. "It seems simple enough."

"It may not be that simple, Serafina," Julia said. "The trail may run warm or cold before we are done."

"Then let's start," Serafina said. "Katherine, where is our cousin Amelia, now?"

"I see a tiny coffin on a pier," a strange, deep, hollow voice said as it issued from Katherine.

"Is Amelia dead, then?" Serafina asked.

"I don't know," came the hollow but decided reply. "It is not a coffin for burying."

"Then what is it for?" Miles asked. "What else can a coffin be used for?"

"I cannot tell. It is curiously made," came the reply. Miles felt nonplussed by the girl's rigid mask-like face. It reminded him a little of the first time he saw her.

"You say you also see a pier," Julia said. "Does that mean that Amelia has crossed the ocean?"

"She has not crossed the ocean," was the reply.

"Then where is she, exactly?" Serafina asked.

"Very close, closer than you imagine."

"Where?"

"Near your house."

"This doesn't seem as if it is going to be very productive," Serafina said. "The replies are direct, in their way, but they really tell us nothing. What can that mean—near our house?"

"Well," Miles said, "If we take it literally, it could mean that Amelia is living somewhere nearby, somewhere in the west end."

"What a strange idea," Julia said.

"Why strange?" Serafina asked.

"Just the thought that after all these years of missing her, she turns up a few streets away. It seems hard to believe."

"It does," Miles agreed. "Something is wrong with all this."

"I agree," Julia said. "But it is not Katherine or her clairvoyance. It is the way we are asking our questions. Let me try a few."

"Please do," Serafina said.

"Katherine, you say the coffin is not made for burying and that it is strangely constructed?"

"Yes."

"If it is not for burying what is in the coffin, then?"

"Cotton."

"Cotton?" Miles said.

"Yes."

"You see," Julia said. "We are not dealing with some omniscient being who sees everything. She only knows what her vision can see. We must frame our questions accordingly. It is like looking through a very long telescope. It can only show what is there, not draw conclusions about it."

"I think you are right, Julia," Serafina said excitedly. "Last week I read an account of Alexis Didier, the famous French

clairvoyant who came to Britain in the forties. He was remarkable for his ability to see things at a distance. I believe he saw
in the same literal sense you are describing, Julia. He could see
whatever was there, like a telescope. He could also see the in-
sides of packages and even people that were put before him."

"Exactly," Julia said.

"So what do we conclude from all this?" Miles asked.

"There is some connection between Amelia and this coffin on a pier. It has nothing to do with death..."

"It is like death," the strange hollow voice interrupted
them.

"It is like death, but it is not death," Julia went on.

"Then what is it?" Miles asked.

"I don't know," Katherine answered.

"Katherine," Miles said, "what else do you see?"

"Ships and the river."

"So it is a real place," Julia said. "It is not the sea but only
the river which tells us that she is in England."

"We need more landmarks," Serafina said. "Katherine,
can you give us some other landmarks?"

"A church."

"What does the church look like?" Miles asked. He
waited some time for a reply but none was forthcoming. "Katherine, can you tell us anything about the church?"

"It is close to the river."

"That's an answer that tells us nothing. We already knew
we were in the vicinity of the river," Serafina said, biting her
lips in vexation. "We must get to the bottom of this. I feel these
answers are genuine..."

"But provokingly incomplete," Julia finished.

"Exactly."

"But I feel," Julia went on, " the fault is ours. It is the way
we are asking the questions."

"Yes," Miles said. "I think you are right, Julia. But what is
the right way?"

"Ohhh," Katherine moaned.

"Oh, dear," Julia said. "I fear she is waking. We have lost

our way and our arguing has roused her."

The girl stirred and life came back into her eyes.

"Was it useful?" she asked.

"Yes, Katherine," Serafina said patting the girl's hand. "But it was also tantalizingly incomplete."

"It is often like that," Katherine said. "I don't know why."

"I think it is because of the way we were asking the questions," Miles said. "No one is dissatisfied with your showing, Katherine."

"No," Julia said. "I have seen clairvoyants who charged a lot of money and offered much less. We have somehow to pursue the clues you have given us."

"There is something tangible, then?" Katherine asked.

"I think so," Serafina said.

"Look," Julia said, "mother is still asleep. Do you think she's all right?"

"I think so," Serafina said looking at her mother closely. "Shall we wake her?"

"Wait," Miles said, "Let us decide what we wish to do next."

Serafina reached over and took Katherine's hand. "Will you meet with us again, Katherine and help us?"

"If it really can be of help, Miss Winstanley, of course."

"Call me, Serafina. When shall it be?"

"Sunday is the only day I have," Katherine said.

"Very well then," Serafina said, "Will that do for you, Miles?"

"Oh, yes, of course. She is my sister, after all."

Chapter 14

A REAL DETECTIVE ON THE CASE

*"The phenomena investigated by Sir William Crookes are so intimate-
ly connected with Modern Spiritualism, that his testimony to their
truthfulness is a vindication of the claims of the Spiritualists. Whatever may be said by the critic there is no doubt that the events tabulated
by the eminent scientist transpired as he recorded them; and what
the materialist may say, the Spiritualist declares that these undoubted
manifestations, with myriads of others of like purport, establish the
certainly of the existence of a world of spirits, with whom it is at
times, under certain conditions, possible to open communication."*

—The Quarterly Journal of Science
Sir William Phillips, ed., 1898

On Wednesday afternoon of the following week, Julia burst
into the house at Twenty-One Cavendish Square much as she
used to do as a child on returning from the back garden with
a captive frog in her little bucket. She was as pink and excited as
a child of ten.

"Mama, where is Serafina? I must tell her the news."
she shouted to Mrs. Winstanley who, like the middle-aged Mrs.
Vesey in the greatest thriller of the age, *The Woman in White*,
was increasingly given to calmly sitting through all the storms of

life. The older woman looked up from her album.

"I believe I heard her castigating someone in the kitchen, Julia. What news? May I be allowed to hear it as well?"

"A detective…" Julia called out as she catapulted herself below stairs, heedless of petticoats, to the servants hall. The rest of her words were cut off as she rushed down the front stairs.

"Serafina, Serafina? she cried, finally catching sight of a mannish figure in trousers who was actually her older sister dressed for the hard discipline of domestic labour.

"Julia? What is it? Fire, flood or revolution?"

"Something much more exciting," Julia said, making a half hearted attempt to retie the ribbons of her disordered shoulder length hair.

"I believe I may have found the perfect man to help us."

"What man? Help us with what?"

"Our investigation with Katherine. Let us go to your room."

The sisters hurried up the front stairs, passed into the hall and crossed to Serafina's little sitting room.

"Now, what is this all about, Julia? I even heard you below stairs when you first burst into the house."

"Yes, well, I just came home from work and was excited. I have made a momentous discovery. I have found the name of a man who tracked the activities of the infamous Mrs. Jeffries, just last winter. In February, Benjamin Scott's committee, set this man on Mrs. Jeffries with a view to shutting her down. He compiled a voluminous report which he gave to the Assistant Commissioner of Police, but which even now has never seen the light of day."

"Well, I am glad that someone is taking action against her, but what does it have to do with us?"

"This detective is a trained criminal agent with extensive experience of the white slave trade. I think we should hire him to follow any clues we may get from Katherine. There couldn't be a better man to help find Amelia. Don't you agree?"

"And he will verify or discredit what Katherine tells us. Brilliant. Yes, I agree absolutely. You are clever, Julia." And

Serafina threw her long arms around the younger woman and clasped her to her bosom.

"Ow, you are too tall to embrace me so tightly, Serafina. My nose hits your shoulder."

"I am sorry, dear. But your intellectual stature more than makes up for our difference in height."

"I am not short, Serafina," Julia said. "You are very tall for a woman and seem to grow still."

"Don't be saucy with me, missy. What is this detective's name?"

"Minahan. And I got his address from our files at work. I shall go to see him, today. Will you come with me and make him swoon and do our bidding?"

"How could I not? Though I think you are certainly capable of making him do your will." Serafina said. "But I must change my clothes if my role is to make him swoon."

"I agree," Julia said. "We are only going to the City. But I think I'll get Rossiter to have the carriage brought round. The brougham always makes a good impression. Don't you think?"

"Oh, yes, but we mustn't let him think we are too rich or he will overcharge us," Serafina said as she slipped from the room."

"Wait, Serafina," Julia said touching her sister's arm. "Why do you think no one has tried to use similar means to find Amelia before now? Hiring a private detective, I mean."

The older girl looked startled for a moment, "You know, I have no idea. Mother would never be capable of it. But, it never occurred to me, before. Perhaps we should ask Miles. His studio is on the way back from the City. We could stop and ask him."

"I think we should," Julia replied. "Hurry, please."

In less than an hour, the girls were riding through the soot and cinders of the City until they arrived at Ste. Mary Axe where, the files of *The Pall Mall Gazette* had told Julia, the former Scotland yard inspector was to be found, wedged into the sooty street among the Jews and moneylenders. It was a narrow, grimy, twisting City street which had enjoyed a brief moment of celebrity as the neighbourhood of Pubsey&Co., the moneylenders who figured in Dicken's last completed novel.

"The City seems more and more dirty each time I visit," Julia remarked to her sister.

"Business always seems to produce dust or smoke or some such noisesome thing," Serafina said. "I am glad Miles is not a man of business."

"He is the perfect antithesis of a man of business," Julia replied laughing. "He is the most unbusinesslike man I know."

"I suppose the City is a good place for a private detective, though," Serafina said. "Oh, this is Ste. Mary Axe. What was the number?"

"One hundred thirty," Julia replied.

"You've memorized it?"

"Yes, I always do when I am going about. Especially somewhere I haven't been before. It saves time with the cab drivers and gives the impression that one knows exactly where one is going. Oh, look, there it is." She banged on the roof of the four-wheeler with her umbrella handle.

Nothing could have been more incongruous than two fashionable young ladies standing in the gray old City street, reading a brass plate etched in black which said: Jeremiah Minahan, Private Detective. Beneath the plate was a bell which Julia pulled.

"Very professional," she commented, looking at the bell and plate.

"Of course. If he's formerly of Scotland Yard."

After what seemed quite a long time they heard heavy footsteps within and finally, the door swung open.

A tall, rather stout blonde man stood blinking at them from the relative darkness of the chambers.

"May I help you?" he asked.

"We are seeking Mr. Minahan, sir," Julia said. "We have a commission for him."

"I am Jeremiah Minahan, ladies. Please walk through to my consulting room."

Both sisters were somewhat disappointed in the appearance of the great detective. He certainly didn't look like a man who had ever swooned at the feet of any woman, no matter how handsome and charming. The fact that he was large-featured and portly with a distinctly venous nose, did not tally with the what either of the sisters had expected from a Scotland Yard detective. He looked more like a not-very-prosperous tradesman in baggy tweeds who probably sat too long over his wine each night. His hands, however, were clean and his nails trimmed, a personal detail which made a good impression on both ladies.

The detective's consulting room reminded Julia of a shabby legal chamber. The seats of the chairs sagged with the weight of the many troubles which had weighed down Mr. Minahan's clients.

Once the ladies were seated the detective said, "May I ask who referred you to me?"

"I work for Mr. Stead at the Pall Mall Gazette," Julia answered smartly.

"So Mr. Stead..."

"No. I consulted my own files, I am a reporter and have conducted several of my own investigations for Mr. Stead. I found your name mentioned in connection with Mr. Scott's commission."

The detective's eyebrow's rose. "That commission is on a notorious..."

"Yes, We know. Mrs. Jeffries. You wrote a report on her which produced absolutely nothing."

"Pardon me, I am not accustomed to discuss police business with young ladies."

"I understand your scruples, sir," Serafina said, "But we are here on our own business. A family member was abducted and never found. We believe we may have some new ideas regarding her whereabouts. We would like to discuss them with you and have you verify or discredit the information we present."

"I see. You are both of age?"

"Yes, sir."

"Your names and addresses, please."

They gave the required information and then Serafina

ended the formalities by charging headlong into the case.

"Now we would like to move beyond our bona fides to hire you to conduct an investigation. We are prepared to give you a retainer, if need be."

"Tell me about the abduction first. Were you living in the west-end at the time of the outrage?"

"Yes, sir."

"I am surprised that I have not heard some mention of the crime, before now. Over eighteen-thousand people go missing every year in the metropolis, but a tiny fraction of those are in the west-end. Yet, I know I have never heard a report of this abduction."

"It happened nearly fifteen years ago," Julia said.

"Good heavens. That is a cold trail."

"Yes, sir. I am not even sure it was reported at the time. Our father and our little cousin's parents were all killed shortly after the abduction."

"The case grows in interest, ladies. What makes you think you now have additional clues to help solve the crime at such a remote date?"

"A spirit medium has given us certain information, sir," Serafina said.

"A spirit medium," the stolid looking detective repeated.

"Yes," Julia said. "And part of your commission will be to tell us how good or how ill her clues are."

"I see. What is the medium's name? he asked, his pen poised over his notebook." Serafina looked over at Julia, uncertainly. "I had not thought of that."

"Nor I," Julia said.

"What is it that both of you had overlooked?" the detective asked with the patient diction of one who had conducted hundreds of interrogations.

"That the medium's name should have to be given," Serafina said.

"Anything you say to me shall be treated with the strictest confidence, I assure you. The only thing I cannot do is hide a crime from the regular police."

"Katherine Green," Julia said.

"Thank you." He paused and looked thoughtful. Both women were impressed for the first time since the interview began. They each began to sense the sharp mind which lay behind the commonplace exterior as the man weighed his words.

" Ordinarily, I would not be free to discuss my earlier investigations for Mr. Scott's committee. However, the report I wrote on Mrs. Jeffries has already been presented and appears to be of no interest to anyone."

"I was told that the Assistant Commissioner did not approve of brothels for the upper classes," Julia said.

The man's thick brows rose once more.

"Your sources of information are surprisingly good. Forgive me, when I look at you, I forget that I am looking at a professional journalist, Miss Winstanley."

"It is precisely because you have investigated some aspects of the white slave trade in English girls that we decided to come to you," Julia explained.

"It seemed to us," Serafina added, "that there was a very good chance that Amelia was abducted as part of that trade."

"This is a delicate subject for me to discuss with two well-bred young ladies—even if one of them is a journalist," the middle-aged policeman said.

"Please do not worry about delicacy on our account, sir." Serafina said sharply. "I have been working with Mrs. Josephine Butler for several years and am well acquainted with many of the grimy details of this trade. I daresay there is nothing you could say that would shock either of us."

The man leaned back in his chair and his watch chain dangled pendulously from the protuberance of his belly.

"Please tell me as many particulars of the abduction as you might know," he said, then he listened carefully as Julia repeated Miles description of the abduction.

"Is it possible," the detective asked, "for me to interview this cousin who was actually present at the abduction?"

"He was only a child at the time," Serafina said, "but if you think it worth while, I am certain Miles, Mr. Winstanley, would consent to an interview."

"And tell me again exactly what your relation is to this man," the detective said.

"He is a cousin twice removed," Serafina said.

"But are you close, distant? Why are you here instead of him if the girl was his sister? I need to understand in great detail the relations between the people who are in any way close to the abducted girl."

"Of course," Julia said. "We understand," and she then gave a full account of the abduction pausing only to cross check certain points in her statement with Serafina. Throughout the narrative, the detective's pen scratched away noisily at his note-book.

"Led away by a colourful tropical bird?" he said, the scratching pen suspended above the page. "That is interesting. You are certain this bird belonged to a neighbour?"

"We were always told that it did," Serafina said. "Miles might know more of it."

"I shall ask," he said smiling for the first time, showing a fine set of teeth. Both the sisters thought the expression gave the detective a rather predatory look, as if he were about to devour his prey.

The only other comment he made was on hearing of the deaths of their father and of Miles' parents.

"Two separate, unrelated incidents, you say? Within weeks of each other? One on the Continental steamer and the other on the Thames? Very strange. Very tragic for your families."

As the narrative wound down, Minahan asked suddenly, "And what about this medium. Is she someone close or distant to the families?"

"She is not connected with the incidents in any way. Miles, Mr. Winstanley, only met her six months ago. They are both photographers," Serafina explained. "We met her by chance at Victoria Park last summer."

Minahan made a few more notes, his pen scratching its way through very large flourishes. Serafina later remembered the scratching as she watched the motes of dust swarm in the winter sunlight which came through the office's single unwashed window. Dust, dryness and method were her chief impressions of their interview with the detective.

Suddenly, it seemed, the scratching stopped. The absence of the sound roused both women. Minahan was now studying them and looking very thoughtful. He leaned across the desk toward them in a confidential way.

"You do realize that there is very little chance of ever recovering this girl?"

"Much time has passed," Julia admitted. "But we thought with the new information we have, we owed it to our niece to pursue the matter."

"Ah, yes, the new information," the detective said picking up the pen once more. "This is from the medium?"

"Yes, sir," Serafina affirmed.

"And this information is?"

"I have thought carefully about this," Serafina said looking at her sister. "I believe there are three key points: first, there was a vision of a coffin which was not built for the purposes of burying. It was filled with cotton. Second, there is a church near this river location. Third, Amelia is in England, somewhere near our house. That is all."

"I cannot hold out much hope," the detective said when he ceased writing. "There is also the matter of how much money you will wish to spend on what is probably a fruitless enquiry."

"How much of a retainer do you require?" Julia asked.

"Fifteen pounds will make a start and I shall give you an accounting of all expenditures. Is that satisfactory?"

"Yes," Julia said. "It is a little high, but I expected you would be more than an ordinary private enquiry agent."

"Your grasp of the fine points of criminal investigations continues to surprise me, Miss Winstanley."

"I have spent hours at the Thames Police Court and the Bow Street courthouse, listening to the testimony of detectives and policemen. The wonder would be if I did not understand the business. We are stopping at our cousin's on our way home so we shall tell him of our consultation with you and prepare him to be contacted by you."

"Let me give you a card to leave with him. When I call, I shall present another and he will know I am who I say."

"Thank you, sir," Julia said. "And here is fifteen pounds."

"And your receipt, Miss Winstanley."

A few moments later and the two sisters were once more standing on the street in the watery sunlight which now seemed almost bright beyond endurance after the detective's dark chambers.

"Well?" Serafina asked, looking at her sister.

"I don't know what I think of him," Julia said. "But at least I know someone has finally done all that can be done for Amelia. Now, let us go and hear what Miles has to say. Naturally, we shall tell mama nothing unless we have good news."

"Of course," Serafina agreed.

"Why do you think he was so interested in the bird Miles saw?"

"I don't know."

Miles was surprised and not altogether pleased to see his cousins arrive unexpectedly. Julia could sense his unease immediately. He was in his shirtsleeves, which were rolled high above his elbow and his hands were stained with chemicals.

"Miles," Serafina said, "we are sorry to intrude on your work but we must tell you something."

"And ask you something," Julia added.

"Yes, well, all right. But can it not wait until dinner tonight? I just mixed some fresh chemistry."

"No," Serafina said firmly, leading Miles to a chair. "We have just come from a private detective."

"A private detective?"

"Yes, about Amelia."

"Amelia?"

"And," Julia added, "in a way, Katherine."

"So it can't wait until dinner because we cannot discuss it in front of mother."

"But why..."

"I came across a name at Northumberland Street," Julia said. "It was the name of a former Scotland Yard Inspector who had done an extensive investigation of Mrs. Jeffires."

"Really?"

"Yes. We hurried along to him and just finished having an interview with him. He wants to speak with you about the abduction. He says you are the only eyewitness and that he must talk to you."

"This is not really a good time to start talking of something so involved," Miles said twisting a little in the chair.

A sound from the doorway drew all eyes toward the interior of the apartment as Katherine stepped into the salon, wearing her hat and a new pelisse.

"I shall go out Mr. Hickenbotham..."

"But the chemistry," he said.

"I do not want to intrude on family business, sir." She walked quickly to the door and went out.

"What was she doing here?" Serafina asked after the door closed. "I thought she worked each day but Sunday."

"She did. She lost her place because I went there the other day to enquire after her. It is just as well, anyway. She needs to assemble a portfolio if she is to start her own practice as a photographer. She couldn't really have done it while working at Bryant & May."

"This must be very recent," Serafina said.

"She came and told me just yesterday and asked if she could use the studio more often. Of course, I said, 'yes.'"

Julia said nothing but looked at her sister and Miles very closely. Both parties, she thought, seemed to be suppressing strong emotions. In Serafina's case the suppression did not last long.

"Good gracious," Serafina blurted out. "What is she going to live on while she is taking pictures?"

"Well, I thought that since she was holding the seances and taking our photographs without charge, I could give her a small allowance to tide her over. Until she started to build a photographic clientele."

To Julia's utter astonishment, Serafina bent down and gave Miles a quick peck on the cheek. "You are a good man, Miles. I believe you have the best heart in the world. I support and applaud your resolution."

"Perhaps I am selfish," Julia thought to herself, "but if Miles were mine I shouldn't kiss him for giving money to an attractive girl so she could loiter in his studio." Serafina's patronage of Katherine must be due to her violent conversion to Spiritualism.

"Miles," she heard her sister say, "tell us about this bird you saw the day Amelia was taken. The detective seemed very interested in it. I am wondering why. It belonged to a neighbour?"

"I have no idea to whom it belonged. We had a neighbour with a remarkable aviary in his house. I have always assumed the bird was his. I must confess that the day is strangely clouded in my memory. Perhaps talking to the detective will help me remember details."

"But you didn't know where the bird came from as a matter of absolute fact?" Julia asked.

"No."

"Well, that is why Mr. Minahan needs to speak with you. We have already misdirected him. I was also wondering if you had any recollection of anyone in the family talking to the police or a private detective about Amelia's abduction?"

"I only remember that one day she was taken. The next day your father was lost and soon after, so were mine. Those events crowded in on one another so that any other memory of that time has been pushed out of my mind."

"I wonder if Katherine could help us?" Serafina said.

"I don't know," Julia said. "I thought that one of the things we hoped to investigate was her accuracy. If we start basing our actions about the abduction on things that can't be confirmed, how can we ever know if she is real or not? I think we should leave it to Mr. Minahan for the time being."

"So we are to think Katherine suspicious until Mr. Minahan says her clues have been verified?" Serafina asked. "That line of reasoning appears to follow the unsound principle of believing in guilt until innocence is proved. It hardly seems fair to Katherine."

"Well, at least we should not assume her clairvoyance is accurate until it is proven so," Julia replied.

"And if it is never proven through no fault of hers are we to think she is a liar?" Serafina asked.

"She is not a liar," Miles said definitively.

"I agree, Miles," Serafina said. "All my instincts are against it."

"Well I say," Julia replied, "the proof is in the pudding. I shall reserve judgement until I have seen more of her and we have heard from Mr. Minahan. By the way, Miles, here is his card. He will present one like it when he comes to call."

Miles took the card and studied it.

"He should get himself a better engraver."

"Like the man," Serafina said, "It is a little unfinished. It represents him well."

"Being a policeman is a rough trade," Miles remarked, "Even in Scotland Yard."

Chapter 15

A DEATH IN THE FAMILY AND SOME SHOCKING DISCOVERIES

I AM the resurrection and the life, saith the Lord: he that believeth in me, though he were dead, yet shall he live: and whosoever liveth and believeth in me, shall never die.

—The Book of Common Prayer

The year '86 did little to reveal new facts about the abduction of Amelia Winstanley, but two events very significant to our history did take place in that year. The first was the death of Mrs. Winstanley, which occurred just after the new year began, and the second was the confirmation of one of Katherine's visions, the first fruit of the investigation which had been taken over by Mr. Minahan.

Mrs. Winstanley's decline could properly be said to have begun on the morning of the publication of the first of the *Maiden Tribute* articles, for she had never fully recovered her strength nor her lively interest in her daughters' activities since that time. The more direct cause of her death began with a chill caught during a holiday visit to her father's family in Yorkshire. The train, which ran along the old narrow gauge line in the snow capped Dales, stalled and sat in the snow for nearly twenty-four hours before a mechanic got it started once more. By that time, the lack of warm food, the icy chill of the air and the enforced motionlessness of sitting in seats through a day and a night was too much for May Winstanley. She arrived home with what her doctor described as 'a serious catarrh' in her chest. The cold rapidly turned to infection and a high fever. A second opinion was called for, but nothing could be done. Mrs. Winstanley was clearly upset about something which preyed on her mind and she kept apologizing to Serafina during the entire course of her illness—some two and a half weeks. Neither Serafina or her younger sister could imagine what lay so heavily on their mother in her last days. Mourning at Cavendish Square lasted into the summer and even then, Serafina did not abandon her simple black dress trimmed with black satin. In fact, to everyone's surprise, it was Serafina who felt the loss most keenly. Her character seemed permanently marked by the sad event. Her demeanour became even more serious than before. She made no more humourous asides about anything and read constantly the day's offices from the Book of Common Prayer. During this time, she also made an intimate friend of Katherine, a fact which made Miles quite uncomfortable. Whenever he visited Cavendish Square, there was a good chance he would find his protégé there, holding a seance. The seances had become the high point of the week for Serafina and she constantly asked Katherine to contact her mother. By the fall of '86 no progress in that direction had been made. However, on a chilly October morning, news was received in the form a letter which, by this time, seemed to have fallen from the sky. It was from Mr. Minahan, the detective.

"Heavens," Serafina said, "I had almost forgotten him and the commission we gave him. So much has happened since then."

Julia, who had just poured tea in the south parlour for her sister and Miles opened the letter at Serafina's request and read it:

"Dear ladies, this note is to inform you that I have un-covered some information which seems to confirm one of the clues you got from the medium, Katherine Green."

"Oh," Serafina exclaimed brightening. "I wish she could be present to hear this."

"Will she not be coming later?" Miles asked. "She had several sittings in the glass room and then I understood her to say that you expected her here, Serafina."

"Yes, that is true. What shall we do? Wait?"

"I cannot wait, Serafina," Julia said. "The investigation has moved at a snail's pace as it is."

"But there is no longer any question of catching out dear Katherine's honest errors, is there?"

Miles and Julia exchanged a meaningful glance which was caught by Serafina.

"Oh, I know you think I have become a religious fanatic since mother's death. But here is Mr. Minahan confirming my own instincts that that sweet girl is honest and that her clairvoy-ance is genuine. Please read on, Julia."

"The item I have been able to verify, I found in a letter written by a notorious trafficker in girls, one Kleberg or Klyberg by name, who until recently, when he was imprisoned, corre-sponded with brothel owners all over Europe. Here is the perti-nent extract from one of his letters which was in the possession of the Belgian Police. I feel quite certain that no civilian could have read it. It is written to one of the brothel owners for whom Kleberg supplied girls. Here is the relevant passage:

'My dear friend, your little package will be delivered some time this week. She is a delightful little thing of eight or nine with the prettiest golden hair and lovely blue eyes. I will use my usual method of delivery which has proved both safe and effective. Who would open a little coffin to find a living girl? Certainly not the Belgian authorities. You need have no con-cerns about the chloroform. It won't hurt her and my agent has become expert in judging dosage. She will need a few days to recover from her trip, but I feel certain that by the Sixth April, you will be able to clasp the little package to your heart. As usual, the package will be delivered to Maison Charles, 18 Canal au Harengs, in Antwerp. It is always a pleasure to serve you my dear Baron'.

The letter from Minahan went on: "I believe that this passage speaks for itself and shows that at least one of the three clues Miss Green provided was entirely correct. I doubt very much that she could have known of this method of delivery by any ordinary means.

I shall continue my researches. There has been little cost to date. I shall write again when I have more to impart."

"But it also contradicts something else Katherine said," Julia commented when she finished reading. "Which was that Amelia was still in England, somewhere near our house. If the girl was shipped this way to Belgium, how could the other statement be true?"

"Does Katherine's vision of the little coffin mean that Amelia was actually shipped that way, or might it mean that she was simply in the hands of people who used such methods?"

"Yes, Miles, yes," Serafina cried excitedly. "I believe you have hit on it."

"Well," Julia said, "We don't have long to wait before we can ask Katherine herself."

"She doesn't always know what her visions mean," Serafina said. "The dear girl is so afraid of being disbelieved that she scrupulously avoids interpretation. I shall write to her immediately and tell her what we have learned."

Miles said nothing, though he felt deeply that Serafina was now too desperate to legitimize Katherine's visions. It was sad, he thought that Serafina, of all people, should be reduced to this kind of wishful thinking. It was odd, he reflected how death can affect people in such different ways. Since Mrs. Winstanley's passing, Julia had become even more self-reliant. She had a column in the PMG with her own name above it and was writing a novel which she kept carefully hidden. Serafina, on the other hand, was much more gentle, sometimes even absent-minded, which was the last thing in the world he would have said of her, before her mother's death. She now often seemed unable to make the simplest decisions, including the important one which involved his own future. He felt increasingly alienated from her and even desired her less than before. Just last year, who could have thought such a thing possible? He thought fleetingly of their argument in her little room off the front hall, which now seemed an age ago. He had not even attempted to kiss her since that night. It was Katherine who had taken over the leading role in any erotically charged fancies that flitted through his mind. It was tantalizing and difficult to have her at the studio every day and know that any advance on his part would be rejected and instantly reported to Serafina, her new confidant. His relations with his cousins had been mysteriously altered during the year. Somehow, Miles felt, he had gone from being a petted and spoiled favourite to a tolerated and occasionally useful male presence. Even Julia had less time for him than she once did. When she was not at the office, she spent all of her time writing in her room. The three women were each more distant from him. There was little interest in the fact that he was getting larger and larger commissions and making more and more money. It seemed that the only things the women ever talked of now were little Amelia's abduction, the franchise for women, the plight of the dockers and Spiritualism.

Once the seances had started, Katherine took no more spirit photographs, but concentrated on taking flattering commercial portraits, and had become skilful in the use of lighting and camera position to erase skin blemishes and double chins. Katherine and her clientele were in Miles' studio every day, so he had no longer any privacy. He could not bring any women home, and because of Amelia he was now loath to go to Mrs. Jeffires again. Only Julia noticed if he did not come to Cavendish Square for his evening meal. More and more often, he told himself that he would take a wife from among the daughters of his wealthy clients, but something always held him back. Soon, Katherine would be able to make her way as a photographer—as soon as her work would support a studio. But as it was, Miles was still paying her a small stipend. He would have been despised by all three women if he cut Katherine off, now. He felt trapped with Katherine in his life every day and frustrated by his own attraction to her. He really felt quite resentful of the exclusive friendship that had developed between Serafina and Katherine. While his relationship with his cousins had diminished, his admiration for Katherine had grown. She now wore lovely, clinging gowns which enabled her to move around the studio easily, as she worked with her clients. The unpadded skirts clung to her figure in a way he found quite distracting. He went to Cavendish Square less and less often. After Mrs. Winstanley's death, the custom seemed to fade away. His only strong bond with the household now was through Julia. She wrote to him every day, even if it was only a line or two. The fact that she now felt free to follow her own inclinations about writing told Miles that whatever understanding had existed between himself and Serafina was at an end. Occasionally Julia stopped at the studio on her way back from the Cage, the fenced off quay at the river end of Nightingale Lane. Through the winter of '87 she worked furiously on a series of articles on the dockers' woeful situation. This state of affairs persisted right through the winter, the infamously cold, hard winter of '87 when dozens of dockers died from drowning and starvation.

All through that terrible winter, Julia went out on the bitterest days and brought beakers of hot coffee and bread to the men at the waterfront. The Winstanley's kitchen was a hive of activity of baking and making coffee and tea, and each time Miles visited Cavendish square, he found the house filled with women and the occasional docker who was helping out and getting a free meal and a hot drink. The beautiful mahogany dining table had been sold to buy an enormous coffee urn, which the sisters transported to the Cage every morning. The change in the house saddened the young painter who found the women strident and the dockers who frequented their house, rough. His only real friend in the house now was Julia. Serafina was so often closeted with Katherine that he rarely saw her when he came to the house. Then a shocking discovery was made by Julia, a discovery that changed the relations between all of them.

Julia had been searching for a present for Miles' birthday

among the second hand bookshops off of Holborn where most such shops were presided over by Jews. The store was one she had visited before to find old photographs of interest to Miles. This time, she found an old family photographic album from America containing beautifully hand-coloured photographs. The album was covered with a heavy wood and leather binding which had carved wooden blocks beneath the leather cover. It had a wonderful mass and feel and the proprietor of the shop, who smelled of garlic and was prepared to bargain aggressively over the price, said it was at least twenty-five years old. There were even several pictures of family members in American war uniforms. Julia took him entirely off his guard when she agreed to the first price he quoted.

"Miles will love this," Julia murmured as she turned the pages, the album resting on one of the crowded tables stacked with books. Then, as she was looking at her purchase, something slipped out of the volume and slid to the floor. Thinking that it was part of the album, Julia bent down to retrieve the pho-tograph. But when she looked carefully, she saw it was a *carte visite*, a photographic advertisement for a contemporary Brit-ish photographer, whose name she knew. The name of Charles Boursnell, the foremost spirit photographer in London and Mr. Stead's friend , was printed at the top of the card. Below the photographer's name was a naked young girl getting out of a copper bathtub from the last century. It was titled, 'The Bathe of Psyche.' It was pornography delivered the way Victorian men liked it, wrapped in the dignity of classical mythology. Julia felt an indignant flush spread through her, but a moment later she turned cold with astonishment. There was no mistaking the fact that the young girl was Katherine, some years younger than she was now, it was true, still a child, but absolutely recognizable— and without a stitch of clothing to cover her nakedness. She smiled at the camera with a coy, inviting look that belied the innocence of the setting and the subject's extreme youth. The overall impression was anything but innocent. Once the initial shock was over, a rapid rush of questions flooded through Julia's mind.

"If she posed for something like this, was she also a prostitute? Had she learned to do spirit photography from Boursnell? And had she lied about having no involvement with spirit photography before? Had she been the middle-aged Boursnell's mistress at the time the picture was taken—as a child? Whatever the answers, Julia felt they had all been deceived.

As she left the shop with the album and the *carte visite* tucked inside, she struggled to recover her mental equilibrium. She did not judge Katherine for doing what was necessary to survive, but she did feel imposed upon, deceived by the girl. It was one thing to support a cause and to know that fallen women were often victims of men, but to discover that a trusted acquaintance might be one of these women was a shock to her. Mrs. Butler, she knew, often had prostitutes staying in her house in Liverpool. But Katherine had been accepted by Serafina as an intimate friend. It was now clear that she had not made her circumstances fully known, whether she was or was not a prostitute. But what else could she be if she posed for such a picture and looked at the camera with such a suggestive smirk? Julia finally concluded that in addition to the uncertainty she now felt about Katherine's past, she was also uncertain about what she felt— and was surprised at her own lack of emotional clarity. She hardly knew how to proceed. She felt she must talk to Serafina and Miles. Then she thought of how close Katherine and Serafina had become and decided that the best thing to do was to see Miles, first. Men were more at ease about discussing sex.

"Oh, yes, she murmured as she walked, "I must show this to Miles without delay. Together, we shall decide what to do about Serafina. Since mother's death, she is not as strong as she used to be. If he does not dine with us tonight, I shall go to him. In fact, I shan't wait to see if he comes to Cavendish Square. I shall just set off from here when it gets late enough. Katherine is so often there during the day. That way I shall avoid her at home this evening if she comes to see Serafina. I don't think I could meet her and look in her face without showing some sign of what has happened. Heavens, if I am affected this way, how, I wonder, will Serafina take it?"

Instead of going home and facing Serafina, she decided to
go to her office at Northumberland Street. Mr. Stead had given
her a dark little room where she could write and think. She had
grown so accustomed to the noise of the double Marioni presses
thundering through the building, that she now hardly heard
them. When she got to her little chamber, she removed the album and *carte visite* from the brief case she had carried when she
went to look for Mile's gift. She opened the album and looked
at the photograph of Katherine once more, and decided that the
most disturbing thing about it was the girl's expression. It was
so confiding and provocative at once, it made Julia think that
Katherine must have posed for many such pictures. There wasn't
a trace of embarrassment in the girl's face. Julia tried to imagine
what it would feel like to stand naked in front of a photographer
and camera, but could not. Sex, as a fact of existence did not
make her shrink. She was not a prude. It was when sex became
the defining element of relations between men and women that
she felt on entirely unfamiliar ground. She had never experienced desire divorced from affection and regard, and she had
only felt passion once in her young life. Miles was the only man
who had ever made her pulse beat faster or her body grow warm.
She disliked prostitution and pornography because she felt
they demeaned women and helped prevent them from becoming equal partners in society. Though she understood the need
that drove many women to prostitution, she felt that prostitutes
harmed the advance of all women. Her feelings about Katherine
before seeing the photograph had been neutral. Julia was interested in spirit phenomenon and had been curious to see what
the girl could do, but she had felt no personal interest in the girl.
She had regarded Katherine as Serafina's and Mile's friend. Now
she felt differently. Looking at the mocking lewdness on the very
young face made her angry. No girl capable of such an expression under such circumstances should be allowed into her family
circle.

She closed the album and took out her own notes on
her novel. *The Maid* was a work of historical fiction inspired by
George Eliot's *Romola*. It was a fictional autobiography of Joan

of Arc. Its major theme was an attempt to analyze the Maid's
individual certainty of God and the mission he had given her.
She wanted to imagine the Maid's mind under threat of death.
Julia wanted to get inside the feelings that could lift a farm girl
from ignorance into illumination. She wanted to understand
and portray the the chief character of *The Maid* entirely without recourse to doctrine, but build her character on principles
of modern psychology. In the course of writing The Maid, Julia
had read Breuer, Freud, Janet and a great many other psychological and religious thinkers. Sometimes she felt that writing the
novel was really a way to focus her reading. Julia was convinced
that essentially the mind was neither male nor female but a
combination of both sexes. Eventually, later in life, this belief
brought her to study with Carl Jung in Zurich. It was not until
then that she realized she had been attracted to Miles because he
was a very feminine man who complemented her own masculine
psyche.

    She worked until she got hungry and then went out
and bought a cup of eel soup from an old man who haunted the
streets off Whitehall with an ancient pushcart. He was a relic
of mid-century London when eel soup and oysters were sold on
nearly every corner of the City. Julia felt herself a more authentic participant in the social history of the City each time she ate
a cup of the thick, greasy stew. Even as a child, Julia had had a
profound awareness of the past and the things which connected
her to it. She often felt that her love of the past was almost an
attempt to fill in some blank spot in the present. When she took
one of the old heavy soup beakers in her hands she imagined
two or three generations of Londoners eating and drinking from
it. The boy who worked in a boot blacking factory and became
a world famous author might have held the same beaker in
his hands. Old things that were man-made, especially humble
things that had enjoyed frequent use, were redolent of history for
her. Such things seemed like a thread connecting her with the
many lives of unknown multitudes with whom she shared the
thousand-year-old city. Buying eel soup from the old man had
the sanctity of a ritual for her. She ate with relish as she stood

on the cold street corner, as the steam was pulled up out of the beaker and into the wind. Then, she went back to her dark, narrow room and wrote several more pages. When she had to light the second lamp in her small narrow office, she knew it was late enough to go to Miles and show him Katherine's picture.

As she walked, she thought about Miles and realized she was going to him because she wanted an ally against Katherine. Serafina would never turn away from her new friend, so she had to try Miles. Julia had never seen her sister so infatuated with anyone. Miles and his cousins had enjoyed a very special bond before Katherine, now it seemed dissolved. In some mysterious way, Katherine had broken into the family's intimacy and changed everything. It made their mother's death seem almost unimportant, and even the investigation into Amelia's disappearance had been allowed to languish. Julia felt suddenly quite angry at Katherine and found her steps growing longer and faster as she walked. She had the dim perception that something other than her own will was carrying her forward, but she was too unclear to examine her own thoughts and feelings. It was easier to be angry at Katherine. In spite of the chill wind, she was quite hot by the time she climbed the stairs to Miles' studio.

"Julia," Miles said in a tone of surprise as he opened the door. "What a nice surprise," and she felt that he meant it.

"I have a surprise, too, Miles. One that is not altogether nice." She threw off her coat before he could help and pulled the album out of her briefcase. "I have a revelation to make about Katherine. It particularly concerns me since she and Serafina have become so close."

"I have never heard you carry a tale before, Julia. You sound out of sorts."

"I suppose I am. I need your help and advice to decide what to tell Serafina. You know she has not been the same since mama's last illness."

"Yes, I have seen that. But what does it have to do with Katherine?"

"Look. I found this inside something I was buying for you," she said as she handed him the *carte visite*.

He said nothing as he looked at the picture for some moments. "The little whore," he finally said, "She certainly is a good liar. She has had us all fooled."

"My thoughts exactly," Julia replied. "But how do we tell Serafina? They see each other every day. And Serafina absolutely dotes on Katherine's clairvoyant 'visions'—especially since the detective explained the use of the tiny coffin."

"Well, for one thing," Miles said hoarsely. "She won't be working here anymore. I can't afford to compromise my own reputation by being associated with someone who has posed for pictures like this. I wonder how many she has posed for?"

"She certainly looks very at ease standing naked in front of a camera. I thought there must be more, too."

"What a little trollop. What astonishing lies she has told me from the first" he muttered, but he said nothing about his very first meeting with Katherine at Piccadilly.

"But do you see whose name is on the *carte visite* at the top?" Julia asked. "It is Boursnell, Mr. Stead's friend and the foremost spirit photographer in London. Mr. Stead says that a large show of his spirit photographs is being contemplated by the Psychological Society. Perhaps that is how Katherine learned the tricks of such photography."

"I am going to have a brandy. Will you join me?" Miles asked.

"Yes, thank you. It is rather a shock."

"It's astonishing," Miles said. "I don't believe I have ever been so imposed upon by anyone. You should have heard her 'confession' about her years in India and how she had been found guilty of theft. What a melodramatic tale of woe. You would have sworn that butter would not melt in her mouth."

"She has been tried for theft? In a law court?"

"In India," Miles confirmed.

"And now she is Serafina's dearest friend," Julia said collapsing into a chair.

"What shall we do?" Miles asked as he tossed off his drink.

"Serafina will not be parted from her, I am certain," Julia

answered. "She may even feel that Katherine as a former prostitute has that much more claim on her. Serafina will do almost anything that is imitative of Mrs. Butler, and Mrs. Butler has made a habit out of making fallen women her personal friends and bringing them to her home."

"Then, perhaps," Miles said slowly, "difficult as it is, perhaps we should keep this to ourselves and try to find out more about Katherine. Use that detective you found. What's his name, Minahan?"

"Oh, Miles, that is an excellent thought," Julia agreed, feeling relieved that facing her sister had been postponed indefinitely.

"Leave the *carte visite* with me and I shall take it to the detective. Just write his address on it. Be careful not to deface the picture."

"Don't you have the card I gave you? It has the detective's name and address on it."

"I had forgotten it."

Chapter 15

A WOMAN OF LOOSE MORALS

"Everything that a woman of loose morals says must be received with caution, and believed under protest."

—Henry Mayhew

While two of her former patrons were plotting to expose her past, Katherine got Serafina's note about the accuracy of her clairvoyance: the little coffins and the children she had seen at the Bowens now fitted together. Now she knew how the Bowens were sending children to France and Belgium: in the coffins with chloroform soaked cotton to keep them unconscious! It was even very likely that Susan had been abducted this way. But how could she prove it, find Susan and put an end to the traffic? She had no idea. The Bowens were respectable pillars of the church. She dared not go to the 'refuge' again. Her strong personal feelings about Susan made it impossible for her to use any of her clairvoyant talents to find the missing girl. Strong emotions always distorted the accuracy of her visions. Serafina's letter was so tantalizing, but it left her frustrated with her own powerlessness.

Miles, too, was feeling frustrated in an entirely different way. He had wanted the girl, and she had stood on very high moral ground and fooled him into thinking she was respectable.

He now felt like an idiot, a man of the world imposed on by a streetwalker! She had obviously been working her trade from an early age, too. It was a wonder she still looked as fresh as she did. When he thought of how Katherine had resisted him with words about her respectability and friendlessness, he felt furious. But it was not just his vanity that was hurt. He could have shrugged that off, but Miles had begun to feel a genuine, even a tender, regard for Katherine and a respect for her abilities—in spite of her station. Now it looked as if she were a complete fraud, not only a whore but also a student of Charles Boursnell and perhaps his mistress from a very young age. God knows what trickery he had taught her. He didn't know what was going on in her seances with Serafina, but he felt certain it was fraudulent. Miles felt bitterly disappointed in her. He began to wonder if anything she had told him was true. Perhaps she had never even been in India. The detective would sift the matter to the bottom. Miles promised himself that he would possess every fact of her past life. Every lie would be exposed and used as a way to separate her from Serafina. He rang for his manservant. He would tell Egbert at once that Katherine was no longer to be admitted to the building. He didn't want her to come to his studio anymore. Oh, eventually, after the detective had gathered evidence that she was a whore, he would confront her at Cavendish Square in front of Serafina and make her burn with shame, but right now, he did not want to see her. He did not trust himself. He felt so angry and hurt that there was no telling what he night not do. Vague images of birching Katherine flickered in his thoughts as he tossed down another brandy. God knew she deserved it. He rang for Egbert, lit a cigar and waited. There was some satisfaction in the thought that barring her from the studio would stop the progress of her photographic career. But another part of him, the part that respected her ability, felt some pain at the thought of ruining the development of her talent. The fact that he could feel such pain made him even more angry at her. It was infuriating that a whore could become so entangled in their lives. It had been the worst kind of seduction. Katherine had seduced their entire family.

Yet, even in the midst of his anger, he kept feeling that he had forgotten something, something connected with Katherine. For the life of him, he could not grasp what it was. Then his ruminations were interrupted by his manservant.

"Yes, Egbert," Miles said, acknowledging the servant's appearance in the doorway. "Do not admit Miss Green to the building any more."

He felt Egbert's eyes on him as the canny manservant weighed the new orders, and added, "I have found some things missing, you see. Under no circumstances is she to get inside. No matter what she says."

"Very well, sir."

For a few minutes after Egbert left, Miles felt some sense of satisfaction over the step he had taken. Tomorrow, he would sacrifice his morning and go to the detective and set him on the girl's trail. For some reason, he thought of Amelia and felt sorry that Katherine was apparently a fraud. But then he felt a moment of confusion: how could she be a fraud and be able to take pictures of Amelia wearing clothing he, himself, remembered?

When he called at the detective's chambers the following morning, Miles, like his cousins was not impressed with the man. But even while Miles wondered about leaving the case with Minahan, he felt it wouldn't do to expose the facts to yet another stranger. He settled into one of the sagging leather chairs and faced the detective across his desk. Miles thought there was something sly about the man which might qualify him for his work.

"What can I do for you, Mr. Hickinbotham?" the detective asked.

"As I told you in my letter, Mr. Minahan, my cousins and I are now anxious to find out more about the antecedents of Miss Katherine Green. I would also like to see if my missing sister could possibly be an inmate in Mrs. Jeffries establishment in Church Street, Chelsea. This is another clue from a recent sitting with Miss Green."

"The medium who has been helping to trace your sister?"

"Yes. And I was also wondering why you had not interviewed me about the disappearance as you told my cousins you would."

"There was, as yet, no purpose to take up your time, sir. I had other facts to gather, first. But now that you are here, we may certainly discuss the matter."

"Facts like the business about the small coffin Miss Green claims to have seen?"

"And others. You see, Mr. Hickinbotham, when someone disappears it is well to know as much as possible about the people closest to them. Usually, the key to the disappearance lies inside the family circle. I have looked into the backgrounds of all the people your cousins named to me, including yourself."

"I see. Then you already know something of Miss Green. I am glad to hear it."

The detective's fleshy face puckered into a frown. "I know less of her than I should like," the man said. "I have traced her to a charitable home for Asian women who were sent here from the subcontinent. But immediately on her release a very strange thing happens." The frown deepened.

"Yes," Miles said anxiously. "What is it?"

"She appears to have crossed paths with a young woman named Francis Coles, whose father is a workhouse inmate. Their tracks become so blurred together that I am no longer sure if Francis Coles and Katherine Green are not the same person. I have shown a photograph of Katherine Green to the old workhouse pauper and he has identified her as his daughter."

"Well, that sounds quite definitive. Can you then tell me anything of Francis Coles?"

"There is not much to tell. She is a prostitute. Her physical appearance bears a very strong resemblance to the photograph I obtained from some girls at the home for Asians where Katherine Green was photographed with some friends. But I should not call the identification definitive. However, before we pursue that point, I should like to understand why this girl has suddenly become of central interest to your family. It almost sounds as if you want to mount a new investigation—into the past of Katherine Green."

"Well, then, let us say that I want to conduct two investigations in parallel. I want to know what Miss Green's past has been—in order to find out how much she has misled us. Here." Miles reached into his breast pocket and dropped the *carte visite* onto the detective's desk. "Miss Green has imposed on my cousins by pretending to be a respectable girl. This photograph shows that she most certainly is not respectable. She has become the great friend of my cousin Serafina and I need information which will prove that she is not worthy of her interest."

"This photograph by itself will not move your cousin to break with her?" the detective asked looking carefully at the image of Katherine.

"Not without supporting facts that clarify the circumstances in which the picture was taken. You say that this other girl, Francis Coles is a prostitute, I should like to have facts in my hands that would allow me to say definitively the same thing of Katherine Green."

At the mention of Francis Coles' name, the detective frowned again. "I don't know if you realize this, sir, but identity is one of the most difficult matters to clarify, in a legal sense. We are making progress with criminal identification. I personally believe strongly in the value of Mr. Bertillion's system of measurements. But unless someone has been measured in that way in the past, there is nothing to compare with."

"You speak as a specialist, sir, and quite over my head," Miles said. "But if the substance does not help us, let us drop it. Are you telling me that there is no way to make certain of the identity of this girl?"

"I am not prepared to make such a statement until I know more. For instance, can you tell me if this photographer, Boursnell, is still in London?"

"Yes. In fact, I understand he is quite well-known in certain circles."

"Then that is the shortest way to your goal, Mr. Hickinbotham. You or I can go to see him and interview him. We can ask him point blank what the conditions of the photographic session were. We do not even need to touch on the more complex questions of identity. Your need is much simpler. You only want to know where the photographer found this girl and what his relationship with her was. Is that not so?"

"I don't know if that shall be enough. It depends on what he says. How damning it is. May I smoke?"

"Of course, Mr. Hickinbotham. I shall join you. I have some excellent tobacco here," he said as he reached out with a humidor in his hand.

"Thank you, I have my own and am a creature of habit as regards my pleasures."

"Most of us are," the detective said as he cut and lit his cigar.

"So," the detective went on after both men were smoking, "you really have two aims in your investigations. First, you want to try to find your little sister. I told your cousins that success in that quarter is extremely unlikely. Especially after all the time that has passed. But if she was abducted by a professional who sells children to Europe, the chances are even less. Your one chance might be that someone closer to home had taken the girl. Depending on circumstances, that is a crime that might be possible to trace. But it is still very long odds after all this time. Your second aim is to detach this girl who has imposed on you and your family."

"Yes, absolutely. I must have a strong, clear case to present to Serafina."

"But if this photograph is not enough to convince her that the girl is not respectable, what sort of facts do you believe may be able to rid your cousin of this girl? Is she asking your cousin for money?"

"No. In fact, she has scrupulously refused to take any money from us."

"Then she is either very clever and is aiming at some much larger fraud or, she is an honest girl—in spite of the photograph. Many women who sell themselves do it out of hunger."

Ignoring the detectives' comment Miles said, "And what that larger fraud is, sir, we must discover."

For some moments, the detective studied Miles through a curtain of blue smoke. Then he put down his cigar and said, "I think we should proceed from the most simple to the more complex investigation. That will be the most economical use of your money and my time. First, I shall go to this photographer and see what I can learn about the girl. Second, I shall spend some more of your money to try to sort out the identities of Francis Coles and Katherine Green. It is problematic because the person known as Katherine Green, according to her own testimony, was born in India where records of births and deaths are virtually nonexistent for someone of her rank. Let us do that much and see where we find ourselves. That is my recommendation regarding Miss Green. Now, as regards the disappearance of your sister, I have several questions I should like to ask."

"I am at your service," Miles answered.

"Tell me in your own words about the abduction of your sister."

Miles plodded through the well-known facts once more. The detective said nothing but wrote while Miles was giving his testimony. When Miles had finished, Minahan said, "I cannot help but be intrigued by this bird you saw. It seems a most extraordinary coincidence that something so exotic should appear at just that moment. You are quite certain about it?"

"Oh, yes. Definitely, exactly as I described."

"Well, I think that is all I need right now, Mr. Hickinbotham. Make it out for fifteen pounds if you please, sir. I shall go and see the photographer and see what I can learn about Francis Coles and Katherine Green. I may also stop at 180 St. George's Street and visit Mr. Charles Jamrach. The old gentleman is as famous as the lions, tigers and other exotic beasts he sells. He's also got a wonderful memory for animals. If we could identify the parrot and its source, it might lead to something. A thin thread, but we do not have much in any direction. You shall hear from me soon about the photographer, and anything I can learn about the connection between Francis Coles and Katherine Green. I shall also interview Charles Boursnell and send a man incognito to Mrs. Jeffries."

Miles left the detective's chambers satisfied that the investigations were well begun. His impression of Minahan had improved as he talked with the man. The detective's suggestions were rational and to the point. Miles felt there would be no attempt to pad the bill. The fact that there was some obscurity about Katherine's legal identity did not surprise him. Nothing about the girl was straightforward, and if Julia had not found the *carte visite* quite by chance none of them would have ever known how murky her past life had been. Even the detective had been quite shocked by the photograph, Miles thought. There was something more about that photograph...Miles felt. Something he had forgotten, but when he searched his memory the clue slipped away into the shadows.

On arriving at home, Egbert informed him that Katherine had tried to gain access to the studio. When she was prevented from entering, she told the servant that she had a sitting scheduled and that she must at least wait for the woman who was expected. She was permitted to wait under Egbert's eye in his apartment. The woman did come and was angry with Katherine. While she was waiting, Katherine tried to question Egbert, but he was as close as his master could have wished and simply said he was under directions to see that no one entered the studio.

"She had a very pretty, pleading way about her," Egbert said. "She asked if no one was to enter or if the directions applied specifically to her. I told her that no one was to enter while you were out, sir."

"Excellent, Egbert. Very good. You have used your discretion well."

"Thank you, sir."

After this dialogue, Miles changed his clothes and put on his studio smock. He picked up a tablet of newsprint and started to draw in an idle way. His thoughts were still on his discussion with the detective, but he had another commission to begin: the daughter of a wealthy Quaker grocer who, with her snub nose and meaty jowls, looked a little too much like one of the creatures that went into her father's sausages. He was working from a photograph of the girl and managed to occupy himself with it for several hours when he was interrupted by the ringing of the bell downstairs.

A few moments later, Serafina's powerful voice rang through the hallway and up the stairs. "No thank you, I shall let myself in. Your presence is quite unnecessary." It was delivered in an imperious, withering tone that at one time or another had terrified every servant in the Winstanley household, even old Rossiter.

Realizing what must have happened, Miles put his draw-ing aside and went to the door. He was just in time to see Serafi-na's tall figure flouncing up the stairs in a green gown of gathered silk. She looked dazzling, but the colour in her creamy skin told him she was very angry.

"Serafina, what a nice surprise," he said holding out his hands as Serafina removed her gloves and coat.

"What are you trying to do to poor Katherine, Miles? Why was she barred from the studio today—when your man was told she had a client? I am quite shocked. I have never known you to be so ungenerous before. You know the poor girl is no longer employed—thanks to you. Her only income is from the career in which you encouraged her. Now, when she needs your studio most, you bar her? What are you thinking of?"

"Please walk in, Serafina, I shall do my best to explain."

"I should hope so." The airy flounces of her skirt brushed by him as she entered the apartment.

Miles and Julia had agreed that Serafina should know nothing of the *carte visite*, not until the detective could reveal more about it. He could not break faith with Julia, his only real ally in the crisis, so he must try to put Serafina off without tell-ing her the real reason. This train of thought flashed through his mind before he had even caught Serafina up at the table which held the humidor. She expertly selected a cigar, rolling it in her fingers to test its freshness, and took a pearl handled knife from her purse to cut the tip.

"You, too, are becoming a regular smoker?" Miles asked.

The pair had not been alone together since the night of

the quarrel on Cavendish Square. The silence was heavy and awkward, the pauses between words too long.

"I suppose I have. These are good. You must give me the name of your tobacconist." She puffed manfully on the cigar and generated a cloud of blue smoke. Miles thought she looked different in some way he could not specify.

"Are you well, Serafina?" he asked.

"Oh, yes. As always."

Neither spoke for some long seconds.

"Now you really must tell me why you are persecuting Katherine, Miles? Surely you realize that situated as she is she must have a studio to use. She really must."

Miles was most alarmed to hear Serafina's voice rise and take on an edge of hysteria. He had never seen her so lacking in self-possession.

"Serafina, what is wrong? I fear you are not well," Miles said.

"I shall be fine if you will let Katherine use your studio," she replied as she carefully rolled the ash off the end of her cigar and into the brass tray next to her.

"Do sit down, Serafina. And let us speak as the friends we are."

"Katherine is my friend, too, Miles. My dear friend. And you are persecuting her for no reason I can understand."

"I am not persecuting her. I have simply learned some things which make it necessary for my own professional standing not to have her in my studio."

"What things?" She shot back, clamping the cigar in her mouth in a gesture that Miles had never seen before. Something about her was changed, but he didn't know what. Again, he feared illness. He must tell Julia about his observations.

"What things?" she repeated in a tone that was aggressive even for Serafina.

"I cannot tell you, yet. But I shall, soon."

"And how is Katherine supposed to eat between now and then?"

"I don't know. It is not my problem."

Serafina looked stung and stared at him in amazement. "I never thought the day would come when you could seem heartless to me. But that is how you seem, now. It is very sad. I feel I have lost a dear friend after many years of close association."

They stared at each other across a gulf, which in that moment, seemed enormous. Miles felt confused. Serafina was angry. How could this be happening? Miles wondered? What hold did the girl have on Serafina that she should turn on him this way?

"Serafina, can you not trust me regarding this matter for a little while?"

"Miles, you simply do not understand all that Katherine has done for me. I must help her now that she is in need."

"How is she helping you?"

"I have had trouble sleeping since mama died. And sometimes I forget the time."

"What do you mean, forget the time?"

"I lose track of time. Sometimes for many hours. I do not sleep, but I seem to wake up and cannot remember the preceding hours."

"Serafina, you are not well." He felt his presentiment about her had been confirmed. "You should see a doctor."

"Katherine is my doctor. She is helping me."

"How? What do you mean?"

"She has mesmerized me on several occasions and it has made me feel much better. I really fear I have not been quite myself since mama died."

"I think that is true," Miles said, as he felt the blood in his body drain downward, leaving him suddenly cold and frightened.

While it was still some fourteen years before the publication of *Trilby*, the most famous book ever written about the power of abusive hypnotism, enough had been written about hypnotic suggestion to frighten Miles. He had quite by chance on a visit to Paris read *Mémoires d'un magnétiseur*, in which Charles Lafontaine, the famous stage hypnotist of the mid century, had described how he became interested in hypnosis by seeing the control exerted on a young woman by her magnetizer. There was another French hypnotist who had also written about using his power to obtain sexual favours from his female subject. Thank God, Katherine was a woman! He remembered the detective saying that Katherine might have a larger, a greater, fraud as her object. Perhaps he had unwittingly uncovered it. Perhaps she was trying to take control of Serafina's mind to have free access to her fortune.

"You absolutely refuse to let Katherine use your studio?" Serafina asked again after the long silence, during which Miles had been mentally referring to his own reading on the subject of hypnosis.

As he reached out and took her hands in his he said, "Serafina, my dearest, I must refuse. My own reputation and livelihood may depend on it. Don't judge me until you have all the facts. I beg you."

She tore her hands from his, turned away and picked up her gloves.

"Good day to you, sir. Until the day you apologize to Katherine for your infamous behaviour, we shall be strangers to one another."

And she opened the door and started down the steps. Miles stood, rooted to the spot, not knowing what to do. He remained in this paralysis of indecision until he heard the outside door downstairs open and close. Serafina was gone. There were only two things now he could do, and he did them both, immediately. He wrote to Julia to tell her what had happened and what he had learned, and he wrote to the detective and told him he must work faster. Then he threw the letter away. Time was now of the essence, he felt. He wanted to impart a great sense of urgency to Mr. Minahan. He would go to see the detective in person. He must separate Serafina from the succubus who had taken control of her. The sooner he could gain his end, the better for all of them. He nearly ran down the stairs on his way out. There was no time to write.

Chapter 16

A PROFESSIONAL'S VIEW OF THE CASE

"It will be best, sir, if you can remain calm," detective Minahan said as he looked across his desk at the distraught young man. "Try to tell me clearly what has led to your sudden reappearance and alarm about your cousin?"

"I should think my alarm was easy to understand, sir. I have just found out that my cousin is under the mesmeric influence of this dangerous girl. For all I know, she may have taken complete control of her. You said she might have some large aim in view. I think she is trying to control my cousin's mind."

"To what end, sir?" the detective asked in his exasperatingly stolid manner.

"To what end? To get her money—to influence her in any way she chooses."

"Is your cousin of age, sir? She told me she was."

"Oh, yes. But can't we lock her up? To protect her—until we get rid of this succubus?"

"It is not so easy to lock up young ladies as it once was. And you are not even her husband. Even if you were, it is no longer a simple thing to do."

"But how can I just stand by and watch my family be imposed upon like this? There's no telling what this girl is after. I just thank heavens that it is not a man who is exercising such an unnatural influence over Serafina."

"I quite understand your feelings on that point, sir. Can I offer you a restorative, sir? Some brandy?"

"Yes, thank you." Miles said irritably. He tossed off the drink before the detective had lowered his bulk back into his chair.

"You mean there is nothing legal we can do to stop this girl?"

"That is correct, sir."

"Good God, I wish I'd never stopped to help her."

The detective watched him with a reptilian immobility, like a lizard watching a fly.

"I quite understand your frustration, sir. On another subject: I have gotten some additional information regarding your sister. Can you answer some further questions, now?"

"I suppose, if there is nothing more I can do for Serafina."

"We could set a man to follow this girl and see what the surveillance turns up. It's expensive but something might appear."

"Yes, by all means. Let's do it," Miles said, brightening visibly. "This is hardly the time to worry about costs. I want to leave nothing undone that might prove effective."

"Very well," the detective pen scratched out a note to himself. "Now, about your sister and her abduction."

"Yes."

"I visited Mr. Jamrasch in the east end. He told me that your bird, as you described it, was a taxonomic impossibility. It does not exist. And, your sister is not resident at Mrs. Jeffries Chelsea establishment, nor at the one in Hampstead. If she went to the one on Kings Road, she must be dead by now."

Miles felt suddenly uneasy, uneasy in exactly the same way he used to feel at times as a child. "When you say the bird does not exist, what are you implying?" The young man could hear the shrillness in his own voice.

"Nothing at all, sir. Merely stating a fact."

"There was a bird. I feel certain there was."

"Memory is an odd thing, sir. I have heard many witnesses testify under oath to things they believed they had seen. Usually, it was because the truth was, literally, something they did not want to see. Did you hear me, sir? Do you understand?"

Miles eyes had become strangely clouded as he listened to the detective. He appeared far away from the seedy office, deep inside himself.

"And if the bird were not there?" Miles finally managed.

"It would mean that something else might have happened and your memory filled it in with this mythical bird."

"And what would that 'something else' be?"

"I don't know, sir. That is a question for you to answer."

"Yes, I suppose it is," he replied distantly. "It is odd the way your questions have dissolved the image of that bird I have carried with me for years."

"Now there is one other point I want to mention," the detective said. "How well did you know Dr. Winstanley when he was alive? Did you see him often?"

"Dr. Winstanley? Why are you bringing him into this? He was a very respectable man. Highly honoured in his profession. A great scientist."

"Yes, he was a doctor, an expert in administering anesthetic, was he not?"

"I see you have been doing some digging into my family's history."

"That's what you are paying me for, sir. Did you ever meet a friend of his, a titled Belgian man he corresponded with in Europe?"

"No. I don't recall ever meeting any European nobility. Why?"

"Your cousins gave me access to some of his papers."

"Really?"

"Yes. Miss Julia Winstanley has been particularly helpful."

"You certainly haven't let any grass grow under your feet, Mr. Minahan. I must tell you that when we first met, I thought you rather a slow man. Now you seem quite the opposite."

"I found among these scraps one letter from a European

gentleman with a title, a Baron Mesnil de Hermann. Have you heard of him?"

"No. Is the letter interesting in some way?"

"Only by the fact that it has reposed in Dr. Winstanley's desk."

"I have never heard of this man, let alone met him."

"It is a thread I should like to follow."

"Do not spare expenses, sir, if, in your judgment, you believe something worth doing. I believe you are an honest practitioner of your trade."

The detective gave a bow of the head in acknowledgement of Miles' words. "I thank you for your good opinion, sir."

"Keep in mind in future that you do not have to clear each small expenditure with me. I want things cleared up. We have had far too much mystery in our family, especially with this dangerous girl involving herself. I wish there was something we could do about her. I have closed my door to her. I wish I had some way of closing Serafina's."

"I shall visit the photographer, Charles Boursnell and interview him. Perhaps something will come of that."

"I certainly hope so."

"I feel we have made a good start."

"Extraordinary, considering the time in which you had to work."

"Thank you, again for your praise, sir. I hope it may all end in a satisfactory manner."

"How do you think it will end, Mr. Minahan? Do you think we shall be successful?"

"I told you at the outset that I feared we'd have little luck in tracing your missing sister. I now feel somewhat more sanguine about the matter."

"Really?"

"I also agree with you about this hypnotist. There are numerous criminal cases involving hypnotism that have been prosecuted on the continent. Usually, though, such cases involve a man and a woman. I think this girl is a danger to your family. She sounds clever, educated out of her class and ambitious, and she appears to have a firm grip on your cousin. And so far, she is doing everything out in the open. Things were different before the Weldon woman came along and turned the law on its head. I still think that women sometimes need to be reined in, sir, if you know what I mean."

"I know exactly what you mean. There couldn't be a clearer case than that of Serafina."

And that was the last bit of conversation with the detective Miles could remember when he found himself strolling along the Whitechapel Road near Aldgate. As Serafina had described, it was somewhat like waking. He could not remember the precise moment when he had slipped into forgetfulness. The journey to the detective's was hazy, but the meeting was clear up to conversation about the bird and Serafina. Then, everything seemed to slip away into darkness. The afternoon seemed covered under a thick haze even though, for once, the air was clear.

"Good heaven's," he muttered. "Could the little witch have hypnotized me, too without my knowing it? I must tell Julia about this. She may have some thoughts on the matter, though I know that, by and large, she is on Katherine's side. I shall go home and write to her. First, I may lie down. I do feel odd."

Chapter 17

TROUBLED RELATIONS

"…the churches are making the discovery that seething in the very centre of our great cities, concealed by the thinnest crust of civilization and decency, is a vast mass of moral corruption, of heart-breaking misery and absolute godlessness, and that scarcely anything has been done to take into this awful slough the only influences that can purify or remove it…THIS TERRIBLE FLOOD OF SIN AND MISERY IS GAINING UPON US."

—Andrew Mearns, *The Bitter Cry of Outcast London: An Inquiry into the Condition of the Abject Poor,* October 1883

On 8 February 1886, Julia and Serafina attended a meeting held by the Fair Trade League in Trafalgar Square. They met to demand protective tariffs and public works to cure unemployment. Roughly 20,000 people, many of them dock and building workers, assembled. Serafina was a member of the Social Democratic Federation which interrupted the meeting and led part of the crowd in the direction of Hyde Park. Julia came in support of the dockers, whose plight she had written about in the *Pall Mall Gazette,* but she, like William Morris, Eleanor Marx and others, had left the Social Democratic Federation because of the dicta-

torial style of H.M. Hyndman, one of the group's leaders. Hyndman advocated the use of violence in demonstrations, a point of
view Serafina supported. A portion of the SDF crowd marched
west, bent on 'getting their own back' from the elegant west-end
shops. In the looting that followed, roughly £50,000 in damage
was done. Serafina went with this group. Julia remained close to
Trafalgar Square. Many of the people in the crowd would have
been described as 'loafers' by the wealthy west-end people —in
the same words used by Beatrice Webb, later Beatrice Potter,
who said they were "low looking, bestial, content with their own
condition." Charles Booth, the famous demographer of poverty
said they were, "Battered figures who slouch through the streets
and play the bettor or bully or help to foul the record of the
unemployed." As in the time of Mayhew, the 1850s, the middle
and upper classes of the west-end could not tell the difference
between those who wanted work and could not find it and those
who would not work. All homeless people were still lumped
together as the 'dangerous classes,' and in 1886, the west-end
of London felt itself surrounded and embattled by what Charles
Warren, Police Commissioner called, "the scum of Europe," by
which he meant the Jewish immigrants who were swelling the
population of Whitechapel and other communities in the
east-end.

　　As the streets around Trafalgar Square filled with marchers, the sisters were lost to each other in the crowd. Serafina
was pushed westward along with the looters. Hours later, when
Julia returned home, there was still no sign of Serafina at Cavendish Square. By dinner hour, Julia became frantic and wrote
to Miles. At nightfall, a thick fog descended on London which
lasted for two days during which, Serafina did not come home,
nor was there any word of her. Miles first went to the police and
then stayed at Cavendish Square with Julia, awaiting news of
the missing girl. The deep fog added to the menace felt by the
inhabitants of the west-end and consequently to the anxieties
felt by Miles and Julia.

　　What then was their astonishment when Virgil, the
bloodhound, began frantically barking just after Miles and Julia

sat down to dinner. A few moments later, Serafina walked through the front door of her home with as little concern as if she had just returned from buying a newspaper? There was a large bruise on the side of her head with traces of blood on it. She refused to talk about where she had been and said only, "Those who have control of capital, whether in the form of money or equipment had better begin to use it for the benefit of those who have nothing."

It was obvious to Miles that she was referring to himself and his studio, as well as the City's ship owners and London's other great employers who had precipitated the demonstration at Trafalgar Square.

"Serafina," Miles said angrily, "You have been most inconsiderate to me and to your sister. How can you behave like this, and allow us to fear for your safety? You should be spanked and locked in your room."

"No. She must see a doctor," Julia said.

A bold, defiant expression took possession of Serafina's handsome features. "You are certainly not man enough to spank me, Miles, or even to attempt it."

"Serafina!" her sister cried. "How can you speak like that to him? You have frightened us both to death. I insist that you see the doctor."

"No, I shall not. It is very easy to criticize me while you sit in our comfortable home with all our luxuries, but what would either of you do if you were poor and hungry and found every door closed in your face, I wonder? I have looked into the lives of the poor as never before. They are a dreadful reflection of our own lives. I am going to my room, now," she said and swept from the parlour.

Miles and Julia looked at one another with astonishment written on their faces.

"What can have happened to her?" Julia asked. "Where has she been? She does not look as if she has been carrying the banner for two days."

"Has been what?" Miles asked.

"'Carrying the banner,' is an expression used by casuals

who have nowhere to go but the workhouse or, preferably, into a grave. It means being forced to walk all night without being able to lie down and sleep."

"I can't believe she has been in the streets for two nights," Miles said. "Her dress was not disordered. Her person is clean."

"No. I agree," Julia said. "I don't know what to do now. Miles, what is happening to my sister? She seems so strange."

"I wonder," Miles said, thoughtfully.

"What, Miles?"

"I wonder if she could have been with that girl, Katherine. That would fit with her comment to me about money and equipment."

"But to go off and leave us like this. It is not like her."

"You know that Katherine has been mesmerizing her, don't you? I have been speculating about why. But now, I am convinced there is some kind of connection between these *conversaziones* and the way Serafina is behaving."

"But Katherine has only been helping her to sleep and feel calm," Julia said.

"So you have known about these 'meetings?'" Miles said.

"Well, I know they have been seeing each other regularly. Often right here."

"Then you have not heard Katherine suggest anything that might be dangerous to Serafina? Because, Julia, mark my words: that girl is at the bottom of this mischief. Mr. Minahan, the detective, agrees with me. And suddenly, he remembered that he had not written to Julia after his last visit to Minahan's office. Surprised by his own recollection he paused and then resumed his tirade against Katherine with renewed vigour. "She is influencing Serafina in some dangerous way, perhaps with mesmerism, which is affecting her mental balance. It is unfortunate we are not married. I would commit her."

"I would never do that to her, Miles. Nor would I permit you to do it. It is not so easy, any more, to lock up a disobedient wife. And for that I am glad. All women owe Mrs. Weldon a debt of gratitude for the way she ridiculed madhouse doctors in a court of law. I have heard Katherine say nothing during their mesmeric sessions but offer the most harmless suggestions about relaxation and sleep."

"After seeing the *carte visite* you found, I feel a profound distrust of that girl in all directions," Miles said.

"I agree that it is a shocking picture. But I think it is less the picture and more an issue of the deceit. If she had told us she had been a prostitute, it would not have been such a shock...and we might still..."

"I don't think," Miles said interrupting her, "either you or Serafina, or I, would have taken her photographs seriously if she had openly presented herself as a prostitute. I doubt I should have spoken to her at all."

"I'd like to think Serafina and I are free of all such biases, but I believe you are probably right. We would certainly have been more on our guards."

"Well, the past is the past. But, what are we to do, now?" he asked himself. "Wait. Let me think. Serafina has already met the detective I am employing. But Minahan must have other operatives whom Serafina has never seen."

"You want to spy on her? Have her followed?"

"If we can't lock her up, do you have a better way to make certain that Serafina is protected?" Miles asked.

Julia's fine featured face grew pale. Her features seemed to shrink into themselves as her face contracted into a scowl.

"That seems such a terrible thing to do," she said finally.

"Would you rather miss her for another two nights—and God forbid, lose her forever?" Miles asked. "We have been fortunate this time. But who knows what might happen if she stays out again. She is an elegant and beautiful young woman who would fetch a high price in the European white slave markets. You know better than I that the trade goes on unabated, in spite of the Criminal Amendment Act. The detective's operative could at least tell us where she goes if she stays out again all night. And watch over her to insure her safety."

"But to set a paid spy on my own sister..."

"Would you rather try to confine her here?"

249

"No. Of course not. It is unthinkable."

"I know that setting a spy on her is a terrible thought. But I would feel far worse if anything happened to her. We have already lost one family member. If Serafina does stay out again all night—on the streets..." he let the sentence hang in the air.

Julia reached over and took his hand. "You are right, Miles. My arguments are based on feeling not on judgement. Serafina's safety is of the last importance in this situation."

"Absolutely. Then, I shall instruct Minahan by post?"

"Yes, Miles. I can see no other way to be certain she is safe."

Shortly after the surveillance was begun, the man who worked for Minhan followed Serafina into the east-end one night, during a march against Whitechapel sweat shops employed in the shoe-making trade, one of the many industries which did not require capital but only an inexhaustible supply of sweated, semi-skilled and unskilled labour. Minahan's operative followed Serafina into a dismal, obscure court where he was violently attacked, beaten and left for dead. Mr. Minahan was baffled at the attack and could not understand how an experienced operative could be caught so unprepared to defend himself. All the man could say for himself was that he never saw his attacker. He followed the young lady into the narrow passage and did not believe anyone else was there. Once in darkness, he was attacked by someone tremendously strong who rushed out of the gloom with a suddenness that caught the detective agent completely unprepared to hold his ground. He was lifted off his feet and flung against an alley wall like a rag doll, his arm broken in the grip of his powerful assailant. After this incident, Minahan's other operatives refused to follow Serafina through the unlit alleys and courts of Whitechapel. All the detective's efforts to watch over Serafina proved futile.

After the incident, in spite of their heightened anxiety, Miles and Julia had no choice but to drop the surveillance. Neither of them wanted to make the family a public scandal by consulting yet another detective, who would probably be less

qualified than Minahan. They could not go to the regular police—with Serafina's well-documented record of socialism and
political agitation. Miles increasingly felt that his own suit with
Serafina was hopeless. The extreme radical nature of her political life, her sojourns into darkest London and her cool, ironic
treatment of him whenever they met left him no choice, he felt,
but to look elsewhere for a wife. He could hardly believe that
Serafina was the same person he had known and wanted for so
many years. He could not discern all the steps of Serafina's transformation, but the changes seemed to date from her seances with
Katherine. He urged Julia to separate the two women somehow,
but the younger sister was at a loss how to do it.

"Unfortunately, Serafina is not a child," Julia replied. " I
cannot just order her to do this or that, Miles, as you very well
know. I am not certain that her character is fundamentally different, in any case. It is more a matter of degree."

"But in character, a matter of degree is everything," Miles
retorted. "An interest in reading the newspaper may be perfectly
normal, but filling one's house with old newspapers is not."

"But Miles," she said placing her hand tenderly on his
arm, "you shall not desert us? I have no one else I can turn to
except Mr. Minahan. Tell me that you will not go away from us."

"Of course, Julia," he said, feeling embarrassed by the
girl's direct appeal. "We are, after all, still family. None of us
have any other close connections. I hope that Serafina regains
some balance in her thinking but if there is a crisis, you may call
on me. I think, too, I must call on Mr. Minahan again. "

The girl did not release his arm but said, "But even if
there is not crisis, you will come to see us?"

"Of course, Julia. You are the best and dearest girl in the
world. I wish Serafina had more of your sweetness."

He completely ignored the short, sharp exhalation of
pain that his remark induced in Julia. There was nothing more
he could say to comfort her.

Next day, after a good morning of working on the jowly

face of his latest commission, Miles walked into the City to see the detective. The man was somewhat chagrined as he greeted Miles.

"I must say, sir, I have not done well for you. I reprimanded my agent in the strongest possible terms. But he stuck to his story and I had to let him off. Such things do happen in police work."

"And the first matter I came about, my little sister's abduction?"

The man pulled at his fleshy lower lip with his thick tobacco stained fingers.

"I have nothing to report, yet, sir. But please note, I say, 'yet,' for I do believe I have hold of some threads that will lead to something worth while."

"And have you made any progress with the identity of Katherine Green? You mentioned someone named Francis Coles. That they were in some way connected. Can you tell me more of this?"

"I'll tell you what I have, sir and I admit it is slender. I have eye-witness testimony of someone arriving on a P&O ship from the subcontinent, name of Katherine Green. That's the name she gave. But in less than a week she meets Francis Coles, a young prostitute and moves in with her. Then, Francis seems to have disappeared. The only reason I got this far was that I happened to know the purser on the P&O vessel. Otherwise, there is no record of Katherine Green having arrived in London. I think she must have shared a cabin with someone else. And there is now no sign of the original Francis Coles, which only means I cannot find her. A girl living at the home for Asians where Miss Green told you she went upon disembarking, died of something whose symptoms sound like cholera, though there were no other cases. There is only someone known mostly as Katherine Green living in the other girl's lodgings. Very obscure, I am sorry to say, sir. If there was any evidence of a felony, sir, I could have the girl arrested, but there is really nothing. However, I did do well with Mr. Charles Boursnell. He told me that the girl, Katherine Green had worked for him for a short time."

"Worked? How?"

"Modeled, charred. He says that the *carte visite* is the only nude photograph he ever took of her. But, I have a hunch she was also a source of sexual favours as well, even though there is a great difference in their ages."

"It wouldn't surprise me at all. I want you to keep on trying to find the true identity of Katherine Green, and, of course, anything more you can learn about my sister. Perhaps you could write to the authorities at Simla and see if they know of Miss Green."

The big man pulled even harder at his lip. "Ordinarily, I should have done that first, sir, but it takes so long to get any reply from the Eastern Empire, and Simla is upcountry, besides. It could be a year before I hear anything, providing my letter does not go astray. I have done it, though, sir. When we shall hear anything, heaven knows."

"And the surveillance?"

"I'll be frank, sir. None of my other lads will do it. The man who was hurt was a big, strong man, experienced, sir. If he can be injured so severely, the others say, it could happen to anyone. A broken arm will stop the injured man having regular wages for a long time. I could recommend another agency, sir."

"No. We have chosen you to wash our dirty linen for us. But I do not want our family to become a public scandal. If your men won't do it, we shall have to let it go."

"A very headstrong young lady, sir, if I may say so. Brave, in the face of such danger. But dangerously headstrong."

"I am afraid I can't disagree with you," Miles answered.

After this impasse was reached, Miles saw less and less of his cousins and concentrated himself more exclusively on his own career, which began to progress by leaps and bounds, thanks largely to the public exhibition of his painting of Amelia, which was chosen by the Royal Society as the year's most promising work by a young artist. His words to Julia notwithstanding, he avoided Cavendish Square. "If I had not talked to Katherine that night at Piccadilly, Serafina and I might have been married by now," he often told himself.

During the Spring of 1887, Serafina and Julia became very taken up with feeding the poor and unemployed who were gathering in ever greater numbers in Trafalgar Square. All through the summer, Serafina helped organize some of the west-end charities that provided food for the vagrants who camped in London's very heart. At first, the police were reluctant to interfere. But by November of '87, the situation had reached a flash point with large numbers of homeless living in the open air beneath Nelson's column. Charles Warren, recently appointed Police Commissioner was a former army man who had little experience dealing with civilian populations. His main recommendation for office was that he had caught the killers who wiped out Palmer's famous Egyptian expedition in '82 and been knighted for it. In November, he finally acted in the heavy-handed way that characterized his tenure as Police Commissioner.

On "Bloody Sunday," 13 November 1887, the Metropolitan Federation of Radical Clubs organized a series of marches and demonstrations to protest the government's policy of coercion in Ireland. Serafina marched in one of them with her radical friends. Julia, sensing trouble, tried to stop her from going, but without success. The police violently dispersed the marchers before they reached Trafalgar Square. Serafina was hit on the head and in return knocked a constable unconscious with a length of pipe. She was arrested on the spot and taken to prison. Because of her height and because she was wearing trousers and a man's hat, the police did not at first realize that they had a west-end lady in their cells.

When Serafina did not return home after 'Bloody Sunday', Julia wrote to Miles and begged him to go to Bow Street Police Court to enquire after her sister.

"Dear Miles," Julia wrote, "for the sake of our good times together and for our family will you find Serafina for me and bring her home? I have no one else I can ask. I feel quite alone."

It was a plea he could not ignore. From the Bow Street Police Court he went to the Bridwell, and from there was directed, to, of all places, the Police Commissioner's office in Whitehall. It took some hours to discover exactly where Serafina was. Miles finally found her in a corridor near Charles Warren's office. She was manacled to a heavy oak bench, apparently awaiting someone, anyone, who would take her home and get her off the hands of the police. Miles was appalled by the blood on her face and in her hair. Her man's suit shocked him and he was horrified to see how roughly she had been handled by the authorities. Serafina's father, who had been well known in his field was also known to the police for his forensic skills. The Winstanley name had been finally recognized and Serafina was brought up out of the cells, against her own insistent cries that she be tried with the other demonstrators. Her behaviour with the police was so aggressive and abusive, no one wanted to come near her once she had been manacled to the bench. Finally, she quieted down and sat by herself for hours. Given the strained relations between the police and the populace, Commissioner Warren was most anxious to avoid a scandal involving a west-end family and the police. All he wanted was to see her gone. This service, Miles willingly undertook to perform.

Anyone watching the pair in the corridor at Whitehall would never have imagined them to be one-time lovers. It was a strained, repressed meeting in a quiet, though busy, public corridor. Miles was shocked by her appearance and could not hide his impression of her. Serafina was pale and silent. At first, she scarcely acknowledged his presence. He was himself surprised at how distant he felt from her. He could hardly believe she was the beautiful and elegant young woman he had aspired to marry. The bedraggled looking creature in man's clothing with blood and dirt on her face seemed hardly like the Serafina to whose graceful hand he had aspired. She looked almost like a common tramp. Then she smiled at him in her ironic, mocking way, and he knew her.

"I shall live to fight another day, Miles. I trust the constable I coshed will, too. So, you needn't look so concerned. They would have turned me loose before now if they weren't afraid I might do something even more scandalous than calling the Police Commissioner an old walrus."

"I don't imagine that went down too well with him," Miles replied, smiling briefly. "I have heard he is something of a martinet and likes to stand on his own dignity. But Serafina, how could I be otherwise than concerned under these circumstances? For Julia, if not for you. She is terrified when you become involved in something like this. You..."

"Miles, please spare me your male opprobrium. I am tired. I ache and I should like to go home and get into a hot bath without listening to homilies meant for my moral improvement."

"I shall get someone to release you," he replied as he quickly stepped away to find someone who had a key to the manacles.

It is a bitter thing when one realizes that one no longer loves. When we love, our feelings seem deathless and permanent. When we lose that illusion, yet again, we are reminded of our own temporal nature and insignificance. This was exactly the kind of grief Miles felt as he strode through the halls, through the apparent somnolence of official power to find the key to the manacles. He wanted nothing more, in that moment, than to be rid of Serafina and forget every trace of the feelings he had formerly felt for her. Having seen her again, he knew it would be possible to expunge their former relationship, for in fact, it was Katherine he thought of as he walked away from Serafina to get the key.

When he realized that Katherine preoccupied him he thought, "That is the strangest bond of all. A kind of malign spell. I wonder if that is how Serafina feels about her? What strange netherworld had that girl issued from that night at Piccadilly? I am not even sure of her real name. Or even what country she was born in. Nor do I understand how she continues to hold any interest for me or my cousin."

But the girl did continue to haunt him. Her face became, for him, a face he imagined seeing intermittently in crowds or in moments before sleep. Sometime he even believed she looked like Amelia. What she had become in his thoughts, he knew, was entirely of his own making, but then, so is everything we perceive, especially when seen among the dancing shadows cast into the mind by the fire of eros.

"Perhaps," he thought "that is why Psyche was supposed to look upon her supernatural lover only in darkness when she could not see him," Miles theorized. "I should have paid Katherine whatever price she might have asked and had her in a dark east-end alley the night we met. Then all of this mystery would have been dissipated by our thrustings and grunts. And I now would be married to Serafina. No woman could remain a metaphysical force once she was known in the biblical sense. If Dante had rutted with his lover, there would have been no divine Beatrice," he told himself, as he finally found the desk of the usher who had the key to Serafina's manacles.

Serafina's wrists were bruised when the manacles were removed. Miles bundled her into a cab and took her directly to Cavendish Square, where Julia met them at the door.

"Serafina, thank God," Julia said as she embraced her sister. She looked over her sister's shoulder at Miles and said, "God bless you. You are a dear friend."

He said nothing but turned away and retreated down the front steps. He heard Julia ask, "Are you hurt, dearest?" As he moved away from them and got into the cab, the sisters' voices became faint murmurings issuing from the darkness. He saw only their silhouettes framed in the doorway by the yellow light within. Then, their shapes and sounds were suddenly cut off as the front door closed and the cab began to roll forward.

He would not visit Cavendish Square again for almost a year but, he thought of his cousins frequently in the privacy of his studio, especially at those times when he studied the nude photograph of Katherine.

"Perhaps," he thought, "all women were interchangeable when examined on the most elemental level. What could any man really know of them? It seems, at times, that we hardly know ourselves."

Chapter 17

A SEASON IN HELL BEGINS

The young men of the middle and upper classes are commended by our social reformers, political economists and Malthusians, for being more prudent and provident than those of the working class because they marry late in life; these expounders and eulogizers of the present system of society conveniently ignore that these prudent and provident young men usually gratify their passions by ruining the daughters of the working class, which economic conditions offer as a vicarious sacrifice of the wealthy classes to whom these popinjays of society ultimately unite themselves.

—*Justice*, east-end socialist paper, 1888

Miles shivered in the unusually wet and cold summer night as the cab drove him eastward to meet one of his wealthiest clients, viscount Michael Adair, a man close to his own age who wanted to go slumming in the pubs, music halls and flesh-pots in the degenerate depths of the east end. He had commissioned three paintings from Miles in the last six months to decorate a new home in the west end, so the painter had no choice but to oblige his patron. He was well aware that the handsome commissions he had been given owed much to the friendly feeling that the young viscount harboured for him. The shy young nobleman had a great admiration for the interest Miles was able to stir in women. On his part, Miles was glad to be known as an artist with a patron whose father sat in the House of Lords.

"Beastly rotten night for a crawl," Miles muttered to himself as the four-wheeler left the City and passed through Aldgate and into the Whitechapel Road. He took out a handsome silver flask and gave it a quick pull. The brandy spread through him with the heat of a comforting fire, and he felt that much more comforted by it while looking out at the passing, sordid streets. It was a route he had not taken since the night he had driven Katherine to her home in the east end. The fog lay thickly on the paving stones and the horses' breaths made small white clouds in the chill, damp air. The preceding winter had been one of the coldest on record and while Miles felt a slight discomfort in the chill of the cold summer night, he was aware that dozens of people had died on the streets and docks of the east end in the season gone by. His long association with Julia and Serafina had given him a social conscience whether he wanted it or not. He thought of a headline he had seen a few days earlier about another drowned docker who had missed his footing on a foggy pier. The news item and the streets through which he was passing made him wonder about Katherine.

"Where is she on such a sharp, miserable night," he wondered. "Is she warm? Has she eaten?" Then to his own musings he sarcastically added, "She had better keep her clothes on in this weather."

Then he thought of his cousins and realized he had not seen either of them at all in the course of the busy winter, not even during the holidays. It was the first time in years that the holidays had passed without the cousins sharing at least one festive meal. He and Julia had written briefly, several times. She now had her own column in the PMG and Serafina was more and more engaged in working with the Socialists in the east-end.

"I wonder that Serafina doesn't find these streets horribly depressing to her spirits," Miles said out loud. "Her tastes have always been so refined. These slimy streets are very ugly, especially on a night like this."

"Everything changes," Miles thought to himself. Then, thinking of Serafina, and the last time he had seen her, "Everything has changed."

The concluding report he had received from Minahan and passed on to Julia had been largely negative. It only asserted that Amelia had probably not been abducted by Mrs. Jeffries, any of her minions or other well-known traffickers in the European slave trade. Like so many thousands on the streets of London, Amelia had simply been 'lost,' no doubt taken by someone for nefarious purposes.

"I have pretty well exhausted my sources here and in Europe," the detective had written."

Minahan's report concluded that the chances of ever finding out anything more did not justify pursuing the investigation. And there, the matter of Amelia's abduction had ended.

The crawl was to begin in Shadwell since, as Miles young patron had told him, "there are four or five of the lowest dens imaginable there, all within a few blocks of one another. And we shall be close to one of the most famous opium dens in the east end, as well." Such were the pleasures of the evening as they had been outlined to Miles by the young lordling. The four wheeler carried Miles down the Whitechapel Road until it was time to turn south toward the river, where the side streets immediately grew narrower and darker with every block. The four wheeler finally came to rest in front of the Hoop and Grapes on the Shadwell High Street. The glass of the pub's front window was steamy and opaque with the breaths of the inmates and in order to reach the door, Miles had to step over a man, dead or dead drunk, who sprawled on the pavement.

"I suppose," Miles thought as he pushed open the swinging door, "he could be an advertisement for the potency of the beverages."

Standing at the bar in front of the rows of red, blue and yellow coloured glasses and bottles was Miles' client, the viscount Adair, elder son of the richest family in Portman Place. He was a very young looking man, made to look even younger by the extremely soft and tentative quality of his ginger-coloured mustachios and sideburns and his very pallid skin. He was narrow chested and was dressed in a crudely made black suit, probably borrowed from a servant's closet, which was still more handsome than any garment visible on any of the authentic denizens of the place. As Miles hailed the younger man, his chief feeling was one of embarrassment at having lent himself to such an outing.

"Adair," he called, raising his stick, whose protection he had refused to abandon for the sake of fitting into the east end crowd.

"There you are, Winstanley. I was starting to think I might have given you too much work, that you were still back in your studio painting away, what?"

That the remark was a veiled threat, there could be no doubt. It could be roughly translated as, "Humour me tonight or lose commissions." It was too bad to have to appease such a creature, Miles thought. But Lorenzo de Medici had been far more dangerous, though less vulgar. Michaelangelo had managed. On that reflection, he decided to get drunk and to take gracefully whatever came.

"You're drinking gin, of course," Adair said. "Must stay in character, what? I've already had three. Tastes like mineral spirits. All part of the ambience. Just a starting point."

"It seems unusually crowded tonight. Not just here, but the streets as well," Miles said.

"Bank holiday, old son," the viscount said.

"Oh, yes. I had forgotten," Miles replied.

Miles was halfway through his fourth drink before he could comfortably dismiss his companion's callow remarks. He was leaning against the bar and observing in the glass behind the bar that the viscount's eyes were very close together and slightly crossed when he felt something soft touch him on his back. He ignored the contact which he assumed was the result of close quarters, but the pressure against his body increased. It felt for all the world that someone was leaning against him. He turned around and found himself looking at a girl of about thirteen.

She looked much like Katherine's lost friend, Susan, only darker and not quite as pretty. The woman-child was drunk and her expression was angry, but when she caught Miles' eye, she looked at him with undisguised lust. There was something perversely attractive about her shameless desire. Serafina would never look at a man that way. Would Katherine? He felt himself stirred by it. For a moment he held himself away from her while her eyes burned into his, and in the suspension of that moment, he was reminded of his first meeting with Katherine. He turned his back to her and faced his drink on the bar.

"Too good for me are you?," a sharp, angry voice with a cockney accent squawked at him from behind, but the pressure on his back ceased and he felt her move away.

"Thank heavens," Miles muttered under his breath.

"You are too fastidious by half, Winstanley," his companion said, "She was a willing little piece and might have paid you into the bargain."

"Is she gone?" Miles asked, not wanting to turn around.

Adair turned to the packed room, "No. She's over in a corner wiping her tears."

"She's crying? Really?" Miles asked.

"Well, her dirty face looks streaked to me. Gad, I think you are quite a fool, myself, Winstanley. She looks as though she just lost her best friend."

"How pathetic," Miles remarked, feeling completely disgusted with the entire situation, his companion most of all. He suddenly downed the rest of his drink. The raw spirits burned his throat.

"Let's get out of here," Miles said. "I need some air."

"Ready to move on to the next, are you? Very well. Let's go then to the chinaman's. It's just around the corner from here. One of the most famous opium dens in the east end. Let's go."

Outside on the high street, the slummers were passed by a man whose wolfish appearance struck Miles. He was above medium height and wore a dangerous looking scowl. Miles watched him for a moment before he disappeared into the darkness.

Neither of the men knew that the current chinaman was

not the original.

Outside, the cool damp air from the nearby waterfront was mixing with the warmer air of the metropolis and the fog was afoot in large brownish-white clumps. The oily clouds shifted in and out of the dark streets which, off of the high street had no lamps whatever. Even so, Miles was relieved to get away from the pathetic child in the pub. What would she be in a few short years? He could not help but think of Amelia and his first encounter with Katherine. He had to admit that Katherine had done better for herself than many of her class. The poor child in the pub would never rise to Katherine's level.

His ankle turned unsteadily on the kerb and his companion took his arm.

"Easy, old son, just down here," and led Miles into a slit between two buildings which opened into the most dismal court the artist had ever seen. The walls of the passage were greasy and so close together that Miles could have reached out and touched both sides. The darkness was stygian but it took only a few steps before they were let out into a foul smelling court.

"Do you come here, often?" Miles asked. "I should think it dangerous?"

"You would be amazed at how many distinguished gentleman from the House of Lords are habitues of the chinaman's parlour." It was the same dreadful parlour where the original chinaman had been found by Katherine two years before.

"My cousins always said that MPs were a dissolute lot," Miles remarked. "But I thought it was mostly sex."

"Watch your step here," Adair said letting go his arm as they stood in front of a completely black hole in the side of the building. The only thing which told it was a doorway was the regularity of its shape.

"The stairs are along the left side. Hug that wall. The bannister is gone, burned for fuel I should imagine."

The gloom and stench of the ancient hallway was unlike anything Miles had ever known. Rat droppings, years of heavy opium and charcoal smoke combined with the sweet smell of dry rot. Treacle melted with glue over an open fire, and flavoured with singeing horse-hoof in a farrier's, might give some idea of the odour. The building seemed abandoned. Rats scuffled across their path as they climbed the stairs, but finally, little thin lines of bluish light shone ahead of them. There was a sudden crash as his companion kicked at a door, which was faintly outlined by some radiance within. A moment later a murky half light oozed out of the room which, in the absolute darkness of the hall seemed almost bright. A yellow skinned man was bent over something on the floor.

As his eyes grew used to the light, Miles could see a frying pan where a chinaman, interchangeable with the former landlord to western eyes, was cooking a dark mass in water over a charcoal brazier. The much-begrimed ceiling was patched with lumps of plaster against rain leakage, and broken here and there, so that the laths were visible. The walls were black with smoke and grease; the shattered upper panes of the foul little window plastered with brown paper. In the years since Susan's disappearance, everything had become even filthier. A white woman was holding a long needle and twirling a brown jelly-like substance which had dropped through the strainer to the bottom of the pan. It was she who had apparently opened the door with her free hand. Even in the gloom, the dirt of the chamber appalled Miles. Ragged banners of torn paper hung from the walls and were alive with vermin , which gave the appearance that currents of air were moving in the close, stifling room. In the centre of the room, a large bedstead held three smokers, lying cross way, side by side, heedless of the insects which fell on the mattress. All the smokers but one stared glassily at the ceiling and held empty pipes in their slack hands. This third man was well-dressed by any standard and he looked at the chinaman with an expression which mixed irritation and expectation in equal measure. Finally, his pipe being ready it was passed over to him and for a few seconds the tiny bowl glowed red as the man's features melted into the same utter lassitude as his neighbours.

"Cavendish Bentinck, MP" Adair murmured as the man on the bed slipped into his dreams. "Say nothing. It's one of the rules of this place that none ever address any other by name. You shall have the next spot when someone wakes."

Miles had not long to wait. One of the dreamers woke, sat up, shivered and got unsteadily to his feet. The chinaman's wife held the door open for him and he disappeared into the darkness of the hallway. He felt Adair's hand on his back pushing him gently toward the bedstead.

Miles had not used opium before and was curious about the effects it would produce on his particular constitution. He had no pain, or moral conundrum which drove him to the drug so he had no fear of it. He was merely curious to see what kind of visions it would induce in him. These were his thoughts as the slender pipe was handed to him, charged with an expertly prepared pellet of cooked opium. His last sober thought was of Coleridge's Xanadu, wondering if he would find such an exalted place in his own imagination.

He pulled the thick smoke into his lungs and idly thought of De Quincey's confessed liking for streetwalkers. Immediately he found himself looking at Katherine in a large oval glass, or pond or some such shining surface. They walked together all over London and felt like two childish playmates, innocent of any idea but pleasure in each other's company. They wandered through many strange countries he had never known existed in London, including Mr. Jamrasch's establishment where they each talked to beasts who were able to reply in perfectly articulated English, and in fact seemed to know all of humanity's languages. Most wise was a giant red bird who sat in a crackling nest of flames. They walked a great distance with these extraordinary companions and eventually found themselves in the neighbourhood near Katherine's home in Dorset Street, Whitechapel. The beat of their steady footsteps grew louder and more constant until Miles was amazed to find himself actually walking alone through the darkened side streets of Whitechapel in the damp fog. Adair was not with him and Miles concluded that somehow he had left the chinaman's without fully waking, leaving the viscount to his own dreams. The strange overlapping of dream and reality was unlike anything Miles had ever experienced. He was befuddled for some moments. Then he saw a gaslight in the distance, walked in its direction and made his way out of the unlit street where he found himself, drawn toward the bright lights of the Whitechapel Road. At the corner of the high street was a lone man. Miles glimpsed him for just a moment and was struck by the rapacious, dangerous character he saw stamped on the foreign face. He walked on. Whitechapel was certainly no Xanadu and the oily fog which clung to the buildings had a raw chill in it. It took some minutes to get his bearings on the high street but then he started to walk west.

As he passed along the high road, the light from its lamps fell a short way into the dark, nearly black, secondary streets and lanes. At one of these intersections, very near the corner, he saw an unusual sign which read, Photographic Studio for Ladies Only. Curious to see if any of the images within were visible, Miles moved a few steps into the side street and looked in through the windows of the shop. He could not see any photographs in the half light. The only illumination was the gas light from the corner some twenty feet away from the shop's windows. The movement of the lamp's flames enlivened every shadow with a dancing motion and made exact shape difficult to discern. But he could see that there was movement inside the shop, figures moving in and out of the shadows. He tried to position himself off to one side of the window so that he could look in and, at the same time, decrease his chances of being seen by those whom he watched. At first it seemed that he was looking at an unintelligible tangle of shadows. He glimpsed a fleeting arm or shoulder and, occasionally, some bare patch of white skin flashed out of the gloom. Gradually, his eyes began to decode the forms in the dark interior. A man and a woman were standing very close together, gripping each other's forearms. When the light fell on the woman's exposed white forearms, her skin brilliantly reflected the gaslight from the street. The man wore a herringbone suit, the woman a long dark costume which left her forearms and neck exposed. Miles felt there was a tension in their stance which indicated that they strained, one against the other, each wanting to pull in a different direction. The man was trying to pull the woman toward him; she was trying to pull away. Miles now became interested in the outcome of the contest and what would happen after the pair drew closer or separated. The movements were not violent. It seemed to Miles that no assault was intended, but perhaps they were having a lovers' disagreement over a kiss. The man moved his grip suddenly to her shoulders and pulled her to him. She lost her balance and teetered toward him and stumbled toward the window into a patch of light which lit her clearly, enabling Miles to glimpse the woman's face just as the man bent to kiss her on the mouth. The woman was Katherine! He rubbed his eyes to shake off what he imagined was an effect of the drug, but the man was now embracing her so he could not see. Now, he particularly wanted to see the woman again and confirm her identity. Could he identify her lover as well? He stared into the shifting shadows trying to get a glimpse of their faces. The man was tall, very slender with something familiar in his movements and silhouette. The woman's shape seemed to confirm the woman as Katherine. The man pulled back from the kiss and Miles had the even greater shock of seeing that the man's face looked very much like Serafina. He could be her twin, except that his expression seemed to reflect an entirely different character. The eeriness of the resemblance and, at the same time, it's contrast from Serafina was uncanny, disquieting and dream-like. It was Serafina, but it was not. He thought himself still dreaming until, a moment later, a sharp blow on the head staggered him and everything became dark. As he slipped into unconsciousness, a figure like Katherine's seemed to be outside with him, standing over him, back lit by the lamp on the high street.

The next thing he was aware of was the rain beating down on him. He was lying in the street where he had fallen. He could feel the clinging dampness of his clothing and a sharp pain in his head. He stood up unsteadily, and was relieved to find he was alone in the narrow lane. The window he had been watching was now completely dark. He looked for street numbers but could find none, and then turned toward the light of the Whitechapel Road, turning up his collar against the light but cold rain which was now falling steadily. The leaden weight of his legs and the pounding in his head made him walk slowly. He had to find a place to lie down and spend the night. His own home seemed impossibly far away.

After being assaulted, he was anxious to find a well-lit street, but there was none such until he got to Commercial Street. By this time, he was staggering and the rain was falling harder. He tried the doors of several doss houses which lined the streets of the district, but none would open at such a late hour. Finally, feeling faint with exhaustion and hunger a burly potboy showed him into a filthy room where Miles collapsed in a corner on the floor. He woke to the kicks of the landlord.

"Get out you, now," the large ugly landlord said, emphasizing each word with a kick. "You're lucky I didn't call the constables, but I'm no nark."

"What? I paid your man last night," Miles said, waking suddenly to his miserable accommodations.

"Aye, but I don't want no bloody chiv in my house. Specially after the murder. Take it and get out." And something clattered onto the floor as the landlord threw it down. It was a wickedly sharp, but common long-bladed knife. He used one like it for cutting canvas at the studio. It was covered with gore.

"What? Where did that come from?" Miles asked, trying to shield himself from the man's blows.

"Come out 'o your kicksies, lad. Fell next to your daisy roots."

"My kicksies?" Miles said, puzzled.

"What 're you, balmy? Your trousers. It fell out of your pocket."

"It couldn't have," Miles answered dodging another kick as he pulled on his damp trousers.

"Coppers 'll be more than interested in your chiv than how it was found. Specially after the murder. But I'm no nark. Take it and get out," the big man finished as he pushed Miles toward the door. "That's what I get for doing a good deed and letting you in last night. Get out," he ended as he pushed Miles out onto the street and threw the knife out onto the pavement.

Then, the door slammed shut and Miles heard the bolt

snapping into place and something metallic bouncing across the cobblestones. It was just light enough outside for Miles to see the gleam of the knife blade on the pavement, but too dark to see it well. He slipped it back into his coat pocket, and within a few moments realized that all his pockets had been emptied. He had no money and would have to walk home through Aldgate and cross the City. Not a long walk by London standards and the early morning bustle on the streets, which Miles rarely saw, lent the ramble a certain charm. If it weren't for the damp of his trousers and the smell of the doss house that clung to his clothes, Miles would have been well-pleased with this end to his night's remarkable adventures.

Two thoughts wound in and out of his mind as he walked up Cornhill and approached the 'Change where, already, a handful of eager speculators dressed like swells were clutching their paper fortunes in their hands, jostling and pushing to be first inside. First, had he actually seen Katherine and a man who looked like Serafina in the shop window, or was it just the vestiges of his opium dreams? Second, where had the gory knife come from—had someone in the doss house put it in his pocket? Of these two mysteries, the first was by far the most tantalizing, at least until he was passing a newsagent in front of the Bank of England.

"Orrible Whitechapel Murder. Woman butchered," the agent cried out as he waved a copy of the Star at passersby. Nothing ever sold as well as murders and hangings. He was doing a brisk business in the early morning gloom.

Miles would have liked to read the article but he could not buy a paper without money. He could only see the headline on the top of the pile of papers that the news vendor had next to him. He managed to read: "A Whitechapel Horror. A woman, now lying unidentified at the mortuary, Whitechapel was ferociously stabbed to death this morning between two and four o'clock, on the landing of a stone staircase in George's-buildings, Whitechapel."

Miles suddenly became sensible of the weight of the knife in his pocket. How had it gotten into his pocket in the first place? It was very similar, perhaps even identical, to one of his own but he had had no reason to take a knife with him the night before. It had to belong to someone else. He felt his blood drop to the pit of his stomach as he wondered if the killer had actually dossed in the same place he had, only a few blocks from George Yard. Perhaps, the killer had slipped the gruesome evidence of his crime into Miles' pocket. Speculations about the crime occupied him as he crossed the City to his home.

When Egbert saw him at the door, the servant became a cross between a clucking hen and a scolding mother.

"Sir, what happened to you? You are filthy. I shall draw you a bath, immediately. Yes, leave those clothes in the hall. I shall have them burned."

"As soon as you draw the bath," Miles said, "Go out and buy today's *Star*. I shall bathe myself."

"Very good, sir."

So it was that by noon, Miles was sitting, comfortably groomed, reading the Star in his own apartment as he sipped a hot cup of tea. The Star made much of the ferocity of the attack, saying that the woman had been stabbed twenty times. Actually, there were thirty-nine wounds on Martha Tabram's body. In either case, the extraordinary violence of the crime could not be disputed. It sounded like the work of a madman, a madman who might have slept in the same chamber with Miles the night before. Suddenly, he remembered the knife. He rang for Egbert.

"What did you do with the clothes, Egbert?" he asked when the servant appeared from downstairs.

"They are in the coal room, sir, awaiting immolation."

"Leave them where they are until I tell you. Do not touch them again."

"Yes, sir. But are you by chance looking for the bloody knife that was in one of the pockets? That was the only thing in the pockets. There was no money or pocketbook"

"Yes, I wanted to look at the knife," he replied, managing to keep his voice level. "I believe someone put it in my pocket last night when I slept at a low lodging house."

"I shall get it, sir."

The fastidious Viennese returned, holding the knife in a

clean cloth. As he handed it to Miles he said, "Isn't this the one you use for cutting canvas, sir?"

"It is very like—a very common sort of knife," Miles replied. "Thank you, Egbert."

Once the servant left the apartment, Miles went into his painting studio and looked carefully at the shelves where he kept various tools he used for framing and other associated work. The knife was not there. He did not remember seeing it for some time, not since he had had six canvases cut, stretched and sized at the framers when he began working on the viscount's commissions. When had he seen it last? He quickly recalled Serafina holding the knife up and commenting on its keenness when he had ordered the feast from Fortnum's. He did not remember seeing it since.

"It is probably somewhere in all this disorder," he muttered as he walked to his dark room and rinsed the gory blade. "It was such a common sort of knife, it was probably not worth tracing in any case. It could have come from almost anywhere."

Arriving at this conclusion made him refocus his attention on the other great mystery of the evening: what he thought he had seen through the shop window. Who was the mustachioed man who looked so much like Serafina? And was it really Katherine with the man? Had he really seen these things or were they figments of a mind stimulated with opium? He might be able to answer that question less equivocally than that of the knife.

He threw off his dressing gown, pulled on his boots and a moment later was rushing down the stairs to the street. The fog and rain of the cold wet summer had persisted from the Bank Holiday into the morning after the horrific murder in Whitechapel. Heavy, pelting drops splashed into puddles and rattled noisily against the umbrella Miles held above his head as he set out to unravel his strange adventure of the previous night. Cabs were hard to find in such weather and his cuffs and shoes were wet before he climbed into a four-wheeler on Oxford Street.

"Where to guvnor?" the unshaven jarvey asked as Miles opened the door

"Drive east on the Whitechapel Road. And don't go too fast."

He really had little idea of where the shop might be along the high street, if it existed at all. He hoped he would be able to catch sight of the sign which advertised a photographic studio "for ladies only" from the relative dryness of the cab, but by the time he passed Aldgate, he realized that the weather and the snarl of wagons, drays, coaches, cabs and umbrellas made it difficult, if not impossible, to see clearly across the street where he believed the sign would be. He had been walking west and the cab was now driving east. He had two options: he could walk in the rain, or he could go all the way to Mile End and have the jarvey drive back on the other side of the street. But even then, he thought as he looked out at the clogged street, the sign could be hidden behind a wall of tall wagons. He decided to walk.

He got out, paid the driver and stepped quickly and mincingly across the wet filth of the street. On the sidewalk, his open umbrella was jostled by those of other people trying to shelter themselves. The crowd was thick and motley, a mixture of east-enders and some City men. The rain bore down unremittingly and the wind tugged at his umbrella as he forced his way through the press of wet, irritable pedestrians. He crossed New Road and was nearly at the London Hospital before he finally saw the sign. It was high up on a wall above a window that only looked onto the small side street of Baker's Row. The sign was neatly lettered in black on yellow and reminded him of the grisly headline he had seen on the Star placard near the Bank. He felt a sinking sensation in himself. It had not all been a dream. He stood, irresolute, looking up at the sign in the rain. How could he get more information about what he had seen in the window? Suddenly, it seemed obvious: he would return that night and keep watch on Katherine and her visitor. He would bring a sword cane with him in case anyone tried to molest him again in the dark lanes.

Chapter 18

A NEW KIND OF TERROR

"Whilst we conventional Social Democrats were wasting our time on education, agitation, and organization, some independent genius has taken the matter in hand, and by simply murdering and disembowelling four women, converted the proprietary press to an inept sort of communism. The moral is a pretty one, and the Insurrectionists, the Dynamitards, the Invincibles, and the extreme left of the Anarchist party will not be slow to draw it. "Humanity, political science, economics, and religion," they will say, "are all rot; the one argument that touches your lady and gentleman is the knife."

—George Bernard Shaw
in a letter to *The Star*

In the world of the twenty-first century, where we sit, night after night, and watch death overtake thousands and even millions of strangers on the television screens in our homes, it is difficult to comprehend the impact of the Whitechapel murders. There were only five or six victims, which by today's standards are only just enough to be classed as serial murder by the Metropolitan Police. But it was the gratuitous brutality of the murders and lack of personal motive that made the crimes horrible in a

273

new way, a post-nineteenth century way, but that was only part of the impact and significance of the killer who became known as Jack the Ripper.

For the Victorians, murder was a crime of almost incomprehensible evil because it violated the holiest of sacred laws, laws which in the 1880s still enjoyed devout acceptance by the majority of all levels of society. When Bill Sykes killed Nancy only fifty years before the Ripper appeared on the streets of Whitechapel, even the criminals who lived on Jacob's Island cried, "Murder" and helped apprehend the killer. Today, we give lip service to the concepts of good and evil, and politicians and terrorists love to invoke the words, but we know that in our own day murder and other crimes will often be defined by public opinion or national policy. Today, we have temporized with good and evil to a point where they are social and political rather than moral values. But the Victorians, even late Victorians, including many who accepted Darwin's theories, still believed that Good and Evil as set forth in the Bible were the mainsprings of the universe, and this view imbued society to a degree we can scarcely imagine. Therefore, taking a human life was a violation of deeply valued sacred principles. But with the random, nearly clinical brutality of the Ripper, the Victorians saw a new and darker spirit make a harrowing entrance into the world, a spirit which gave sinister and terrifying evidence that the new sciences could be right: God and his creation might be nothing more than a myth. Perhaps all was merely what it appeared to be and no more. The Ripper, incarnation of this nihilistic spirit, lurked in the unlit noxious lanes and courts of Whitechapel where "foreigners" lived. The murders were sexual in some inverted, diabolical way which was only dimly understood, since the Ripper appeared several years before Freud published his seminal works, and many years before the first criminal profile had been developed. There had been other sexual serial killers before 1888, but none who had the circulation of metropolitan newspapers to spread his terror for him.

As G.B. Shaw noted in his letter to *The Star*, it was the Victorian media that made the Ripper what he became: the

world's first terrorist. Osama bin Laden and his kind walk where
the Ripper went before them. If bin Laden did not have the
help of the media to disseminate the knowledge of his acts, they
would be fruitless. The phenomenon of the Ripper murders was
a defining moment in the transition to the modern era, and the
first step on the darkest road mankind has yet taken. It is not
difficult to liken the Ripper's virtual dissection of Mary Kelly, the
fifth victim, to the "experiments" of Joseph Mengala, perpetrator
of scientific torture, the most personal and heinous of Nazi war
crimes. We have tried for over a century to discover the identity of this Victorian killer, whose exploits have mesmerized us,
showing us the worst in ourselves, fascinating us with our own
darkest reflection, making it impossible to look away from his
crimes. Even after nearly a century and a half, each generation
gives the Ripper its own face. So it is not to be wondered at that
Miles, having found himself only a few streets away from the
scene of the Ripper's début and discovering a bloody knife in his
own pocket should become one of the first to speculate about
the "horror" as he stood in the damp lane on the night after the
murder, watching the window of the photographic studio.

According to his pocket watch, which Miles had to turn
to catch the illumination of the street lamp on the high street, it
was some time before ten when he saw a light shine, very faintly,
through the curtain at the back of the shop. A moment later, the
curtain was pushed aside and Katherine entered the shop area
carrying an old fashioned oil lamp of indian design, a figure of
Siva, cunningly made in what Miles recognized as Benares metal
work. It was the ruddy light of the lamp that permitted Miles a
view of the interior. Katherine was dressed in traditional Indian
costume. Her long close-fitting sari of small-patterened cotton,
worn over a pair of pajamas gave her elfin figure the appearance
of a supernatural character out of Burton's recent translation of
The Arabian Nights. Her long black hair was brushed out and
hung down in a cascade of darkness to her waist. She now appeared entirely oriental to Miles, endowed with an altogether
foreign and exotic character. Her long, dark eyes were the shape
of almonds. She sat at the table and looked around the room.

Then she began breathing in one nostril by closing the other with the last two fingers of her right hand. She switched nostrils and used her thumb to close the other nostril as she exhaled. She continued this strange breathing for some time. Gradually, her eyes became glassy and empty of expression.

"She has entranced herself," Miles thought.

Her face might have been a carved mask of light brown wood. She picked up a small Indian bottle on the table, removed its stopper and poured a black and silver liquid into a cupped hand. Her blank eyes looked downward into the liquid and stared at it for a long time. Then her lips moved and she smiled very faintly. Her eyes became animated with life once more and she picked up the bottle and poured the liquid back into it from her palm, replacing the stopper when she was done. Miles felt certain that Katherine had just used her clairvoyant powers to see the person for whom she waited. If Miles had ever had lingering doubts about the autobiography Katherine had sketched for him, there were now dispelled forever. In her face that night, he had seen the impersonal, hieratic essence of a knowledge that passed ordinary human thought. He had never thought her so strange, nor so fascinating. Her face alone had confirmed his belief in her supernatural abilities.

For whom, he wondered did she wait? Was it for Serafina's male twin? He hoped so. He would like to know more of the alien person who wore the features of his own cousin—the woman he still, under certain conditions, might marry. Who was he? Could there be a male family member of whom he knew nothing? It seemed impossible and yet...

Just as he had reached this point in his speculations, the curtain in the shop was thrown aside and Katherine's lover of the previous evening appeared.

He was dressed in very elegant evening clothes, as good or better than anything Miles had in his wardrobe. The orange flame of the pagan oil lamp gave a fiery tinge to the faces of the two actors within. The man bowed to Katherine, took her hand and kissed it in a formal, respectful way. The fiery glow gave his tall slender figure and pale, pale skin gave him a character not unlike Faust's adversary. Then, Katherine lightly touched him on the forehead and the man's figure became suddenly immobile and rigid, a living being turned instantly to stone. Then, Katherine took his hand and led the man to the curtain at the back of the shop and gently pushed him through while she remained in the area which was visible to Miles. A short time later, Katherine picked up the oil lamp and followed the man through the curtain. For the better part of an hour, Miles was able to see little else but the flame of the oil lamp through the cloth of the curtain. Then, suddenly, it was extinguished, and all was dark.

Night after night these same rituals were repeated in the shop. Miles learned the interval of the constable's round in Baker's Row and avoided being seen. For nearly three weeks, Miles watched the players go through their strange pantomimes with little variation. At times during those weeks, Miles was tempted to believe that the man really was Serafina, but at other times the expression and character of the man was so different that it seemed impossible. Finally, on the night of August 31, a dramatic scene was enacted in front of him as he kept his vigil in Baker's Row.

Hour after hour passed and the usual time of ten o'clock came and went. A man and a woman walked down Baker's Row at about eleven in the evening. He sported a small mustache and was wearing a leather apron, the woman was a worn looking prostitute. Miles ducked into a doorway as they passed and then resumed watching the shop window after they had gone. Katherine glanced continually at the clock and at the stroke of twelve began pacing up and down the shop. She was clearly anxious about something. The quarter hours became hours. The night crawled into the small hours of the morning while Katherine kept her vigil inside and Miles kept his in the lane. Finally, there was a loud noise. Katherine started to her feet, looking anxiously to the back of the shop, her eyes dilated with fear, her lips parted and her finely chiseled nostrils flaring. A moment later, Miles saw the man come staggering into the shop through the curtained entrance at the back. He moved as if he were drunk. Katherine ran to him as soon as she noticed his condition, her

face reflecting profound concern. She touched his forehead in
the usual way, he became rigid and she removed his jacket and
waistcoat. Katherine started to undress him. Then she moved
away from the man and afforded Miles a veiw of him: His white
ruffled shirt was sprayed with blood. The cuffs were soaked in
red. The ruffles of his shirt front were marked with great diago-
nal slashes of scarlet. Katherine wrapped the man in a blanket
and kept him covered while she removed the stained clothing,
gathered it up in a heap and took it through the curtain. The
man's eyes were vacant, empty of all expression as Katherine
worked. He might have been made of brass. Miles noted that
the time was some time after four a.m.. It seemed an impossibly
late hour. He couldn't have been standing and watching for so
many hours!

     Once Katherine had carried off the stained outer cloth-
ing, she wrapped him in a robe and began making mesmeric
passes in front of the man's immobile figure, drawing her open
hands back and forth across his body without touching him.
Then she began to speak. From her expression, Miles could see
that her words must be earnest. She moved to one side of the
man and Miles was able to see his face for the first time since the
trance had been induced. The eyes were no longer vacant and
the face no longer expressionless. Miles started, for he had never
seen such a terrible, cruel expression on a human countenance,
and it was doubly shocking because the man's features were so
like Serafina's. The mouth was twisted in a sort of mocking smile
as Katherine spoke, but it was his eyes, reflecting the flame of the
lamp, which revealed a character that was both enraged and icy
cold. The eyes made Miles shiver involuntarily, as if they were
able to touch something deep inside him. He felt that a cold
fist had been put inside his chest and was squeezing the warm
blood out of his heart. He could almost believe that such eyes
could kill with a glance. Katherine, however, showed no signs of
trepidation. She continued to speak to the man without pause
and without waiting for a response. She seemed unaware of any
danger to herself. One part of Miles wanted to rush inside and
tear her away from the man. But his concern was overwhelmed

by curiosity and by the realization that Katherine was exercising mesmeric control over her visitor. He only hoped that the invisible bonds would remain strong and not snap. The man sat only inches from Katherine. Miles could only speculate wildly at the nature of the relationship between Katherine and the dangerous looking man. Doctor and patient? A powerful hypnotist attempting to keep a criminal in check? He knew Katherine well enough to know that if she had this special relationship with the man, she would not thank Miles for trying to interfere. She might even think him jealous. In any case, as the pair rose and walked to the curtains at the back of the store, Miles knew there was nothing more for him to see or do, unless he was ready to burst in upon them. Who was the man, he wondered as he gained the high street? Why did he look so much like Serafina? This part of the secret he might uncover by talking to Julia, which he resolved to do as soon as the hour was decent. Feeling utterly done up and exhausted, he walked home up the Whitechapel Road and through Aldgate, where the slaughterers and meat cutters were already starting work. The City was just beginning to stir, and as he reached Cornhill, he heard the news vendor in front of the Bank cry, "Second horrible murder in Whitechapel. Read all about it."

The cry sent shivers through him as he immediately thought of Katherine and her strange visitor. He rushed up the street to the news vendor and bought a copy of the Times. Standing under a lamp near the massive columns and steps of the Bank he read the following:

Another Murder in Whitechapel. Another murder of the foulest kind was committed in the neighbourhood of Whitechapel in the early hours of yesterday morning, but by whom and with what motive is at present a complete mystery. At a quarter to 4 o'clock Police-constable Neill, 97J, when in Buck's Row, Whitechapel, came upon the body of a woman lying on a part of the footway, and on stooping to raise her up in the belief that she was drunk he discovered that her throat was cut almost from ear to ear. She was dead but still warm. He procured assistance and at once sent to the station and for a doctor. Dr. Llewellyn, of Whitechapel Road, whose surgery is not above 300 yards from the spot where the woman lay, was aroused, and, at the solicitation of a constable, dressed and went at once to the scene. He inspected the body at the place where it was found and pronounced the woman dead. He made a hasty examination and then discovered that, besides the gash across the throat, the woman had terrible wounds in the abdomen. The police ambulance from the Bethnal Green Station having arrived, the body was removed there. A further examination showed the horrible nature of the crime, there being other fearful cuts and gashes, and one of which was sufficient to cause death apart from the wounds across the throat.

Miles thought of the splashes of blood he had seen on the man's ruffled shirt front. They might easily have been caused by such wounds as those described in the *Times*. And if ever a face revealed the character of a murderer, it was the face he had seen through the window in Baker's Row. What was Katherine doing with the man? What did she know about the murders? Was she somehow involved in the atrocities? He couldn't believe it, and yet...Who was the vicious looking man whose features had been stolen from Serafina? Could he be a relation about whom Miles knew nothing? There had to be some connection, for the resemblance to Serafina was uncanny and pointed to a close relationship of blood ties. His mind whirled with guesses, suppositions and anxieties, and by the time he reached his home, he was wide awake and utterly exhausted at the same time.

He changed his clothes, bathed and decided to go to Cavendish Square immediately. He wanted to talk to Julia at the earliest opportunity to see if she knew anything about a male relative who bore such a close resemblance to her sister. Fortunately, Serafina usually slept late and Julia was customarily an early riser. He would be able to have a *tête à tête* with Julia without Serafina being present. He had not seen his beautiful cousin in nearly a year, but the nature of their last meeting did not suggest that she would be glad to see him or be ready to listen to speculations about Katherine and her strange visitor.

After a bath which he drew himself and a change of clothes, Miles felt fresh and ready for any difficult discussion he might have with Julia. He strode quickly through the west end streets just as the earliest clerks were arriving for work and found himself at number twenty-one Cavendish Square at an early but decent hour. Rossiter would undoubtedly be in the front hall. The old man slept little, sometimes passing the entire night in his chair near the door with his loyal friend, Virgil, at his feet. After so long an absence from the house, Miles had taken care to have a sugar cube with him.

The door was opened immediately after Virgil released a mournful bay into the quiet of the gray morning. But once he scented Miles, the dog nuzzled his waistcoat pocket, the customary hiding place.

"Good morning, Rossiter—here Virgil" Miles said.

"Good morning, sir. It is good to see you on our doorstep. Sad changes here, sir. Sad changes."

Before Miles could enquire about the sad changes, Julia appeared at the back of the hall from the dirction of the south parlour.

"What a lovely surprise, Miles. How good to see you."

"Julia, you look marvelous. What is different. No. Wait. Don't tell me. You changed your hair. And that is a new dressing gown."

"If all men were as observant as you, Miles, there would be many happier homes in London. It is too long since I saw you in our house."

"It is too long," Miles agreed taking one of her hands in both of his. "But tell me, Rossiter just alluded to sad changes in the house. To what was he referring? No one is ill, I hope?"

"No. Though Serafina is still having somnambulistic dreams. Katherine's mesmeric abilities have helped. But it does worry me sometimes. It's over a year since mother died and I would have thought the effects of grief would have diminished by now. Yet, she is still having somnambulistic dreams during which she walks all over our house and out into the garden. You know, when we were little, she used to have dreams about the garden, about the maze in particular. I have tried to speak with her about it but she just dismisses my concerns."

"And you?" he asked. "You are well?"

"I am impervious to illness, no matter how much I smoke and no matter what late hours I keep. Rossiter was probably referring to the sale of the dining table. We sold it to buy an enormous urn we used to take hot coffee to the dockers last winter. Rossiter decided that the table's loss was the beginning of a general deterioration. We never sat at table anyway. Now that there are just the two of us, we eat in the parlour in a very Oriental fashion, sitting on cushions on the floor. Come," she said, reaching out her hand to him in the manner of a playmate as she led him into the parlour which always managed to capture any sun that might have pierced London's dark fall days.

"Serafina is still asleep?" he asked.

"Of course. If you wanted to see her, you should have come after twelve."

"So late? That is new, is it not?"

"She is keeping very late hours these days. She does a great deal of visiting in the east end."

"Well I hope she will exercise some caution with these recent atrocities."

"It is terrible," Julia agreed as she sat down next to him on the settee. "The violence of the assaults is dreadful. Like the work of a madman. That's what Mr. Stead thinks. I have asked Serafina not to go to Whitechapel until the killer is caught, but she is adamant about continuing her visits to the poor and to Katherine."

"Well, if the killer is mad, he has some slyness about him. He is not simple."

"Why, what do you mean, Miles? Do you know something about the atrocities?"

"Perhaps," he said, feeling grateful he had found an impersonal way to the questions he wished to ask. He first described his night out with the dissolute viscount; his doss in the east end and the finding of the gory knife in his own pocket.

"How dreadful, Miles. He might have been in the same room with you."

"Very likely. Of course, there is no way to be certain that the knife was used in the murder of Martha Tabram. But it was certainly a disquieting coincidence, at the very least."

"I should say," Julia agreed. "And where was this doss house? Which street?" she asked reaching for a notebook and steel-nibbed pen beside it.

"Ah, I should have remembered I am talking to a journalist," he said with a smile. "It is so very good to see you again, Julia. I didn't realize how much I missed you until this moment."

"Out of sight, out of mind, does, I am afraid, describe my place in your thoughts," she said ruefully.

He leaned over and kissed her on the cheek. "Please forgive me," he said in a serious tone.

"That too, has always been my problem. I have always been ready to forgive you anything—as well you know. Perhaps if I were more demanding, you might think of me more often. Perhaps that is the secret of Serafina's hold on you. She grants you no favours and you fawn on her. While I..."

"While you are the one I have always turned to if I had great need," he finished for her looking at her very seriously. "That is what I am doing now."

In a moment, her quick, mobile face had shifted from a teasing smile into an expression of sympathetic concern.

"What is it, Miles? Are you in some kind of trouble?"

"No, but I have seen something recently and I must speak with you about it, with the understanding that what I tell you shall not be repeated to Serafina."

"I should have to know what it is before I could make such a promise. If I can withhold it from her without hurting her in any way, you have my promise of silence."

"That is enough," he answered, and then he told her about the two nights he had visited Katherine's shop on the Whitechapel Road.

"What a very strange and alarming tale," she said when he had finished. "I know of no male relative with a strong resemblance to Serafina."

"Could it have been she?" he asked.

"Miles, what are you saying?"

"I don't know. I know only what I saw—a man who

looked like Serafina's twin with blood on his clothes in the vicinity of a gruesome murder. You say her mind has been disturbed of late."

"She has difficulty sleeping, that is all." But in spite of her denial, her face wore a troubled look.

"Are you sure she was here last night—all night?" Miles pressed.

"I was writing last night and I rather lose track of time when I am working. She was in her room, with the door closed. To get out without being seen, she would have had to climb down from the leads of the porch. Difficult but not impossible— especially in trousers. Though, it would be much more in character for her simply to announce she was going out and wish me to the Devil if I objected."

Suddenly she stopped and looked up at Miles with her small face fixed in a fierce expression of determined resolve.

"Miles, I love and trust you. But under no circumstances shall I ever believe that my sister is a brutal murderer."

"I did not say she was."

"But you think it a possibility."

"No, of course not. But this man must be a relative. His resemblance to Serafina is uncanny. There must be some connection. Look through your mothers papers, old letters, anything that might shed light on this. The blood stained man I saw could be Serafina's twin."

"And are you asking me to enquire about her whereabouts last night?"

"No. And I do not want her to know that I am watching Katherine's shop, in any case. Remember what happened to the detective who tried to follow her?"

"Surely, you don't think that attack had anything to do with Serafina? You think this twin was involved in that?"

"I frankly do not know what to think. But I must find out who this man in bloody clothes was. If there is some connection between this man and the murders, as I believe there is, it will become a police matter. If you could make certain that Serafina was in all night, without arousing her suspicion it would remove her from any remote connection with these horrible crimes. The fact that I saw this man at Katherine's and that Katherine and Serafina have been birds of a feather, also makes me uneasy. If the police ever establish a connection between Katherine and this man, Serafina would surely become involved."

Julia's light gray eyes became fixed in a distant stare, an expression she wore whenever she was thinking deeply on something.

"I will need some time," she said, finally. "Serafina is very clever and perceptive—as well you know."

"I shall leave it then in your capable hands, Julia. Let me know immediately if you learn anything."

"I certainly shall. What are you going to do?"

"I shall continue to keep watch on Katherine's shop."

"But if there is a connection between Katherine, the man and the Whitechapel atrocities, you could be in danger."

"I know. I am going to carry my swordstick. And brush up my fencing at Colonel Foster's establishment."

"Do please be careful, Miles," she said putting her hands on his shoulder. "I—we could not bear to lose you. Serafina and I both need you."

"You do agree, though, that I must follow this up? We don't want the family to be connected in any way with these atrocities, yet we cannot just stand by."

"Yes. Of course not. If you can do anything to prevent another of these horrors, it is your duty. But I agree that talking to the police might put the family in the middle of a terrible scandal. It might even create the scandal. If the police are desperate for an arrest, they might do anything—especially under Commissioner Warren's direction. Serafina is already known to him as a suspicious and dangerous character."

"That's true. I had forgotten."

"Let her name come up just once in connection with a difficult investigation where the police are floundering and Serafina would certainly be questioned, at the very least. I'm sure that I am also on some police list of suspicious characters."

"Why?"

"Because I am a woman, a socialist, a journalist and because I consort with dockers. All of our comfortable neighbours in the west-end are very worried by the disaffections of the poor right now. They smell the brimstone in the air. Especially after Bloody Sunday and the way Mrs. Besant helped the Bryant & May match girls beat their rich employers. After that success, I believe a massive dockers strike is only months away. Who knows what might happen, then? The ruling classes and their footmen are fearful. Anything that adds to these fears will also frighten the police and make them ready to act precipitously. I could almost believe the police are behind the murders themselves."

"What do you mean?"

"These sensational murders are a perfect way to distract the public from the real problem facing Britain—the poverty of the working people."

"But surely, Julia..."

"I rule out nothing when it comes to the Commissioner and Mr. Matthews, the Home Secretary. It is unlikely that the government would stage such crimes, I agree, but I do not think it impossible."

"Your politics are too radical for me, Julia. But we must know if Serafina, or anyone who might be related to us is even remotely involved in the Whitechapel atrocities. If there is a connection, we must do everything in our power to erase it."

"Don't forget, Miles," Julia said wagging her finger at him, "After having been arrested for coshing a constable, Serafina would be the perfect Socialist scapegoat for any violent crimes the police can't solve. The police could easily cast her as a someone who has a history of violent assault. Her politics would provide the ideal motive."

"I had not considered that," Miles said slowly. "It certainly does make Serafina's situation even more dangerous—especially, if she is connected in any way—which I am certain she cannot be."

"Or is even thought to be," Julia added. "That's the reason we must find out the identity of this man who resembles her. She could be blamed for his crimes, especially if the police become desperate for a solution. I may even have to confront Katherine directly. Though, I find it very hard to believe that Katherine would help a murderer escape justice."

"Talking to Katherine should be the last thing we do. Once she knows we have interested ourselves, she may warn the man she is mesmerizing. He is probably her lover. We still really know nothing about him. We must move carefully until we are sure of our ground. If you do try to find out if Serafina went out last night, do it in some way that will not alarm her. And it is of the last importance that she does not know I am watching Katherine's shop."

"I understand, Miles. I shall do my part."

Little else remained to be said. Julia walked with him to the door and then suddenly put her arms around him and pressed him to her.

"Do be very careful dear Miles," she said, brushing his lips with hers.

Later the same evening as Miles walked through the City to take up his post near Katherine's shop, a *Star* placard carried by a news vendor stopped him in his tracks. The headline rooted him to the spot, just as he was passing the 'Change. The placard read: A REVOLTING MURDER. ANOTHER WOMAN FOUND HORRIBLY MUTILATED IN WHITECHAPEL. GHASTLY CRIMES BY A MANIAC.

After buying a copy, Miles found the article exactly agreed with his own idea that the two crimes were committed by the same person. After seeing the expression of the man in Katherine's shop, Miles, too, believed he could be dangerously insane. It was possible he was not the killer, but he was in the area at the time of both murders. He had been covered with blood and he certainly looked the part. As he read over the article, Miles thought, "And I may know where to find this monster. Why does he so closely resemble Serafina? He must be a relation."

He dared not go to the police with his observations. He could not disagree with Julia's analysis. An official investigation of the man he suspected would certainly involve his cousins and

Katherine. With the increasingly shrill tone of the press and the current state of hostility between the Socialists and the police and the radical politics of both his cousins, talking to the police could be dangerous for them and Katherine. Yet, he could not stand by while murder was done. Catching the criminal seemed the only option left open to him. He would have to act alone. There was no one to aid him. As a former policeman, Minahan could not be trusted with what Miles had seen. His duty and allegiance would be to his fellow officers.

"Not only must I catch this madman, I must also watch over Katherine and try to grasp what lies behind the remarkable resemblance between Serafina and the man I believe to be the fiend. " Miles muttered to himself as he walked east.

Chapter 19

MURDERS MOST FOUL

One may search the ghastliest efforts of fiction and fail to find any-
thing to surpass these crimes in diabolical audacity. The mind travels
back to the pages of De Quincey for an equal display of scientific
delight in the details of butchery; or Edgar Allan Poe's "Murders in
the Rue Morgue" recur in the endeavour to conjure up some parallel
for this murderer's brutish savagery.

—The Times, Sept 10, 1888

For a week and a day, Miles wandered the streets of Whitechapel every night, always beginning and ending his peregrina-
tions outside the window of Katherine's shop. During these
early weeks of the killings, the newspapers, particularly *The Star*,
had begun to run articles about Jack Pizer, a man whom east
end prostitutes called 'leather apron'. Pizer had given up earning
his living by making slippers and was known to live by bullying
prostitutes with a knife. In early September and October, he was
the primary focus of police attention. But Miles was not satisfied
with any solution which did not explain the bloodstained man
in Katherine's shop, of whom the police seemed to know nothing. As far as Miles was concerned, 'leather apron' was a blind
alley which would lead nowhere, and so it eventually proved.

Pizer was eliminated from the enquiry by October. During the 'leather apron' episode, Miles saw nothing of Serafina's twin, nor anything else of interest. Several times, he was tempted to knock on Katherine's door and ask her directly who the twin was and what she was doing with him. Had Katherine had his confidence, questioning her would have been the most direct way to get answers. But he still smarted from her pretence of virtue and the contrary evidence of the *carte visite*. He did not trust her, so he did not try to speak to her. Julia said that she had refused to speak about what she called, "her work" with Serafina, citing the necessity of absolute trust and privacy if she was to help Serafina. Miles believed all this was a blind, and if she warned the blood stained man, he might disappear into the dark Whitechapel lanes and rookeries. On several occasions, the hunter almost became the quarry: Miles was almost stopped by constables but each time, he managed to slip away before he was seen.

It was not until the early morning of September 8, that Miles' efforts were rewarded, though not in the way he had anticipated. At about 6:00 am, the sun having risen just a short time before, he was crossing Commercial Street, walking east, leaving the noise and congestion of the early morning merchants at Spitalfields Market behind him when he saw Serafina. She was walking toward him, carrying a carpet bag of a very poor quality whose garish floral pattern clashed badly with her silk print walking costume and stylish pelisse. She looked straight ahead and seemed to pass through the crowd without seeing anyone. Miles had to call to her to attract her notice.

"Serafina, what are you doing here at this ungodly hour? I thought you never rose before noon."

At first, she did not reply. Her eyes continued to stare straight ahead of her.

"Serafina," he called again as he pushed through morning crowd to take her arm.

She seemed to him like one waking from a dream. In a moment her eyes became focused on him and appeared normal.

"Miles, what are you doing here?"

"I just asked you the same question," he replied.

"I am on my way home from an all night meeting at the International Working Man's Club on Berner Street. We were discussing ways in which Socialist organizations could help put an end to sweating, particularly in the shoe making trade."

"Is that where you got that dreadful bag?" he asked with a smile.

"Yes. Pamphlets. You know. My usual weapons," she said, suddenly making the morning more radiant with her smile. It was a light he had not seen for many months.

"It's been ages since I've seen you," he said. "How strange that it should be here. Perhaps we could have some tea and breakfast together."

"What a good idea. There is a very clean Jewish shop on Jubilee Street, not far from here," she said as she took his arm. "Their baked goods are excellent. Well worth the walk of a few blocks."

They walked further east on the Whitechapel Road, crossing the railroad near South Raven Street. Not far from the old Mile End Gate, they turned into Jubilee Street. Serafina led him to a large, glass fronted shop which offered tea, coffee and chocolate in English and Hebrew. The letters of both languages were quite handsomely painted on the shop windows in gold. The strange Hebrew letters gave the place a very exotic look. A clean white curtain suspended from a polished brass rail covered the lower half of the windows. Inside, the tiled floor was clean, reflecting the sunlight pouring in through the windows.

"Well, what do you think?" she asked. "Is it acceptable."

"It looks clean enough," Miles answered, opening the door and holding it for Serafina.

"They make wonderful baked goods here," Serafina said as they were shown to the table by a waiter.

"Now, why are you here, Miles?"

"I have been slumming, too," he said, giving the answer he'd been preparing ever since he saw her. "I've been inspired by Degas' portraits of the Parisian bohemians. I have been visiting some of the pubs on Commercial Street with a view to capturing the ambience on canvas. You know, the tawdriness of the flesh-pots."

"Yes," Serafina said, taking off her gloves. "I have heard that that sort of thing was becoming popular. The American, Mr. Whistler, is chiefly to blame for the vogue, I believe."

"Well, you are certainly up on your painters. But I should say Whistler took his cue from Degas, and I think the word 'blame' is unnecessarily hard. Whistler is very skilled in his way. He has trained himself to work quickly because of his subject matter."

" I don't want to be disputatious. That's what I've been doing all night. I am too tired, and it is nice to see you after so long. I'm sorry, Miles. I have not exactly been myself since mama died," she said taking his hand and giving it a squeeze.

He felt suddenly quite sad about his relationship with Serafina, meeting in a tea shop as two mere acquaintances instead of what they had once been. What had happened to them, he wondered? His life and hers had been so bound together and suddenly their connection had withered and died. He remembered a milk weed pod they had opened together at the top of a high cliff on one of their painting day trips. All the earlier years they had shared had scattered like the soft, white down they had released over the sea from the pod.

"How do you mean, 'not like yourself,' Serafina?" he asked. "Is it the same trouble sleeping?"

"That and more. Excuse me for complaining."

"You are not complaining," he said. "You are giving me your confidence."

"Katherine has been very helpful. I know I should have been worse if not for her."

"You trust her so completely, then?"

"Yes. She has proven her value, in many ways."

"But as a physician?"

"She knows a great deal about—about the mind. Perhaps not theoretically, but practically."

"I can still recall a time when you thought her a fraud."

"That was long ago— long ago in terms of our relationship. I hardly knew her then."

"And you are so certain of her now?"

"She has my complete confidence."

"But you still do not 'feel yourself?' How?"

"It is hard to explain. But for one thing, you know how methodical I am in my habits..."

"Yes."

"Well, now I find myself losing track of time. I don't know if I've been day dreaming or have fallen asleep. I miss appointments. It happens even when I am being active, walking, riding, any time. I return to myself and wonder what I have been doing for the last half hour. Truthfully, it is a little frightening. You and Katherine are the only ones who know the extent of my concern. I have tried to make light of it with Julia, though I couldn't altogether hide it from her."

Miles thought of his own peculiar incidents but said nothing. "What about a medical specialist? There are excellent men here in London."

"I have done an enormous amount of reading, Miles. And actually the best men for nervous disorders are not in Britain but on the continent."

"Then why not go there?"

"My concern is that any professional man who specializes in nervous disorders will simply tell me my problem is hysteria— a vague diagnosis usually given to women with almost any kind of nervous complaint. We know so little about the mind, and I don't think the medical profession has yet outgrown its own prejudices about my sex. That's why I prefer to let Katherine treat me."

"But she has no qualifications."

"She had some rather unusual training in the Eastern Empire. And she has already helped me to some considerable degree. Her skill with hypnosis has been very useful."

"I don't know whether to feel reassured or alarmed by what you are saying about her. I hope your trust is not misplaced. It could be catastrophic."

"I do appreciate that you are concerned about me, but I believe I am in the best hands right now."

"Perhaps a change of air would do you good. A holiday."

Serafina shook her head. "I have too many people who are relying on me to help them. I could not possibly let them down. The conditions they live and work under are appalling. And especially now, with this mad man loose. "

"Yes, you must be careful, Serafina."

"Ha, I should like him to attack me. I would tear him limb from limb. I believe I should be more than a match for him. I go armed, now. I will not let a bully like him impede our work."

"What do you mean ''armed?"

"Look," she said as she struck the edge of the table. A slim, deadly looking blade seemed to jump into her hand.

"One of my Jewish friends from Pesht made this for me. He is a first-class mechanic," she said. "The blade lies hidden in my sleeve but is in my hand instantly. It is operated by a powerful spring."

"Perhaps you are working too hard. This talk of weaponry..."

"If I could, I should arm every woman in Whitechapel. Then the monster would get his just deserts. The police are proving to be even more stupid than I ever thought they could be."

"But Serafina, you sound quite bloodthirsty. I've never heard you talk like this."

"Has there ever been anyone like this fiend?"

"No. I imagine not. But you must not be over confident. You must take care of yourself—for me, for all of us, please. Put off your work for a while. Until the monster is caught."

"Miles, I have long known that you are a man with a good heart, and that your concern for me is genuine, but I've come to realize that your priorities and mine are very different. You are focused on personal achievement and its rewards. I am interested in Society as a whole. The gulf between the lives we aspire to live is enormous."

"You think art frivolous, but you think it all right to risk your life?"

"Not frivolous, and I do think that the work we are trying to do is worth fighting for, if it comes to that."

"You are wrong," he said, rubbing his unshaven chin thoughtfully. "The artist is the leader of society. He or she shows what is possible. Political groups are followers, usually followers of the lowest common denominator. The artist gives form to ideas which have not existed before. Society follows his lead. But, truthfully, right now, I am more interested in some practical improvement in your state of mind."

"And that is just what Katherine gives me: a practical improvement in my state of mind. Her hypnotic treatments make me feel better, clearer and more relaxed. From my point of view that is eminently practical."

"And is there nothing I might do to contribute to your well being?" he asked as he took her ungloved hand. "I have never seen you like this. I really think you are working too hard."

"Many others work harder than I," she replied as she removed her hand from his.

"But it is affecting you, Serafina. I can see that it is."

"It is not hard work that is affecting me," she said standing up. "It is something else."

"Then, you know what it is."

"Not in a way that I can put into words. I really can't say anything more about myself. I must go, Miles. I have been up all night, and right now I am feeling rather fatigued." She picked up her gloves and began coaxing them onto her large slender hands.

"Do be careful, Serafina, while these ghastly murders are going on. Do not go about at night. I beg you."

"Actually, these murders make my work more urgent than ever. How can I serve the people I want to help if I flee when they are threatened? They are being driven out onto the street by poverty and the greed of lodging house landlords. If these killings were taking place in the west end, the killer would already have been caught. You know that as well as I. Good bye, Miles," she said pulling her pelisse around her before picking up her ugly carpet bag. Then she pushed through the door and was gone.

He watched her straight, slender back framed for a moment between the double wood and brass doors. In her green pelisse, her back reminded him of an early spring shoot, a crocus, and then she was gone.

Miles saw her disappear into the motley crowd outside and had to agree that she did seem to have aims very different than his own. She was becoming absolutely wild in her radicalism. She would never offer him the tenderness and emotional support which he had craved from her almost since childhood. She was completely absorbed in political concerns, without any feminine feelings for marriage or family. She had so little of the feminine gift of providing emotional nourishment, he wondered how he could have ever imagined her as a wife. Then his own gift of emotional awareness, which was often more like a delicate sense of touch than thought, felt rather than understood that Serafina would always be emotionally remote and that much of his former desire for her lay in that fact. He had always been questing for her emotional essence, in search of a perfect tenderness which had been an article of faith rather than an experienced fact. He now realized that the thing he had quested for never existed. He had invented it as a correlative of her physical beauty, charm and wit. He had hypothesized her heart, a heart which now seemed far from the feminine ideal he had sought. They were better off as friends and cousins, though because of their history she would always have a unique place among any amours he might have. A love that has taken root among the vivid events of childhood and which interpenetrates early experiences of colours, sounds, and memories will remain green into old age. His early feelings for Serafina would, he knew, as he looked at the fugitive sunlight and shadow falling on the white tile floor, never entirely fade away. His feelings for her had deep roots made even stronger by the loss of Amelia and his own family. Thinking of her and writing to her had helped ease his first years at Oxford. He had needed what he made her into and that creation had been extended from childhood into adult life. Memories and feelings that he associated with his idealized image of Serafina had been wound together to become a central strand of his inmost life. The inner constellation formed by memory and his make believe child love would be with him as long as he lived, in spite of its illusory character. He felt these things just as certainly as he felt that he and Serafina could never be married. It was a moment of sudden realization that flashed out from the interstices of his mind like a gem in a setting of dull metal. He would remember this moment, the hexagonal white tiles of the coffee shop floor spanned by the shadow of the brass curtain rail, as vividly as any event of his life. He would remember the foreign smells of thick oriental coffee mixed with the odor of spices and unwashed men in crudely made black suits. But the thing that became fixed indelibly in his mind was a thin broken line of red near the place where Serafina had rested her carpet bag when she sat down. It looked like as if the bag's bottom seam had been dipped in red paint or blood. The shock he felt on seeing this mark on the floor caused his stomach to contract and brought a sour taste to his mouth. He glimpsed it and his body reacted to the mere possibility and made him feel ill before his mind could even form the thought. From that day forward two of the predominant smells of Whitechapel, pickled fish and dark roasted coffee, would make him nauseous and call to mind the 'Jewishness' which East End papers would claim was responsible for the murders—since no Englishman could possibly commit the ghastly murders which were still to come in the autumn of 1888.

In realizing Serafina's unique place in his life, and remembering his failure to protect Amelia, Miles felt more determined than ever to watch over her and discover whether Katherine's influence was really for good or ill. Was Serafina's blood-stained twin really the Whitechapel killer—or was there some less dramatic and dangerous interpretation of what he had observed? What could it possibly be? There seemed little he could do except wait, watch and hope that he would be able to act before more lives were lost. At the very least, he would guard Serafina and not let her slip away from him any night she was going into Whitechapel. He would arrange with Julia to let him know whenever Serafina was out at night and, if possible,

where she was going. The more he could anticipate her movements, the more effective would be his protection. Under the
circumstances, he did not think that Julia would object to spying
on her sister. Neither of them wanted to lose Serafina to the
fiend. Though Serafina was strong and determined, she would
be a conspicuous target for the madman who was roaming the
east end. Unfortunately, it was clearly impossible to persuade
Serafina to give up her visits to the east end until the monster
was caught. Her sense of obligation to her work had, if anything,
been increased by the murders.

If the killer was Serafina's blood-stained look-alike, it
would give Miles the advantage of knowing at least one place
where the killer went to ground, and knowing that Katherine
was, in some sense, the killer's conspirator. If Serafina's twin were
not the killer, then the fiend could be anywhere. He could appear out of any of the dark lanes and courts which grew like ugly
tendrils from Whitechapel almost into the City itself. If Serafina
were alone at night on the streets of Whitechapel, it was of the
last importance that he follow her as closely as possible. Daily
communication between himself and Julia would be an essential
aid in keeping Serafina safe. All of these thoughts about Serafina
took less time than the passage of a wren's shadow as it flickered across the white floor, the bird itself darting back and forth
outside, fascinated by the reflections of the shiny cooking pots
within.

Miles suddenly felt the full weight of his sleepless night
and the suspense of his vigil outside Katherine's shop. He looked
once more at the red line on the floor, lurched to his feet and
pushed his way out onto the pavement. He did not know the
street and was not altogether sure of his direction, but once he
realized he was south of the Whitechapel Road, he easily found
his way to the High Street. He walked at a leaden pace noticing
little of his surroundings until he reached the large intersection
of Commercial and Whitechapel Roads. Here, he noticed a sudden increase in the movement of the crowd on the sidewalks. He
heard shouts that had a ring of urgency and alarm about them.
He stopped one man who was running north on Commercial

Street.

"What is it? What is the alarm?"

"Another murder," the man answered breathlessly. "Hanbury Street," and then ran off again.

"Good God," Miles murmured to himself. He unwittingly hastened his own step and soon began to see pairs of constables who were obviously watching the streets closely. He followed the crowds to Hanbury Street and when he approached No. 29 at the end close to Spitalfields Market, constables were preventing people from entering the premises. A large crowd had collected on the sidewalk and as far as the eye could see the street was a jumble of costers, loafers, merchants and constables. Two tired-looking women of the night stood smoking on a corner and were trying to see over the heads of the impenetrable crowd.

"Ee got another one, bloody fiend."

"Ee's a monster, ee is. How are we supposed to work? And if I don't work, I can't pay for a doss. I wouldn't want to be on the street tonight. Not with 'im out there. Have you got a doss I could share for one night, Chlöe?"

"Me? I'm same as you. If I don't get my 4d , I'm out on the street with the monster."

"Ee's going to kill us all and...," the first woman's voice trailed off as Miles walked away from the crowd.

"I must get some sleep so I can be out again tonight," Miles thought. "If Serafina goes to the east end again, I must be ready with a hansom and track her from her doorstep. The new murder on Hanbury Street and the excitement on the streets added a new sense of urgency to his thoughts. As soon as the papers were out, he would order them in and see what he could learn about the Hanbury Street outrage.

By the time he got home, wrote to Julia, slept and was awakened by Egbert for an evening meal, he was able to read the following leading article in the *Times*:

The series of shocking crimes perpetrated in Whitechapel, which on Saturday culminated in the murder of the woman Chapman, is something so distinctly outside the ordinary range of human experience that it has created a kind of stupor extending far beyond the district where the murders were committed. One may search the ghastliest efforts of fiction and fail to find anything to surpass these crimes in diabolical audacity. The mind travels back to the pages of De Quincey for an equal display of scientific delight in the details of butchery; or Edgar Allan Poe's "Murders in the Rue Morgue" recur in the endeavour to conjure up some parallel for this murderer's brutish savagery. But, so far as we know, nothing in fact or fiction equals these outrages at once in their horrible nature and in the effect which they have produced upon the popular imagination. The circumstances that the murders seem to be the work of one individual, that his blows fall exclusively upon wretched wanderers of the night, and that each successive crime has gained something in atrocity upon, and has followed closer on the heels of, its predecessor--these things mark out the Whitechapel murders, even before their true history is unravelled, as unique in the annals of crime. All ordinary experiences of motive leave us at a loss to comprehend the fury which has prompted the cruel slaughter of at least three, and possibly four, women, each unconnected with the other by any tie except that of their miserable mode of livelihood. Human nature would not be itself if these shocking occurrences, all taking place within a short distance of one another, and all bearing a ghastly resemblance, had not thrown the inhabitants into a state of panic - a panic, it must be feared, as favourable to the escape of the assassin as it is dangerous to innocent persons whose appearance or conduct is sufficiently irregular to excite suspicion.

The details of Chapman's murder need not be referred to here at length. It is enough to say that she was found, early on Saturday morning, lying, with her head nearly severed from her body, and mutilated in a most revolting way, in the backyard of No. 29, Hanbury street, Spitalfields. She was not an occupant of the house, which is a tenement let out to many families of lodgers. It is nearly certain that she made her way into the yard, which is easily accessible through the house at all hours of the night, in company with her murderer, for the purpose of privacy, and that she was not killed in another place and then carried to the spot where she was found. The fact that no cry from the poor woman reached any of the inmates of the house shows that the assassin knew his business well. The wounds inflicted by him were exactly similar to those which caused the death of the woman

Nichols eight days before. Nichols, it will be remembered, was found with her throat cut, and frightfully mutilated, upon the pavement of Buck's-row. Rather more than three weeks previously Martha Tabran [Tabram] was picked up dead on the stairs of George-yard-buildings, Whitechapel, with 39 stabs on her body. It is important to notice that, although some of the stabs might have been inflicted by an ordinary knife, others, according to the medical evidence, were far too formidable to have been produced by anything but "some kind of a dagger." The case of Emma Smith, who died from the effects of a barbarous assault in the early morning of Easter Tuesday last, is different, and possibly it ought to be entirely dissociated from the murders of last month. Smith lived long enough to describe the outrage, and her account was that at half-past one in the morning she was passing near Whitechapel Church when some men set upon her, took all the money she had, and then inflicted the most revolting injuries upon her. If this murder is to be classed with the three recent ones, then the theory that they were the work of a gang of blackmailers is more than tenable. But the crimes of August and September naturally separate themselves from the other, both by reason of the considerable interval which elapsed and by the more determined method of the later assassin or assassins. Probably SMITH'S assailants did not mean to kill her outright. But there is no room for doubt that the slayer of TABRAN, NICHOLS, and CHAPMAN meant murder, and nothing else but murder.

After reading this terrifying summary of the crimes, Miles finished dressing and was about to return to Katherine's shop when a letter reached him from Julia.

"Dear Miles," the short note read, "please come to Cavendish Square as soon as you receive this."

"Poor Julia," he muttered to himself as he put on his frock coat and made ready to leave.

Chapter 21

THREE BRASS RINGS AND A WALK
IN THE LABYRINTH

It is a long walk down Brick Lane…Enormous warehouses, looming up in the distance, vaulted railroad tunnels of the Great Eastern Railway, broke the monotony of the crowded streets. Odours alternated: decaying fish, onions and fat, pungent vapours of roast coffee, the foul air of filth, of decaying matter…Shops with bloody meat, stuck on prongs…

—East End 1888

Julia met him at the door, looking very distraught. Her hair was disordered and her flushed complexion showed that she was in the grip of some strong emotion. It was the first time since she was a child that he had seen her long brown hair falling loosely to her shoulders. The lids of her eyes were red and swollen. He assumed she had been crying, something he had never seen her do even as a child.

"My dear girl, what is the matter?" he asked.

"Miles, I am at my wits' end."

"Why? What is the matter?"

"Serafina will go out into the east end, no matter what sort of fiend is lurking there."

"I know. I was going to Katherine's myself when I got your letter," he said. "Has Serafina already left the house?"

"Yes. I let her go. I have decided that we must approach her," she paused, "her condition, in a more direct way."

"What do you mean? How could you let her go so soon after the outrage on Hanbury Street? Do you know about it? I met her very near there, early yesterday morning. We breakfasted together. Did she tell you?"

Julia nodded. "Miles, we must talk to Katherine. She has Serafina's confidence and I feel certain she knows far more about her movements than we do. And," once again she paused, "and I found these on the floor of her room right after she left." She held out her hand and Miles saw three dull gold coloured rings lying in her palm. "They are the reason I wrote to you."

"They look ordinary enough. Cheap. I believe they are brass. Surely they are not Serafina's?"

"One of them is inscribed. Read it."

"Annie Chapman. Chapman. Good God, Chapman, is the name of the woman who was murdered in Hanbury Street this morning. I was just reading a Times article about the outrage."

"I know, Miles. I,too, read the newspapers. That is why we must get Katherine here and make her talk to us. I thought it would be easier if Serafina were gone."

"I still don't think you should have let Serafina go."

"Really, unless I had forcibly restrained her, I had no choice. We must find out how Serafina comes to have the rings with a murdered woman's name inside one of them."

"Yes, I agree but..."

"No, wait. There is more. Come with me."

She turned and led the way to the upstairs bedrooms. Miles had not been in this part of the house since his boyhood. These were the entirely feminine and private rooms of his cousins and aunt. Without a pause, Julia pushed open the door of a

303

room which he vaguely remembered as Serafina's bedchamber. She crossed to a large wardrobe which stood near a handsome cheval glass and opened it. Miles noted the details of Serafina's personal sanctum: the finely patterned silk on the walls, the bed curtained in white and the dressing table with brushes and combs neatly arranged on it. There were no paints or powders anywhere. The purity and simplicity of the almost virginal furnishings made him think of the carpetbag he had seen Serafina with that morning. He could not imagine it in this setting.

"Have you ever seen Serafina carrying a large, ugly carpetbag?" he asked.

"Perhaps. I think so, but look at this," she said pulling a man's suit of clothes out from among Serafina's gowns. "What do you think of that? Is it like the suit the man at Katherine's wore?" she said, as she placed the suit across the bed.

Miles regarded a well-cut black jacket, waistcoat and trousers of a fine salt-and-pepper tweed. It was not the suit he had seen on Serafina's twin. He opened the jacket and found the tailor's name.

"Poole is an excellent tailor," he said. "There should also be a label with the customer's name, as well. Ah, here it is, 'Made expressly for Mr. Jack Winstanley.' Who is 'Jack Winstanley?'"

"I have no idea. Our father's name was John, but I never heard of him using 'Jack' instead as some men do. Besides, this suit would never have fitted him. He was a much bigger man." Julia answered scowling at the inappropriate garments which lay across her sister's bed. "You see why we must talk with Katherine. She is the only one who might be able to tell us about—about—whatever Serafina is doing in the east end."

In the privacy of his own thoughts, Miles felt that the suit pointed to a connection between Serafina and her blood-stained twin. Perhaps Serafina was hiding the suit for the culprit. He dreaded any revelations that might come now. It seemed to him that they could only involve Serafina in some connection with the ghastly crimes.

"Do you think she will tell you?" Miles asked. "If they

have both gone to such lengths to keep all of this hidden, do you think Katherine will expose Serafina just because you ask her?"

"She must. I shall beg and plead with her, if I must. I do not believe she is a hard hearted girl."

"Perhaps not. But do not forget she has lied to us once before—about her checkered past, if it deserves such a polite euphemism. And if Serafina has asked her to hide her secrets, what claim can we make for betraying her friend's confidence?"

"I am her sister. I am a woman who is suffering over my sister's dangerous behaviour. Surely, she will talk to me."

"Perhaps," Miles answered, obviously not convinced. "But we know nothing of the relationships between this man and Serafina or Katherine. He could be Katherine's lover. I hardly know how to proceed when we are so much in the dark."

"I think it would be best if I went to see Katherine alone. I shall attempt to bring her back here, if she will come. You will wait here and she will not know of your presence until she is in this house with the door bolted. Together, we can cross question her. That is my idea."

"You would go into Whitechapel by yourself?"

"Not by myself. We still have our barouche, and Joshua, our coachman, was a noted *shikari* in the eastern empire. He is old but still a tiger of a man. He and young Edgar, the footman, will keep me safe for the short time I would be down there. The killer only strikes when women are alone. It won't take long to ask Katherine to come. Either she will come or not. A few minutes. Not more."

"Are you certain you are feeling well enough to go? You looked very upset when I came tonight."

"I was. But I can do anything needful to protect Serafina."

"We are fortunate that tonight's fog does not prevent you taking the carriage."

"So you will wait for me, here?"

"I don't like to let you go alone, Julia. But I agree that if Katherine saw me in the carriage, she might refuse to come. We did not part on good terms. Yes, of course, Julia. I shall wait. And tomorrow, I shall visit the tailor and see what I can learn about Mr. Jack Winstanley."

"Thank you, Miles. Of all the things that have fallen away from our early lives, you are the only one that remains true and unspoiled." She reached up and kissed him and then turned abruptly and went for her wrap in the front hall.

Moments later the door slammed. A few more moments and the horses' hoofs could be heard, clicking on the paving stones as the carriage pulled away from the kerb. As the absolute silence descended on him, he felt it very odd to be alone in the familiar house which he associated with so many family events and with his very long attachment to Serafina. He had never known the house to be so silent. It gave him an ominous feeling, a feeling emphasized by the heavy dull ticking of an eighteenth century clock on the mantelpiece, one of the only antiques Serafina had ever purchased.

Miles walked the length of the large salon where, only a few short years ago, the whole family had read *The Maiden Tribute* articles together.

"It is sad," he thought, "that objects, dead things, outlive other people and our own affections." It seemed somehow wrong that things which had the highest value should be the most perishable. So many things had sprung from the time of the *Maiden Tribute* publication: Julia's work as a journalist, his separation from Serafina, Mrs. Winstanley's decline and his meeting with Katherine. As soon as he thought of her, his thoughts reverted to her impending arrival. What was the best way to get her to speak ingenuously? Obviously, she had to be convinced that he and Julia were acting out of concern for Serafina. She must believe in the disinterestedness of Julia's intentions. His own part in the interview should, therefore, be largely passive. He interrupted his flow of ideas to take his pocket watch from his waistcoat and open it. The time showed as ten, the hour when Serafina's male twin usually came to Katherine's shop. He should have said something to Julia. Now, he could only hope that Julia and the man did not arrive at the shop together. How could he have been so stupid? He shrugged off the thought and walked the length of the room once more. Time began to hang heavily on him and he wondered if there was something useful he could do before Julia returned with Katherine. He thought of Serafina's bedroom and what they had found there. They had not made a very thorough search. He at once resolved to search the room carefully. Another chance might not present itself. He even picked up Mrs. Winstanley's reading glass so that he could more closely examine the man's suit they had found for blood marks. In the hallway, he passed Rossiter and Virgil as they made their evening rounds, examining the locks and latches on doors and windows. A sudden inspiration struck him. It was an idea that the police themselves would use within the month to try to catch the Whitechapel killer. But Miles must have the credit for having had the notion first.

"I say, Rossiter," he called out after the man and dog had passed him.

"Sir?" Rossiter replied, retracing his steps.

"Is Virgil a very good bloodhound, Rossiter? I mean, can he actually track a man?"

"He's champion, sir," Rossiter said proudly. "By birth and by training. Mr. Mackusick of Surrey, biggest breeder in the world, picked him out for us. 'Keen as mustard,' he told us. And he is. Give him a good scent and he could follow a man clear across London."

"And why haven't the police used dogs like Virgil to track this east end maniac?"

"I don't know, sir. But he do need a scent of the man's blood or clothing to get on the track. Maybe they've not got anything belonging to the madman."

"I don't believe they do. I am sure you are right. Thank you, Rossiter."

"Not at all, sir."

Man and dog turned to go but Miles spoke again, "If I could put him on a track, would he go with me to find the man?"

"I don't know why not, sir. You've been giving him sugar cubes since he were a puppy."

"All right. Thank you, again, Rossiter. May I have the

lead? I wish to take him upstairs."

"Here you are, sir. Go along with Mr. Miles, Virgil."

The dog obediently climbed the stairs to Serafina's room and once inside immediately began sniffing near the bed. When Miles removed the man's suit from the cabinet and laid it over the edge of the bed, Virgil ran his long nose up and down the pants, stopping repeatedly near the cuffs. Miles knelt down and examined the cuffs minutely with Mrs. Winstanley's reading glass. On one he could see a small scarlet mark.

"Well done, Virgil," he said to the red and black hound. "I believe you could follow this man from one end of London to the other. Come with me," he said as he grabbed the pants and put them over his arm.

Hearing the excitement in Miles' voice, the hound lunged toward the door nearly knocking over the man.

"Wait, Virgil," he said sharply, holding onto the heavy leather lead for dear life as he was pulled precipitously down the stairs.

"Rossiter," he called out.

"Yes, sir? Is he doing his duty?"

"Admirably. But I shall need you to hold him for a few moments while I write a letter to Julia."

The older man took the lead, but Virgil watched Miles closely as he walked from the front hall to Serafina's little room where there was certain to be writing materials. As Miles entered the room, he had a sudden uprush of memory of his fight with Serafina in this very place. He stepped to the desk and wrote rapidly.

"Julia, I have taken Virgil to the east end to see if he can trace the killer from the man's clothing we found in Serafina's room. Find out what you can from Katherine. I shall come later, no matter what the hour. Miles." He scratched out the words, threw down the pen and met Virgil and Rossiter in the hall.

"I may be late, Rossiter. But don't worry, I shall take good care of him. Let me have your latchkey, please. And give this letter to Julia."

"Very well, sir. Here it is."

"As I say, I shall watch over him."

"And he will watch over you, sir—he will watch over you."

With that, Miles lunged out into the night with his four legged companion.

Several cabs would not take him with the dog, but finally he hailed a shabby four wheeler whose driver did not object.

"Whitechapel Road and Baker's Row," Miles called to the driver. A short time later, Miles and Virgil were standing near Katherine's shop at the corner of the High Street and Baker's Row. "Here, Virgil," he said to the dog as he held the tweed trousers to the dog's nose.

The hound plunged at once into Baker's Row and in his eagerness jostled several pedestrians. In moments they stood in front of Katherine's door and, before he could be stopped, the dog pushed his way through the door which should have been latched but was not. Miles tried to look around the unlit premises as the large animal pulled him through the shop, through the curtains at the back and to another unlatched door at the very rear of the building. Without even a pause, Virgil pulled Miles into the lane. There could be no doubt that the scent was a hot one. Man and dog walked and ran up to the point where Old Montague Street converged on Baker's Row and Hanbury Street. When Miles realized where they were, how close to the scene of the last murder, he was very excited.

"Good dog, good dog," he cried to Virgil.

Then, in spite of the hound's eagerness, hours passed while the dog led Miles up and down the courts, alleys and rookeries of the Whitechapel streets which lay between the City and Spitalfields. The darkest and most confined passages were those off of Flower and Dean Street or along the north edge of Dorset Street. In a matter of a few months, the Ripper would make these ugly, narrow lanes and courts remembered forever as the ghastliest streets in the metropolis. So violent and shocking were the crimes of the Ripper that the killer single-handedly destroyed the very places which gave him refuge. The public, the police, even the queen, herself, would demand better lighting, better sanitation and the rebuilding of the area so that it could never again spawn such a fiend. For years prior to the killings, bill after bill had been floated in a vain attempt to have the area improved. But the profits from the substandard lodging houses were too great to tempt middle and upper class landlords to demolish them. The Ripper would succeed where all reformers had failed, and after the killer's disappearance, the area would be completely rebuilt. But on the night that Miles and Virgil walked the streets, the dark buildings of dirty brick and the stench of open sewers was still very much in evidence, providing a dreadful setting for the terrible crimes, a labyrinth which allowed the killer to mutilate women while crowds of vigilantes and police searched in the next street.

As Miles walked, the bells of Nicholas Hawksmoor's Georgian Baroque masterpiece, Christ Church, Spitalfields, tolled the hours. As with many older parts of London, architectural magnificence and utter dilapidation stood side by side in Spitalfields. Up and down, back and forth, through the narrow unwholesome passages, sometimes measuring less than six feet between three storey buildings, Miles was towed by his canine companion. Then, all at once, the dog seemed to turn eastward, doubling back on his own steps. He appeared to be following the way they had come. Finally, he stopped at the rear of Katherine's shop where they had begun their long circuitous walk. The dog sat down at the door and looked eagerly to Miles, who could make nothing out of the canine's behaviour. Exhausted and thoroughly disappointed with the results of his experiment, Miles and Virgil finally caught a cab back to Cavendish Square.

Julia met him at the door with an eager expression on her face.

"The dog led me through nearly every street in Whitechapel and then some. I do believe it is worth trying again. But..."

"I have had more luck than you, Miles," Julia interrupted him eagerly. Come inside. I have spoken with Katherine, too. She has left something for you to see."

"You certainly sound uplifted," he said somewhat grudgingly. "Is Serafina home? It is very late."

"I know. Yes. She is upstairs in bed, thank heavens. She came home hours ago, shortly after Katherine left."

"Did they meet?"

"No. Katherine was gone when Serafina came in."

"What shall I do with Virgil?"

"Leave him here. He often sleeps in the front hall."

"Very well," Miles said slipping off the lead. "He should sleep well after pulling me all over the east end. Now, what news do you have?"

"Let us go into the salon," Julia said, taking his hand. "Would you like some tea? You must be frozen."

"I am, but I am more eager to hear what you have learned."

"You know, Miles," Julia began as she led the way to the salon, " I must say that I think Katherine a very brave and unusual woman. Wait until I tell you what she has done."

"I could not be more expectant," he answered as they sat down.

"I don't know if you realize it, but Katherine's shop is only steps from the Whitechapel Mortuary where Annie Chapman's body was taken by police."

"No," Miles answered. "I hadn't even thought of it. Why?"

"Well, when I got to Katherine's, the gas was unlit. The only light came from the street. But the door was ajar, so I went inside."

"Julia," Miles exclaimed. "It was dangerous. I must have just missed you there. Virgil and I were there as well. We know too little about what is going on at that shop."

"But surely you realize, Miles, that as a journalist who has written about the dockers and stalked the streets of the east end, I have more than a large dose of curiosity. If I let imagined dangers stop me, I should do nothing. I have even worn the costume of a hallelujah lass so that I could penetrate some of the abysmal thieves' kitchens on Dorset Street and interview the inmates. A dark photographic establishment would not stop me."

Miles believed that Julia felt too much trust for Katherine. She did not seem to realize that Katherine could be an accomplice to the ghastly crimes. He wondered if he should caution her, dropped the idea and continued listening to Julia's narrative.

"...so I found her dark room at the back. I lit a small lamp and looked around. I saw immediately that she had been working very recently and had not cleaned up. Then, I found what she had been working on. At first, I didn't recognize them, but then I realized that they were ghastly photographs of a face, more particularly, the eyes. As I was poring over these horrifying images, the door at the rear of the building seemed to burst open. My heart jumped into my mouth but it was only Katherine, carrying her camera. How such a tiny little woman can carry all that equipment is amazing. Anyway, after we had greeted each other and I explained my errand, I asked her about the gruesome photographs I had found. She told me, 'Those are the eyes of the first two victims. Annie Chapman is lying dead at the mortuary a few paces up this lane. I just came back from photographing her eyes.'"

"Why, Katherine? Why would you want to haunt such a ghastly place?"

"I know it does sound ghoulish," she said, "and it was, but *The British Journal of Photography* recently had an article on how the retina can retain the image of the last thing a person has seen just before death. I have photographed all three women to see if my camera could capture any image of the last thing they must have seen in this world, the Whitechapel murderer, their killer.'"

"I've never heard of such a thing," Miles said derisively.

"Well, sir," Julia said in her most pert tone, "perhaps you should read more. I am only telling you what *The British Journal of Photography* has said about the eyes of the dead.

"Besides, what about Katherine's pictures of Amelia? They were even more astonishing to me. And what about the fact that the police in America have used precisely this method to find a killer. It was reported in *The Tribune*. They believed the camera could record the person last seen by the victim. They identified a man, tried him and put him in prison," Julia said, thrusting out her sharp chin. "We live in a time of scientific wonders."

"I really don't know what to think about those images, nor about this criminal case. Perhaps their techniques are more advanced than ours. This picture is very strange. It looks more like a death's head than a living face. Why is that? And, good God, look within the orbits of the eyes—within in the skull sockets there is a faint face. It almost looks like one exposure printed on top of another. This is amazing. I, myself, have seen this man in Whitechapel. On the night of the first atrocity. Get me a glass, Julia, a magnifying glass."

Dim and small though the images were, Miles was nearly certain that in the orbits of the skull he was seeing the wolfish, predatory looking foreigner he had seen on the night he smoked opium and found the bloody knife in his pocket after being assaulted outside of Katherine's shop. Julia quickly picked something out of her mother's knitting basket which was still near the chair she had always used.

Miles took it and bent over the image. "There can be no doubt," he said, "that is the man I saw on the high street on the night of the first murder. How did she take these, I wonder?"

"Katherine said she just set up the camera and took the picture."

"Well, perhaps Katherine's clairvoyance would enable her to capture some bizarre spirit image—in this case imprinted in the woman eye sockets rather than her retinas," he said.

" The old man at the mortuary told Katherine that the police wanted to photograph the dead woman's eyes, too, until the police surgeon stopped them. He told them it wouldn't do any good in this case."

"Before seeing these, I shouldn't have thought it could do any good in any case."

"Miles," Julia said taking his hands in hers, "You do not have an open mind. You assume that everything works in one way."

"My dear Julia, it is not a matter of an open mind. It is a description of the laws which underpin the physical universe."

"But you do admit that our grasp of those laws can change? For centuries people believed the world was created in seven days. Since the great railway excavations and the fossils they unearthed we know differently."

"Yes."

"So we don't know everything there is to know," she said. "Why should it be utterly impossible for a certain person to do something which ordinarily is against what we know of nature? We must always keep an open mind and be neutral observers. To say we know all is to put ourselves in the place of God."

"All right, Julia. But what is the result of all of this? Where does it get us in our pursuit of the Whitechapel killer?"

"It gets us this," she said, suddenly turning to the table behind her and handing him another photographic print.

At first, Miles had difficulty understanding what he was looking at. Then he realized there was a woman's forehead and open staring eyes. But superimposed over these was a face. The face inside the eye sockets, not captured and reflected by the retina as some people believed the final image of life would be. Each eye socket was filled with the head of the same man's bearded face. The features were too out of focus to be identified. The photograph suggested a death's head with a luminous face of the dead woman superimposed on it. Grisly as the photographs were, Miles felt a sense of relief. In neither image did the man's face within the orbits look anything like the blood-stained man Miles had seen with Katherine.

"So she's taken two of these, of different victims?"

"Three. Somehow she's take photographs of Annie Chapman, Martha Tabram and the most recent one."

"Well," he said, "I would certainly know this man if I passed him on the street, but the overall effect of the image is certainly grisly enough. But he looks nothing like the man I saw at Katherine's. He had no beard. It looks as though Annie Chapman's face has been peeled from her skull."

"I asked Katherine about that and she said she didn't un-

derstand it, either. There seems to be something in the clairvoyant process of photographing these dead women that causes that
gruesome effect on their faces. Look, here are some other photos
which Katherine took of the victims. They are quite ghastly, yet
fascinating in their horror. They are all death's heads. I have no
idea how she got them. It is quite an achievement. That little
woman must be fearless," and she showed him three, quarter
plate prints of the first three ripper victims. They were similar
but different from the police photos of the victims which were
later so widely published.

"I think you should forget about the man who resembles
Serafina. We know nothing about him. He could be anyone."

"But his clothes were bloodstained—and the resemblance was striking. I believe he was Jack Winstanley—who is
very likely a relation of ours."

"Even so, that does not mean he is the killer. Unfortunately, none of what we know qualifies as evidence in a legal
sense. Except the brass rings we found in Serafina's room. They
might. Especially if someone identified them as belonging
to Annie."

"But we found them in Serafina's room. Imagine the
construction the police would place on that. After this last murder, I believe the authorities will be even more desperate for a
plausible suspect. From what I saw this morning, east enders are
starting to panic."

"What can we do?"

"I must get some sleep before I can think," Miles said.
"Virgil dragged me over most of the east end. Or so it seemed. I
am thoroughly done up."

"You must stay here, then," Julia said. "You can sleep in
mama's room. I shall wake you before Serafina wakes and we
shall hold a council of war."

"Right now, I should agree to anything that allows me to
lie down," Miles said yawning.

"All the servants are already in their own chambers so I
shall show you to your room. Come."

315

Chapter 22

VISIONS OF MURDER AND WORSE

...the success of the Victorian detective largely rested upon a thorough knowledge of the local villains, upon the evidence of informers, and upon much legwork, tracing and interviewing witnesses. The Whitechapel murderer, however, may not have been a professional villain and probably worked alone.

—Philip Sugden
    The Complete History of
    Jack the Ripper

Miles woke from his tangled dreams feeling disoriented and uneasy. He had been running in the dark Whitechapel Streets once again, running until he nearly tripped over a bloody, torn up corpse which lay unavoidably in his path. When he forced himself to bend down and look closely at the decaying face, he saw that it resembled Serafina and then, Amelia. What was worse, it gave off a stench worse than rotting fish. The shock of recognition and the smell had wakened him. The horror of the dead, stinking body lying in the gutter faded slowly, in spite of the fact that Mrs. Winstanley's room was the sunniest and most cheerful of the house's bedchambers. It was decorated in yellows and light mauves and pale greens, colours which seemed even lighter in the watery sun reflecting off the large looking glass mounted above the dressing table. The mahogany wood of the table and mirror was too heavy and ornately carved for Miles' taste, but he remembered Serafina telling him that Mrs. Winstanley was attached to it, in spite of the fact that it in no way complimented the new decoration Serafina had done in the room. He thought of his Aunt May as he looked around. She had liked the colour yellow. He was almost more aware of her now through the emptiness of this chamber than he had been when she was alive. He sat up in her bed. Even after he was fully awake, he felt heavy and fatigued and could still feel a thrill of horror from the images of his long, extraordinarily vivid dream.

He bent over and felt under the bed for the chamber pot, used it and put on a dressing gown which had belonged to the late Mr. Winstanley, whom Miles scarcely remembered. The head of the family had never been seen clearly by the boy Miles had been. Something about the man had intimidated Miles in spite of his broad, face and his voice with traces of a north country brogue still in it. He saw a sudden, still image of Dr. Winstanley leading him toward the maze in the back garden. It was so clear, it was like a photograph.

"What an odd thing to recall after all this time," he murmured. "And what an odd moment to recall it."

There was a soft knock at his door. "Miles?" he heard Julia's voice say.

He opened the door. Julia was wearing a peignoir of white chiffon and pink silk which gave the illusion of transparency without revealing any distinct outlines.

"I thought I heard you," she said in a stage whisper. "If you come downstairs, we could talk over tea before Serafina wakes."

"Yes, of course. I shall be down directly."

A short time later, as Miles descended the stairs, he pulled Dr. Winstanley's dressing gown around himself more tightly. As he opened it to make it more snug, he noticed the tailor's label on the inside pocket. The dressing gown had also been made by Poole's of Savile Row. Though, Poole's had been a popular tailor since the '40s, a strange sense of forboding crept up his spine and recalled some of the images from his dreams.

The cousins met in the dining room at the centre of the main floor. A much smaller table with folding leaves and oriental motifs had taken the place of the massive mahogany dining table. Julia, with her hair unbound, was fetchingly pouring tea as he entered the room. The shape of her figure was made more distinct by the light which came from a French window opposite the table and passed through her diaphanous peignoir.

"This is very handsome, Julia."

"You like the new table?"

"Yes, I do. And your costume."

A sudden pink flush lent charm to her small face and finely cut features.

"I have been thinking about our problem, Miles."

"Yes?"

"I think the idea of going to the tailor an excellent one."

"You know," he said, "I noticed while I was putting on this dressing gown of your father's, that he used the same tailors as those who made the suit we found in Serafina's room."

"And that means?" she asked, turning pale.

"I don't know. But it is one more connection between this family and the crimes in Whitechapel. We are not certain that this man you saw really has anything to do with the outrages."

"No. We are not certain," Miles agreed. "But I tell you that the resemblance between this man and Serafina was astonishing. I feel there must be some—pardon the word, blood connection —between our family and the man. He must be a relative of some kind. And he was covered in blood. With what has been occurring in the east end, that seems more than a coincidence to me. A well-dressed man with blood all over his clothes is no Aldgate slaughterer. But surely in your talk with Katherine last night you learned the identity of this man."

"No. She wouldn't tell me. She said it would violate a confidence."

"Good Lord, what astonishing cheek under the circumstances."

"She regards herself as a doctor and feels that she cannot violate a client's confidence."

"That makes a visit to the tailor even more worthwhile," he answered. As he finished speaking, the door pushed open and Serafina stood next to table, smothering a yawn. Then, she sat down.

"Miles, how curious to find you here at this hour."

"Not curious at all, Serafina," Julia said. "I was uneasy about you last night and I asked Miles to stay. By the way, I found these after you left. Where did you get them?" She put the brass rings on the table. Serafina looked at them and her eyes widened in what was clearly an expression of horror. Then her countenance became fixed and immobile, lifeless. She had slipped into a cataleptic state.

"Oh, dear Lord, what have I done?" Julia exclaimed.

"She has gone into a cataleptic fit or a trance," Miles said evenly.

"What shall we do?" Julia answered.

"We'll wait," Miles said, buttering a slice of toast, which he took from the warming rack.

The seconds dragged by and Serafina sat at table like a wooden idol. The expression in her eyes remained one of horror, as if witnessing some terrible eternal moment.

"I cannot sit here like this," Julia said. "I can't bear to see her like this. I am going to fetch Katherine. I know she is able to bring her out of trance states, but I've never seen her like this. You shall stay with her while I dress."

"Didn't you tell me that this kind of thing has happened before?"

"Not with that dreadful look of horror frozen on her beautiful face. It is too terrible. I must go to Katherine."

"Very well, Julia. I think you are rushing things a little."

Without replying, Julia jumped to her feet.

"Tell the servants to stay out of this room until they are informed otherwise," Miles said.

"Oh, yes. Thank you, Miles. I don't want her to be seen

like that, even by our own servants." A few minutes later, Julia could be heard rapidly climbing the stairs to her room.

Miles looked over at his former lover's beautiful, horror stricken face and thought, "It is said that madness runs in families. First, Mrs. Winstanley had nervous attacks and now this. And even I have started having odd memory lapses. And there is the family resemblance to the man in Katherine's shop. Once we get Katherine here, I shall get the truth out of her, one way or another. We must find out everything that little witch knows. My poor, lovely cousin. What a terrible thing to be cursed with. Would the illness overtake Julia, as well?" he wondered. What about himself? He had to fight his own impulse to touch Serafina and comfort her. He had no idea what the effect would be. He felt some of the same horrible feelings engendered by his dreams, only now, he could not wake from them. After what seemed a very long time, he finally heard Julia leave the house. Serafina's rigid, horror stricken countenance was beginning to tell on him. He, too, wanted Katherine to come and release Serafina from whatever terrible thing that had taken possession of her.

For the first quarter hour after Julia left, Miles remained in the dining room with Serafina and tried to study her. But her complete immobility defied any attempt to divine her inner condition. Finally, Miles had to accept her as nothing more than an object.

"How dreadful," he said softly. He moved close to the frozen girl, looked in her face and said, "Dear Serafina, can you not hear me? Give me some sign, please." But the girl remained rigid and absolutely motionless. Though he looked right into her eyes and could see the many colours of her iris that made up a distinctive shade of blue, she gave no sign that she saw him. She did not even blink. He sat down directly across from her and tried through sheer force of will to enter her thoughts. Every effort was met with complete neurasthenic paralysis. Finally, the girl's immobility forced the young man into motion: he stood up and began pacing the long, narrow room.

After walking back and forth a few times he noticed a small, bright reflection on the table, appearing and disappearing as the clouds outside scudded back and forth across the sun. The brilliant highlight radiated from the brass rings where they had dropped from Serafina's nerveless hand. He picked up the carefully polished metal trinkets and held them in his hand. Could Serafina have been present when these rings were taken from the dead woman by the killer? Had she witnessed the brutal crime? Was that why she had been frozen in horror when she saw them again? If Katherine really had access to Serafina's mind, she must be made to tell what had happened to Serafina. Then, an even more horrible thought came to Miles. What if Serafina had been violated by the fiend but not killed? What if she had escaped, afterward? Perhaps that was the true meaning of the horror they saw frozen in her eyes. Compared to the other victims, Serafina was young, beautiful and strong. Might not these factors have affected the behaviour of the Whitechapel killer and caused him to spare Serafina's life while perhaps taking something of even greater value? Most women of Serafina's class would feel that being raped was a living death, a crime which, through no fault of their own, would cut them off forever from polite society. During the Indian Mutiny, excerpts from women's diaries published in British newspapers, told of family discussions about precisely when the wife wished to be shot by her husband rather than risk being ravished. Had Serafina suffered a fate worse than death at the hands of a murderous madman? Would she believe she was irredeemable? Miles did not know. He had often heard her say that no woman should bear the shame for the crimes of men, but would she really believe that in her own case? Her personal standards of physical purity were very high. He really could not predict whether she would take the shame of violation on herself. If only she had listened to everyone who had tried to dissuade her from visiting the east end while the madman was loose. But perhaps the worst had not occurred. She was alive, uninjured, and where there is life there is hope, Miles told himself. She may even have seen something which could help catch the killer. He remembered that she had been very annoyed with him when, after Amelia's abduction, he could not describe the perpetrator. And then he drifted off into memories of their early years together when he had admired her with a sublime, childish passion. In particular, he remembered her in a pink dress which resembled an opera dancer's costume. How he could have been so emotionally inflamed and yet know nothing of physical passion was a mystery.

The time Miles waited in the dining room with the stricken Serafina was an eternity of dread mixed with memory and impatience, but in fact it was just over an hour by his own watch when he once again heard footsteps in the front hall. Moments later, Julia burst into the dining room.

"How is she?"

"Unchanged," Miles answered.

"My poor dear," a higher, softer voice said. Katherine was momentarily hidden behind Julia as the women entered the room. For a moment, the *frou frou* of skirts and petticoats was the loudest noise in the room.

Miles and Katherine had not met face to face for over a year. She looked very well and Miles found her extremely attractive. He blushed deeply but the woman showed no sign of unease. She threw off her cape and went immediately to the side of her patient and began making mesmeric passes over her. In a few minutes, Serafina sighed deeply and relaxed. She was no longer rigid but slumped in her chair. She appeared to drift into a deep sleep.

"She will be all right now," Katherine said after watching Serafina's slow, even breathing and taking her pulse. "Allow her whatever she asks for when she wakes. She will be entirely herself." Then Katherine picked up her cape and place it over her shoulders as she turned to go out of the room.

"And that is all?" Miles said sharply.

"Yes, what more did you expect?" Katherine replied.

"A great deal more," he said. "See here, Miss Green, there are things we must know about. What are you and Serafina up to?"

"Up to?"

"Yes. What is the purpose and meaning of all this memerism that the two of you are engaging in? We must know what is happening to Serafina. You are going to tell us. And these grisly photographs you've taken. How did you do it?"

"I'm sorry, but as I've already told Miss Winstanley, I cannot. Serafina's confidence must be protected. I can only add to what she herself has already said."

"Oh, no you don't," Miles said as he grabbed the girl's wrist to prevent her from turning away.

"Unhand me, Mr. Hickenbotham."

"You have much to explain," he replied truculently.

"Not if it touches on Serafina. She can divulge whatever she likes, but I cannot say anything without her express permission. She has asked me to be silent about our work together. My pictures are my own business. You will not believe me in any case."

"Miles," Julia said, "please let her go. She has told me all that Serafina has given her leave to say. We must talk to Serafina if we want more."

"Do you realize, Miss Green, that you may be endangering Serafina's life by not speaking plainly?"

"You do not seem to understand, Mr. Hickenbotham, that preserving Serafina's confidence is the only chance I have to, to help her. If she loses confidence in me, there will be nothing anyone can do for her."

"Oh, only you have the power to make her well?"

"Only I have her confidence. That is necessary to do the work I believe she needs to do."

"And what is that work?"

"Ask Serafina."

"Miss Green, do you know that there is a homicidal madman running around the east end? Do you realize what risks Serafina runs when she goes to Whitechapel to visit you? I really think you have an exaggerated idea of your own powers."

"She doesn't come to Whitechapel to visit me. She has many there who need her help."

"That may be but if you would help convince her to wait until this mad man is caught..."

"I cannot say more. I must leave." Then she turned to

Julia. "If Serafina needs me again, please come anytime— day or night."

"You are very kind, Katherine. We do appreciate your help."

"And who is the man in these images? Where did you find him?" Miles went on querulously.

Miles felt quite desperate to stop the girl from leaving. He would not reveal that he had been watching her shop, so he could say nothing about the bloodstained man he had seen there, but perhaps there was something else that he could force from her.

"Miss Green," Miles said, "how do you explain this." From his dressing gown he pulled the *carte visite* with Katherine's nude photo on it. "Is this how you earn your livelihood, while you pretend to be respectable?"

Katherine took the card from him and blushed deeply.

"This picture was taken some years ago," she said in a very soft voice. "I thought they had all been destroyed."

"Well, as you can see that is not the case."

"It was taken in exchange for food and lodging and to keep me from starving to death when I first arrived from the subcontinent. I had no other way to earn money—except prostitution, to which I would not resort."

"So you give hunger as an excuse for behaviour like this?" he asked, flushing angrily.

"Yes," the girl said quietly.

"Miles," Julia said, "You should know that everyone in this house supports women who are driven by starvation to grant sexual favours to unprincipled men."

"Yes, but she pretends to be far above such things."

"What do you mean?" Julia asked.

"It means that I would not accept his advances," Katherine said, blushing furiously. Miles also coloured at the revelation.

Both Katherine and Miles watched Julia closely to see what her reaction would be. For a moment it appeared that she, too, had become paralysed. Then she sniffed and dabbed at her eyes and looked at her cousin.

"What?" Miles asked.

"I am disappointed, dear Miles," Julia said softly. "I had thought you better than other men."

"I am only a man, Julia. Your sister would grant me no freedom nor would she set a wedding day."

"I know. But, but...Oh, I suppose it is foolish. I certainly have no right to remonstrate with you. You were never really pledged to anyone in this house."

"Julia," he said. "You make my heart ache when you imply that I do not have a deep bond to both you and Serafina."

"And you, dear Miles, have made mine ache today."

"I am terribly sorry, Julia. But we musn't digress. Miss Green, you must tell us what is wrong with Serafina. Never mind what has passed between us. Serafina's recovery is all that matters."

Katherine looked thoughtful for a moment and finally said, "I do not know that there is actually something wrong with her, in the sense you mean. Do you remember my telling you when we first met that we each have multiple selves? Serafina is more aware of some of her other selves than most of us are. I agree that it can be confusing and inconvenient. But I do not view it as a disease."

"What then?" Julia asked.

"A greater sensitivity, perhaps. A kind of Amfortas wound," Katherine replied.

"But isn't there a reason for that?"

"That is what Serafina and I have been exploring. I cannot tell you more than that without violating her confidence. I shall only say that there is one very strong secondary personality who makes its appearance frequently."

"What is going on, here?" Serafina's sharp, clear voice suddenly asked.

"We were just trying to decide how we could best help you," Miles said.

"Help me? You could order lunch. I am famished. What time is it?"

"The clocks have just struck two, Serafina," Julia replied.

"Oh, dear. I do believe I have lost some time again."

"That is what we want to help you with, Serafina," Miles said seriously. "Surely you want to find out what happens during the time you lose?"

"Katherine and I are working on that problem," Serafina said. "Right now, I want to eat."

Julia and Miles looked at each other and shrugged slightly.

"I shall ring," Julia said. "You'll stay to lunch, of course Katherine?"

"Thank you, no. I should feel my presence was an imposition."

Serafina reached out for Katherine and seized her sleeve, "Thank you, dear friend," she said in a fervent tone as she kissed the other woman's hand.

"It's all right, my dear," Katherine answered in a soothing tone as she stroked her head. "You can send for me any time you need me. You know that."

"Yes, dear friend. Thank you. What should I ever do without you."

"It isn't necessary that you should do without me, Serafina. Goodbye."

"I insist on seeing you out," Serafina said, getting to her feet. The two women left the dining room, arm in arm.

When they were alone, Miles turned to Julia. "Does that look like a relationship that should be encouraged?"

"Miles, you keep talking like a father. Please remember that Serafina is a grown woman who must do what she thinks right."

"Even if her thinking is part of her disease?"

"That same argument was used against Mrs. Weldon in court. It is wrong to curtail personal freedom unless a person is demonstrably doing harm to others."

"And are we certain that Serafina and her friend are not involved in the murders in some way? I am not."

"That is a dreadful way to put it," Julia said. "You make it sound as if they could be actively taking part in the crimes."

"No. That is not what I meant. Excuse me."

Julia frowned and said, "That Serafina is dependent on Katherine, I have known. That is the worst I can say about their relationship."

"I think there is something unnatural about it," Miles said. "Something else is going on which we know nothing about."

"If Serafina does not want to tell us, we cannot force her confidence, Miles. Please remember how fond of her I am. I must trust her. Otherwise, I rob her of all dignity."

"I shall continue to watch her," Miles said, somewhat hoarsely, obviously suppressing the full force of his feelings. "You will tell me when she goes to the east end?"

"Yes. It is a sound precaution, as long as the killer is loose on the streets. Will you stay to breakfast?"

"No. I shall go to see the tailor, now. Poole's will have a list of clients and their addresses. I shall go and beg an introduction to Mr. Jack Winstanley—whoever he is and wherever he resides. I want to know who he is—who his antecedents are—and what he was doing in Katherine's shop, covered in blood, on a night when one of the outrages took place. I also want to know who this man is who appears in the photographs—who I saw on the street in Whitechapel on the night of the first murder. I insist on having the truth about those things, one way or another. If Katherine will not explain it to us, she can explain it to the police."

"But Miles, you told me yourself that you couldn't see that clearly and that you had been smoking opium. Even if they are desperate, do you think the police will take you seriously?"

"Perhaps I'll omit that fact."

"And what about the danger of involving Serafina with the police?"

"I'd forgotten. Julia, I am only trying to force the truth out into the open. I believe it is the best way to protect Serafina."

"I disagree," she replied, her sharp little chin thrust upward in an expression of determined defiance.

They looked at each other for some moments and finally Miles said, "The real difference between our positions is that you trust Katherine and I do not." Then he turned, went up to Mrs. Winstanley's room and got dressed. When he came downstairs, his two cousins were waiting in the front hall.

"By the way, Serafina," he said suddenly, "Where is that garish carpet bag I saw you with the other morning, right after the Chapman murder?" Perhaps, he thought, there was something in that bag that had stained the floor. If it were still in the bag...

"What bag are you talking about, Miles? I have never even owned a carpet bag. Have I Julia?"

"I don't remember one."

"You told me it was filled with pamphlets."

"I'm sorry, Miles. You are mistaken."

"Then, I wish you both a good day," he said as he pulled one of his gloves on with a sharp jerk which expressed his irritation with both women. Then he turned and left the house.

Chapter 23

A DIFFICULT PERSON TO FIT

Henry Poole, son of the first tailor to set up shop on Savile Row, had a passion for the hunting field, and made his elegant, Italianate premises a recognised meeting place for the young bloods and swells of the later nineteenth century. The premises were crowded with customers being measured for hunting pinks or the new Court dress (introduced by Poole) in bottle green or mulberry velvet. Miles Winstanley, himself, had several suits in his wardrobe from the famous tailor, though he tended to favour an even softer line in the cut of his clothes.

As he rode through the west end, Miles felt more than a little irritation with his charming cousins. Serafina, of course, was not to be blamed for her unbalanced state of mind, but Julia he felt, should have a cooler head and be able to see through Katherine's questionable character. Instead, she treated Katherine as the most trustworthy of allies in a matter where lives might hang in the balance. He felt in his pocket and found the brass rings he had taken with him. That was one piece of tangible evidence which was not going to disappear like Serafina's carpetbag. Julia had made it impossible for him to press Katherine about the man in her shop and force the truth from her. Whoever he was, he had to be a leading player in the grisly

drama which was unfolding in the east end and, with his startling resemblance to Serafina, he had to have some connection
with the Winstanley family. Julia seemed willfully to ignore
those facts. Without saying anything to Julia, he had also appro-
priated some of Katherine's death's head photographs.

"At least," he said to himself, "she did show me the suit."
A thought which brought him back to his present errand. He
would not be able just to walk into an establishment such as
Poole's and ask for the address of Mr. Jack Winstanley. A gentlemen's clothier wouldn't think of giving out private information about one of their patrons. And Poole's was perhaps the
most distinguished gentlemen's clothier in all London. By the
time of Miles' visit in 1888, Pooles was already an institution, a
place where gentlemen not only came to be fitted for the finest
clothing but also to gossip, drink hock and puff on 'old pooley's'
cigars. The patronage of Edward, Prince of Wales, had made the
tailor an arbiter of what should be worn since the 1870s. Henry
Poole's talents and good character even earned him a place in
Disraeli's novel, Endymion, where he was described thus as Mr.
Vigo:
"The most fashionable tailor in London… consummate in his
art…neither pretentious nor servile, but simple and with becoming respect for others and himself."

Dickens, the most celebrated man of his time bought
suits at Poole's. It was evident that Jack Winstanley was a man of
substance if he bought his suits there, but why had Miles never
heard of him before, and how had his suit had turned up in Serafina's wardrobe?

Perhaps, Miles thought, he could pretend to buy a gift
for Jack Winstanley, something which would then have to be
sent to a home address. He could then simply ask the clerk to
confirm the address to him, saying that his 'cousin' had recently
moved. He could see no reason why the stratagem wouldn't
work. Though Miles was not a good customer, he was known at
Poole's. So having settled his line of attack, Miles was entirely at
his ease when he got out of his cab and entered the elegant store
which had been the cornerstone for the reputation of Savile

Row. A quarter hour later he walked out of the store feeling
stunned and baffled. According to Poole's, Mr. Jack Winstanley lived at 21 Cavendish Square! When the clerk read off the
address, Miles had felt a shiver of apprehension. The only other
information he had gleaned was that, "Mr. Jack Winstanley was
a difficult man to fit." A vague, cloudy suspicion which had lain
at the back of his mind coalesced into a terrible idea: Jack Winstanley and Serafina were one and the same person! It seemed
incredible, but no other hypothesis seemed to fit the facts. And
if that were true then Serafina's mental condition was even more
deplorable than Julia imagined. If the man he had seen with
bloodstains on his clothes was actually Serafina—and that might
also explain the stain her carpetbag left in the cafe—could she
be implicated somehow in the Whitechapel killings? Good lord,
if madness did run in the family, what might it mean for Julia, or
even himself?

"I must think," he muttered to himself as he walked
along Old Burlington Street. He did not want to alarm Julia
further but, she would certainly ask about the suit. What should
he say? He felt a sense of panic and then told himself, "Wait,
I am reacting to the hysteria in the newspapers and on the east
end streets. I must not be swept up in all that. I must think
clearly about what to do next." Then, in one of the curious leaps
the mind sometimes makes, his desire for an interlocutor made
him think of an acquaintance he had not seen in some time,
another painter named Walter Sickert. In later years, Sickert
would develop a sizeable reputation as a painter of lower class
people and settings. He would even be put forward as the 'real'
Jack the Ripper by a writer of 'true' crime books in the late
twentieth century. But Miles knew Sickert as a man fascinated
with mystery, strongly imbued with Symbolist esthetics and very
much under the influence and shadow of the American painter,
Whistler. Miles and Sickert both shared a taste for Degas and
other french Impressionists. During the early 80s, the two men
had undertaken several journeys into the demimonde of Paris,
once when Sickert brought the now famous painting of Whistler's mother to Paris. Sickert's marriage had muted their friend-

ship, reducing opportunities for male camaraderie and they had not seen each other in some time. Miles was wealthier than his friend, but Sickert's reputation was growing more quickly. He lived in the west end in South Hampstead. It suddenly occurred to Miles that Sickert would be a good person to use as a sounding board for the mystery in which he found himself involved. Sickert was also an avid photographer. Miles could show him the photographs Katherine had taken. Naturally, he would hide the real names of the people involved. He had kept the photographs of the murder victims which he'd taken from Julia. They were in his pocket. He resolved to visit Sickert immediately.

Since Sickert lived very near the West Hampstead station, Miles took the expedient of hailing a cab to the nearest Metropolitan train station. As he rode north, he looked forward to having another male mind to shed light on the mystery. Was there any flaw in his reasoning? Did it not seem most likely that Serafina and the man in Katherine's shop were one and the same? He wanted someone else to arrive at the same conclusion based on the same information. If he and Sickert agreed on his conclusions, then Miles resolved to force the truth from Katherine and find out what was really taking place at her shop. He also wanted to know how she had managed to take photographs of the victims without being questioned by the police. Serafina was incapable of looking out for herself, and Julia's faith in Katherine made her a questionable ally. He must take charge of the investigation and get definitive answers. It was all very well for women to have an equal say in politics, but there were some situations where women were at a serious disadvantage. They allowed sentiment to colour investigations of hard fact. Any time that clear, completely balanced thinking was required, one could not count on a woman, not even one as intelligent as Julia.

Miles had not seen Sickert since his wedding in 1883, almost five years earlier. They had always been somewhat uneasy companions and now the long hiatus in their relationship would no doubt make the meeting even more awkward. It was their mutual womanizing and interest in photography and painting that had stimulated the relationship. The emotional bond between them had always been weak. Miles found Sickert, like his painting, too dark, almost sinister. When Sickert had gotten married, Miles, as a former partner in sexual adventures, became *persona non gratia* with Mrs. Sickert. But Miles knew that Sickert's interest in sensational crime would guarantee him a warm welcome and an attentive hearing. The gruesome photographs Miles had would be sure to fascinate the anglicized Dutchman. Miles knew he was in town because a mutual acquaintance had just seen him at the Tate.

On arriving at the West Hampstead station, Miles crossed the tracks and walked south to Broadhurst Gardens, where Sickert had been living since his marriage. Miles rang the top bell of number 59, which was marked, 'studio.' In a few moments he heard a bolt snap inside and the entrance level door swing open. As Miles stepped into the dim hallway, he noted the clever lock and rope which enable Sickert to open the outer door without coming down the stairs.

"Who's there?"

"Miles Hickenbotham," Miles called, looking up to the top landing. "I have a murder mystery in my pocket which I thought you would appreciate." When he reached the top landing, the big man was waiting for him.

"It's been a long time, Hickenbotham." The two men shook hands.

"Yes, it has, Sickert" Miles agreed. "And I wouldn't bring an apple of discord into your comfortable nest now unless I had something of interest to show you."

"You make too much out of my wife's possessiveness. I told you that at the time. Besides, she is better trained now."

"So have you seen any of our little friends in Paris?"

"Often," Sickert said showing him into the studio. "I have convinced my wife that my trips to Paris are essential to my art. Degas is getting old and I wouldn't miss seeing his work and speaking with him for the world."

"You are fortunate to have such a friend. He will be remembered longer than any of us. One of the true giants of our age. What about our little friends, the dear flowers we used to pluck from the muddy streets of the left bank?"

"Oh, yes, I always look in on them when I go."

"And little Elaine? Do you see her?"

"She has disappeared. Who knows where she is. She could be dead from disease or absinthe by now. There was actually some talk that she was murdered."

"I prefer to think of her as having found a rich husband, living comfortably in some pleasant Parisian suburb with children and a garden."

I think you were really enamoured of that little whore," Sickert said. "Though I will admit she had the most exquisite breasts in the world, two perfectly ripe, delicious melons. I was just about to have some very nice Hock with my lunch. Will you have a glass?"

"Thank you, Sickert."

Once seated, both men regarded each other across the table, looking for signs of change after so long a time.

Miles thought that the sharp planes of Sickert's face were even sharper, his chiseled nose and forehead more definitively modeled.

"You will look like a boy when you're fifty, Hickenbotham," Sickert commented as he poured the Hock. "You'll keep the ladies happy well into old age. Now, what is this murder you were telling me about?"

"The Whitechapel killings. I have some photographs."

"Really?" Sickert said, brightening suddenly. "Let's see them."

Miles passed over the prints and Sickert flipped through them.

"Oh, these are a gruesome bunch. He doesn't choose them for their looks, does he? These are wonderfully ghastly. How did that Death's head get into them? Somebody must have tampered with these."

"Tampered how," Miles asked. How do you think they would have been taken?"

"Don't you know?" Sickert said looking closely at the prints.

"Well, these are hardly official police pictures. How do you think the photographer took them?"

"How did you get them?"

"From a friend of the photographer," Miles answered.

"Why not ask him."

"I'd like your opinion."

"Hmm. Well, the police would certainly be anxious to clear the streets, and they could hardly do it as long as the body remained. It is hard to tell where these were taken. They are so tightly framed it is difficult to tell. There seems to be three layers in the image. The original face, the death's head and the diapha-nous top layer— but the face in the death's head's eye-sockets!" He spread out the photographs and bent over them. "Yes, he's in all three of them. It is certainly a killer's face. A dark, dangerous looking man. Very strange. I should think it's a least three plates exposed onto one image."

"So you think they are fakes?"

"Fakes? How else would one get a multiple exposure like this?"

"There was a recent article in *The Journal of British Photography* that talks about dead people having their final look at this world impressed on their retina. The article claimed that the impressions could be photographed. *The Tribune* talked about using such images for criminal identification."

"Now I see where you're going with all of this. You want to identify the Whitechapel killer. Gad, Winstanley, you have gone in neck and crop for the outré. I have never seen any such images. And if they came off of the retina, I can't imagine how they could look anything like these."

"No. I know."

"Then how do you explain them other than as fakes?"

"Have you seen Charles Boursnell's work?"

"Spirit photography. Now we go from the merely bizarre to the supernatural. Now that you mention it, yes, I have seen a few of Bournell's images. These do look wonderfully like, don't they? But Boursnell's are simpler, not so many parts. One thing I can say definitively, the police would never leave a body lying in the street like this. They'd want to clear the street. Who took these? Not you?"

"No. They were taken by a young Eurasian woman I know."

"Peculiar taste for a lady."

"I did not say she was a lady."

"Ah, at last, the plot thickens with love interest. A woman, an attractive woman and deliciously low, as well, took these really gruesome photographs. Why and where did she take them?"

"I think they were taken in the two morgues where the bodies were eventually carried—the City Morgue and the Whitechapel Morgue." Miles said. "As to why, she wanted to identify the killer. She is a pupil of Boursnell's. "

"Ah, ha. I heard he had a young girl hanging around his studio a couple of years ago. I think he took some nudes of her. Don't have any of those, do you?"

"No. But there is something else. I have seen the man who appears in the orbits of the death's head."

"What do you mean you've seen him?"

"I've seen him on the streets in Whitechapel. Once on the night of one of the murders."

Sickert looked carefully at each of the prints again. "My guess would be that they were taken indoors at night with a great deal of powder. Difficult to get the right exposure, I should think. These really are marvelously ghastly. You have seen this man, you say, in the flesh."

"Yes, on the night of the first murder."

"So you believe these really could help identify the killer?"

"I don't know. A picture might have been taken of the man I saw at some time and double exposed into these. What do you think?"

"This would be a very difficult double exposure, that's what I think," Sickert answered. I say, do you have the plates?"

"No. But I might be able to get them."

"Look, old man, these are right up my street. I should

love to paint these. What a sensational series they would make. Even more sensational if this fellow in the eye sockets really is the killer."

"I should be careful, Sickert. The police are very touchy right now about these murders. They are eager to arrest anyone with the slightest connection to the crimes."

"Yes, the murderer has made Warren look rather a fool, which I suppose he is. Especially with all his military posturing."

"Bloody Sunday didn't help things, either," Miles said.

"No," Sickert said still gazing at the photographs. "See here, Hickenbotham, can I buy these from you? They are not your kind of thing at all. To paint, I mean."

"Are you painting from photographs, now? I have thought about it, but it seems rather a cheat."

"No. Why is it a cheat?"

"The camera has already reduced everything to a single plane."

"But one still has to catch the mood, the lights and darks. That challenge remains. And those are the things I am most interested in."

"The photographs are not really mine to sell. However, if you'll give me your opinion about some odd circumstances and swear to be discreet, I might be able to manage it."

"You know that nothing stimulates me more than knowing the story behind the report of sensational crimes. But I can keep what I learn to myself. I am a painter, not a writer."

"There were times when I have thought you'd like to be both," Miles remarked. "You like titles that imply a story, a narrative style more in keeping with an earlier age. I used to think sometimes that you would like to make up stories."

"Just good business, Hickenbotham. People don't respond to abstractions. The more narrative a painting is, the better it will sell. But I give you my word I won't reveal anything you tell me about the Whitechapel murders."

"Very well," Miles replied. He paused and finally went on, "There is a west end family I know..." and so he told his story as anonymously as possible. When he was done Sickert looked closely at him.

"I can hear that you have only told me an approxima-
tion of the truth. But I'd really like to see the plates to see if we
can determine if this fellow who appears in the orbits was added.
Especially since you say you have seen him in Whitechapel,"
Sickert said, "but it is a good tale and just knowing it actually
happened makes these photographs even more interesting. It
seems obvious that the wealthy young woman and the blood-
stained man are one and the same. I can see no other explanation for the facts of the case. Can you?"

Miles shook his head. In recounting his story to another
person, the pieces fitted together even more neatly. The suit had
to have been made for Serafina and it was she, wearing a false
beard whom he had seen in Katherine's shop.

"Do you think this girl could be the killer?" Sickert asked
him. "I'd want to rule out this fellow in the photographs, first.
He is the one I would suspect, first."

"Could you tell if they were faked if I can get my hands
on the plates?" Miles asked.

"I won't lie to you. I'm not sure. But I'd certainly like to
try. There is something really dangerous looking about this fellow. Wild, wolfish."

"He looks even more that way, late at night, on a dark
street in Whitechapel."

"I don't see how the west end woman would have the
strength to subdue these women and inflict such terrible injuries," Miles answered. "Though if she were in a deranged state..."

"No. It does seem unlikely. The *modus operandi* of the
Whitechapel murderer is not the type usually chosen by female
killers. It is hard to imagine any woman being so deliberately
brutal. I cast my ballot for the man in these photographs. "

"Especially this particular woman," Miles added.

"Yes, well I'm sure that if I knew this girl, it would be
very difficult to believe that she and the Whitechapel killer were
one and the same. In this case, familiarity breeds a reluctance to
admit even the possibility. I can understand why you wanted to
discuss it with me—even though you have kept me in the dark

about true identities. Get the plates and lets see what we can make of them."

"I'll try."

"Now, what about these prints?"

"I have one more question, or set of questions I should like to put to you," Miles answered. "Do you believe in spirit photography in a general sense?"

"Do you mean taking pictures of someone who is not physically present, or specifically, someone dead?"

"Either."

"Boursnell's are quite credible. The others I've seen are just trash, obvious fabrications."

"And what about the eyes' ability to register the last thing a person sees, just before death overtakes them?"

"You mean for something to actually show in a photographic print of a person's eyes taken after death? It seems unlikely."

"My thought as well."

"Now, what about these photographs?" Sickert said as he patted the prints with his large hand.

Miles was quiet for a moment and finally said, "You could photograph the prints," Miles suggested. "That way, you would have your images right away and I could still return them. Of course, the quality would suffer."

"I am not so concerned about that. It is the feel, the mood that I find so evocative. The gruesomeness is what matters to me. A photograph of a photograph wouldn't destroy that. Shall we do them, now?" Sickert said, rubbing his hands together.

"Why not?" Miles asked.

Several hours later Sickert had rather fuzzier versions of the dead women: Martha Tabram, Polly Nicholls and Annie Chapman. He had paid £50 for each photograph, £150 in all.

"If you should get a hold of any more photographs like these," Sickert said, "Please let me know. I shall certainly buy them from you. I don't care if they are only prints or, as we have just done, photographs of prints. I know that this is not the sort of thing you like to paint, so I shall have a clear field for turning them into paintings. But what I would really like is to see the plates. Perhaps we can catch the killer."

"He doesn't look easy to catch. And I really don't know if I can get the plates. In any case, remember what I said about the police," Miles replied. "I shouldn't be in a hurry to exhibit paintings of these pictures. You could find yourself in a prison cell, or worse."

The two men shook hands once again at the top of the stairs, each feeling that he had made a good bargain. But for Miles the conversation had only been a preliminary. Now, he had to discover why Serafina was dressing as a man. It seemed likely that she and Katherine were lesbian lovers. That would go a long way toward explaining the male clothing and the doting quality of their relationship. It pricked his vanity slightly, but it also explained much about Serafina's feelings about sex. It was much more difficult to imagine that Serafina had some submerged aspect that was a monster, a vicious and brutal killer of prostitutes, the very women she had worked so hard to protect. Perhaps her illness had caused some terrible inversion in her attitude toward such women. Or, maybe a part of her interest in prostitutes had always been malign. Who could interpret this kind of gross irrationality? Sickert was right. In spite of the source of the photographs, the man who appeared in them looked like a dangerous killer. Besides, if *The British Journal of Photography* could write about the eyes of the dead preserving an image, why couldn't these be real? He thought of Julia telling him he had a closed mind. If only he could get the plates. If he could find out who this man was, who he was and where he lived. Even the police wouldn't know that. He dared not go to them in any case: there were too many connections between Serafina and these killings, and as a violent socialist, she was already a suspicious character. The plates must be in Katherine's shop, but there were now so many police on the streets of the east end, it would be very difficult to break into the shop. He knew nothing about where Katherine slept. Julia had implied the darkroom was somewhere near the back. If he simply asked

Katherine for the plates so they could be examined, she could destroy them. She might not even be the author of the images. Perhaps Boursnell, himself, had made the plates and wanted to profit from the notoriety of the murders. Somehow, he and Sickert had to get their hands on the plates. Who was the man? Was he just a local man who had been photographed and used to make the plates? Or was he the Whitechapel killer?

The element which made the Whitehall killings so obscure was a lack of motive. Without a motive, the very primitive state of forensic science left police helpless. It would not be until 1892 that the Sherlock Holmes stories would emphasize the importance of such medico-chemical police methods in the public mind. When Holmes gleefully spoke about finding a reagent for human blood in *A Study in Scarlet*, it was clear that forensic science had a very long way to go before a killer like the Whitechapel murderer would be caught in a laboratory retort.

Miles shared the problem of motive with the police. If he thought the unthinkable: that Serafina was involved—the question of motive was a tremendous stumbling block. Why would Serafina want to kill prostitutes even if she were unbalanced? Why would she help the killer dismember other women when she spent almost every waking moment crusading for women's rights? Imagining Serafina in a suspicious role, made motive even more of a puzzle. Whoever the Whitechapel killer was, it was clear that the key to the crimes lay in an understanding of the killer's mind. There was some terrible malformation of the killer's personality that made him— or her— butcher the hapless Whitechapel prostitutes. Serafina obviously believed in Katherine's knowledge of the human mind. But did the chit really have such knowledge? Was Katherine distorting Serafina's mind with hypnosis and actually harming her? Could the killings be the result of a malevolent hypnotic control exercised by Katherine? The extent of mesmeric control was still debated in Europe and Britain among such leading experimenters as Milne Bramwell and Alfred Binet. What could an ignorant girl like Katherine really know about obscure questions of the human mind? Perhaps she was actually causing the Whitechapel murders with her mesmeric treatments. From what Julia had said, Serafina would not trust a male practitioner, which ruled out a visit to any of the leading authorities on mesmerism. If only he and Serafina had been married when she was well, he could have taken control of the situation, now. As he arrived back at his own studio, he felt clearer but had really made very little progress in discovering anything substantial about the Whitechapel killer. He knew what he must try to do, but how many more women would die before that happened? That Serafina was somehow involved in the murders could not be debated after finding the brass rings engraved with the last victim's name. She had to have been present at the scene of the crime in order to have the rings in her possession. Beyond that, he could say little with certainty. The one thing that really haunted him, however, was the glimpse he had had of a face that appeared very similar to the one in each of the photographs.

Chapter 24

JACK THE RIPPER

25 September: 1888

Dear Boss

…The next job I do I shall clip the lady's ears off and send to the police officers just for jolly wouldnt you. Keep this letter back till I do a bit more work then give it out straight. My knife's so nice and sharp I want to get to work right away if I get a chance. Good luck.

> *Yours truly*
> *Jack the Ripper*
> *Dont mind giving the trade name*

—Excerpt from letter received by the Central News Agency Ltd of 5 Newbridge Street on September 27, 1888—the first and one of the few Ripper letters regarded as possibly genuine.

During the weeks immediately after the first three murders, the east end seethed with fearful anticipation of the Whitechapel killer's next outrage. The Hanbury Street murder brought London to an early peak of fear and speculation. The police had detained various men for questioning but had released them all, as Miles knew they were bound to do. There were butchers and barbers, nearly an even dozen men thought to be likely suspects. One by one, each was eliminated from the investigation. By mid September, as Miles walked the east end streets, the journalists and citizens of the metropolis were becoming openly hostile to the Home Secretary. Mathews had his secretary get a report from Commissioner Warren on the progress of the case. But official business took place behind the scenes, hidden from journalists and the public. Miles was mostly occupied with getting the answers he wanted about Serafina, Katherine and the blood-stained man. He paid little attention to newspapers in the first weeks of September, feeling that his own first-hand knowledge was better than the distortions of sensational journalism.

He called several times at Cavendish Square and was warmly received by Julia, but Serafina declined to see him on each occasion.

"Why do you think Serafina is so set against me, Julia?" he asked during one of these visits.

"I have given up trying to fathom my sister's motivations, Miles. I think you only give yourself pain to no purpose when you speculate about her."

"It is very hard to come here and find myself received as a stranger."

"I can imagine, Miles. But I do not treat you that way, do I?"

"No, Julia. We remain good friends."

"I am glad that you can still feel that way."

"Serafina's behaviour is not her fault or even responsibility, in my view," Miles said. "We must all be prepared to forebear and try to lead her to better understanding. But it is not always easy." He deliberately said nothing to inflame Julia's suspicions of Serafina involvement in the crimes. Julia had been tenderly solicitous of her sister ever since the night that Serafina had gone into a cataleptic state. His speculations were still too vague and the results of his investigation too indeterminate to place them before Julia. If he were able to prove his case against Serafina, he would compel Julia to send her sister to an asylum. At times, he felt like a traitor. Yet, he could not sit by and let the murders continue. If Serafina were involved in the outrages, she and the killer must be stopped, though, in spite of all incriminating indications, he found it impossible to believe that Serafina played more than a secondary role in the gruesome crimes. If involved, she was a helper, there must be someone else—the bloodstained man he had seen. That man held the key to solving the crimes. With this conviction, Miles continued to haunt the streets of Whitechapel at night. The more time that passed, the more he thought Katherine's prints clumsy frauds. If he could only get his hands on the plates he might loosen Katherine's grip on Serafina.

By 11 September, the Mile End Vigilance Committee had sixteen men on the streets in an effort to assist the police. Other such groups also helped to watch the east end streets. So from an early date, the streets of Whitechapel were closely watched for anything suspicious. All the more reason why the Ripper's dismemberments were extraordinary. All but one were performed out of doors. From the timing of patrols it is known that the Ripper often achieved his bloody purpose in mere minutes while police and vigilantes were searching streets on every side of the crime scene. Even when men were searching the very next street, no one ever heard any of the Ripper's victims make a sound as she was butchered. Even from a modern vantage point, the elusiveness of the Ripper is astonishing. To Londoners of the late Victorian Age, his feats seemed almost supernatural.

For Miles, the killer's need for elusiveness was a major argument against Serafina dressing in male clothing if she were actually participating in the crimes. She would have been much more elusive in a dress. Because of this, Miles hypothesized that if she were involved, it was as an accessory, a helper for the killer, hiding his clothes and picking up any clues, such as the rings, that might help the police. Some nights when Julia wrote to Miles, announcing that Serafina was going out, she never appeared at Katherine's. But most nights when she was out on the street, Serafina would turn up at Katherine's in the small hours of the morning. Katherine would mesmerize her and the pair would disappear into the back of the shop. Sometimes the man who looked like Serafina's twin would appear, but he was a rare visitor—and Miles never again saw him besmirched with blood.

During that dark September, the streets of Whitechapel became empty of all but constables and vigilance committee members. It was more and more difficult for anyone to move through the streets at night unchallenged. Miles knew that if he was to continue visiting Whitechapel to watch over Serafina, he must somehow make himself as invisible as the killer. After several near encounters with constables, he had tried without success to find a cellar or passage where he could hide near Baker's Row. As he thought over the problem, the man's suit hidden in Serafina's wardrobe gave him the idea of getting some women's clothes for himself. In the dark lanes, a dress and a bonnet would be enough to let him pass muster and allow him to walk freely. It was firmly fixed in everyone's mind that lone women were the chosen prey of the killer. No one would imagine that a lone woman would be the Whitechapel murderer, so no one would question him. If the real Ripper did attack him, Miles would have no compunction about dispatching the fiend, and if Serafina was acting as an accomplice for the killer, Miles might have a chance of getting her home before the authorities could learn of her connection with the crimes. So it was that by mid-September, Miles walked the streets of Whitechapel in a cheap but respectable gown. On his head he wore a bonnet and wig. His face he lightly powdered. With his slender build and handsome, regular features, he made a credible woman in the half light of the streets. His only danger lay in being attacked by the Ripper, himself, but he carried the sharp, straight knife that had been dropped into his pocket on the night as he'd slept in the cheap lodging house. It would be fitting, he felt, if the same knife were used to dispatch the murderer. He felt no doubt that he would not shrink from the task if the opportunity presented itself.

Most nights were damp, dreary and uncomfortable in the unusual clothes he wore. Miles sometimes felt half asleep as he walked the dark lanes. During the days the rest he needed often prevented him from painting. In spite of his fatigue, he frequently found himself thinking of Amelia, planning more paintings of her. His patrols became a kind of grim routine to which he acclimatized himself. He swore to himself that no evil would touch Serafina as it had his own sister. He thought of them both as he walked his beat along the dark lanes. Suddenly, however, he was jolted out of his nocturnal rut by the stunning events of September twenty-ninth.

The night began like many others: he went to the City stable yard, picked up his hired four-wheeler and drove it himself to the east end yard he used. There, he pulled down the blinds and put on his female costume over his own shirt and trousers. Julia had written to him during that afternoon saying that Serafina planned to go out that night. He left the rented horse and vehicle in the stable yard and walked to Baker's Row. He reached his post near Katherine's shop and began his watch at about midnight. Serafina had told Julia that she was going to a meeting in the neighbourhood of Berner Street and Commercial Road. He later remembered looking at his watch once and seeing that it was twelve thirty. Moments after noting the time, Miles was suddenly struck from behind. He heard and saw no one. His assailant was as stealthy as a shadow. Miles was only aware of the stunning blow on the back of his head which immediately cut off all consciousness. Curiously, when he later examined himself, there was no cut or wound. When he fully recovered his senses, he was standing and could see his watch gleaming on the ground in Baker's Row where he had dropped it, a few feet away from where he was standing. The gas that had earlier illuminated the interior of Katherine's shop had been turned off. By the light of the Whitechapel street lamps, his watch told him he had been unconscious for more than two hours. Several seconds later, as he stood swaying in Baker's Row, the gas in Katherine's shop was suddenly lit.

The sight that met Miles' eyes caused him to gasp: Serafina, pale as death itself, was dressed in a dark cashmere walking costume which was dribbled with long blood marks. Her eyes were blind and staring, reflecting the same kind of horror he had seen in them during the trance she had fallen into at Cavendish Square. The extreme contrast of light and dark caused by the poor interior lighting made Serafina appear even ghastlier than she was. Miles was so upset that without reflection, he grabbed the door handle of Katherine's shop and put his shoulder to the door. Katherine shrieked as the door broke open, the ancient wood suddenly splitting in the quiet lane with a sound that seemed as the report of a gun. Serafina remained lost in the horror of her inner world. She did not even look toward the door as Miles burst into the shop. Her eyes were blind to all in the shop, staring at some dreadful inner landscape only she could see.

"Katherine," Miles shouted, "What has happened? What is the matter with Serafina. You must tell me all or I shall blow a police whistle in the High Street."

Katherine, too, was momentarily blanched with terror at this sudden incursion. When she realized that it was Miles who addressed her, she visibly relaxed.

"I don't know. I was not with her, Mr....Miles. I know as much as you about how she comes to be in this condition."

"But you do know something of how she comes to be nearly out of her senses. You must tell me what is wrong with her. You must tell me now—otherwise, I shall call the police and all will be forced into the open." He spoke in a loud voice, raised in anger.

The sound seemed to jolt Serafina into a momentary awareness and she screamed piercingly. "It's him," but the gaze of her eyes was not outward at all. Her beautiful, luminous eyes, ordinarily so reflective of her thoughts, were fixed in a stoney, rigid stare.

"You must let me quiet her," Katherine said in a pleading tone.

"Do whatever is necessary to her comfort. But then you shall tell me what has been taking place here. Things are clearly out of hand."

Katherine nodded in reply and took Serafina's arm, leading her to the chaise where customers usually sat. Touching Serafina lightly on her forehead, the blood spattered young woman immediately slumped into complete unconsciousness and relaxation. Katherine gently lowered her softly to the chaise. Miles could read great tenderness in the care with which Katherine handled the unconscious Serafina. Finally, Katherine covered her friend with an afghan and turned to face Miles.

"Now," he said, "speak, or even at the risk of her reason, I shall call the police. I have heard more than one whistle tonight. From the blood on Serafina's costume, it is obvious that more dreadful murder has been taking place."

"Sit down, Miles," Katherine said in a firm voice, "and I shall tell you what I am willing to do. Serafina must speak for herself. She will explain herself to you while she is in a trance."

"I just want the simple truth, Katherine," Miles said.

"But it is best for her if she speaks from a trance. And you may learn more as well. And remember that the truth is not always simple."

"Like your fraudulent photographs, which are made up of three exposures at least."

"You may think what you like about me. I know you have been angry at me ever since I refused your advances, but the critical thing now is to take care of Serafina—and stop the fiend."

Katherine made a few passes above Serafina's recumbent figure and almost immediately the eyes of the entranced woman opened.

"Serafina," Katherine said softly, "I want to speak with Jack. Let him talk with me now."

As he watched, Miles felt the hair on the back of his neck prickle with apprehension. Then, the apprehension turned to horror as Serafina was transformed into someone else. It was more than merely seeing her expression change. Her features were rearranged in a way that reflected a different soul, a soul that belonged to an alien presence, a soul with different thoughts, feelings and experience than the young woman Miles had known. It was someone totally other than Serafina Winstanley.

"Hello, my adorable girl," boomed a deep male voice as

the gaze of the former Serafina fixed on Katherine.

"Hello, Jack," Katherine said as 'Jack' took her hand and kissed it like a lover.

"What is he doing here?" Jack boomed, looking at Miles, who sat staring, transfixed by what was taking place in front of him.

"He wants to meet you, Jack, and understand what we are doing together."

"That is easy," Jack answered, standing suddenly and taking Katherine in his arms and planting a passionate kiss on her mouth.

What Miles found most astonishing was that he had no trouble believing in Serafina's lovemaking as the acts of an authentic male. All softness, suppleness and femininity he had seen in her face was now re-cast into harder, graver masculine lines. She was the man he had first seen through the window on the first night he had watched Katherine's shop. There was no question about it, now. Though the shape of her features remained, Serafina's face was changed because, Miles felt, the gender of the mind behind it was changed. He could not believe it, yet he saw it clearly. It was weird and perverse beyond description. There was something terrifying about seeing a familiar face which reflected an unfamiliar person. It was the most uncanny thing he had ever seen.

Jack and Katherine sat down next to each other on the chaise, Jack with his arm around Katherine's waist in the perfect semblance of an adoring man holding his lover. Jack leaned over to Katherine and kissed her neck greedily, repeatedly, obviously becoming more and more passionate with each kiss.

"No, Jack. Wait. We shall do that later. Not now. I want to talk to Serafina again."

"No," the voice boomed.

"Jack, you must—or I shall not let you make love to me later. Do you understand?"

Jack got to his feet and lurched threateningly toward Miles, "I could just cosh him again and he would go away."

"No, Jack. You must let me speak with Serafina. Come

here, you great boy. Don't be bad, now." Then she reached over, touched his forehead and the figure slumped once again.

For some moments after Jack had receded behind Serafina's sleeping face, Miles was too shocked to say a word. Finally, he looked closely at the little woman who sat next to someone he could recognize as his sleeping cousin.

"What, what does it mean? I see you are lovers..."

"Yes and no," Katherine said quickly. "That is, I do let him make love to me but not for the reasons you might imagine."

"I am lost," Miles said simply. "I cannot grasp this."

"Sometimes it is useful to play a role with someone I am trying to help. I pretend to be what they wish me to be. I let them treat me as they would like."

"But her, his face—it changed."

"I told you we each have more than one soul within us, did I not?"

"Yes, but I never imagined... To see such a transformation is quite another thing like, like"—he struggled to find an analogy— "like Jekyll and Hyde."

"It is quite dramatic in Serafina, I agree. But do not make it melodramatic."

"But what are you doing with her, him—allowing him liberties with your person? You act like lesbian lovers and yet you say you are not."

"I have never done that before now. Jack, Serafina, is unique."

"But what is the meaning and purpose of all this? Do you claim that this is some kind of bizarre treatment?"

"Yes, it is, Miles."

"And what exactly are you treating? I don't understand any of this."

"Remember when I once told you about how we may have more than one self, that a human being could be made up of different persons?"

"Yes."

"You have seen the truth of that tonight."

351

"You mean that Serafina's soul is somehow divided into two?"

"Yes."

"And one part is male?"

"That's right. He calls himself, Jack Winstanley."

"Good Lord. What a dreadful pit you open before my eyes. You are telling me that someone I have known all my life is a complete mystery to me. That she has a side about which I knew nothing for all these years. It is horrible. It is as if, as if, someone else, other than her was always watching us. Perhaps interfering with us."

"Did it not sometimes feel that way?" Katherine asked.

"You mean he is why she would not marry me?"

"Yes. I think it may be so."

Miles leaned forward, placing his elbows on his knees and wrung his hands. His next words were spoken in a rough, cracking whisper, "Is Jack Winstanley, the male soul who lives in Serfina's body actually— the Whitechapel killer?"

"I'm not certain," Katherine said, meeting his pleading eyes with a pitiless equanimity.

"Oh, God save us," Miles croaked.

"Yes. These murders make everything much more difficult."

"Difficult! How can you say that. They are horrors. I see the same horror at times in Serafina's eyes. You terrify me and speak like it is only a difficulty, a minor inconvenience."

"I know. But from my point of view and from Serafina's, that's true. When one tries to heal an injured soul, nothing else we may encounter has any significance. If we are turned away from our goal for even an instant, the soul will break in pieces and slip away from us."

"You speak as one with a definite point of view, the product of a school of thought. Where does all this talk about healing and souls come from?"

"From many sources. From India, from modern medicine and from hypnotism and European metaphysics."

"And everyone is like Serafina? With several distinct

souls within?"

"The possibility for that always exists, I believe. But it is not always brought to fruition."

"I listen to you and look at Serafina's sleeping face and I fear I am in a nightmare. One minute, you seem to make sense, the next your words slip through my thoughts in a meaningless jumble."

"I understand how difficult it is. Really."

"How?"

"Because I have been somewhat as Serafina is. I have known some of my other selves, what in India might also be called other lives, lives my soul lived as other people."

"Great Scott! I have read of the Indian belief in the many births and incarnations of a single soul. You are telling me that these fantastic speculations are fact?"

"Yes. I know their truth from my own experience. Can you say that much about the resurrection of Jesus?"

"No. Of course not. It is a matter of faith."

"In the east, faith is only the beginning of awakening. One must know reality through experience."

"And you have done that?"

"I have experienced other lives I have lived."

"And this double soul in Serafina, is this connected with a past life?"

"Say with something that happened in the past of her present life."

"And can any of this dubious metaphysics reveal the connection between Jack Winstanley and Jack the Ripper? Is there a connection? That is what you must tell me. Otherwise, what good is any of this?"

"Discovering the Whitechapel murderer is your goal, Miles. It is not necessarily mine. I want to heal Serafina."

"But if she is the murderer? What then? We just let her go on killing?"

"No. We must find out what has divided her. We must bring the two parts back together and see what happens."

"Ahh," Miles said in disgust as he stood up. "The murders

are real. The killer is real. If Serafina is the killer..."

"No. Never. If she is involved, it is as Jack Winstanley. They are two different people, two different souls."

"What practical difference does it make? If she is caught, Serafina and Jack Winstanely will both die on the gallows as surely as we sit here. No one will excuse these murders for any reason. Oh, this is impossible. I might as well be talking with a character from the other side of Alice's looking glass."

"Together, Miles, we can watch over her. You and Julia can help me, now. Now that you understand."

Miles paced up and down the shop from front to back several times. "This is madness, lunacy," he muttered. "And what about those fake photographs?"

"They are not "fake" in the sense you mean."

"How were they produced then? I know you were Charles Boursnell's whore while still a child. You must have learned the same photographic techniques he used."

Katherine looked at Miles searchingly for a moment and then said, "Forgive me, Miles," And she touched him as she had touched Serafina. Like her, the man slumped in his chair.

Sometime later, he awakened. "For being an imposter he continued..."

"No, for not realizing how much you care for me. The bitterness in your voice when you just mentioned Charles Boursnell finally made your feelings clear to me. I thought you were merely angry because your pride was hurt by my rejection."

He looked up at her from where he sat, next to the un-conscious Serafina, "I confess, other than the pressure of work, these killings and worry over Serafina, I have thought of little else but you since we met."

"Then I shall tell you that the pictures were produced clairvoyantly. Before going to the mortuary, I entered a trance which made me more sensitive to clairvoyant influences. I then went with my equipment, mesmerized anyone who was present and took the picture. Still in the trance, I would come back here and develop the plate. When I began, I only knew what I had read in *The British Journal of Photography*. I did not

at all expect those death's head pictures. I found them
quite shocking."

Miles tugged reflectively on his lower lip and was silent for a long time. Finally, he said, "The one thing that gave
me pause about your pictures is the fact that I have seen the
man who is in those photographs, the one in the orbits of each
death's head. I saw him the night of the first murder. I saw him
very near the George Yard where Martha Tabram was killed."

"You saw him? Do you know who he is? Where to
find him?"

"No. I caught only a brief glimpse of him passing on the
Whitechapel Road."

"So you have no name? No clue to his whereabouts?"

"No."

"What do you think we should do?" she asked.

Miles got up and began pacing back and forth. "May
I smoke?"

"I'd rather you didn't in my shop. Many ladies object to
tobacco."

"Yes, of course. I quite understand. I'll do my best unaid-
ed by my usual stimulant. These are my thoughts: These murders
are real. There is nothing metaphysical about them. Women are
dying and will continue to die until this madman is stopped. I do
not know if the murders are being done by Serafina's alter-ego.
I don't know what her involvement is. We must try to find out.
But first, we must do whatever we can to put a stop to these killings. That, and protecting Serafina are the greatest imperatives.
Thanks to your photographs we do have a suspect, other than
Serafina. We know he is a real person for I have seen him. I can
say as much. I think we should give your pictures to the police.
We can leave Serafina out entirely. They may question us both
very closely, but it's worth a try, I think. All we have to do is tell
the absolute truth, only leaving out anything that touches on
Serafina. We met without her, we were working together because
of our shared interests—how was this shop paid for, by Serafina?"

Katherine nodded.

"By cheque, by draft, how?"

"She gave me the necessary cash."

"Good. Then all we have to do is say is that the money came from me. The police will think you are my mistress, but that is the only damage you will suffer. It seems a small thing if we can stop this devil by giving the photographs to Detective Abberline."

"Who is that?"

"The man in charge of investigating the killings. He's reputed to be the best detective on the force. The police are stumped. If we can help Abberline put his hands on the fiend, we must do it. Not to act may mean that we are contributing to other deaths."

"I had not thought of that. You are right. We must go to the police with the photographs. Do you know this detective?"

"I have met him once or twice, but only as a west end slummer. I daresay that if I send my card in to him, we shall be given an audience."

Miles stopped in mid stride of his restless pacing and looked down at the sleeping Serafina. In repose, her features were once more her own. Whatever creature had taken possession of her was gone.

"Have you ever seen such a thing before—such a transformation?"

"It can be part of magnetic sleep. Serafina has other powers as well. Such powers are often referred to as the 'higher phenomena'."

"What powers?"

"For one thing, there is the degree of the distinctness of her other self. He has exceptional physical strength. Jack Winstanley does not need to eat or sleep for days at a time. Sometimes, he can put himself in rapport with another person and compel them to do what he wants. Sometimes even I have trouble resisting him. He is very penetrating about lies. He knows when someone is speaking falsely to him. He can even be clairvoyant."

"He sounds like what a German philosopher recently called das Ubermench, the Superman. But that would explain how some of these murders are done—at once so violent and silent. She could be mesmerizing her victims, put herself in control of them and then...God good, what a horrible thought," he finished as he looked over at Serafina's sleeping face. I can drive you both to her home," Miles said. "If she does not return tonight, her sister will be in an agony of suspense about her safety."

"It is not necessarily horrible. Jack Winstanley is also what enables Serafina to accomplish so much for the women of the east end."

"I suppose that is true," Miles said. "But I would happily let all that go if Serafina could just be a lovely young woman once again."

"Her strengths would daunt any man."

"Especially if her second self could be a fatal companion. But it is very strange that no men have died. Why is that?"

"You are assuming that she and the Whitechapel killer are one. I am not yet ready to make that assumption."

The little woman bent down and touched Serafina's forehead. Serafina opened her eyes as herself.

"Katherine," Serafina said as soon as she saw Katherine, "my dreams become stranger and stranger. Oh, Miles. What are you doing here?"

"He is helping us, dear," Katherine answered. "He is going to take us to Cavendish Square."

Chapter 25

ON THE TRAIL OF THE WHITECHAPEL MURDERER

There are strange phenomena that are frequently seen and observed in Multiple Personality Disorder patients. They are accepted as Multiple Personality Disorder dynamics, and are often present with some personalities and absent with others. In different patients, they may or may not be linked with a subjective sense of "being evil" and are clearly linked both to trauma and attempts at adapting to that trauma. These phenomena would include at least the following: Susceptibility to hypnosis and an unusual ability to cause others to enter hypnotic or trance states.

—Study by Dr. Fraser
The Royal Ottawa Hospital, Ontario, Canada

The above paragraph is a distinct anachronism in this narrative of four people who lived through the Ripper crimes. They were written from a point of view which benefits from twentieth century writing about multiple personality disorder." Yet, there is nothing here that would be entirely foreign to Miles, Katherine, Seraphina or Julia. In 1888 the lines between science, religion and magic were extremely blurry. Today, the definitions of our inner life are actually still just as blurred. We still know very little of our inner life. We may laugh at the idea of a photo-graph recording something non-material, and many nineteenth century "spirit photographs" are obvious fakes. But photographs have been taken which have no rational explanation, such as the famous "Brown Lady of Raynham Hall." Annie Besant, who led the Bryant & May match girls strike wrote one of the first books on birth control, and also produced several books with the medium C.W. Leadbetter, containing detailed descriptions and explanations of "the etheric body." And there is the fact of multiple personality disorder or dis associative identity disorder which can be accompanied by extraordinary phenomena. Clair-voyance is a fact proven in the laboratory of J.B. Rhine. Yet, we are no closer today to understanding these manifestations than Alfred Binet was in the1880s when he wrote *Double Concious-ness*. F.W.H. Myers, a contemporary of Freud's, was the most highly respected psychologist of his time. He tried to construct a psychology that admitted all the facts of hypnosis and spiri-tualism (ESP, today). Today, he is practically unknown, largely because of the title of his great posthumously published book, *The Human Personality and its Survival of Bodily Death*. In the materialistic certainty of the twentieth century, such a title made all his conclusions incredible. Yet many of Myers' ideas have reappeared in the writings of experimental scientists at Duke University's ESP laboratory. Some of today's experts even believe that certain aspects of mental phenomena were better under-stood at an earlier time than in our own century. For example, some writers have argued that Anton Mesmer's idea of magnetic fluid explained certain of the so called, higher phenomena (ESP) which the modern model of hypnosis does not. The truth is that modern psychiatry could add little to Katherine's attempt to unravel the connection between Serafina and the Ripper murders. Miles and his cousins are at no scientific disadvantage to the modern reader in grappling with the psychology of the monstrous crimes that confronted them. We know little more than they did, in spite of the fact that we have had another one hundred years to theorize and gather data. Profilers have been able to create a taxonomy of murder, but they couldn't catch the

deadly Zodiac killer, who wrote to police even more voluminous-
ly than Jack the Ripper.

The basic idea of the underlying psychological dynamic
of 'splitting' of which Janet wrote were known to Katherine,
though she was not acquainted with , Gurney, and perhaps most
importantly, F.W.H. Myers. She did not have the counsel of
Ralph B. Allison, leading twentieth century forensic expert on
crime and multiple personality, nor the doctors who treated the
serial rapist, Billy Milligan, who was the first multiple personality to be recognized by a court of law. So we must remember
that Katherine was a pioneer and that each step she took was
on ground where no one had stepped, let alone, walked before.
Today's workers in these fields are still pioneers.

Miles marveled at the complete change in Serafina since
Katherine had used her hypnotic power to return her to a normal state. The cool air he felt as he sat on the box of the coach
and drove through the streets gave him much needed refresh-
ment after the scenes with Serafina and her alter-ego. What he
had seen that evening of Serafina's other self was terrifying. No
matter what explanation was offered, there was no question that
her behaviour demonstrated the degree of the disturbance in
Serafina's mind. To become another person, of a different gender,
showing physical as well as emotional change...it staggered him.
Unfortunately, it also seemed to indicate that Serafina could herself, be the Whitechapel killer. Or did it? She could behave in
a male way, that much was proven. But why would she kill—so
violently, murdering only the gender she ordinarily championed?
Or were the brutal murders a terrible inversion of her normal
feelings and part of her strange condition? Perhaps she was horribly unique in her monstrous behaviour. No matter which way he
looked, he saw nothing but intellectual quicksand, but he reaf-
firmed his determination to do whatever seemed best for both
cousins. He must see them through this bizarre, horrific quag-
mire. And that meant he must trust Katherine as fully as they
did. He resolved to do that, as long as his own judgement didn't
force a change. He would follow her lead without flinching as

long as she appeared to have some resource with which to meet the crisis. After seeing the *carte visite* nude photograph of Katherine he would never have imagined giving her his confidence again, but in present circumstances, he had no alternatives.

They passed through Aldgate and into the City, then up through the quiet streets of the darkened places of business and into the west end. Soon they were on home ground near Cavendish Square.

Julia met them at the door. She embraced her sister eagerly and to Miles' surprise, Katherine insisted that Serafina go to bed while the rest of them adjourned to the salon.

"I shall just tuck her in," Julia said, unable to part from her dear sister so quickly. She disappeared into the hall leaving Miles and Katherine alone in the big room.

Miles stood in front of the fire to warm himself and with his back to Katherine he said, "These are deep waters in which we find ourselves, Miss Green, Katherine. Can you pull us out?"

"I?" she said. "It is not up to me, alone, but to all of us—especially Serafina."

"But you are the only one who has any practical experience with whatever it is we are facing. I confess that I am entirely out of my depth. Julia may be better informed. I don't know."

At that moment, Julia reappeared in the doorway and joined the others.

"Tea is coming," she announced as she sat down and smoothed her skirt over her knees. "I suppose we all know that this is a council of war?" she ventured.

"Definitely," Miles said turning to face the room. "We must catch this fiend to protect Serafina. Otherwise, she could be implicated in the Whitechapel killings."

"How?" asked Katherine. "How could the police ever know anything of Serafina's movements during the nights of the killings. You are the one who has been following her, Miles."

"Yes, but if she continues..."

"So you are saying you believe Serafina is the killer?" Julia asked in a flat, even voice.

"I'm saying that if the police had seen what I have seen,

they would think so. And if Serafina persists in, in, whatever it is she is doing, she would certainly be implicated. I don't pretend to know what the truth of all this is. Katherine, I believe you have more of the truth about Serafina than any of us. Can you really deal with this or should we be talking to a medical man or a vicar? I, for one, don't know."

"Wait," Katherine said. "We must tell Julia about going to the police."

"What! You are thinking of the police with Serafina's history of violent assault and socialist affiliation. How..."

"Wait, Julia," Katherine said. "Miles has thought all this through quite brilliantly. Miles, will you please explain your reasoning?"

At first, Julia was argumentative but once she saw that Serafina could be kept out of contact with the police, she agreed that they must offer the only genuine suspect they did have.

"When will you go to see Inspector Abberline?" she asked. "I should like to go with you."

"Absolutely not," Miles said. "That begins to involve the family and possibly, Serafina. We should keep her and the police in water tight compartments."

Julia scowled but finally said, "Yes. You are right. It is just difficult to be left out at this critical juncture."

"You won't be left out, Julia," Katherine said. "We still have to heal Serafina. You will play an essential role in that."

"But it seems to me that hypnosis is the most powerful tool there is for dealing with the kind of thing that Serafina is undergoing."

"I believe your love for her is the thing most essential to her getting well."

"Can you describe how this recovery is to take place?" Miles asked.

Katherine showed her unease by getting to her feet. Her hands fidgeted with one another, two small nervous white birds fluttering against her dark dress.

"It is so difficult..." she began and then stopped. "There are so many ways of describing the same thing. Medicine and hypnosis are our ways of trying to cope with this, but in India there is a wealth of knowledge which includes what we would call a religious as well as medical point of view. Let us put it in terms of religion. It is the oldest attempt to come to grips with this kind of phenomena."

"You mean what a priest would call possession?" Miles asked.

"I think it is the largest view we can take right now. I mean, we won't be leaving out anything important, which we might do if we tried to define Serafina in purely medical terms."

"So are you telling us that Serafina is possessed by another spirit? I thought you said this Jack Winstanley was part of her?"

"He is part of her and he is separate at the same time," Katherine answered slowly, her inward gaze showing her care in choosing her words and thoughts.

"But I mean, Katherine," Julia broke in, are you speaking about a demon, a creature from hell who has taken control of her? I have read an account of the nuns of Loudon in sixteenth century France. I admit that these murders invite such an explanation even if it does fly in the face of modern thinking."

"I think I should answer with a quotation which was a favourite of one of my teachers in India, 'The art of healing comes from nature, not from the physician. Therefore the physician must start from nature, with an open mind.' To put it another way, we are on ground here where none of us has absolute answers. What we need is an answer that is good enough to heal Serafina," Katherine said.

"Isn't that from Paracelsus?" Miles asked. "An Indian quoted Paracelsus to you?"

"And Shakespeare," Katherine said. " Remember, the English have been in India for nearly three hundred years."

"Isn't this all rather beside the point?" Julia said. "I understand that we are trying to define things we don't really understand fully, but I am interested in what we can do, here, tonight, for Serafina."

"And for any future victims of the killer," Katherine

added.

"Yes, of course," Julia agreed. "The killings must stop, and we hope that the photographs will help the police put a stop to them."

"Let us confront the unthinkable for a moment," Miles said. "What if the only way to stop the murders is to lock Serafina up in an asylum?"

"I shall not believe my sister is the Whitechapel killer. I don't know how you could think so, Miles, you, who wanted to marry her."

"That is because you have not met Jack Winstanley, has she, Katherine?"

"No. But I do not think Jack Winstanley and the Whitechapel murderer are one."

"You don't?" Miles said, a sharp tone of disbelief in his voice.

"No, I don't. That he is somehow involved, I won't argue, but I do not believe that Serafina's other self is committing these crimes. And I believe, Mr. Hickenbotham, that if you were ruthlessly honest with yourself you would agree with me."

"Are you accusing me of some dishonesty?"

"Not deliberate dishonesty."

"I don't like the line you are taking, now, Miss Green," Miles said petulantly.

"Can you offer proof that Serafina is not the killer?" Julia broke in. "Is it because she is not strong enough, physically?" Julia asked.

"No. Jack Winstanley and other secondary souls can bestow immense physical strength," Katherine answered. "Serafina is a strong woman. As Jack Winstanley, she might be extraordinarily fast and strong, stronger than most men. You see, based on what I know and avoiding the metaphysics of past lives, someone like Jack only comes into existence as a response to a threat of death or something worse. There must be tremendous pressure on someone to cause such a split."

"But what if it does have to do with past lives—or some form of possession?" Julia asked.

"No." Miles shouted bringing the flat of his hand down on the table. "That is the other side of the looking glass. We must stay on this side, where the murders are occurring."

"All right," Katherine said, "I am willing to stay on this side of the looking glass but we may still be pulled into a darker realm."

"There's quite enough darkness inside most human beings," Miles said.

"All right, so on this side of the looking glass I shall explain what I believe. A second soul may come about in response to a life and death situation. It is because of such a threat that the soul splits in the first place. It happens when there is an event that is so threatening or terrible that the mind of the single person cannot encompass it, so it separates from itself and creates a self that can cope with the horror of the situation. The fact that human beings have such a mechanism has been amply demonstrated by hypnosis. The somnambulistic self is the result of the same separation between the ordinary mind and the somnambulistic mind, which is often much wiser and stronger than the usual person."

"And you think Jack Winstanley superior to Serafina?" Miles asked.

"Not superior in all ways, but in some. I believe, he will have the memory of the terrible event that has brought Serafina to her present state. I have been looking for that event, but stumbling around in a darkened room. I have been afraid of injuring her with my clumsiness."

All were silent for some moments and finally Miles said, "Thank you for your candour, Katherine."

"Wait," Julia said, "remember what happened to the detective who tried to follow Serafina into a dark lane? He was knocked down and injured by an extraordinarily strong attacker. Could that have been Jack Winstanley, her other self?"

"And what if it was?" Miles said. "How can we help her—right now—what can we do this minute? That is what I want to know."

"Hear, hear," Julia said. "What action can you recommend now? I think we've all had enough theory, Katherine. What can we do, now?"

"I must ask you both a question, the answer to which shall determine what I say. You have both known Serafina all her life. Can you think of any unusual phenomenon or event that took place during her childhood?"

"The kidnapping of Amelia and the deaths of Dr. Winstanley and my own parents" Miles said immediately.

"The dream!" Julia suddenly cried leaping to her feet. "The dream."

"What dream?" Katherine asked.

"A dream about a labyrinth and a mythological monster who chased her. She had it over and over again until...I can't remember exactly when they ended..."

"Might it have been around the time when Dr. Winstanley was drowned?" Katherine asked.

"I'm not sure...wait, let me think, the beautiful doll's house Serafina got for her twelfth birthday...yes, I think that's about when they did stop. I don't understand the connection."

"Are you suggesting that there is one solution to all these old family mysteries that will also solve the identity of the Whitechapel killer?" Miles asked. "That could only be if Serafina were the killer."

"Never mind about the killer for a moment," Katherine answered. "Tell me about the dream you have mentioned. It may be the key for which I have searched in vain. It gives me a better starting point than before. Now I can question her other self, Jack Winstanley, about it," Katherine said. "I was not sure she was ready, but after seeing her tonight, bedaubed with blood once again, I believe it must be attempted. We must not lose sight of the fact that like it or not, she is somehow involved in these killings. She had Annie Chapman's rings and she has had blood on her clothing on two occasions. But if we should lose her..."

"What do you mean, 'lose her'?" Julia asked.

"I think I know what she means," Miles said abruptly in a strange tone of voice. "She means that Serafina could remember the dreadful event that gave birth to Jack Winstanley and it could drive her mad, permanently. And she could become... what?" he said turning to Katherine.

"Perhaps a lost soul who sits silently rocking in a corner, oblivious of the world around her," Katherine answered.

"Uh," Julia cried covering her small, delicate mouth with her hand as she bit her lip.

"What a dreadful possibility for someone as strong and independent as Serafina," Miles said.

"It would be terrible—unimaginable," Julia said her face ashen. "We must save her from that. Can you do it, Katherine?"

All eyes in the room were on the little woman, who seemed lost in her own thoughts. After some long moments she appeared to return to the discussion.

"I think my relationship with both aspects of Serafina is very strong. That is good. Because, I believe that the strength of her feelings for each of us will determine the strength of her desire to become whole again. Does that make sense to you both?"

"Yes, in a way," Julia said. "But I haven't the faintest idea of what to do to bring it about."

"We must get her to return to the circumstances that split her into two distinct souls. We must get her to remember it—and that is probably going to be very unpleasant for her."

"But are we proceeding on the assumption that Serafina, or some part of her really is the Whitechapel killer?" Miles asked.

"We are keeping our minds open to that possibility," Katherine said, "And open to any other explanations for the crimes that might make sense to us."

"And what if there is no connection between Serafina and the crimes? Suppose she is completely innocent?"

"How did she come to have the brass rings with Annie Chapman's name engraved in it?" Miles asked. "There must be some link between her and the killer, Julia. We must be prepared for that at the outset."

"I had forgotten the rings," Julia said, looking sad.

"And why was 'Jack Winstanley' wandering around

Whitechapel apparently within steps of each of the crimes?"
Miles added.

"There is a great deal we don't know," Katherine admitted, looking worn."

"I think we all need a good night's sleep first," Julia said. "And I think we should also fulfill the duty of taking the photographs to the police and informing them about the other suspect. Miles, could you and Katherine go first thing in the morning? Once that is over, we can do whatever is necessary for Serafina."

"I agree," Miles said. "Night seems to exalt the powers of darkness, whether they be of the mind or of the devil."

"Then, everyone will stay," Julia said, and Miles and Katherine can leave after breakfast?"

"I think that is a good plan," Katherine said. "Do you have room for us all, Julia?"

"Of course, Katherine. Miles knows where he can sleep. The bed has not been changed, Miles. I can sleep with Serafina in her room and Katherine, you can sleep in mine. Come, I'll show you the way."

As he lay in bed waiting for sleep, Miles asked himself yet again, if there were anyone other than Katherine who could help them. He could not help but feel apprehension about her lack of formal training and her strange early life. But, of course, they wouldn't dare discuss Serafina and the killer with any highly respectable practitioner. He would be bound to give them all up to the authorities. Everything would then be taken out of their hands. At the very least, Serafina would be imprisoned for a time, especially given her behaviour with Commissioner Warren after bloody Sunday. There really was no option but to trust the strange girl. They had no other resources with which to meet present contingencies. For all they knew, Katherine might have caused Serafina's condition with mesmerism. That idea haunted Miles as he fell asleep.

He woke with a start, bathed in a cold sweat. The killer was dismembering another woman. Pieces of her had been hacked off and thrown in every direction. Blood was everywhere. The horrible slaughter seemed absolutely real as he woke, and for some time afterwards. He lay awake, staring into darkness as presentiments of the killer's future crimes nagged at him, like taunting devils in a Bosch painting. The gray light of morning was filtering into the room before he could close his eyes again, but sleep eluded him. Finally, he rose and resolved to walk into the City and buy an early copy of *The Times*.

After dressing and stealthily making his way to the ground floor, he could hear the servants stirring below stairs. Then he heard the clicking of Virgil's toenails on the steps. As Miles reached the front door, the dog emerged from the stairs to the servant's hall and, placing himself between the man and door, sniffed at the right hand waistcoat pocket which usually harboured a sugar cube.

"Sorry, old man. I don't want to stop now." Miles said in a stage whisper. "I'll get you one later."

Out of doors it was a blustery morning, everything freshly scrubbed from the storm of the pervious night. Miles found it invigorating and walked with a lightened heart down toward the news agent at Charing Cross where even the ancient marker itself seemed polished by the weather. It was Monday, October 1 and the streets were as still as they ever got on a weekday morning. The wind and droplets of rain blew away the remaining night images which had followed Miles out of his bedroom and he enjoyed the walk like a young boy on an illicit but harmless errand. As he crossed the street to the news agent's Miles even felt sanguine about the experiment with Serafina. But as he arrived at the kiosk he saw the leading article of *The Times*, which read, "MORE MURDERS AT THE EAST-END. *In the early hours of yesterday morning two more horrible murders were committed in the East-end of London, the victim in both cases belonging, it is believed, to the same unfortunate class. No doubt seems to be entertained by the police that these terrible crimes were the work of the same fiendish hands which committed the outrages which had already made Whitechapel so painfully notorious. The scenes of the two murders just brought to light are within a quarter of an hour's walk of each other, the earlier-discovered crime having been committed in a yard in Berner street, a low thoroughfare out of the Commercial-road, while the second outrage was perpetrated within the city boundary, in Mitre-square, Aldgate.*

"Good God," Miles exclaimed, thinking of Serafina's sudden blood stained appearance at Katherine's shop the night before. "Two of them in one night. What can we do? We must make an end of it."

Chapter 26

DETECTIVE INSPECTOR ABBERLINE AND THE PAST UNCOVERED

"…time is of the greatest importance in this case, not only with regard to the question of identity, but also for the purpose of allaying the strong public feeling that exists."

—Detective Inspector Abberline
from his report of *September 19, 1888*

The above excerpt dates from nearly two weeks before the morning when Miles and Katherine went to see Inspector Abberline . There is no doubt that by the time they entered his office, the detective's concern about time was even more acute and it showed in his haggard face. Nonetheless, he was civil to Miles and Katherine. His curiosity had been roused. Before Miles had sent in his card he had written on it, "I believe we have photographs of the Whitechapel killer." The name, "Jack the Ripper" would not become public for another three days, on October 4 when police would print and post facsimiles of the famous "Dear Boss" letter where the killer's *nom de geurre* was used for the first time.

"Mr. Winstanley," the detective said in an affable tone to Miles. "Your note is quite bizarre. I hope this is not a joke."

"No, sir, it is not."

Katherine opened a small portfolio and pulled out three prints and two plates of she had taken of the victims.

"Excuse me, Inspector Abberline, this is Miss Katherine Green, the photographer."

While the detective studied the prints and plates, Katherine studied him. He looked nothing like a great detective. His whiskers were soft, he was balding and slightly overweight. Miles compared him to Minahan and thought that Abberline looked even less like a policeman than the other man. Abberline picked up a glass and looked closely at the prints and then at the plates.

Finally, the detective spoke, "Certainly gruesome, Miss Green. But how do you know this man in the photographs is our man?"

Katherine again looked into her portfolio and pulled out a copy of *The Journal of British Photography*.

"I took these photographs in the Whitechapel Morgue, sir. My studio is in Baker's Row. They are each a victim of the Whitechapel fiend."

"I, myself, saw this same man on the Whitechapel Road on the night of the Tabram murder," Miles added.

"If you will just look at this article, sir," Katherine said. "I have marked the places. It is not long. I am certain your time is very valuable."

The detective took the magazine and read silently for some minutes.

"It says here that a dead person's last vision of this world is imprinted on the retina. That's what this article says. This man appears in the eye sockets. I can't even see the retina."

"We are both aware of that anomaly," Miles said. "But I did see this man myself on the Whitechapel Road."

"And do you know him?"

"No sir, I know nothing of him. I just saw him as he

walked past. Even before I saw these pictures I thought him a most singular looking blackguard."

"Hmm. Excuse me, please," the detective said as he got up. "I want to show these to the police surgeon."

The minutes dragged by as they waited for Abberline's return. He returned holding more photographs.

"The surgeon says that anatomically, at least, these could be the skulls of the murdered women, though how they were exposed to the view of the camera neither he nor I can guess. I suppose you realize, Miss Green, that taking these without police permission is breaking the law? A serious offence."

"I—I saw the article and, and I was only trying to help. The old man at the morgue told me that the surgeon had said it would not work in this case. I could not understand why not."

"But these are certainly not images taken from the retina. The likeness is much larger and more evident."

"I know, sir. I have no explanation. This is how the photographs came out. In each instance."

"How did you get the morgue attendant to talk to you, then? Did you flirt with him? Come, come, I shall have the truth out of you, my girl."

Apparently, Miles thought, the Ripper was starting to undo the normally polite police official.

"Miss Green is a highly skilled hypnotist," Miles said. "She has nothing to hide. She must have used her skills to get the old man to talk to her."

"And these plates, have they been tampered with? Are they faked, in other words?"

"What does your own man say? The plates are right here. Isn't that part of why you showed the photographs to him?" Miles asked. "You have no right to intimidate citizens who are trying to further your investigation by offering cooperation. Miss Green and I came here in good faith."

"Well, you see, sir, I have no way of knowing that. It could be that you simply want to get your name in the papers. It could be that this man is an enemy of some sort."

Miles and Katherine looked at each other. They were

dumbfounded. Both had been primarily worried about Serafina somehow coming into the conversation.

"I could put you in prison, Miss Green, for interfering with my investigation but," he held up his hand to forestall Miles' protests. "I shall not do that. I do know you slightly, Mr. Winstanley. I shall keep these," he nodded at the plates and prints, "and consider what you have both said. Now, I apologize but I have very heavy calls on my time, just now."

Miles got to his feet and the two men shook hands.

"I trust I shall find you at the address on your card, Mr. Winstanley?"

"Yes. I live and work at that address."

"And you Miss Green?"

"At the same place," Miles answered before Katherine could speak.

"Very well, I'll contact you soon about your property when I am finished with it. I may or may not return it. Good day."

"Good day."

Outside it was raining again. The streets were wet and slimey.

"Why did you imply that I lived with you?" Katherine asked. "I can think of several imputations that Inspector Abberline could make as a result."

"Isn't it better than to find you living right in the area where the murders are occurring? In a lodging house? That is hardly respectable, and it makes you more suspicious."

"I hadn't thought of that." She was quiet for a moment and then said, "Do you think he will use the photographs?"

"I think he will examine what we said from every possible vantage point. He needs a break in this case, especially after the double murder last night. He will certainly try to find the man in those photographs. I hope he succeeds. At any rate, we have done all we can on that score."

"In that case, let us go back to Cavendish Square and meet with Serafina and Julia. Julia will be anxious to hear what has happened. I should rather not tell Serafina about the photographs until after we have talked with Jack Winstanley."

"I think Julia is going to be shocked when she sees him," Katherine said.

"Yes, she very probably will."

When Miles and Katherine arrived at Cavendish Square, Julia was sitting in the dining room with Serafina at breakfast.

"Well, I am glad to see that the ill will between the two of you has ended," Serafina said as Miles and Katherine came into the room. There was a slight smile on both their faces.

"Serafina, would you allow me to entrance you, now? There are some questions I should like to ask."

"You know I place myself entirely in your hands, Katherine. Is it wise to have all these other people here?"

"I think it might be a very good idea," the girl answered.

"Very well," Serafina said as she sat back in her chair. "I am ready."

Katherine touched her friend and Serafina became rigid and unseeing. Then Katherine turned to Julia. "Julia, this will be rather shocking for you, I am afraid. Serafina may look and even sound different than usual. Do you understand?"

"I think so. Something like she used to do as a child?"

"She used to do that as a child?" Katherine repeated. "Her face changed?"

"I have seen it quite a few times. At night when she was having bad dreams. When she would wake, I would brush her hair and she would eventually fall asleep, peacefully. Is it important?"

"It could be."

"I always thought it was just part of the dream about the little girl and the monster."

"The person you're going to meet now is no little girl," Miles put in.

"But there could be a little girl as well," Katherine said. "I have not met her. Jack is always so forward."

"Jack, you mean this 'Jack Winstanley'?" Julia asked.

"Yes," Miles said. "He is in love with Katherine."

"Good heavens," Julia exclaimed. "How frightfully odd."

"Very odd," Miles said.

"I am very ready to meet him if it will help Serafina—and very, very curious," Julia said.

"Jack," Katherine called softly.

"Well," Jack's voice boomed, "Look at this gathering. How did the police like your pictures?"

"How do you know about those?" Miles asked. "We didn't tell Serafina."

"I have other sources of information. Now, I hope this meeting is about us, me and Serafina."

"That's exactly what it's about."

"Good. Come on, then. Let's go out into the yard."

"The yard?" Katherine asked as she stood up.

Julia too rose from table. They began to file out toward the hall.

"Why are we going outside?" Miles asked.

"I don't know. I am just following Katherine's lead and she is following Serafina's."

"Somebody get the gardener," Jack ordered.

"Julia, would you go?" Katherine asked.

"I think he is in the back yard. Cook told me he was working back there this morning."

"Does he have a shovel?" Jack asked as he fell back and walked behind Julia.

"He should have one," Julia answered. "When I saw him this morning, he was planting some annuals."

"Good," Jack said. "I'll do the digging, now."

The group entered the formal garden behind the house and walked a round the outer perimeter of the maze. On the far side of the hedges they saw the gardener digging and planting flowers. Serafina walked up to him and said, "Lend me your spade and I'll give you some port that you won't have to steal."

The startled look on the man's face could have been Serafina's strange voice or it could have been that his pilfering was known to her, or both. She took the shovel from his limp hand, turned and led the way into the maze. The three others followed her.

Miles had not been in the maze for many years. He felt strangely reluctant to enter. The closer they got to the hedges, the more he perspired. He felt suddenly extremely nervous and uneasy. He began having pains in his stomach and began to feel faint.

"I shall wait here," he said, stepping aside and stopping at the entrance to the maze.

"No, you won't dear cousin," Serafina said as she encircled his arm in a grip that felt like a band of iron. "Come." And she pulled the reluctant man into the hedges. There was no way he could break free.

"Remembering, are you?" Serafina boomed at him.

"N-no," but his teeth were chattering as Serafina dragged him after her. Suddenly, Miles fainted. His whole body went limp but Serafina easily kept him from falling by retaining her grip on his arm. She dragged him a few more steps and then let him down onto the turf.

"Good lord," Julia said rushing over to the fallen man.

"He's all right," Jack said. "He'll come out of it. Don't worry about him. What you need to see is right here under a couple of feet of dirt."

"What is he talking about, Katherine?" Julia asked.

"I don't know."

"Oh, she's here, all right," Jack said as, with demonic energy, he ripped up the sod and began to throw great piles of black earth away from the hedge. A couple of minutes later Jack spoke, "Look, I've already found the skull."

"Oh, my heavens," Julia cried out. "Who's skull?"

"Amelia's, of course," Jack replied.

"You mean she was buried here?" Katherine asked.

"Yes, I saw the whole thing. So did he," he added nodding at Miles.

"How ghastly," Julia said, blanched white as a ghost.

"Tell us, Jack," Katherine said. "We need your help, please."

Serafina's strangely masculine form stabbed the spade

into some loose earth and left it. She picked up the skull in her hand, shook out the loose soil and looked at it.

"Poor little mite," Jack said, sounding almost tender. "She never had a chance."

"Tell us what happened, Jack," Katherine repeated.

"Very well. It's almost too bad it isn't night as it was then."

Miles sat up and Julia helped him get to his feet.

"Did I miss anything important?" he asked.

"Not really," Jack called to him. "You were pretty scared that night weren't you?"

"Terrified. I still am."

"You remember what happened here, Miles?" Julia asked.

"It's been coming back to me in bits and pieces. But there are still gaps."

"Jack, please go on," Katherine said.

"Well, it is too bad it isn't dark, now. That night there was some moon, but not much. These hedges cast deep shadows. The little one was brought out here."

"Who, brought her, Jack?" Julia asked.

"Whom do you think? Yes, she was brought out here. In case she should cry out, I suppose."

"Oh, my God," Julia said, becoming pale. "My father— Dr. Winstanley assaulted Miles' little sister. Is that what you are saying?"

"She was ravished right where this earth is and her face was covered so no one might hear her cries. I suppose that's how she died. Probably covered her nose as well as her mouth."

"It's too horrible," Julia said staggering against Miles.

"Ask him," Jack said pointing to Miles. "He was there, too."

"Miles, were you?" Julia asked.

Her cousin's face was ghostly, drained of all colour. He nodded. After a few moments he said hoarsely, "I could never quite remember it until a few moments ago when we were approaching the maze. Everything Serafina has been saying has seemed as if it were taking place while I was sleeping. I feel I have been watching my own dream. I remember now that I heard Dr. and Mrs. Winstanley carrying Amelia out of the nursery that night and I followed them down the stairs and out into the garden to the maze. I had no idea what they were going to do, really I didn't. It all seemed rather exciting at first, being out in the yard in the moonlight. It seemed like some kind of fascinating game Dr. Winstanley had devised. They knew I was there, but they seemed possessed. By the time Amelia was ravished by Dr. Winstanley, she was already dead. I remember seeing the moonlight on her still features. I didn't know what to do, I didn't know what to do, really I didn't," and he started sobbing. "What should I have done? Tell me, someone, what should I have done? Could I have stopped him?"

"No. Miles," Katherine said, hurrying to his side. "It wasn't your fault at all."

"Then," Jack continued, "Dr. Winstanley left the maze and didn't return. I never saw him after that. Mrs. Winstanley beat Miles and made him dismember the dead girl and bury her. Then she raped Miles and Serafina. She had a male member strapped onto herself."

For some moments the four figures formed an odd tableau: Miles leaning on Katherine, sobbing on her shoulder, Julia blanched and horror stricken, Serafina, as Jack, leaning on his shovel as he contemplated the little skull.

"Poor little mite," Jack muttered several times. "There's another one back here, too," he said softly."

"Another?" Julia exclaimed.

"On another occasion that fat foreigner took a little girl in here who never came out. He got her somewhere down near the docks. I heard the foreigner and Dr. Winstanley talking about what a nice little package she was."

"Oh, my God," Katherine said out loud.

"What is it, Katherine?" Julia asked.

"Recently I found something dreadful down near the water, parts of a child hacked to pieces in a bucket."

"How vile, how frightfully disgusting" Julia said.

"I was looking for a young girl I knew who was abducted

and my search led me down near the river. In Wapping. I broke into a building and was nearly abducted myself."

"I wonder if there could be an even closer connection than we have yet imagined," Miles said. "Was this warehouse near a place where five corners meet off of Wapping high street?"

"Yes, how did you know."

"Katherine, that is the neighbourhood where I saw the man in your photographs."

"Do you think he was involved somehow in the trafficking?" Julia asked.

"I don't know," Miles said. "But you said this child was cut in pieces?"

Katherine nodded, looking rather ill at the memory. "I was looking for a young friend who had been a prostitute. It was in an opium den..."

"The chinaman's," Miles cried.

"That's right," Katherine agreed. "How did you know?"

"Because on the night of the Tabram murder I was down there with a client who wanted to go slumming. It was on my way back from there that I saw the man in your photographs. It was also the first time I saw your shop and I suppose, Serafina, Jack, hit me and laid me low in the alley."

"I still don't understand the connection between our suspect for the Whitechapel killings, this trade in children and Katherine's friend," Julia said.

"You know I am rather afraid that the damp of these hedges does not agree with me."

Everyone turned in the direction of the voice. It was Serafina speaking in her own voice.

"Serafina!" Julia cried rushing to her sister's side.

"Where's Katherine?" Serafina asked.

"I'm right here."

"But you didn't bring her out of it, did you?" Miles asked Katherine in a whisper.

The girl shook her head in the negative.

"Let's go inside, Serafina," Julia said, taking her sister's arm. "I shall make you a nice hot pot of tea."

"Oh, yes. I should like some gingerbread, too, please." Serafina replied in a soft child like voice.

Miles and Katherine were left standing in the maze. The thick hedges did seem to hold every drop of moisture in the air.

"I still don't understand the connection between the traffickers and this man you saw, the man in the photographs," she said.

"I don't have all the answers either," Miles replied, "but I do know someone who may. Would you ride into the City with me? *Sotto voce* he added, "You don't have to overact your part. We are quite alone."

"I would ride anywhere if there was the least chance of finding out what happened to my friend, Susan."

As the pair walked arm and arm out of the maze, Miles said, "I suppose it is a good sign that Serafina came out of it on her own—that Jack seemed to fade into Serafina?"

Katherine nodded.

"Is she cured, then?"

"I don't know. Every person is different, especially when they have had such a terrible shock. Jack is very strong. If he leaves, Serafina will inherit some of his strength."

"Then she will surely be a power to be reckoned with for the suffragists."

"She is a remarkable women," Katherine agreed.

"You could go inside and join them," Miles said. "While I go and speak to the groom about the carriage."

"I think I shall."

"I'll come and get you," he said, taking her hand and giving it a squeeze. Then, the pair turned away from each other. Within the hour, Miles and Katherine were riding into the city toward the shabby offices of Jeremiah Minahan. As they rode, Miles explained where they were going and why.

"You see, I believe that Minahan gave us an important piece of the puzzle which may connect our family history with the mysterious man in your photographs and the Bowens. I want to see what he thinks about it."

"Yes, but we must follow Susan's trail, too, if we can."

"Yes, of course, Katherine. After all you have done for us, I shall have Minahan sift the matter of your friend's disappearance thoroughly."

"Thank you. You are kind."

"So, you no longer think I am a bad man?"

"I never thought you were bad—only confused."

"Confused?"

"Yes. Your feelings for Serafina were dreadfully mixed up. I see now that your bond with her was connected with the horror you had both experienced. I didn't understand that before. I thought you were a fine gentleman who wanted to trifle with me because I was poor and ignorant—and—" she paused as she looked up at him with shining eyes "— in love with you. I didn't understand that you and she were bound together and yet had few real feelings for each other."

"I only realized very recently how close and yet how distant Serafina and I really were. It was the morning after the woman was killed in Hanbury Street, Annie Chapman's murder, actually. And that's another thing we must still clear up. What was Jack Winstanley doing on the streets of Whitechapel every night? Why did he have Annie Chapman's rings? We must completely understand Jack's connection to the Whitechapel atrocities. I do hope Serafina is not connected in some way in the crimes. It would be horrible even if she didn't know what she was doing and played a very minor role in the horrors. We must make sure the police never know anything about her. But first, Mr. Minahan may set us on the track of your young friend and help connect my family with the man in your photos with the horror at the chinaman's. If I am right in my guesses he will."

The pair had to wait some half hour in the dark waiting room of the detective. It was a shabby little space, ill-lit and confined. Miles had never been in it before. There was a second door which was odd for a room the size of a large closet. There was hardly enough room for two chairs. It smelled of soot, as if the fireplace hadn't been cleaned for years. After what seemed a very long time the door to the dismal room was opened and the detective led them into his chambers.

"I apologize for keeping you waiting. I have been rather busy and I take it that you have some urgent developments you want to discuss."

"This is Miss Green, Inspector Minahan."

"I thought so. Do please sit down. It's a rough place and is not arranged for fashionable young women."

"Here's the situation Mr. Minahan. We have been working a puzzle. We now have two opposite edges done. I believe you may have the middle portion that might connect what we have—a portion you have gleaned from an official investigation you were once engaged in. May I ask some questions, sir?"

"You may ask, but if the information is from another investigation, it may be confidential."

"I understand."

"Then, proceed."

"You once told us about a letter which confirmed one of Miss Green's visions. It spoke of small coffins in which children were going to be shipped to Europe for immoral purposes."

"Kleberg's letter. Go on."

"I should like to know sir, how did they keep the children quiet in these coffins while they were in transit? Surely ten children in ten coffins would make an awful noise—even if they were terrified."

"Yes."

"So the traffickers would have used chloroform or ether to quiet the children, would they not?"

"Some sort of powerful sedative. One of those two. Yes."

"And with a child," Miles said excitedly as he leaned forward in his chair toward Minahan, "If the dosage was not exactly correct there would be a real risk of death, would there not?"

"It is very possible."

"We have recently learned, sir, wait, I must ask you to assure me once again that anything we say is in complete confidence. This must never be revealed."

"As long as no laws are violated."

"They have been violated, sir. But the criminal is dead. Disclosure could only unleash a scandal on a respectable family."

"I see. Very well. In that case, I shall promise that what you say will remain confidential."

"My stepfather, the respected medical specialist, Dr. Winstanley, raped and murdered my sister and buried her in the back yard at number twenty-one Cavendish Square."

Miles had the pleasure of seeing the unflappable detective entirely bowled over.

"My God! Excuse me, Miss. How do you know? Are you sure?"

"I have witnesses and I have remains. I was forced to bury my own dead sister."

"Heavens!"

"So much for one side of the puzzle," Miles went on with some satisfaction.

"It sounds like a very complete case to me," the detective remarked, lighting a cigar. "Oh, pardon me, Miss" and stubbed it out.

"So far as it goes. But we have some other pieces that I want to connect with what I just told you."

"I am all attention, sir," and the detective was literally sitting on the edge of his chair. His head was cocked to one side. His expression at that moment reminded Miles of Virgil on a scent."

"I also know that Dr. Winstanley had an—ah—associate with similar tastes who was reputed to have buried another child at number twenty-one Cavendish Square. I have not seen the remains of this child, but my source is a reliable one. He is reputed to have procured this other child down near the docks in Wapping—the very area where an attempt was made recently to abduct Miss Green by someone we believe is connected with the Bowen Refuge for Indigent Children."

"So you believe you have uncovered a ring of traffickers?"

"Yes, sir. And I believe that Dr. Winstanley was probably working with them as their anesthetist to ensure the healthy delivery of their packages to Europe, and perhaps taking his payment in trade! It seems likely that the rapacious Mrs. Jeffries was also somehow involved, though I have no way to prove it. How do you like that, sir? What do you think?"

"Your surmises sound quite plausible to me," the detective said, once more lighting his cigar, this time forgetting or not bothering to stub it out. "What do you want to know from me?"

"Could Mrs. Jeffries be getting fresh girls from the same source? In other words, can you, from your exhaustive investigation of her, confirm that fact?"

The bulky detective suddenly stood up and began puffing on his cigar rapidly. "Now you tread on dangerous ground, sir, I must tell you. In spite of months of documented evidence I could get no one in government to move against her. But yes, you are right. The same power that protects her, protects the Bowens. They work hand in glove, sir. I was told to leave the Bowens out of my report, altogether."

"My poor, dear, Susan," Katherine said.

"Is there any way, Mr. Minahan that you can think of that would allow us to find a girl who might have passed through these hands? I know you tried with my sister and failed, but is there any way that you could use the threat of exposure to find another girl who may be in Chelsea, or one of the other bad houses?" By the time he finished speaking, Miles was also standing up, smoking and gesticulating.

"I shall do my best, sir. Of course, you realize, that these people are so well protected that even with the Criminal Amendment Act, which is now in force, we are not likely to get much satisfaction out of punishing the guilty parties."

"I don't care about them," Katherine broke in. "I just want Susan back and to know that she is safe and healthy."

"I shall do my best, Miss, to find your friend."

"Now," Miles said re-lighting his cigar. "There is yet another matter, one that you may find too hot to touch, Mr. Minahan. The regular police are already on the case. Do you, by any chance know Inspector Abberline of H division?"

"I know him well. He is the best man on the force. No one else comes close. He is what I call a real brain worker. But the case he is now on..." And before he finished the thought, the big man sank back into his chair. "My God, is anything you told me somehow involved with the Whitechapel fiend, the killer that everyone is now calling, Jack the Ripper?"

Miles nodded and Minahan held up his beefy hand.

"Before you say a word, sir, I must tell you I cannot protect your confidence in a matter that touches on an active police investigation."

"There is no need, Mr. Minahan. Look." And to Katherine's astonishment he dropped prints of her death's head image onto the detective's desk.

"Where did you get those, Miles, Mr. Winstanley?" Katherine exclaimed. "I thought Inspector Abberline had everything."

"These are poor copies of your original work, Katherine. I got them from a friend who kept them for me. Can you see the man's face in the orbits of the skull, Mr. Minahan?"

"Yes. What grisly pictures these are. Where did they come from?"

"Miss Green took them in the morgue."

"But the skulls..."

"I don't know. I have no explanation. I can only say that Miss Green is clairvoyant as well as being a photographer. Inspector Abberline has copies of the same photographs."

"Amazing."

"I have seen this man in the flesh, Mr. Minahan. In the neighbourhood of the chinaman's opium den."

Clearly, even the hardened detective was agog.

"Now suppose that the Bowens had some connection with the chinaman and were using his premises to dispose of children who didn't have the benefit of Dr. Winstanley's skill and so died—inconveniently. And further suppose that Jack the Ripper is the man that they hired to get ride of the evidence for the traffickers. I believe it would take quite a bit of skill to butcher a child. Does this killer have such skill? This man whom I saw only for a moment under gaslight had a rapacious look about him. A few moments later, I was struck on the head and when I woke the next morning I found a bloody knife in my own pocket."

"Great Scott," the detective exclaimed.

"Yes. It was the night of the first murder and I was slumming in Whitechapel. Scared the life out of me when a potboy threw me out of a lodging house the next morning and tossed the knife after me and said it fell out of my pocket. I had been smoking opium you see...and on the way home I heard about the murder which took place only one street away from where I woke up."

"And you thought..." the detective said.

"I'd never smoked opium before, you see. After I left the chinaman's that night, I found myself wandering around Whitechapel where I saw this man. He was a very sinister looking fellow in the flesh, especially under gaslight in a slum." he waved his hand at the pictures on Minahan's desk.

"Did you tell this to the police?"

"No, sir, I did not. I did tell Inspector Abberline I had seen the man and I did give him the pictures. But I did not tell him about smoking opium nor that I found a bloody knife in my pocket."

"Is the knife still bloody, sir?"

"No. I washed it off."

"Tampering with evidence, sir, bad. Very bad. Are there any more prints of versions of these photographs? Are these the only ones other than what the police have?"

"Those are the only ones and Inspector Abberline has the plates."

"That's good, sir. And I am going to do you a favour and burn these right now in my own grate."

"But why?"

"Because if this fellow did turn out to be the killer and it became known that photographs of him had been circulated before he was proven to be the culprit, a clever barrister might get the case thrown out of court. These photographs could ruin the prosecution of Abberline's investigation. Even if this fellow is the man and his guilt were proved, these photographs might set him free."

"Good God!" Miles exclaimed. "Burn them, then, by all

means. Katherine, you have no objections?"

"Of course not. I should not want to do anything to help the fiend get away with his crimes."

Minahan was already walking toward the grate with the photographs in his hand.

The three people sat around the small grate in dingy little City office and burned the only photographs of Jack the Ripper outside of the set that had been left with the police. However, earlier that same morning, Inspector Abberline had made a similar fire in his office. He had finally received a cable from M. Nadar of Marseilles, widely recognized as the world's greatest living authority on photography, the man who had successfully lit and photographed the Paris sewers.

Nadar had written, "They could be fakes or they might not. You will end up fighting over the photographs instead of the merit of your case. As a journalist and a photographer I advise you: Burn them."

And so it was that the only photographs of Jack the Ripper were deliberately burned by the sage judgment of Messrs Abberline and Minahan, two experienced men of the law. During the period of the Ripper investigation, the man in the photographs was known only to Inspector Abberline and the police surgeon. It was only some years later that his identity was uncovered.

When the images had become fluffy white ashes, the spell of silence that had fallen on Minahan's office seemed to grow deeper. For a moment everyone stared into the dead fireplace. Then, Miles and Katherine wordlessly took their leave of the detective, each shaking his hand as they passed out onto the City street. The bulky detective held Katherine's hand a little longer than necessary and said, "If she is alive, I shall find her, Miss Green."

Chapter 27

SERAFINA AND JACK THE RIPPER

"...Dr. Fraser from the Royal Ottawa Hospital in Canada.. reached several conclusions:

> *...exorcisms had an effect in that they produced a change and had an impact on the personality system.*

> *Alternate personalities can be, at least temporarily, "banished" and new personalities can be created in response to the sense of trauma.*

> *The effect in each case was severely destructive.*

> *At least in cases where MPD is present or may be present, exorcism is contraindicated."*

"Now, we are all quite certain we want to try this?" Katherine asked Julia, Miles and Serafina as they sat at the dining room table after returning to Cavendish Square from detective Abberline's office at the police station. Serafina's eyes were wide and staring. She was in a deep magnetic sleep.

"We must find out why Serafina was present at Annie Chapman's murder—and we must make certain she is not present again during any future crimes of the Ripper," Julia said.

"What does it matter why she is following the killer?" Miles said. "She must be stopped. It is in the identity of Jack Winstanley that she is tracking the Ripper. I say, let us get rid of Jack Winstanley and Serafina will stop at home."

"I also feel that it is paramount that Serafina be kept off of the Whitechapel streets," Julia said. "The Ripper has not been caught and we must keep Serafina out of harm's way. Twice Serafina has gotten perilously close to the monster. She has had blood on her clothing and Miles still has Annie Chapman's rings, which Serafina could only have taken from Hanbury street. We must, we must prevent any future episodes. She could be at risk from the monster or from the police. We must put a stop to it. That is my thinking," Julia finished.

"I agree," Miles said. "Get rid of Jack Winstanley and we get rid of the problem. Don't you agree, Katherine?"

"Yes. I think that is sound, as far as it goes. However, I don't know what the effect of eliminating or suppressing Jack Winstanley will be."

"Surely, there cannot be as much danger as that which threatens her now," Miles said.

Katherine looked over at Julia who nodded her agreement.

"Yes, all right. Let's go forward. Let us see if we can do away with Jack Winstanley."

"That's an odd way of putting it," Miles said.

"It's just that he does seem like a part of Serafina."

"How do we go about getting rid of Jack?" Miles asked. "Do we need a priest, do we say prayers?"

"No," Katherine answered. "If Serafina were very religious it might be useful. In India, one wouldn't dare try to exorcize part of the self without some religious ritual. But not with Serafina. No. I shall ask Serafina to suppress Jack. I shall tell her why it should be done and I shall use her affection for us to force her to suppress him. I shall make it an "us or him" situation for her."

"And what do you want us to do?" Miles asked.

"Nothing. She will know you are here. I shall try to focus all of her attention on me and on my will. Please just remain quiet and relaxed, no matter what I or Serafina says."

"We are in your hands, Katherine," Julia said.

"Serafina," Katherine called.

Instantly they all saw an alteration in the young woman seated with them. Her eyes were no longer dull and blank. She regarded them all in a completely characteristic mocking manner—each one except Katherine.

"So you want to make me a good girl—no more nights out?" she asked.

"It is not a joke or a game, Serafina," Katherine said quietly. "We are trying to keep you safe. If you really care for us—for me—you will banish Jack Winstanley from your mind—forever. You will not allow him to take over again. He must be stopped. Do you understand?"

"Yes, but..."

"No. If you care for me, if you care for Julia, or any of us. You must do as I say and completely suppress Jack Winstanley. You must. Your life and perhaps our lives may depend upon it. You must suppress Jack."

Serafina's eyes had once again become veiled. They became more distant. "All right, Katherine" she said in a hollow voice, "I must suppress Jack Winstanley. But he is not the kill.."

"No!" Katherine said forcefully. "You must do as we ask. There is no other way."

Tell her, Julia," Katherine said.

"Dearest Serafina," Julia began, "please, take care of yourself. Do not follow the monster any more but stop at home with us. Please push out Jack from your thoughts. I believe it may also eliminate your dream forever."

There was a long silence and finally Serafina said haltingly. "I—I shall do as you ask. But..."

Katherine leaned over and touched Serafina's forehead.

"I am hungry," Serafina said in her usual forthright manner. "What time is it? Isn't it past time for luncheon to be served?"

Everyone at the table laughed heartily after their long period of concentration.

Katherine rose to leave and tied her shawl around her shoulders.

"You are not leaving, my dear?" Serfina asked.

"I must. I have my living to earn. Saturday is usually my busiest day and half of it is gone." She bent down and kissed Serafina's cheek. Miles walked out of the room with her and saw her to the door. He stepped out onto the veranda with her.

"Well?" he asked interrogatively.

"I think you'll be safe, but I would not do anything to provoke her. Can you do that you strange, beautiful man?"

"Of course, I can. I shall see you tomorrow night."

She started to touch his cheek but he drew away.

"Are you mad? Not here," he said. "Tomorrow night."

Katherine turned without another word and walked down the steps.

It rained all day Sunday and Miles was listless in his studio. He was bored and out of sorts. He decided, finally, to surprise Katherine in her shop. He would go an hour early. She would have nothing to do on Sunday. He dressed carefully and preened in front of the glass in his studio.

"How strange it all is," he said to himself. "If we had not met that night perhaps none of this would have happened." Then, after a final inspection before the glass, he threw on his waterproof and went out into the rain.

When he got to the shop in Bakers Row, he noted with pleasure that although he was early, Katherine was waiting for him. She sat on the chaise in her shop fidgeting with her hands for a few moments, then jumped up and walked back and forth, looking toward the door. Her air of eager vigilance was unmistakable. He thought of how distant she had been the night they met and smiled. Miles watched his pretty little bird flutter back and forth a few times before knocking on the door to end her suspense. In some corner of his mind, he wondered if it would end with her as it had with the others. It had already lasted longer than ever before. How could he have known about her powers when they first met?

At the sound of his knock, Katherine wrenched open the door and flung herself into his arms, kissing him deeply on the lips as she pulled him inside. Clinging to him like a limpet she took him into the chamber at the back of the shop. She pulled off his streaming waterproof and pushed him onto the pretty bed. She pulled off the oriental burnoose she wore and stood naked before the smiling man, her perfect little figure revealed.

Miles chuckled as she drew close to him. "That is what I like about you," he said. "You are like a cat in heat."

"Touch my skin. I am in heat—as you well know."

And it was true. Her fingers were burning as she undressed him. He did little to assist her but lay passively on the bed as Katherine threw his things onto the floor. Only when they were both naked did he move and begin to fumble with the top draw of a pretty little chest next to the bed. He pulled it open as he rolled onto his stomach, reached inside and drew out an odd confusion of leather and ivory. Katherine took it from him, reached over him and took some cream from a jar which she rubbed on Miles' backside. She slipped the last clasp around her thighs and began to slide the smooth ivory into Miles.

"Ohh," he cried out. "It hurts."

"Of course it does, you bad boy. Now, you will do exactly as I say."

"Oh, God, yes, Katherine, darling—anything."

"You know what you must do, or not do," she replied as she thrust deeply into him.

"Oh, yes—anything, you know I am your slave."

"That's right," she said thrusting again.

"Uhh."

"I have suppressed Serafina's memories for you, though she almost told everyone that she had been following you when we exorcized Jack," she said, biting his ear. Now, you must give up the pleasure of your nights out. If you don't, I shall really hurt you." And she pushed downward, ramming the entire length of the smooth ivory piece into him with a single hard thrust.

"Mother, mother, please don't hurt me," he shrieked. "I'll be good."

"Yes, you will," she said as she moved her hips faster and faster.

When both were finished, Miles lay curled against her in a tight ball. He was just dozing off when Katherine bit his ear, again, hard.

"Ouch."

"You will stop going out at night, won't you? It could ruin both of us. And all my efforts with the photographs would be for nothing. Even the good fortune I had in photographing the barber from George Yard. All those hours of printing the death's heads. All my art would be useless if you are caught in the act."

"I know. I shall do my best, if you will help me," he said rolling over to look at her.

"Haven't I always done everything for you? From the very first time you barred your soul to me and asked for my help?"

"Yes. Though it still amazes me that anyone—let alone the police— could believe that the man you put into the orbits of the skulls is an afterimage of the Ripper."

"Thanks to *The British Journal of Photography*," she said, slipping her arms around his waist. I told you that people were in awe of photography. Just as they are of spiritualism. As Krishna once told me, 'people want to believe. They want to believe in the reality of spirit."

"Do you think Jack Winstanley is gone for good?" he asked. "Do you think there is the remotest chance that Serafina will remember what Jack knows about the nights she followed me?"

"Do you think Jack the Ripper is gone for good?" she asked.

"I think so, now. But, if I feel the beast stir in me again, it seems there's little I can do. He came out the night I had the opium..."

"Thinking so, isn't enough. You must stay off the streets

at night, even if you have to lock yourself in. You must take precautions by avoiding the things that trigger his appearance."

She took his flaccid penis in her hand. "If you do not. I shall cut off this delightfully useless thing."

Mary Kelly, the last of the canonical Ripper victims was murdered almost a month later. Around that time, according to Julia Winstanley, Miles and Katherine both disappeared from London and defied all attempts to trace them. But in 1891 another women was found with her throat cut in the manner of the Ripper. A terrified young constable walking his beat alone for the first time found her under a railway arch near Swallow Gardens. She was wrongfully identified as Frances Coles, Katherine's look-alike room mate. In fact, it was Katherine, herself. Miles had finally fulfilled his own speculations about "how it would end." He could not help but hate the woman who humiliated him sexually, nor could he give up that perverse pleasure either.

Eventually, Serafina regained her full memory and completely integrated "Jack." In spite of Katherine's efforts, she eventually had an unclouded picture of Miles stalking his victims through Whitechapel. She also remembered that on the night of Amelia's murder, when Miles had finished dismembering and burying Amelia, Mrs. Winstanley used the same implement on Miles and Serafina that Katherine had used on the adult Miles. At the time of the double rape, Dr. Winstanley was on his way to the continent and would soon die while trying to dump overboard the body parts of another dead child, the accident which finally ended the monstrous crimes of the "Minotaur of Modern Babylon." Serafina never told Julia what she knew about Miles. The truth would have broken Julia's heart.

For reasons known only to herself, May Winstanley ceased abusing her elder daughter and Miles after the night of the double rape. Perhaps her appetites changed, perhaps she was afraid of discovery after the death of her husband. Perhaps she knew of Mr. Stead's interest in her husband's business and feared, long before the *Maiden Tribute* articles, that he had learned too much of the family's bizarre and grisly history. Perhaps he even threatened her with exposure. No one will ever know. Julia was never able to get her employer to tell her anything about the true identity of "the Minotaur." Mr. Stead took what he knew about the Minotaur of Modern Babylon to a watery grave on board the famous ship, *The Titanic*.

In spite of all the horror in their family life, Serafina and Julia lived long and useful lives. They both lived long enough to see women get the vote. The man Katherine had printed into her photographs in the orbits of the skulls, and whom Katherine had seen at the chinaman's was Stanislas Koslowski (a.k.a. George Chapman). He was, ironically, hanged for the murder of three wives at Wandsworth prison on April 7, 1903. He was also a leading suspect in the Ripper case first, because of his surgical training in Poland and later, the fact that he was a convicted multiple murderer. He was the perfect man to take over the disposal of the bodies of children after Dr. Winstanley's demise. Baron Mesnil de Hermann, the infamous Belgian paedophile contacted him after he tried to sell body parts to one of the London hospitals. Of course, Dr. Winstanley was, himself, the person referred to by W.T. Stead as "the Minotaur of Modern Babylon."

By the time the Ripper murders ceased, the only sign that the suppressed photographs had ever existed was Abberline's remark to Inspector Godley. When Godley arrested Chapman for the murders of his wives, Abberline told him with the certainty of one who had seen incontrovertible edvidence, "You finally got Jack the Ripper." Whether Abberline told Godley about the suppressed photographs he had seen is entirely unknown.

The End

A NOTE ABOUT ALAN MCKEE

Alan lives with his family in Toronto but spends time writing at his second home in Nova Scotia. He studied violin in New York City for ten years. His special interests are British history and nineteenth century literature. He has been inspired by E.P. Thompson and Eric Hobsbawn, both great British historians.

OTHER TITLES

The Iron Beast
Shadows of Empire

www.hudsonhousemysteries.com